MR SIDHU'S POST OFFICE

AMMAN BRAR

Juniper

Juniper
An imprint of HarperCollins*Publishers* Ltd
1 London Bridge Street
London SE1 9GF

www.harpercollins.co.uk

HarperCollins*Publishers*
Macken House, 39/40 Mayor Street Upper,
Dublin 1, D01 C9W8, Ireland

This edition 2026
1
First published in Great Britain by Juniper,
an imprint of HarperCollins*Publishers* Ltd 2026

ISBN: HB: 978-0-00-872223-4
TPB: 978-0-00-872222-7
INDIES EDITION: 978-0-00-883813-3

This book is set in 10.7/15.5 pt. Sabon by Type-it AS, Norway

Printed and bound in the UK using 100% Renewable
Electricity by CPI Group (UK) Ltd

MIX
Paper | Supporting
responsible forestry
FSC® C013604

Amman Brar is a writer and theatre maker. He has an MA in Creative Writing from UEA. He was one of the inaugural winners of the BBC Writers Room 10 Award for his play *Punjabi Boy* with the Tamasha Theatre Company where he was also Artist in Residence.

Amman's father was a sub-postmaster during the 1980s and 1990s, and as soon as he was able, Amman was 'encouraged' to work in the shop after school and at weekends. He saw how respected his father was and how the locals loved having a post office as a hub for the community. *Mr Sidhu's Post Office* is Amman's debut novel and pays tribute to his father and the community he served for decades, while also honouring the struggle of the victims of the Horizon scandal.

For Dad – thank you for everything

G.S. BRAR (1939 – 2017)

Prologue

One day as Mantinder Singh Sidhu walked home from tending to his fields, he tripped and fell over. It was the same path he used to follow his own father on when he was a boy, and falling over like this now, as a man of forty, was quite unexpected. He was not far from his house, which was only around the corner, but as he attempted to lift himself up, he felt a jab in his back.

'You might as well stay down, old man. There is no one to help you up.'

He heard the man to whom the voice belonged laugh along with the other men who were idling on that particular corner, where men had been idling for centuries.

Mantinder knew who these men were. After getting up and dusting himself down, he smiled his childlike smile and started to walk again without saying anything. Bala raised his stick, barring Mantinder's path. He stared at Mantinder and with his other hand twirled the ends of his moustache.

'You have no sons – who will protect you, Munni?' he said.

The other men glared silently at Mantinder. After a few moments Bala dropped his stick and let him go.

For the rest of the evening Mantinder was deep in thought. He was not a man prone to thinking about things; his daily routine of walking to the fields and overseeing his workers, eating his lunch and returning home did not require any kind of deep thought, yet now, today, something had happened.

Mantinder walked through the big wooden double doors to his house. Bitu, his daughter, came to greet him but stopped short. She looked at his kurta pyjama which was covered in dust on the front.

'Something happen, Daddy?'

Silently Mantinder gave Bitu his cloth-covered bundle containing his empty lunch dishes and went to sit on his charpoy. Mantinder remained silent. He sat in his courtyard, walled off from the rest of the village. Small trails of smoke rose as fires were lit for the evening meal. Each house had the same design with little variation: a mud-walled compound with a one-storey building and a courtyard where buffalo were kept for milking. The entrances too were the same, thick wooden double doors, with steel plates on the front and steel hinges and locks keeping them secured.

Bitu had not expected to see her father like this. She hurriedly made him his food, giving him his tea first. She sat silently near him – not moving but watching and listening. She ate only once he had finished.

The house was silent, the village was silent, the sun set over the flat horizon of the Punjab and all around was darkness. Mantinder and Bitu slept outside in the courtyard of their house, as did most people in this dry season in the month of March. The only sounds were of insects and occasional grunts from the two black water buffalo. The whole village was asleep by 8 p.m.. Around 9 p.m. the village dogs barked and howled for ten minutes and then promptly fell silent again.

The next morning, at 4 a.m., the village priest started to recite the words of a morning prayer from the Guru Granth Sahib, the Sikh holy book. The words were written to be sung, in keeping with ancient oral traditions, yet the village priest recited them quickly and monotonously, making no attempt to follow the carefully crafted rhythm. The village woke to get ready before the sun rose. Men got up from their slumber, their voices low as they told their wives to make tea. Their beards were wild and untamed, and hair poked out at all angles from the loose half-turbans they wore to sleep. After washing, the men sat on charpoys waiting for their tea. The wives and daughters busily prepared the morning fare. Mothers shouted at daughters from behind chunnis clenched into their mouths to stop them falling and letting the cold morning air onto their heads and faces. Crouching in squatting positions, they milked the buffalo and then heated the milk in blackened steel vessels on dried buffalo manure pancakes which had become red-hot from being heated up with kindling. Busily, they cooked the parathas, which they wrapped up in cloth to be taken to the fields along with a pot of curd, a smaller pot of pickle and a big vessel of lassi.

Bitu had no one to shout to. She undertook all this in silence, first giving her father a cup of tea and then cooking the parathas.

A week later Mantinder told Bitu to put on her nice salwar kameez.

'We are visiting your bhua,' he announced.

Bitu did as she was told. She washed herself with soap and oiled her uncut hair, combing it thoroughly all the way down to her knees. She plaited it tightly into a single plait which draped down her back like a tail. Wearing her best blue salwar kameez, she carefully placed her chunni over her head, tucking the sides behind her ears. She and Mantinder got onto a neighbour's bullock cart which would take them out of the village, past the fields and onto the road to the next town where her paternal aunt lived. Bitu tugged at the front of her chunni until there was enough material to hold on to with her teeth and cover her face from the light wind of the dry, dusty plains.

Once off the bullock cart and on the road, Mantinder walked at a steady pace. Bitu had to skip every few steps to keep up with her father. They walked silently; the sun was starting to get hot and Bitu was sweating. Mantinder knew this path well and did not have to look up to see the flat fields, full of kanak all around him. The flat, straight road ran between the two districts of Moga and Faridkot. The wheat would be harvested in a few weeks, and there was expectation in the air as farmers waited for the right time. The weather had been good; there had been no late rains to damage the harvest and this would mean Vasaki would be celebrated with great gusto.

Bitu dared not ask why they were going to her bhua's house, but she knew it had something to do with the day her father had fallen over. Since that day, women in the village had started to make snide remarks as they passed the house.

'Oh Bitu, where are your brothers to protect you?'

'Watch out, here come some dacoos! Who is going to protect your honour?'

The comments were followed by laughing.

Some of the small, half-naked children dared each other to shout obscenities outside their door. 'Koothi!' they shouted and then ran away laughing. Mothers pretended to scold the children but did so laughingly, without any of the usual harshness.

Bitu was not sure how to deal with these antics. She was alone at home and her father seemed far away in his thoughts and she did not wish to disturb him. Mantinder was kind and gentle with her. She had always felt lucky that she had her father all to herself and did not have to share him with anyone. She trusted him and did all she could to make him happy. But now it seemed there was something wrong and there was nothing she could do about it. She kept walking.

Mantinder's sister, Gudi, lived in a similar-sized village to theirs. Mantinder walked through the village, while Bitu made sure she completely covered her face and kept close to her father. When Mantinder reached the house, he called out to his sister.

'Gudi!'

Gudi – a fat, rotund figure who could move surprisingly fast if called upon to do so – sat on a charpoy inside her house. She was watching her servant collect buffalo dung off the ground, scooping it up with her hands into fat round pancakes and smacking them onto a wall to dry. Gudi was making sure the servant girl wasn't upsetting the buffalo, which would happen if she wasn't there to supervise. She knew these servants were liable to kick the buffalo when she wasn't around and, if the buffalo was upset, it wouldn't let anyone get its milk in the morning. When she heard her brother's call, she ran to the door and shouted at the girl.

'Leave that! Make some tea!'

The servant girl did as she was told and, as if startled by all the sudden noise and commotion, one of the buffalo lifted its tail and started to urinate. The dark yellow liquid splattered on the ground, weaving in between the cobbles and finally forming a nice puddle.

Mantinder entered the house and smiled his childlike smile at his sister. Gudi went to Mantinder and hugged him side on. Bitu greeted her bhua then followed her father into the house and sat next to him on a charpoy. The servant girl came to give them tea.

'Show Bitu the house,' Gudi said in a much nicer manner than her servant was accustomed to so far in her employment. Bitu followed the girl. The servant wore a dirty, dark-green salwar kameez and her complexion was dark too, compared to the fairness of the Sidhus. Bitu looked at her face and noted a prettiness. Her walk was busy and her back was tall and straight, as was her figure. The muscles on her bare forearms rippled as she opened the door to go inside.

'How old are you?' asked Bitu.

'Fourteen. And you?' she replied quickly.

Bitu hesitated at the servant girl's forward manner. The girl kept her eyes on Bitu for a few moments, then turned away. Bitu followed her as she led her deeper into the house. It was empty. The children were at school and her uncle, Gudi's husband, was working. Bitu looked into the bedrooms; the walls were brown, made of mud and straw. There was a picture of Guru Gobind Singh astride a white horse in one of them. In a smaller room an old man was asleep, his thin body wrapped up in bundles of white cotton, a baggy turban on his head. His mouth was open and Bitu could only see two teeth on his bottom jaw. He breathed deeply, nearly snoring, but not quite.

'This way,' whispered the girl.

Bitu followed the girl up a rickety wooden ladder, held together with twine. The wooden rungs were smooth through use. It was bright outside after the darkness of the house. Bitu looked at the village from her vantage point and saw two peacocks pecking at something on the roof of the house next door. The servant girl lay down on the roof and indicated to Bitu to do the same.

Bitu saw her father and aunt talking below them. They had fallen silent and were looking away from each other.

'If you want to marry, she must be married first. It would be bad for a new bride to be in competition with your daughter.'

Bitu's heart dropped. She looked at her father hoping for something, a sign perhaps that he wouldn't do such a thing. Mantinder nodded.

'Find out. Do it quickly,' he said.

'Do not worry. I will arrange everything. I will talk to her,' Gudi became animated as the task became part of her.

'Bitu!' Gudi cried out.

Bitu and the servant girl ducked their heads down and scurried back into the house.

'Coming!' Bitu shouted as soon as she was back down the ladder. She held down sad thoughts as she approached her father and aunt.

'Do you like the house, Bitu?' Gudi asked, her eyes now looking at her in a different way: searching, scrutinising.

'It is a very nice house, Bhuaji. I was hoping to see your lovely children.'

'Don't worry, beta, they will be home soon.' Gudi turned to the servant girl and shouted, 'Make the food!'

The servant girl sprang into action. In a squatting position, she started up the fire in the open-air kitchen. The stove was built out of the wall at ground level, with the same mud–straw material. Inside, the stove was blackened by years of use. Once it was hot, she warmed the dhal she had made earlier and heated the thuvva to cook chapatis on.

Mantinder was served first and the women waited until he had eaten before eating themselves. There was silence in the house – punctuated only by screaming kingfishers, peacocks and crows.

For the rest of the day, Bitu felt eyes were on her more than usual when visiting relatives. She was polite and ready to do the smallest task, even though she knew the servant would do it anyway.

Once she had been told by her bhua that she would be married, Bitu kept looking towards the servant girl who was now on her haunches, sweeping the floor. She used a brush made out of long, thin reeds tied at one end with tight string, balancing on one leg and brushing with the opposite hand, then swapping hands and balancing on the other leg, gathering the dirt on the floor between her legs. Once or twice she looked up to see Bitu, silent, looking serious and nodding to her aunt. When Mantinder and Bitu were ready to leave, she paused her work to look at her. Bitu looked in her direction and for a millisecond broke into a smile. The servant girl dared not smile back but kept the image of Bitu's smile in her head and would think about her when she curled up to sleep that night.

Bitu was married two months later to the son of a local family, a week after her sixteenth birthday. Now the way was clear for Mantinder himself to be married. And with Bitu gone, the memory of Mantinder's first wife, who died in childbirth, was forgotten.

The first child Mantinder bore with his new wife, Harbajan, was a boy, and celebrations were held. Two more boys completed the family and Mantinder did not need to worry any more. Now that there were no more comments or threats against him, Mantinder continued as he had done before. He got up, drank his tea, washed, ate breakfast, went to the fields and then walked home – stopping on the corner with Bala and the others, who felt more comfortable with him again.

As the boys grew up into teenagers, Mantinder Singh Sidhu did less and less work in the fields and spent more and more time idling on the corner with other old men who had no more cares in the world.

'But what about Sukhdev? He is dry like hay, he cannot work in the fields,' said one of the men.

Mantinder stopped. He had to think again. He looked at the others, hoping for some kind of guidance. He knew it was true. Sukhdev, his third son, was a runt. He had always been ill as a child and was regularly bullied by his brothers; it was only Mantinder's intervention, with his natural aversion to any kind of conflict, that stopped the bullying. Yet he also knew this was making Sukhdev soft.

'You should send him to school, he will be useless on the farm,' another man said. All the men nodded and grunted in approval at these words. They held on to the staffs which they carried around with them everywhere, all looking towards the sun, which was setting over the chuppar, where buffalo bathed in the afternoon heat. They each popped a small ball of opium into their mouths and silently listened to the noise of the village they knew so well, watching the flights of the birds swooping low over the surface of the water and a bullock cart moving slowly along the road, its wheels kicking up dust off the dry, flat land of the Punjab.

Chapter 1

Mr Sidhu held a pencil tightly in his hand as it hovered just above the page. His turbaned head was bowed down over his accounts book. The columns and rows he was meant to be filling in were all blank. He would have to fill them in later, it was something he always took pleasure in. However, right now, all he really wanted to do was stare at Rose and watch her as she unpacked the goods he had laid out for her that morning.

The shop was narrow. As you entered, the counter was on the left and on the right were shelves filled with boxes of fresh fruit and vegetables. Further on were dairy cabinets containing cold drinks and sandwiches, single samosas in plastic packets, cheeses and milk. More shelves of canned goods and household products led up to the post office end of the premises. The stock was stacked in small piles around the front counter. As Mr Sidhu tried not to stare, Rose busied herself with her work, arranging the stock and putting it out on the shelves. Her thin cardigan and cotton dress moved easily over her lean frame. She looked young for her age.

Rose stopped to set the correct price on the handheld price gun. Mr Sidhu watched her from behind the reinforced glass of his post office as she rotated the dials until the correct price appeared. She started to stamp the small adhesive price labels onto the slim rectangular tins of sardines in tomato sauce – twelve hard stamps. Mr Sidhu's breath became shallow and his mouth opened slightly. Something stirred within him. Rose stopped, placed the price gun down, looked up at him and smiled. Startled, he quickly returned to his accounts, unable to meet her gaze.

These moments in the shop were happening more and more often. When there were no customers for either the post office or the shop, Mr Sidhu found himself unable to focus on his work. He felt safe locked inside the bulletproof, reinforced glass of the security-locked post office, but he still had to go to the toilet and cover Rose on the till while she took her lunch break.

'Cup of tea, David?' called Rose, standing by a box full of crisp packets. The shop was empty and the words hung in the air. She had said his name again. *David.*

Mr Sidhu's first name was Sukhdev, but everyone who came to his shop and post office called him David. Ever since he was first asked all those years ago.

'Sook *what*?' they'd asked.

'Sukh-*dev*. Like *Dave*,' he'd said hurriedly, not wanting to dwell on his difference.

'Oh, David?'

'Yes, yes, David,' he'd said. And so it stuck. Dave. Or David.

He liked David as it sounded more respectable than Dave. However, it happened that the more respectable customers *did* call him David, and the less so called him Dave or even Davey, as Bill, the Scotsman, liked to call him. Rose called him David. And to Mr Sidhu, when she said it, it sounded like nothing he'd ever heard before. Sukhdev meant something else to him, especially after being called Sukhdev by his wife for so many years. David and Sukhdev had nothing in common. They lived in different worlds with different sensibilities. It used to embarrass him when his wife called him Sukhdev in front of his customers. So much so that he'd asked her not to do so. They never discussed the reason why, but they knew it was good for business and so 'Sukhdev' was never called upon in the post office again. Sukhdev was relegated to his home and community back in Hounslow (TW5), not Richmond (TW9).

Rose was still waiting for his reply.

'Yes, thank you, cup of tea, lovely . . . thank you, Rose,' said Mr Sidhu and then again pretended to go back to his accounts, marking figures randomly on the page in an effort to look busy. He would have to rub out his scribbles later.

The post office and shop were empty. It was Wednesday, which was balance day, so the post office closed at 1 p.m.. It was a quiet time anyway, as it always was between the last day of post for Christmas and the Christmas holidays. The darkness outside made the shop cosy, a kind of sanctuary. Outside the small parade of shops where Mr Sidhu's post office was situated, the street was empty. Most people were either in the pubs for their extended Christmas lunches or rushing around the high street buying last-minute presents.

Mr Sidhu could hear the kettle boiling and he knew he would have to open the post office window to receive the cup of tea from Rose. And then there would be nothing between them, no glass, no door, just air.

The shop door opened and the noise of the cars passing on the road outside made Mr Sidhu look up. A scruffy young man strode in, holding something out in his hand.

'Hello, mate, I'm not too late, am I?' he called out.

Mr Sidhu looked at the man, who appeared about thirty but could be younger, his jeans ripped and his tired white trainers grubby with dirt.

'Need to cash my old dear's pension before Christmas. Don't tell me I'm too late?'

The man's eyes pleaded to Mr Sidhu.

'She can't come herself. She's going a bit, you know,' he added, tapping his head. 'Lucky I was coming to see her. Not too late, am I?' he repeated.

'Let me see,' said Mr Sidhu, indicating for the man to pass the pension book under the security glass. He examined the book, which was Min's, a regular who was indeed going a little senile. Rose came to give him his tea.

'I'm her nephew, Simon. Thank you, I appreciate this. Just want to get it cashed before Christmas.'

'The post office is closed, I'm afraid. You'll have to come in the morning,' said Rose. It was something she was never afraid of telling the customers who'd come late. Mr Sidhu liked that trait in her.

'It's OK, Rose, it's for Min,' said Mr Sidhu. 'I'll deal with it.'

'David, you can't serve anyone who comes at any time. You've got your work to do,' Rose said, shaking her head as she went back to the shop counter.

'Thanks, mate. I appreciate that,' said the man, smiling. His mouth revealed yellowed teeth and some gaps where teeth should have been.

'Do you have some identification, Simon?'

The man made a show of checking his pockets and put his hands to his head.

'I was that much in a rush to get here I left everything.'

Mr Sidhu and Rose exchanged a glance.

'It's OK, you can go and get it, I will still be here,' said Mr Sidhu.

'It's just I'm in a bit of a rush, actually.'

'No problem, I will be here,' repeated Mr Sidhu.

'Can you give us the book back, then?'

'The pension book will stay here,' said Mr Sidhu, looking directly at him.

'I think Min would want it back.'

'You see, Simon, this pension book, just like your driving licence and passport, is government property. It is my duty to keep it here, but once you have your or Min's ID, I can give you the pension.'

Mr Sidhu shrugged and opened his palms to the ceiling as if to say 'this is out of my hands'. The two men looked at each other. Mr Sidhu, who had dealt with men like this for many years, held his stare.

'Fuck you, you fucking Paki,' the man blurted out, slamming his hand onto the counter. Mr Sidhu glanced at Rose and then spoke to the man.

'Just go before I call the police. They will be here in minutes.'

Mr Sidhu nudged his foot closer to the foot alarm which he could press easily if he needed to. The alarm was connected directly to the local police station.

The scruffy man turned to leave – but not before pushing over a slim wire card carousel. It fell, leaving birthday, anniversary and engagement cards mixed up with bereavement cards on the floor. This last action angered Mr Sidhu the most. He could have called the police and made things worse for the man, but he hadn't, and he knew it would be Rose who would clear it all up. The man walked to the shop door and Rose stood behind the counter, one hand out of sight. Mr Sidhu was sure she was holding on to a rounders bat that was hidden under the chocolate counter. He himself had picked up the hockey stick he kept inside the post office in case he needed to use it.

'I'm not a Pakistani. I'm Indian!' declared Mr Sidhu as the man, who might have been called Simon, left, never to be seen again in his post office.

Mr Sidhu opened the post office door, making sure he locked it behind him, and walked over to Rose. He peered out of the window.

'You OK, Rose?'

'What a rude man,' she replied. 'I'm fine, but how did he get Min's book?'

'Not sure. I will go and see her.'

'We're lucky to have you, David.'

Mr Sidhu's heart started to beat loudly in his chest and he felt his face go red. He said nothing and went to pick up the fallen greeting cards.

'Leave that,' said Rose, touching his arm and making him jerk slightly. 'Are you OK, David?' Her spectacled eyes peered into his and for a moment he had no idea how he had arrived here. Had she asked him a question? Her blue eyes sparkled at him. Then he saw the cards on the floor and remembered what was happening.

'I will go to see Min,' he managed to say.

Min's two-up, two-down worker's cottage was around the corner from the post office on a small cul-de-sac. Mr Sidhu knocked on her door. He heard some shuffling and then the door opened.

'Hello, dearie,' said Min, a huge smile on her face. Mr Sidhu looked down at her; she was five foot nothing and nearly as wide. She used a walking stick in the house and two when she made her way to the Shaftesbury Arms for her early evening gin and tonic.

'Come in, come in.'

Mr Sidhu smiled and walked into her lounge. He was amazed to see the walls covered in framed paintings. They were all different sizes, some of them obviously of a tree or an animal, others an abstract mix of colours and shades. Mr Sidhu had never seen a house with so many pictures covering the walls. It took him a moment to remember what he was there for.

'Min,' Mr Sidhu said loudly like an Englishman abroad, even though Min wasn't deaf, 'I have your pension book!'

Min looked at the book.

'That lovely man from the council said he was going to get my Christmas money,' she said happily.

Mr Sidhu shook his head. 'This man is no good,' he said, shaking his finger left to right.

Min looked confused. Mr Sidhu sighed. It made him feel anxious that she lived alone like this. He got her pension money out of his pocket. He'd stamped the next two weeks with the official Post Office stamp, '23Dec2007' and '30Dec2007'. The Post Office allowed people to collect two weeks' worth of pensions over the Christmas period.

'This is two weeks' money, but I am taking twenty pounds for the book,' said Mr Sidhu, taking twenty pounds from the pile of notes he was giving to Min. Mr Sidhu had a credit book in the shop but only for the customers who received their pension or benefits from the Post Office. In that way he was sure to get his money back and the money was spent in his shop, too. It was an idea he and his wife had come up with in the early days to make their business thrive. Min owed him money from the previous week. She took her money and then gave Mr Sidhu another twenty pounds.

'Is that enough? Do you want more?' She stared at him like a child.

'No! It's OK. It's enough.'

Mr Sidhu walked back to the post office with her book in his pocket. He would keep it in the post office and give her the money when she needed it. She'd already lost the book a few times and he didn't want to risk her being without it. As he opened the door to the shop, he was met by a crowd of locals including Richard the retired solicitor and Bill.

'Here he is,' exclaimed Richard as the crowd looked at him.

'You should've seen him. Cool as a cucumber, weren't you, David?' said Rose.

Mr Sidhu was embarrassed by all the attention. And by habit, he scratched his head with a pencil from his pocket, sliding it underneath his turban, behind his ear, and mumbled that anyone would have done the same.

'Nonsense, Sidhu,' piped up Richard, 'you stood up to the dacoit! Like a proper Sardaarji. I hope you gave him a good thappar,' he chuckled.

Richard had been born in Lahore when it had been the

capital of the unpartitioned Punjab as it had been when Mr Sidhu was a child. Richard liked to speak to Mr Sidhu with smatterings of Punjabi, Hindi and Urdu, which Mr Sidhu always enjoyed.

'Anyone comes like that, you tell me, Davey. They can deal with me,' said Bill in his thick Glaswegian accent, grinding a fist into his other hand to show he meant business. The crowd looked at Mr Sidhu, waiting for him to say something.

'Thank you. Please, it was nothing,' he said but the locals still looked at him expectantly. He didn't like being the centre of attention and added quickly, 'I have work to do,' and then walked back to his post office counter. He sat down and pretended to work again as he watched Rose talk with the locals. He could tell she was talking about him and could feel butterflies in his stomach. After a while they all started to leave.

Once the shop was empty, Rose came up to the post office window.

'Was Min OK?' she asked.

'Yes, she is fine, but we need to keep an eye, make sure she is OK,' said Mr Sidhu.

He explained what had happened at the house and showed Rose Min's pension book.

'I will keep it here. It is better.'

'Good idea. And we can even tell Gerry in the Arms to get her bar bill paid from you,' said Rose. Mr Sidhu nodded in agreement. It was the right thing to do. Min had a son, but he lived far away and Min needed looking after.

Rose turned the open sign to closed on the door. It was time for her to go. She'd tidied up and made everything ready for

19

the next day, and all Mr Sidhu had to do before leaving was vacuum the floor.

'You doing anything nice for Christmas, David?' asked Rose as she busied herself putting on her coat, scarf and gloves.

Mr Sidhu nearly always spent Christmas alone at home. Meenu, his daughter, usually went to her fiancé's parents for Christmas in Shropshire (SY5) and Raju went wherever he thought it was 'cool' to go with his actor friends. Meenu would try to persuade him to go up to Craig's parents', but Mr Sidhu could not bring himself to go alone without Sarabjit, and he actually enjoyed being on his own at home, something Meenu didn't understand.

'Lots to do, Rose. Have to get ready for the new computer system. They are installing it before the new year,' he said, hoping that would be enough of an explanation. In reality he had little to do. A team from a company called Fujitsu were coming in to wire up the new terminal and he'd already had a few days' training – it all seemed simple enough.

'You can't be working over Christmas, David, it's not right,' said Rose, taken aback.

Mr Sidhu wanted to say that it was perfectly normal to work over Christmas in India and that it was on Diwali that he found it hard to work here in England. However, he also knew that he didn't want to disrespect the English customs of being with family and drunk at Christmas. Years ago, when money had been tight and he and his wife had opened the shop on Christmas Day, customers had been shocked to see them working even though they still bought cigarettes and milk. Nowadays money wasn't tight, so he could afford to close and lean into the English ways.

'What are your children doing?'

Mr Sidhu explained that they would be away. Rose's gaze softened and she came close to him.

'David, why don't you come to mine for Christmas lunch?'

'No, no,' said Mr Sidhu with a thin smile, wanting Rose to leave so he would not have to refuse her too directly. His head felt hot under his turban and he could feel beads of sweat trickling down his forehead.

'It'll only be for a few hours. It would be an honour, David. You look after us lot here – you need looking after too, you know.'

Mr Sidhu swallowed, unable to think of anything to say.

'Think about it, David. See you tomorrow,' she said before touching his arm and flashing him a smile.

Mr Sidhu heard the door close. By that time the world had become a blur and the sweat had seeped into his eyes. He took off his glasses and wiped them with a tissue. When he put them back on again and the world came into focus, the shop was empty with only the humming of the dairy cabinets to keep him company.

On the drive home, Mr Sidhu told Sarabjit about his day, including the bit about Min and her pension book. Then he got onto the topic that came up again and again in their conversations: the settling of their children. 'Meenu is still the same,' said Mr Sidhu. 'I haven't seen Craig for a long time. She says he is busy. I don't know. I want to ask her, but she gets angry if I say anything. So I think at least she has a good job; Craig earns good money too. But no marriage. Raju, I don't know what he is doing. He is still doing this acting business. He makes everything into a joke or an argument. He thinks I am an idiot. Sometimes I wish you could visit him, talk to him. He would listen to you. These children, they think they know better than us, hunnah?'

Mr Sidhu smiled to himself. When his children had finally left home and he and Sarabjit had the house back to themselves, they'd enjoyed a period of calm where they were not awash with the moods and latest dramas of their two children. He and Sarabjit had never known that kind of peace before. They'd started to tend to their garden which had been neglected for so long. Building up their business and bringing up two children had taken its toll on them and their marriage. The recessions of the Eighties and Nineties had nearly bankrupted them, but somehow through hard work and luck they'd survived. The time they'd shared together when it was just the two of them now felt like a time of preparation for what happened next. Sarabjit received the diagnosis out of the blue. 'Just a precaution,' the doctor had said, but the scan and tests had come back positive for breast cancer. He'd taken her to a hospital in Chelsea for her course of chemotherapy. He'd juiced beetroots, apples, celery and carrots for her in an effort to give her body all the nutrients she needed. But in the end, after a short remission, the cancer took her away and he accepted it. She told him that it was not in their hands; they had to do what they could but if she had to go then she had to go, and that was it. Then it would be up to him to settle the children. So, he thought fondly of that time, the time they'd had briefly when they'd become so close.

But now what? Why did he have these feelings for Rose? Was he lonely? He didn't seek out those feelings; they were just there, pulling him towards something. He didn't dare utter anything about them to Sarabjit, but something told him she knew. She was always with him in his heart, so why was he thinking about Rose all the time? He didn't want to do that; he didn't want to betray his love for Sarabjit. He knew something needed to be done. But what?

Chapter 2

Meenu and Raju were already at his house when he arrived home in Hounslow. Meenu came every Wednesday without fail. It wasn't something they had arranged or planned; Meenu had decided that that was what she would do. Mr Sidhu assumed it was convenient for her and he appreciated her making food for him. He was surprised that Raju was there too. Raju's appearances were sporadic and he never came this early. Perhaps he had some news. He might have even got a proper job.

'Hello, hello,' Mr Sidhu said, trying to be as welcoming as he could.

'Hi Dad,' Meenu smiled at him as he stood in the doorway of the kitchen. Her dyed blonde hair was up in a ponytail with two strands coming down either side of her face, and she wore slim-fitting jeans with a grey hoodie. She was making the rotis on the thuvva and using a chimta to flip them over. It was the same one Sarabjit had used.

'Sat Sri Akal, Pitaji,' said Raju, approaching him and bending down to touch his feet. He held his hands together as he stood up. Raju was being silly, trying to make his sister laugh. He'd always been like that. Mr Sidhu looked at Meenu who shook her head and sighed, not joining in with his joke.

'Hello Dad,' exclaimed Raju, holding Mr Sidhu's shoulders while looking into his eyes. Mr Sidhu didn't like his neat, trimmed beard and long, shoulder-length hair. He should be wearing a turban, thought Mr Sidhu, but he'd learned that forcing your children to do what you wanted only made them resentful. You had to let them make their own mistakes, which they would blame on you anyway.

'Tell me all your secrets,' Raju whispered. Mr Sidhu blinked and tried not to think of Rose. Raju burst out laughing. 'Oh Dad, you are so . . .' he started rubbing Mr Sidhu's beard, '. . . hairy!' Raju let go of him and turned his attention to the kitchen.

'I've got a lovely bottle of wine, Dad. It's a Châteauneuf-du-Pape. I know you have no idea what that is, but I shall explain.'

Mr Sidhu and Meenu exchanged a quick glance. She smiled at him and immediately Mr Sidhu regretted the look. It was not good that Meenu was so at home in his house. As a daughter she should make her house with her husband, if only she would get married.

The three of them sat down to dinner. The kitchen was still a kitchen in his house; it wasn't joined into the lounge like so many were. The smell of smoked aubergine in the partha, coupled with the lamb curry and melting butter on the fresh hot rotis, made Mr Sidhu's mouth salivate. Meenu placed the dishes on the table while the two men sat.

'As I said, this is a Châteauneuf-du-Pape.' Raju held the bottle in the way waiters did at restaurants. 'It means, roughly translated, "the Pope's new house", which is what Avignon was in the south of France at a time when the Pope fled the Vatican.

And why, you may ask, am I bringing this wine?' Raju paused for effect. 'Because I am going to Avignon this July for their annual festival. They've invited us to put on a show. Voilà!' And with that he gave a small bow. Apart from his acting work, Raju also ran a small theatre company with two friends. It was a world that neither Mr Sidhu nor Meenu ever really understood or cared much about.

'Very good, Raju,' said Mr Sidhu.

'How much are they paying you for that, then, Raju?' asked Meenu without looking up.

'Not as much as the compensation they pay you for sitting for hours in front of a metal box with a light in it, obviously, darling sister. This is just red wine to you, I suppose? Want some?' Raju held the bottle out to Meenu.

Mr Sidhu knew Meenu drank, but for some reason she didn't like drinking in front of him, even though he didn't care. Raju, on the other hand, drank too much in Mr Sidhu's opinion, but didn't ever hide it. He never got out of control, but once he started, he didn't stop. Mr Sidhu enjoyed a whisky after getting home on his own, but these days he didn't really socialize like he used to with Sarabjit. He didn't really miss it either.

Mr Sidhu nodded and Raju poured him a glass. Mr Sidhu didn't like the idea of Raju drinking alone. He would have one glass.

They ate in silence, something Mr Sidhu was very used to these days, but he could see Meenu and Raju exchanging looks. They were up to something. Raju cleared his throat.

'This is delicious, Meenu, thanks. What do you think, Dad?'

'Yes, very nice, beta,' said Mr Sidhu smiling, but thinking that it wasn't as good as Sarabjit's cooking.

'So, Dad. I was thinking,' said Meenu, 'that it might be nice for us all to go away somewhere for Christmas as a family. We've never done that. Let's do something different. Get out of London. We could visit Craig's parents in Shropshire, I've rented a little cottage nearby. We could all stay there, or you could stay at his parents' house if you prefer,' her eyes looked at him earnestly.

'That sounds nice,' said Raju a little mechanically. They both looked at Mr Sidhu.

Mr Sidhu was eating and didn't want to stop, because that would mean he'd have to tell them it was the last thing he wanted to do. He was confused as to why they were asking him. He quite liked the deal they had where they all did their own thing.

'What do you say, Dad?' asked Raju, smiling at him. Meenu was also smiling at him. This was not going to be easy. Mr Sidhu took a sip of the wine. It was pleasant.

Mr Sidhu had visited Craig's parents, Douggie and Sue, a couple of times with Sarabjit during the summer months, but in recent years he hadn't seen Craig much, and Craig's parents hadn't come to see him either. They were good people, both recently retired professionals, and their two sons were also both professionals. Craig was a journalist and his brother a chartered surveyor. Mr Sidhu and Sarabjit had decided early on in their marriage that they would not be like the backward types who insisted that their children only marry Punjabis from the same caste and all the other silly things that people held on to when they emigrated. They would look at the person and their family. And so they had accepted Craig into the family. Meenu and Craig had got engaged after Sarabjit's passing, but since then nothing had happened. Mr Sidhu tore off a piece of roti and used it to scoop up some partha from the bowl. He loved anything with peas in it.

'It's really nice in winter. They've got a big fireplace and the local pubs are great,' Meenu continued.

'Something happened, beta?' asked Mr Sidhu. Raju and Meenu both looked at him as if he'd just berated them.

He changed tack, thinking he might not have struck the right tone.

'No, I was just thinking maybe there is some news? And that's why you are inviting me,' said Mr Sidhu, feeling hopeful and trying to smile. He looked at Meenu, hoping for good news. But Meenu's face gave nothing away.

'No, why?' she asked, looking serious. 'No, nothing's happened, Dad. I just thought it would be nice for us all to be together.'

'Haven't set a date, then?' chirped Raju, smirking. 'Or is there something else?' he asked mysteriously, his eyebrows raised. Meenu's face hardened for a moment before softening again.

'It's not nice for Dad to be on his own at Christmas,' she said quietly.

'It's OK, beta. I don't mind being here, really. It's a very nice thing you are saying, but there is a lot to do with the new IT system coming in. I have to get everything ready,' said Mr Sidhu, hoping he looked earnest. In fact there was nothing to do. He placed a piece of roti in his mouth and let the flavour envelop it.

'Maybe next year we go, hunnah?'

He turned to Raju. 'Everything OK with the flat?'

Mr Sidhu was proud that he and Sarabjit had been able to

give deposits to both his children to enable them to buy their own property.

'I can come and have a look at the IT system if you want, Dad? I can help,' said Meenu, ignoring his question to Raju. Meenu worked with computers. She was successful but Mr Sidhu had no idea what she did. He agreed that she could come and have a look. He was pleased with himself for getting out of this attempt to disrupt his plans. Of course, it also meant that he could, if he chose to, see Rose.

'Everything OK with the flat?' he asked again. Raju was prone to paying workmen too much when anything went wrong, so Mr Sidhu liked to keep abreast of such matters. Mr Sidhu had various Punjabi builders whom he would call when he needed anything done, but because Raju was unable to speak Punjabi properly, he floundered whenever he had to deal with them. They laughed at his inability to speak his own language, which Raju took as a personal slight, so instead Raju would use English builders who would charge double or triple what a job was worth, fleecing him. This annoyed Mr Sidhu for two reasons: firstly, it reminded him that his only son was a bit of an idiot, and secondly, Mr Sidhu didn't like paying for things he knew he could get for a cheaper price. It hurt his business pride.

When he and Sarabjit had broached the subject of buying a flat for him, Raju had been dismissive. The idea of mortgage repayments and the responsibility of owning a property had filled him with dread. Mr Sidhu remembered that a couple of times, when his children were young, he and his wife had told them that the banks might repossess their house and that they might have to close their business because of high interest rates and recessions, so he understood Raju's anxiety. However,

Raju also claimed that he didn't need their help and that he would do it all himself once he was an established actor. He and Sarabjit didn't laugh out loud in front of him, but instead found a lovely three-bedroom flat in Putney, after tactfully asking him where he'd like to live in West London. They gave him a deposit and even introduced him to a friendly mortgage advisor who got Raju a self-certified mortgage. At the time, Raju didn't understand the nature of property.

'Why do I need three bedrooms?' he glared at them as if they were trying to imprison him, rather than setting him free. They had told him that by renting rooms to his friends, his mortgage would be paid for and any money he earned he could keep. They had been right, of course, and did not receive any gratitude for it, but that was not why they did it. They did it because they wanted the best for their child.

'Yeah, flat's all fine, Dad.'

'Still making money off your friends?' asked Meenu.

'Just providing top-notch accommodation at a fair price.'

'Is that what they taught you at drama school?'

'Craig happy with your flat, is he? Pays his way, I hope?'

They looked at each other while Mr Sidhu ignored them and settled himself in his armchair to watch the news. Meenu cleared the dishes while Raju came to sit with him.

'You going to be all right on your own this Christmas, Dad?'

'Of course I am fine, Raju. Every year I am fine. Why you are both asking me suddenly, ha?'

Raju leaned into his father. 'It's Meenu. She thinks you need looking after – you know, because you're getting old and everything.' He smirked.

Even though it was a nice thing that his daughter cared about him, the idea irritated Mr Sidhu. He'd prefer her to get married to Craig and start a family rather than worrying about him. He pretended to be interested in the news.

'You are going?' he asked Raju.

'Course not, not if you're not going, Dad.'

'Why is she making a fuss?'

'I dunno. She's been going on about how we need to make sure you're OK. That living all alone isn't good for you. You seem OK to me, though,' said Raju matter-of-factly. Mr Sidhu was touched at his son's comment. It was the nicest thing Raju had said to him for a long time.

'Maybe she is missing her mother,' Mr Sidhu said more to himself than Raju. He knew how much Sarabjit had missed her own mother when she'd left India. Perhaps Meenu needed to talk to him. The thought sent a shiver down Mr Sidhu's spine. He wasn't good at talking to his daughter.

'And what about you, puttar? You have any news?' Mr Sidhu asked Raju gently.

'I told you about my Avignon commission.'

Mr Sidhu was irritated. 'No, any girlfriend yet?'

'Leave it out, Dad,' said Raju, turning his head to the television. 'There's a lot more to life than just getting married. Jesus.'

Mr Sidhu was transported back to when Raju was a teenager and he'd ask him to work in the shop. He got the same reply then: *'Jesus, Dad. There's more to life than working in the shop!'*

'I've finished, Dad,' said Meenu, coming into the lounge, drying her hands. Raju was drinking his third glass of wine.

'Thanks, sis, bohot acha!' said Raju.

'Hope you liked it too, Dad?'

Mr Sidhu got up and looked at Meenu. 'Thank you, beta. Tell Craig's parents I am sorry I can't come. You explain to them that it is a busy time, hunnah?'

'Yes, of course, Dad.'

The two of them remained standing for a few moments before Meenu spoke again. Mr Sidhu was thinking about what he could wear for Christmas lunch at Rose's house – if he decided to go, of course. He decided he would wear what he normally wore. Trousers, shirt, tie, pullover and jacket.

'Well, it's a shame you can't come, Dad. Is there really no way you can come?' Her eyes implored him.

'The computer system,' he managed to say, 'I need to be here, beta.' He felt bad that he was putting his own needs ahead of Meenu's. She doesn't know what it's like for me, he thought, being there and talking to Craig's parents but then not having Sarabjit there to gossip about them with afterwards. There was hardly anyone he could joke about the English to anymore.

'We're leaving tomorrow so I won't see you before I go,' said Meenu.

'OK, beta.'

'I'll come over after New Year's to look at the new IT system.'

'Yes, beta.'

'It must be exciting having this new computer system, Dad?' said Meenu. Mr Sidhu could tell she was trying her best not to show her disappointment.

'Yeah, really exciting,' interjected Raju.

Mr Sidhu shook his head. 'Beta, you come after New Year and you can show me how to use the new system, OK?' He made a mental note to try his best to talk to her then.

'I will, Dad. Merry Christmas.'

'Merry Christmas, beta.'

They hugged each other side to side, which was the usual way, and then Meenu left. Mr Sidhu closed the door behind her, wondering how his daughter really was. And for some reason his mind wandered towards Rose. Was he being foolish? Mr Sidhu started to rub his kara on his right wrist, then looked at his son, his leg resting on the armrest of the sofa while he drank his wine. Raju turned to him.

'Go on then, Dad, tell us about this place you're thinking about.'

Mr Sidhu had told Raju that he'd found a house in Richmond he wanted to buy. A small cottage, not far from the post office. He placed the details on the dining table.

'Very nice,' said Raju, 'Meenu won't like it, though. She loves coming here, making food and all that.'

'She can come to my new house,' said Mr Sidhu. 'I don't want to drive all the time; I want to walk and see the parks in Richmond. Here there is nothing,' he said, meaning Hounslow.

Raju looked at Mr Sidhu for a few moments and slowly nodded his head, 'Fair enough.'

Mr Sidhu was pleased to know Raju approved. Suddenly he wondered, am I just moving to Richmond to be closer to Rose?

He cleared his throat.

'The rooms are rented out?' he asked, trying to focus his mind.

'What? Oh, you mean my place. Yeah, you know, it's actually brilliant having spare rooms to rent out. There are always actors who need a place to stay. It helps,' said Raju, his face looking solemn, which was rare.

'Good,' said Mr Sidhu, feeling satisfied all was well.

Raju looked down at his feet and twirled his long hair around a finger. 'What if interest rates go up, Dad? What if house prices collapse?' he asked. 'I think about that, you know. About you and Mum and the interest rates and everything.'

'Beta, in good areas prices never go down,' Mr Sidhu said proudly. It was true. It was what he had observed during the recessions. He knew other Punjabis who had properties that lost a quarter or more of their value at the end of the Eighties. And what had been even more problematic for many had been their inability to sell those properties. Many had gone bankrupt, but miraculously Richmond prices stayed level. He and Sarabjit had admittedly overstretched themselves a little by buying a second investment property in Richmond in the Eighties. However, they had been surprised to be able to sell it and still make a profit and secure deposits for their children, while others had simply handed their house keys back to their banks, being unable to sell or pay the mortgage. It was probably at that moment that he'd developed a new level of respect for Richmond. The fact that most people were polite had already endeared him to it, but now there seemed an even bigger strength in the place.

'Don't worry, Raju. You will be OK,' he said.

'How do you know?' asked Raju.

'I know. You are in a good position, Raju, you don't have to worry like we had to worry,' he said and left it at that.

Mr Sidhu lay in bed wearing his kurta pyjama, his long grey hair spread out on the pillow. After a day wrapped up in his turban it felt nice to give his scalp a good scratching. He couldn't get Rose out of his mind. He'd forgotten to tell his children about the fraudster, he realised. Perhaps because it involved Rose. He was scared that he might give something away. Meenu would pick up on it. Women were like that in his experience. Sarabjit would know he had something on his mind, even when he thought he was hiding it well. She probably knew about it now. Sometimes when he closed his eyes before sleeping, he imagined floating away into space and finding Sarabjit in some other universe, floating and reaching out her hands to his. They never needed to talk to each other, it was as if they knew everything that had happened and that would happen. Just being together was enough. They would hold hands and fly over planets and stars and suns. He would often fall asleep like that. But not today. Today he could feel his heart beating and when he closed his eyes, he could only see Rose smiling at him, with her lovely blue eyes. He stopped and opened his eyes.

Chapter 3

It was Christmas Eve, which meant the post office closed at 1 p.m., but the shop remained open until later. Mr Sidhu sat in the basement having his lunch, which lasted until 2 p.m., when he would relieve Rose, whom he would not ordinarily see again until after the Christmas break. The basement housed stock along with miscellaneous items relating to Post Office business: an old set of scales, a safe, Special Delivery envelopes and lots of out-of-date paper forms. Mr Sidhu sat on a chair that had already been there along with a few others when he'd bought the post office. He liked the chairs, which were wooden and sturdy. Through years of use the seats had become curved, smooth and, more importantly, comfortable. He looked at his lunch – a chicken salad sandwich from the dairy cabinet, a samosa and a packet of chilli flavoured crisps – pushing away all thoughts about the potential Christmas lunch that he'd been invited to by Rose. Ordinarily, the post office was closed all day Christmas Day and Boxing Day. Then it was back to work for the rest of the year until New Year's Eve. This year things were being done differently: the post office would stay closed after Boxing Day while the new computer system was being installed, but he would still need to open the shop. Some years the dates conspired against him and Christmas Eve would fall on a Thursday. This would mean a three-day weekend and half the stock of milk going off, something that Mr Sidhu would rather do without. A regular week meant that the milk and bread would sell and there would be no need to reduce them to half price once the mould had started.

For the last five years, Mr Sidhu had done the same thing every year for Christmas. As a Christmas treat, he would go to Southall and order three days' worth of food: lots of tandoori chicken, chole, gosht, saag, keema muttar, karela and bhindi. For chapatis he would use the Mexican fajita wraps from his shop. He had never got the hang of making chapatis, which was his wife's domain. His always came out square and thick. It was why he didn't mind when Meenu came over to cook.

Mr Sidhu wasn't sure whether he needed to say anything to Rose about her invitation. He wasn't used to arranging things in this way. The morning had passed without incident and there had been no awkwardness between them. He didn't know why he was getting so worked up about this. Perhaps he should just go with Meenu and stop all this nonsense. He looked down at his uneaten sandwich and unopened packet of crisps. But what if Rose had already bought the extra food for the meal? He would be letting her down. Mr Sidhu was lost in his thoughts when Rose called down to him from the entrance to the cellar.

'Dav-id, it's ten past.'

He hurried up the stairs.

'Fell asleep, did you?' asked Rose, her blue eyes staring at him, her face smiling. Mr Sidhu could not meet her gaze.

'So what time shall I expect you tomorrow?' she asked.

Before Mr Sidhu could even answer, he heard his daughter's voice coming from the shop.

'Hi, Dad,' said Meenu, coming into the small alcove which led down to the basement. The three of them stood silently for a few moments before Mr Sidhu could get his tongue to work.

'Hello, beta.' He smiled, hoping it looked authentic.

'Hello, Meenu,' echoed Rose.

'Yes, fine, thanks,' Meenu answered to the question she thought she'd heard.

Rose walked back to the counter, leaving Mr Sidhu and Meenu alone together in the alcove. On the wall were a couple of hooks with Mr Sidhu and Rose's coats hung up, and there was also a small shelf which held a kettle, tea bags and mugs. Meenu had been making these sudden visits to the post office recently. They were unannounced and Mr Sidhu didn't know what they were about.

'I wanted to see you before I left, Dad.' She paused, looking around as if someone might be listening, then added, 'Did Rose say something about seeing you tomorrow?'

'Hahn?' said Mr Sidhu, with what he hoped was a confused expression. Meanwhile, he frantically searched his mind, trying to find something to say that would sound legitimate.

'Oh,' he said, as if just now understanding what Meenu was referring to. 'You know these goreh. I told Rose I was doing some work tomorrow here, getting ready—'

'For the new IT system, yes,' said Meenu, interrupting him and looking concerned.

'So she was saying,' Mr Sidhu cleared his throat and lowered his voice, 'that if I wanted to pop over for a break or food, then she doesn't mind.'

'That's nice of her, Dad. Nice that she's looking out for you.'

Mr Sidhu maintained a neutral expression even though the idea that Rose was looking out for him made his heart leap. 'What time are you going?' he asked, hoping to change the subject.

'Not for a while, Dad. Craig's just finishing off some work before we leave, so I thought I'd come and see if you needed any help.'

'You don't have to worry about all that, I can do it myself. You work hard, you can relax now,' said Mr Sidhu, heading back into the shop. The proximity to Meenu and her questions was making him feel uneasy.

'So do you, Dad. You should relax, take some time off.'

Mr Sidhu was not listening to her.

'What is it, Dad?'

Mr Sidhu was looking at Rose as she measured out some Liquorice Allsorts for a customer, her small, thin, pale hands handling the plastic jar, letting the confectionery spill into the metal measuring bowl which she lifted off the scales, opening a small paper bag and letting the contents fall into it. She swung the bag around to twist the ends and gave it to the pensioner. Mr Sidhu gathered his thoughts.

'I need to take over in the shop. Rose is going now,' he told Meenu.

Mr Sidhu strode over to the shop counter followed by Meenu. Rose was struggling to get the lid back onto the jar. Mr Sidhu took the jar from her hands gently, screwed on the lid firmly and placed it back on the shelf with all the other jars of sweets.

'It's the sugar that makes those lids stick, David. You need to make sure you wipe them after you use them,' said Rose, getting a cloth, taking the jar down again and wiping it clean. Mr Sidhu felt a sense of pride about how Rose made these small adjustments in the shop, making it run more efficiently.

'It's lovely to see you, Meenu,' said Rose. 'Your father mentioned you were going up to Shropshire for Christmas.'

'Yeah, I wanted Dad to come with us, but he said he's busy.'

Mr Sidhu's ears burned. He drifted away from them, pretending to be busy doing a stock take while he eavesdropped.

'And how's your lovely boyfriend? What's his name again?'

'Craig's fine. Working, busy, you know,' said Meenu quickly and then, almost as an afterthought, smiled. Rose smiled back at her.

'It's nice you come and see your dad,' she said.

'That's what a family does, Rose. We look after each other. It's part of who we are,' said Meenu. Rose looked at Meenu, who held her stare. Rose nodded and smiled silently, taking out a tissue from the sleeve of her cardigan and trying to unravel it until she was able to blow her nose into it. Mr Sidhu overheard all this while he pretended to be counting the tins of tomato soup. He noticed the severity in Meenu's voice and Rose's silence. He dared not say anything. This was not the kind of conversation he was used to hearing, especially about him. Mr Sidhu moved out of earshot.

Meenu took over serving in the shop while Rose went to gather her coat and handbag. Mr Sidhu waited until Meenu was busy with a customer and then went to see Rose by the basement entrance, which was out of sight of the shop counter.

'Everything OK, David?' asked Rose.

'Yes. Have a nice Christmas, Rose,' said Mr Sidhu, wringing

his hands and wondering if he could say that he might pop in briefly for Christmas.

'Thank you. You too, David.'

Rose leaned into Mr Sidhu, whispering, 'I don't blame you if you don't want to visit the in-laws, but if you are at a loose end, feel free to come over. There'll be plenty of food. Merry Christmas, David.'

She leaned in a little further and kissed Mr Sidhu on his bearded cheek. Mr Sidhu stumbled back into the small shelf that held the tea, mugs, sugar and kettle, sending them clattering onto the floor. He tried to catch the sugar, which was actually just a paper bag of sugar with a teaspoon in it, but fumbled it and sent the packet spilling past the open basement door and into the shop.

'Oh, David. Are you OK? I'm so sorry,' said Rose, aghast.

'Fine, fine. Everything fine,' he blurted out, interrupting Rose. He hastily dusted himself down to get rid of the sugar granules which had rained all over him. He looked up and saw Meenu looking straight at him from the shop counter.

'Everything OK, Dad?' she asked, coming over to him, her brows furrowed, her eyes serious.

'Yes, the sugar.' He pointed vaguely while Rose got out the vacuum cleaner and made a noise that didn't allow for any more conversation. Eventually everything returned to normal, except that Mr Sidhu was unable to ignore the feeling of Rose's lips on his beard.

'You need to be more careful,' said Meenu, coming to him.

'It's fine, beta,' said Mr Sidhu, unable to stop her as she picked sugar granules out of his pullover.

'What happened?' Meenu asked.

'I'm afraid it was my fault,' interjected Rose as she placed the vacuum cleaner in its place, under the shelf. 'I was tidying up and the sugar slipped out of my hands.' She smiled at Meenu and Mr Sidhu. 'I'm so sorry, David,' she added, giving him a wink.

Mr Sidhu froze, hoping that Meenu hadn't seen it.

'Well, I'll be off then, David.' Rose buttoned up her bright red woollen coat and put her green hat on. He watched her as she walked to the door, adjusting her hat and gloves.

'Merry Christmas, Meenu,' said Rose.

'Yes, Merry Christmas, Rose,' said Meenu. She paused and added, 'Thank you for inviting my father to your house for Christmas lunch.'

Rose was about to reply but Meenu continued, 'I tried to get him to come with us, but he said he was,' Meenu and Rose both said 'busy' at the same time. They turned to Mr Sidhu, who stood smiling at them.

'Busy,' he managed and wiggled his head side to side, surprising himself.

Meenu offered to wait in the shop while Mr Sidhu locked himself in the post office, clearing away the last of the papers and forms which would become redundant after the computer system came in. He didn't know why Meenu was coming over to see him so often. He'd love it if Raju had the same impulse, but he didn't. Raju told him he felt sick every time he came into the shop.

'It's awful, Dad. I don't know how you can hole yourself up in that place all day, all week,' he'd say, without a thought about how much it had helped the family. And never mind that it paid for his deposit and his university expenses so he wouldn't

have a loan hanging over his head. It never occurred to Raju that the business would one day be his, Mr Sidhu mused. He'd probably sell it for a low price too. Mr Sidhu missed being able to discuss such matters with Sarabjit, who always tempered his impatience with Raju. He also missed not having to deal with Meenu. She had always been the more intelligent one. Raju, being the boy, had been spoiled by Sarabjit, of course, but she'd also been able to handle Meenu. He looked at Meenu, who was a successful IT project manager (which he proudly told everyone about), standing in the shop serving customers with the politeness that the Sidhus were known for, apart from Raju, who would become impatient with anyone who didn't do things the way that he wanted them to.

Quite often, elderly customers would simply hand over their purse or wallet to them; some couldn't see very well, hear very well or move very well, and they trusted the Sidhus and now Rose, whom all the locals knew, to take what money was needed. This was something that Mr Sidhu prided himself on. It was how he and Sarabjit had built up a small post office with a meagre shop, selling only a few cards and envelopes, into a busy, thriving post office and convenience store, serving the local businesses and community. It was the hub of the area, which local estate agents said had a villagey feel. Apparently, this was an asset to any area in London, but Mr Sidhu knew what a real village was, and this was nothing like that.

The chime sounded as the shop door opened.

'Get in!' a mother shouted at her two young children as she lifted the front of her pram and pushed her third child into the post office. It was Rita. Mr Sidhu knew her well and immediately came out to see her. She was always coming at the wrong time and always looking distressed.

'Hello, Rita,' said Mr Sidhu.

Meenu looked at Rita with disdain. Her lipstick was applied untidily on her lips and her children looked like they had not had clean clothes on for an age and their noses and faces hadn't been wiped for a long time either. Sensing judgement in the air, Rita extracted a cloth from beneath the pram, took hold of her toddlers and forcibly wiped their noses, then applied saliva to the cloth and wiped what looked like chocolate from their mouths. They screamed out at this sudden scouring of their faces, which then made the baby in the pram start crying too.

'Look what you've done,' she cried, as she picked up the baby. The two children immediately left their mother and ran around the shop.

'I'm sorry, Mr Sidhu,' she pleaded, cradling her crying child.

Mr Sidhu looked at Rita. She was short with black hair tied at the back of her head and wore a leather biker's jacket and a denim miniskirt. Her eyes pleaded for help even when she wasn't talking.

'It's OK, Rita,' said Mr Sidhu, aware that Meenu was eyeing him disapprovingly.

'Am I late?'

'No, it's OK,' lied Mr Sidhu.

'They're driving me crazy,' she said, referring to her daughter and son who were tearing around the shop playing tag. Mr Sidhu tried his best to ignore them despite all the noise they were making. 'Stop running around,' she shouted, but the children ignored her while the baby in her arms went quiet.

She handed Mr Sidhu her giro and he went into the post

office to stamp it and give her the money which she'd need over Christmas. It was actually his own money he gave her as the Post Office safe worked on a timer for security reasons. It opened once in the morning to take out money and stamps to use in the day and then once again in the evening to put everything away again. Otherwise it was locked, so when certain customers came in needing their cheques cashed he would give them his own money, which he would get back when the safe was opened the next day.

'Thank you, Mr Sidhu, you're a lifesaver,' said Rita, unaware of what Mr Sidhu had done for her.

'It's OK. Try and rest, Rita,' he said and immediately felt the hollowness of his words.

'You're lucky to have a dad like him,' she said, turning to Meenu who gave her a strained smile. Mr Sidhu spied the two kids who had become quiet kneeling by the penny sweets at the entrance to the shop, putting some into their pockets. He saw Rita looking at them too.

'It's OK,' said Mr Sidhu softly. 'Christmas present.' He smiled. Rita wiped away a tear from her eye, unable to look at Mr Sidhu.

'No. You can't do that. I have to make sure they understand. They need to know right and wrong,' she said, fishing out coins from her purse.

The door chimed and in came a balding man wearing a dark grey suit peppered with dandruff on his shoulders, and carrying a brown leather briefcase. It was Alan Dankworth, the Post Office area manager. Mr Sidhu had been expecting him but didn't want him to know that he'd just cashed Rita's giro. Suddenly, Alan put his briefcase down and grabbed the children by the wrists, sweets still in their hands.

'Caught 'em red-handed,' he barked, looking gleefully at Mr Sidhu. 'Stealing is against the law no matter how old you are,' he told the two terrified kids.

Rita looked paralysed with fear, her fingers holding the coins for Mr Sidhu.

'It's OK, Alan, they already paid for them,' said Mr Sidhu, trying to keep the atmosphere as calm as he could.

Alan let the children go and they immediately ran to Rita and held her legs as she wrapped her arms around them.

'Sorry, I saw them outside, I didn't know. Looked like a couple of tea-leafs to me,' said Alan, smiling. Meenu smiled back at him. Rita ignored him.

'Come, I'll help you with your pram,' said Mr Sidhu, wanting Rita to go and not mention anything about cashing the giro. He helped her out and ruffled the hair of the two children. Outside, Rita knelt down to speak to them. They turned to Mr Sidhu and, looking at their feet, said 'Thank you' in unison.

'No problem,' said Mr Sidhu.

'Thanks again, and Merry Christmas,' said Rita. The children gobbled down their treats and Rita pushed the pram into the winter evening, leaving Mr Sidhu alone outside on the pavement. He hoped she would be OK.

Inside the shop, he could see Alan speaking to Meenu. He handed her a business card, smiling and lingering a little too long on her hand as he handed it to her. And Meenu didn't seem to mind as she smiled back at him.

Mr Sidhu strode back into the shop, interrupting their chat.

'Dave, me old mucker, how are you? Sorry about that – didn't mean to scare them like that. You know what some of these people are like,' grinned Alan.

'One moment, Alan,' said Mr Sidhu, heading back to the post office to get the carrier bag he'd been keeping ready for him. It contained a bottle of Johnny Walker Black Label whisky and two hundred Rothmans cigarettes. This was a present he gave Alan every year. Mr Hodgson, whom Mr Sidhu had bought the post office from in the mid-Eighties, had told him to, 'Keep the area manager sweet, they hold a lot of sway.'

Mr Sidhu approached Alan with the bag.

'You didn't tell me your little Meenu is an IT whiz. You were only that high, and now look at you, project manager this, infrastructure project that, my word. Don't worry,' Alan winked at Mr Sidhu, 'I've given her my card. She can come work for us. She knows what she's doing and if she's anything like you, Dave, she'll be brilliant,' he laughed, showing off his yellow stained teeth and a couple of gold crowns.

Mr Sidhu silently passed the carrier bag to him. Alan made a show of thanking Mr Sidhu, his eyes peering into the bag to check the contents.

'All ready, Dave?'

Mr Sidhu didn't like being called Dave by Alan, but as it wasn't his real name, he found it hard to tell him to call him David, like Rose did.

'Alan's been telling me about the new IT system,' said Meenu.

'Oh, the Post Office might be old but we move with the times. Did you know the Post Office is the most trusted brand in Great Britain? Which probably means the world.' Alan laughed at his own joke. His forehead was sweating. Mr Sidhu could also smell alcohol on his breath. It was something he was accustomed to at this time of year. The English didn't need much of an excuse to have a drink, and Christmas seemed to be the time of year when this was normalized behaviour – apart from rugby days, which also made the whole of Richmond smell of beer.

'Right, I need to have a little chat with your father. Lovely to see you all grown up.' Alan's eyes lingered on Meenu as he clutched his carrier bag and briefcase. Meenu smiled and straightened her top. Mr Sidhu didn't like the over-familiar way Alan spoke to Meenu, but he didn't say anything. There was important work to do. He indicated to Alan to follow him into the basement.

'This way, Alan.'

Mr Sidhu and Alan descended into the basement and sat down on the wooden chairs Mr Sidhu liked so much. Alan pushed a pile of paper held together with a bulldog clip to Mr Sidhu.

'I need you to sign this,' he said, offering Mr Sidhu a pen. 'It's an updated contract, to take into account the new system.'

Mr Sidhu looked at the pile of papers. It seemed unfathomable that he would be able to read it all and sign it here this minute.

'Everyone gets one and everyone signs it,' said Alan in his normal business-like manner, seeing Mr Sidhu's expression.

'I should read it,' said Mr Sidhu.

Alan exhaled. 'Well, yeah, sure you can read it, but that means I'll have to come to get it off you once you've read it, and I'm a busy man, Dave, and to be honest I need you to sign it now, otherwise you can't get the new computer system and you don't want to delay that, I promise you.'

Mr Sidhu flicked over a few pages; each page had dense print all over it. Even the idea of reading it made him feel tired.

'Remember, Dave, the Post Office is where Joe Bloggs and

government money come together,' said Alan, clasping his hands together. 'Can you imagine the amount of money that the government shifts in post offices every day? Tens of millions of pounds. Billions every year.'

The numbers were staggering to Mr Sidhu. The Punjabis he knew only wanted to be millionaires. Many were, but only on paper, through the ownership of property. None of them had a million pounds in the bank.

'The new system saves the government billions, because for each transaction they save money. Now you don't need paper books any more and the money can only be collected by the person with the card. There's no book, no date stamps, no fraud, no filling out forms – everything is electronic.'

Mr Sidhu made a mental note to keep Min's new payment card in the post office. She would not know what was going on.

'So I need you to sign this now, please, Dave, otherwise you will be in breach of contract.'

Mr Sidhu had never been accused of anything, and he knew if he was in breach then the Post Office could take away his licence. He couldn't really remember signing the initial contract back in the Eighties, but he signed it now and gave it to Alan.

'Well done, Dave. Now I hope you've told everyone the post office will be closed until the new year. They can use the main one on the High Street in the meantime. The IT guys will come in to set everything up and you should be up and running by the time you reopen. You will get paid for the days it's shut, so there you go, a bit of free money. Don't say I don't look after you.' Alan winked and examined the contract to make sure he had Mr Sidhu's signature.

'Shall we seal the deal, eh, Dave?' Alan pulled the bottle of

Johnny Walker out of the bag and sat it on the table. 'Got any glasses?'

Mr Sidhu got a couple of the clean mugs he and Rose used for tea. Alan poured a measure each and then got out a packet of cigarettes, flicking open the packet and drawing one out.

'You don't mind, do ya?' he asked after he'd lit it.

Mr Sidhu waved his hand as if to say he didn't mind. He did mind, he hated the smell of cigarette smoke and there was hardly any ventilation in the cellar. Within minutes his eyes were stinging.

'I have to go and make all the subs sign the new contracts. You're all right, Dave, but some of them want to read it and then this and that. Makes my life hell. And if I don't get it sorted then them upstairs give me hell. To be honest, this new system is gonna be the death of me,' he chuckled.

Mr Sidhu was glad to finally be out of the cellar.

'Well, that's all sorted now. So the technicians'll come in and hook you up to the new system. Exciting times, eh, Dave?'

Mr Sidhu nodded and smiled silently.

Alan looked across at Meenu. 'And lovely to see you, my darling. Have a lovely Christmas, won't you? I know I will be,' he said, winking at Mr Sidhu and lifting up the carrier bag.

And with that he left Mr Sidhu and Meenu alone together.

'Might as well close the shop, Dad, no one's coming in,' Meenu said, looking at the darkness outside. Mr Sidhu didn't hear her; he was leafing through the new contract, unable to understand much of what it said.

'Everyone's probably getting ready for Christmas,' she added.

'Craig is coming here to pick you up?' asked Mr Sidhu, not understanding why she wasn't leaving.

She shook her head and a silence descended upon them. Normally, Mr Sidhu would keep himself busy in the shop. There was always something to do: putting stock on shelves, flattening boxes, old stock to be thrown away, the floor to be vacuumed . . . but right now Mr Sidhu knew he needed to talk to Meenu.

'When are you going to get married?' he blurted out, aware that his direct Punjabi way of talking grated with his children.

'Dad, you're being old-fashioned,' Meenu replied, with a light smile on her face. 'Why are you asking me?' she added, as if it was a strange question to ask.

He was asking her because he'd made a promise to Sarabjit. 'When you marry, then you can start a family. It is time.' He hadn't been this direct with Meenu since she was a child.

'Dad, we'll do things in our own way, the world's changing.'

'Of course, beta, you do it in your own way. No problem, but you need to marry, then I can stop worrying,' he said, trying to be light-hearted, but even he could tell it wasn't coming across in the way he intended. There was an impatience in his words.

Meenu snorted and looked away, shaking her head, 'It's all about you, isn't it, Dad?'

Another silence.

'Raju doesn't even have a girlfriend; you should be more worried about that. I mean, he's going to have all this one day, isn't he?' she said, her hands indicating everything around her.

Mr Sidhu didn't say anything. This was something he never talked to Meenu about. He knew that Sarabjit had told her about Raju's position as the boy, the heir of the family name and wealth. It was also true that while Meenu was unmarried, he was still responsible for her. Was she doing this on purpose? Mr Sidhu stayed silent. Whenever he or even Sarabjit had tried to explain this to Raju, he'd been dismissive of it all. And in all these years Meenu had never said a thing about it, until now.

Meenu nibbled at her bottom lip and looked at Mr Sidhu.

'Alan told me there's nothing for you to do while the new IT system is being put in. He said you didn't even need to be here, Dad. Maybe you *can* come with us? You can go back after Boxing Day to open the shop. I can drop you back.'

Meenu looked at him hopefully.

'Beta,' he said slowly, trying to find the right words to say, 'I don't know anything about this computer thing, but all the old forms that we are not using any more have to be packed away and sent off to head office and I have to do a last balance before the installation. He probably meant the computer system. Yes, I don't have anything to do with the installation,' he breathed and looked at Meenu, thinking he'd done a pretty good job of explaining. It wasn't true about the forms; he'd been told to throw them all away. But it was true about the balance. It would be the last balance he did in his trusty account books, written with his hands. But it would only take a couple of hours.

'You understand?' he asked.

'I thought that maybe you'd misunderstood. It doesn't matter. Merry Christmas, Dad.'

Meenu handed Mr Sidhu a present. He was given Christmas presents by his children most years, but he never desired them and never really liked them. If he needed socks or a scarf, he could quite easily buy them himself. As it was, they liked to buy these things for him and he had even tried to be a bit more enthusiastic about them since Sarabjit's passing, but it wasn't something he grew up with and he couldn't really muster up the enthusiasm he saw a lot of people displaying for Christmas presents.

'Thank you, beta.'

'It's nothing,' said Meenu and then added, 'you're too nice, Dad. People take advantage of you.'

'Hahn?' he said, not understanding.

'That woman who came in, she must have been on drugs or something. She didn't come at the right time and then her children were stealing sweets and you did nothing.'

Mr Sidhu shook his head. He didn't like the way his children thought the worst about people. Especially when they had none of the stresses someone like Rita did.

'Beta, you don't understand. You don't know what other people are going through.'

'I don't know what story she's told you.'

'Not story, beta,' Mr Sidhu interrupted. 'Her husband is dead. Only a few months ago. She has three children and no other family. She is all alone.'

'Oh. I didn't know. What happened?'

'They found him in the river. Near the bridge.'

They both stood silently. The memory of Sarabjit lingered in the air. Not because of what happened to Rita's husband, but because it reminded them of the hole in their own lives.

'I better go, Dad,' said Meenu finally. They did their sideways hug and Meenu started to open the door and then stopped.

'Are you going to Rose's tomorrow then, Dad?'

'Hahn?' Mr Sidhu replied, trying to sound confused. Meenu said nothing as she waited for him to reply.

'There's so much to do, I don't know,' he said finally. Meenu nodded and left. Mr Sidhu sighed deeply.

'Jaldi, jaldi, Sidhu!' shouted Richard the retired solicitor at the empty shop. 'I've got an important letter to go first class.'

Mr Sidhu smiled to himself. Richard was what Mr Sidhu would call a real Englishman. He had a smooth, plummy English accent, like the one that Mr Sidhu had thought all English people would use when he'd arrived all those years ago. Mr Sidhu was making himself a cup of tea and was out of sight. Richard continued to call out to Mr Sidhu.

'I've got to get this chithi to the council before the new year. Will it go in time, Sidhu saahab?' Richard stood leaning against the counter brushing his floppy white hair away from his forehead.

'Possible, but not sure,' Mr Sidhu walked back with his tea, slurping it unashamedly loudly as if this were the only way to drink tea. 'The post is not reliable this time of year.'

'I see. Damn. Well, just send it first class, there's a good man.'

Mr Sidhu kept a few sheets of stamps behind the shop counter whenever the post office was closed in order to serve the needs of his customers. He tore off a first-class stamp from the main sheet which held forty-eight stamps.

'Twenty-seven pence.'

Richard counted out his coins onto the counter, and Mr Sidhu held the stamp out to him.

'What are you doing for Christmas, Sidhu? With the children, is it?'

'No, I actually . . . you know, might go to Rose's house for Christmas, she invited me,' Mr Sidhu replied in as casual as way as he could muster.

'Well I never. You're a dark horse, Sidhu.'

'Her son and Min will be there too,' said Mr Sidhu hurriedly, making sure Richard understood he wasn't going on his own. Rose had told him earlier and it had made it feel less anxious knowing that there would be others.

'Ah, yes, her son. You've met him?'

'No,' said Mr Sidhu.

'Nice chap,' Richard paused and looked at Mr Sidhu, his eyes narrowed. 'Mmm, yes, he's a nice chap. If you come to the Arms after lunch I'll see you there. I'll buy you a pint, although with you Sikhs, it's whisky, Patiala pegs and all that, isn't it, eh?'

Richard smiled at Mr Sidhu. He liked him more than most other people he had to deal with. For Richard, Mr Sidhu reminded him of some of his fondest memories of growing up in Lahore in the Forties. A big, hairy Sikh man called Bupinder was employed by his family as a guard to protect the house. Bupinder used to carry him on his shoulders whenever he liked, wherever he liked.

With that, Richard took the stamp off the counter, licked it, placed it in the corner of a white envelope and brought his fist down on the stamp. Without waiting for a reply, he winked and was about to leave when Mr Sidhu had a thought.

'Richard?' he said.

'Yes?'

'What should I bring? To Rose's, I mean, for the lunch.'

'Ah well, Sidhu, if I were you I would get a nice bottle of port. It's all wine and champagne these days, but a good bottle of port at Christmas, can't beat that. That'll do it.' Richard waited for Mr Sidhu to reply. Mr Sidhu had never tasted port before.

'Which is a good one?' he asked.

'You want to make an impression, eh?' said Richard, smiling at Mr Sidhu.

Richard wrote down which brands to go for, and that night on his way home Mr Sidhu stopped off at Threshers off-licence and bought a bottle of Taylor's Port as advised by Richard. When he got back, he placed the bottle of port on the small console table next to the front door. It was where he put anything that was important for the next day. After he'd eaten his dinner and checked all the doors and windows were locked before he went upstairs to bed, he picked up the bottle from the table and gave it a polish with his handkerchief.

Chapter 4

Mr Sidhu woke up as usual at 6.30 a.m.. It was Christmas Day and dark outside. He woke up thinking about Rose. She'd been in his dreams. They were best friends, driving on a day trip to the seaside. They were in the first car he had bought when he'd come to England, an Austin 1300 GT Mark II. It was the Fifties, a time he'd never known in England, but which he'd seen on television and films. In the back seat was Mr Sidhu when he was eight years old. He was wearing the shorts and short-sleeved shirt that he'd worn to his school, as well as being barefoot. The landscape was a strange melange of Punjab and the Home Counties. It hadn't seemed strange when he'd seen his younger self sitting in the back, in the way that things didn't in dreams, unless they were meant to. His dreams were always in Punjabi, but he couldn't remember if Rose had spoken in English or Punjabi. He remembered how he'd felt. Happy. When he awoke and had that moment of realization that he'd been dreaming, he stretched out his hand to the other side of the bed, but it was empty.

In the kitchen, Mr Sidhu stirred his porridge and threw in some raisins. When Meenu had asked him whether he would go to Rose's, he'd said he didn't know. But he did know. Wouldn't it be better to keep things as they were, he thought. Rose worked in the shop with him, it would be unprofessional to go to her house for Christmas lunch. What if something happened? He felt his thoughts whizzing around his brain. He lifted his hand and felt his cheek, where Rose had kissed him. It's just the way the English are, he thought. Kiss on the cheek and drinking at Christmas. There was a French woman who used to come to the post office, and when she was going back to France, she would kiss him on both cheeks, as had her husband, too. He'd been in shock for hours after, not understanding that it was normal, as Richard had explained to him later.

Mr Sidhu turned the gas off and the bubbling subsided. He put on his down-filled, hooded parka over his kurta pyjama and went into the dark garden to begin his morning exercises. He rotated his arms round and round by his side and then jogged on the spot, raising his knees as high as he could, as well as standing on tiptoe and reaching his fingertips to the sky. These motions were second nature to him. He did not consciously start one exercise and finish it to start another; they all flowed from one into the next. Mr Sidhu's mind would awaken to absorb the birds fluttering in the sky, the growing buds on the branches and the different types of trees – trees he did not know the names of. His senses absorbed the smells of the plants and trees and finally he would forget where he was. But today all he could think of was Rose.

Rose had worked in the post office with Mr Sidhu for seven years. And ever since she'd come in with her no-nonsense way of dealing with everything – from the cleaning to the credit book – he'd admired her from behind the post office counter. She'd been brought in when Sarabjit was too ill to work any more. Min knew her and recommended her. She had worked at Selfridges for most of her life and had retired early. She still claimed her pension and he paid her in cash so that she didn't have to declare it. He didn't know if she'd married, but she mentioned her son a few times and Mr Sidhu was curious to meet him. She must trust him enough to meet him, he thought.

Mr Sidhu kicked Raju's old, heavy, wet, deflated football from one end of the garden to the other. He felt the leather give as his foot kicked the ball. It flew into the air and landed with a dull thud. Standing in the post office and shop all day meant exercise was limited, but Mr Sidhu, a practical man, used the morning to move his body and make himself breathless. This was what one of his customers, a Harley Street doctor, had told him to do so his heart would work harder and therefore be stronger. However, right now his heart felt strange, unlike anything he was used to. He gave the football one final kick and then he went back inside to eat his cooling porridge. He ate it straight out of the saucepan with a spoon.

After showering, the light of the day edged its way into the sky. The Christmas Day rain had stopped and by eight o'clock it was a crisp, sunny winter's day. Mr Sidhu started to get ready.

He chose a trouser, shirt and tweed jacket combination, with a cardigan too. He polished his shoes and ironed his turban cloth, putting it on last so that nothing would disturb it, change its angle or loosen it. He toyed with the idea of letting his beard hang down like Father Christmas, which is how it looked naturally after having a shower. However, he decided to keep it matted. This involved combing his beard downwards tightly against his cheeks and tucking the excess hair under his chin, using gel to keep it in place. Then he placed a cloth under his chin and pulled it up over his cheeks and tied the ends on the top of his head. After using a hairdryer to set the gel and hair, he untied it and the beard was neatly matted against his face. It would stay like that all day. This was how he normally wore his beard, which he'd never cut or shaved his whole life.

Before he left the house, he picked up the bottle of port and got into his van. He drove as calmly as he could to Richmond. The streets were empty and he passed the odd car, probably on its way to a Christmas lunch. Is that what he was doing?

He parked and sat for a few moments, trying to understand what he was doing. He got out and marched to Rose's cottage. He would give her the bottle of port and then go home and have some chicken tikka with a whisky and forget all about this. As he reached Rose's house, another one of those small workers' cottages, Mr Sidhu realised he'd forgotten the bottle of port. He raced back to his van, even though there was no rush to get it. He arrived again outside Rose's cottage with the bottle in his hand and beads of sweat forming on his forehead.

There was the smallest front garden, containing a blue and black recycling box and a green wheelie bin. He noted that the recycling boxes were a different colour to the ones in Hounslow. In the front window was a small Christmas tree decorated with tinsel and blinking lights. Mr Sidhu took a deep breath and rang the doorbell. Rose opened the door and as soon as she saw him, her face lit up.

'David! You came. I mean you're here. What am I saying? Merry Christmas.'

Rose leaned into Mr Sidhu to hug him or kiss him, he wasn't sure which, because at the same time he thrust the bottle of port towards her. They stopped, unsure who should move first, the bottle between them. Eventually Rose peered down and asked, 'Is that for me?'

She was wearing a dark-blue dress with silver embroidery on the collar and a pearl necklace around her neck. Mr Sidhu stopped himself from staring at her necklace.

'Yes,' he managed, looking into her spectacled eyes, her name for some reason not coming out of his mouth as he'd wanted it to. They untangled themselves and Rose accepted the bottle of port.

'Thank you, David. That's very kind,' she said and then smiled at him. With her other hand, she took hold of his hand and led him into the house.

'Come in, David. Say hello.'

He was nervous. He'd never been to an English person's house for Christmas. He wasn't sure what was expected of him. Should he have brought presents for everyone?

The house was small. He walked straight into the living room which had bare wooden boards and a rug where the small round dining table was. The house was tidy but everything looked a little tired. He noted the wooden sash windows weren't double glazed and needed a lick of paint; the skirting boards were old and painted over many times.

'Hello, David,' called out Min. She sat in a worn armchair, looking pleased with herself.

'Hello, Min. Merry Christmas,' said Mr Sidhu, relaxing a little at seeing another of his locals. Rose took his coat and he sat down, looking at the pictures on the wall which brightened the room up. One of them was of the bridge he drove over every day but had never seen from the angle of the river, and another of a regal-looking stag with orange leaves everywhere.

'What are you doing here, David? Who's in the post office?' asked Min.

'No. It's closed today. Christmas. Open Monday,' he half shouted as he always did to Min to make her understand, even though he knew the post office wouldn't be open on Monday either, due to the IT system being installed.

A black shape ran towards him and before he knew it, he could feel a wet sensation all over his hand. Mr Sidhu instinctively started to slap the animal which was doing it. The dog, as Mr Sidhu realised it was now that he could see it properly, flattened its ears and lowered its head. Mr Sidhu looked at it, daring it to lick his hand again. A tall, dark-skinned man with a bald head approached him.

'Sorry about that. He's a licker, can't help himself, just his way of saying hello,' said the man in a strange northern English accent that he couldn't place.

Mr Sidhu continued to look at the man, who looked familiar. He was unaware that his mouth was hanging open.

'Sorry, how rude of me,' the man continued. 'Merry Christmas. I'm Jay, Rose's son.' He held out his hand and Mr Sidhu took it limply.

'Merry Christmas,' Mr Sidhu replied softly.

Rose came and stood beside Jay, taking his arm and leaning into him. 'Ah, I see you've met the boys.'

Mr Sidhu nodded slowly.

They all sat down to eat the Christmas dinner Rose had made and Mr Sidhu felt as if he was floating above the proceedings as an observer – not involved in any way with what was happening. Rose served up turkey with the best roast potatoes he had ever tasted. The ones he'd eaten in canteens in the factories he'd worked at when he'd first arrived in England in the Seventies were cold and heavy; these were light, fluffy and crunchy, with gravy poured over them which tasted delicious. Mr Sidhu smiled when everyone was smiling and ate and sipped wine (more often than he normally would) but didn't say a word at the table, which wasn't difficult as everyone was talking to each other and over each other. Rose glanced at him a few times and smiled, asking him whether the food was OK. Mr Sidhu carried on eating and drinking, nodding his head from time to time. He didn't want to say anything because if he did, he might say the wrong thing. His mind was a whirl of activity. Of course he'd seen Jay many times in the shop and post office, but in his mind he was one of those locals you just don't get to know much. He could see them now, talking to each other at the shop counter. He'd say hello if he saw him but it never occurred to him that he was Rose's son. His eyes were the same blue as Rose's but his skin was dark brown like his. His features looked West Indian to Mr Sidhu. He'd worked with a few West Indians in Southall in the early days. In those times everyone had been curious about where everyone was from and they all exchanged stories about their backgrounds: about the farms in Punjab and the plantations in the West Indies. But as time went on, the different tribes of immigrants settled into their groups. Mr Sidhu's world became Punjabi and he lost touch with those men. He wanted to say something to Jay but words failed him – and the more the words didn't come, the more he felt as if the world was spinning off its axis and he was hurtling through space. He wasn't sure how much longer he could remain sitting on his chair; his mouth was dry and suddenly the world started to fall away. His vision was no longer on the table and the food; instead he was looking at everyone's feet below the table and the dog was licking Mr Sidhu's mouth. What was going on?

Mr Sidhu slapped the dog away again and sat up. He could see the others standing up; the dog had its tail between its legs and was being held by Jay. Min was laughing uncontrollably. Rose came to him.

'David, what happened? Are you OK? Come with me.' She led Mr Sidhu to the kitchen. He saw that his chair had fallen over, which explained why he'd been on the floor. She dabbed a wet cloth on a gravy stain on his cardigan.

'It's OK, David, just an accident,' she looked over her shoulder to the lounge. 'And don't fret about Tubby. He can be quite annoying with all his licking, I have to shoo him off me all the time.'

'I'm sorry,' said Mr Sidhu, regaining his composure and feeling embarrassed. 'I will go. You enjoy your Christmas.'

'Hey,' said Rose and held Mr Sidhu's hands, as if they were about to dance. 'Everything's fine.'

He dared to look up into her eyes and without saying anything more she held him and he let his body press into her.

Chapter 5

He didn't know how long he'd been at Rose's. The house was quiet and it was dark outside. Had he fallen asleep? His head felt heavy and his eyes sore. His shoes had been taken off and he was lying on the sofa with a blanket over him. Rose sat in the chair opposite, watching television.

Mr Sidhu cleared his throat. Rose looked over to him and turned off the television.

'You're back with us,' she said.

Mr Sidhu sat up and smoothed down his beard with his hand, something he did all the time without thinking.

'Sorry, Rose, I don't know what happened.'

'It's OK, David,' Rose handed him a glass of water, which he gulped down. 'You sat down after lunch and fell asleep. You aren't the first and won't be the last,' she said, smiling at him. 'I took your shoes off. I hope you don't mind?'

Mr Sidhu wasn't sure what to say to her.

'Min and Jay have gone to the pub,' said Rose.

'Toilet,' blurted out Mr Sidhu.

Rose led him to the toilet which was next to the kitchen at the back of the house. While he urinated, he tried to see if he could remember anything. He remembered Rose hugging him.

He needed to go home and stop embarrassing himself. He zipped up his trousers and stopped to look in the mirror and adjust his lopsided turban, straightening it. Rose had looked after him. He should repay her kindness. But how?

'All better?' asked Rose as he re-entered the lounge.

'Yes, thank you, Rose.'

'Are you hungry? There are plenty of leftovers.'

He shook his head. 'I should go. I am sorry, Rose.'

'Hey, it's OK, David, there's nothing to be sorry about.' She handed him another glass of water. He hadn't realised how thirsty he was.

'Why did they go to the pub?' he asked, thinking he might have done something to make them leave.

'That's what we do on Christmas, David. We have lunch and then go to the pub to see everyone. We can go too if you want?'

Mr Sidhu didn't move or say anything. Then he remembered Richard telling him that he'd buy him a drink in the pub. He relaxed and smiled.

'We could go for a walk, get some fresh air if you like?' said Rose.

'I need to go to the bathroom again,' said Mr Sidhu, remembering that the dog had licked his lips.

'Are you sure you're OK?' asked Rose, her face looking concerned.

He nodded and hurried to the bathroom, washed his lips and beard and rinsed his mouth out until he couldn't feel the memory of the dog on his mouth.

'So, ready for a stroll?' asked Rose when he came back. She looked at him with her kind eyes.

'Yes,' he replied.

*

The Shaftesbury Arms was on the same parade of shops as the post office. Mr Sidhu had walked past it many times, but because of the frosted windows it was impossible to see what was happening inside. He'd never been inside, so he was a little nervous as they approached the entrance, where a few people were smoking cigarettes. Most of them he recognized as locals, so he nodded politely as he and Rose entered the pub. It was the first time he'd been into an English pub since 1970.

It was noisy, and there was some music playing but it was hard to make out because everyone was talking over it. The bar was at the centre of the pub, like an island. A brass footrest followed the curvature of the bar all the way round. Gerry, the landlord, magically rose up like a genie from behind the bar. It was only when Mr Sidhu got up close that he realised there was a staircase to the cellar there.

Gerry was Northern Irish and when they'd first met it had taken a few goes before Mr Sidhu understood that Gerry was actually speaking English. Gerry deposited the takings from the pub into the post office on Mondays. Mr Sidhu had been shocked at how much money the pub made. On a rugby weekend, Gerry might deposit upwards of twenty thousand pounds. Gerry always apologised for the amount of money, knowing Mr Sidhu would have to count it all himself. But Mr Sidhu never minded; he felt that it was a reflection on him that the pub made so much money and that by helping, somehow he was part of its success.

'Well, well, well, Dave. How many times have I invited you for a pint and nothing doing? Now here you are. What's she got that I haven't, eh?' Gerry grinned at Mr Sidhu and nodded his head towards Rose. He had a serious face and his voice was always loud as if he was shouting, but he was actually only talking.

'Merry Christmas, Gerry,' replied Mr Sidhu, ignoring his question. Around him he heard voices saying, 'Look who it is' or calling out 'Merry Christmas, Dave!'

Mr Sidhu pretended not to have heard the voices, but he had, and every single one made his ears burn.

'Watch out for the mistletoe, Dave, she might kiss you,' said Gerry, indicating mistletoe hanging from the bar above Mr Sidhu's head.

A slight panic in Mr Sidhu's eyes launched Gerry into more laughter. Mr Sidhu looked around the pub and saw mistletoe hanging in a few places. Like Valentine's Day or the four-leafed clover, mistletoe was one of those things Mr Sidhu knew about but had never really understood.

'Gerry,' he called out.

'What is it, Dave?' Gerry asked.

'Min, she is a bit . . .' He struggled to find the words.

'Yeah, I hear you. Everything OK?' said Gerry, turning to give Mr Sidhu his full focus.

'I have her pension book in the post office. She keeps losing it. So when she comes here I will pay or Rose will come to pay her bill. OK?'

Gerry leaned his arm across the bar and patted Mr Sidhu on the shoulder.

'You're a good man, Dave.'

'Ah, everything OK now?' asked Jay once they'd got their drinks and sat down at the table with him and Min.

'Yes, thank you,' said Mr Sidhu. He paused, trying to find the correct words to say, 'The dog is OK?'

'Tubby? Yeah, he's fine,' Jay said, rubbing Tubby's neck, the dog looking worried in Mr Sidhu's presence. Jay said nothing as Mr Sidhu and Tubby eyed each other. The dog had its ears flat on its head, looking intently at Mr Sidhu.

'He wants to say hello,' said Jay.

Mr Sidhu had never thought that a dog might want to say hello to him before. He tentatively placed his hand on Tubby's head and his tail started wagging at speed. Mr Sidhu looked up and saw everyone looking at him. He felt his face go red and he managed a smile. He was just about to get up and disappear to the toilet, even though he didn't want to go, when he felt something soft and warm enclose his hand. It was Rose. She held his hand under the table. Rather than pulling away he let it melt into his until all his thoughts and worries lifted. He looked around the pub at the swirl of activity and noise.

Rose started to speak to him in a low voice.

'I was young,' said Rose. 'I was eighteen when I got pregnant.' An impulse to take his hand back from Rose's came and went. Instead he nodded a little to indicate that she should continue. Mr Sidhu couldn't picture her as an eighteen-year-old; the way she was now was how he knew her.

'They made it seem normal to give away your baby for adoption. I regretted it immediately, but everyone said the same thing – that it was for the best. The nurses said they had a home all set up for him.'

Mr Sidhu looked at Jay talking to Min. He seemed happy and relaxed. Surely he would be angry at Rose.

'And then, ten years ago, he just turns up out of the blue. As soon as I saw him, I knew. And he's just the nicest boy you'll ever meet.'

'What does he do?' asked Mr Sidhu.

71

'He's a gardener. Tree surgeon, properly qualified and eve-rything,' said Rose proudly. Mr Sidhu had never heard of a tree surgeon before but didn't say anything. He spotted Bill the Scotsman making his way over to him. Bill had an expression on his face like a child who'd been given a present.

'Fucking hell, Davey, never thought I'd see you down here.'

Bill was a former long-haul driver from Glasgow (G1) who had miraculously settled in Richmond. Mr Sidhu gave him odd jobs to do in the shop like taking out the rubbish on a Wednesday. His eyes were glassy and even on Christmas Day he was unshaven, matching his grey, Brillo-pad hair combed over his bald head. He took Mr Sidhu's hand and shook it violently. Everyone knew he was a drunk, including Mr Sidhu, but nevertheless the community accepted him as one of them. He seemed to know Jay, too, and Mr Sidhu wondered what else people knew that he didn't.

After an hour their table was full of locals and customers. Mr Sidhu kept being offered a drink and kept having to refuse until a glass of whisky was put in front of him.

'Chak de phatte,' said Richard.

Mr Sidhu grinned. Richard never ceased to surprise him. When Richard had first entered the post office after Mr Sidhu had bought it and he and Sarabjit were wondering whether they'd made a mistake buying a post office in such a white area of London, Richard had greeted them with a 'Sat Sri Akal'. It was the first time either he or Sarabjit had ever heard an English person speak Punjabi. They'd taken it as a good omen, something auspicious.

'So, Sidhu Saahab, you've finally succumbed to the allure of the Arms?'

Richard was different to most of the locals Mr Sidhu knew. He didn't have to collect a pension at the post office, but he was a prolific letter writer, especially to the council, and bought his stationery and stamps there. Mr Sidhu liked having Richard around, because he was what Mr Sidhu had imagined England would be like when he'd arrived. Of course, it hadn't been anything like that.

Mr Sidhu naively offered everyone a drink, to which they all responded with a resounding 'yes, please' or 'nice one, Dave'.

'Need a hand?' asked Jay. Mr Sidhu nodded and turned to look at Rose, who winked at him. It caught him by surprise and his mind started to wander. What did Rose winking at him mean? Jay put a hand on his shoulder, 'Those drinks aren't going to order themselves, David.'

At the bar Mr Sidhu and Jay waited for one of Gerry's bar staff to get the big order of drinks: two G&Ts ('they'll want doubles', Jay informed him), a glass of white wine (large), two pints of ordinary (Mr Sidhu had no idea what that meant), three whiskies (doubles, of course). Luckily for Mr Sidhu, Jay remembered the order. Mr Sidhu wanted to say something to Jay about the gardening but wasn't sure what.

'You're surprised that I'm Rose's son,' said Jay as Mr Sidhu contemplated what a tree surgeon did. Mr Sidhu looked at Jay. His head was smooth, but little black hairs poked through the brown skin. He wore jeans, leather boots and a thick shirt. He looked very comfortable and at ease as he leaned on the bar. He was taller than Mr Sidhu, but you couldn't tell because Mr Sidhu's turban added a few inches to his height.

'Rose told me you are a tree surgeon,' he replied, not wanting to say anything about what Rose had told him earlier.

'Yes, I am.'

'What is it?'

Jay explained it to him and as they took the drinks back to the bar, they carried on their conversation.

'I have some work in my garden. The trees, they are too big. They need cutting. Can you do it?' asked Mr Sidhu. The drinks were starting to make him more at ease in the pub and he was feeling more at home.

'Yeah, sure. Bit busy this year, though, maybe talk next year. How does that sound?'

Mr Sidhu looked doubtful for a moment before the laughter in Jay's eyes made him realise it was a joke.

Mr Sidhu felt pleased with himself that he'd been able to talk to Jay. He'd discovered that Jay had grown up in Yorkshire with his adopted family and that was where his accent was from. Even better was that Mr Sidhu would be able to see him work, which was how Mr Sidhu judged people. It was one of the reasons he liked Rose so much. She worked effortlessly without complaining. He sighed as he thought about her. He might tell her about the job he had offered to Jay. It might make up for the earlier incident at the house with the dog. He saw Min and Rose putting on their coats and for a moment Mr Sidhu felt panicked. The idea of being in the pub without Rose seemed to him unthinkable; they'd come together and they would leave together.

'David, I'm going to take Min home,' said Rose, coming over to him.

'I will come too,' he replied, hastily picking up his coat.

'You don't have to, David. You can stay if you like.' Rose was close to him now and he wanted to tell her how he felt about her. It was unbearable.

'I want to come with you,' he said.

Rose nodded and the three of them left after saying their goodbyes while fending off Bill, who was trying to get Mr Sidhu a drink before he left.

Min was talking but not making much sense. She was a little unsteady on her feet, but between them they were able to navigate her towards her house. A man in a duffle coat stood blocking the pavement with his hood up and Mr Sidhu was about to say something when Rose spoke up.

'Michael, is that you?'

Min pricked up her ears at hearing the name. And the man took off his hood and smiled. He wasn't very tall but had a thick head of mousy hair and pale skin.

'Merry Christmas, Rose. Hello, Mum.'

Min plunged herself into Michael's chest and closed her eyes.

'Oh Michael, you came, my darling, you came. Thank you, thank you,' Min cooed.

'Always have time for my mum, haven't I? Come on, let's get you home.'

'This is David, he runs the post office here.' Michael put out his hand and shook Mr Sidhu's hand.

'I want to thank you, David. My mum always talks about you, and I know you help her. It's appreciated.'

'No problem,' said Mr Sidhu, feeling self-conscious.

'I can take her from here,' said Michael, 'unless you want to come in for a drink?'

'No, that's fine. I'm sure you've got lots of catching up to do,' said Rose. Mr Sidhu smiled his thin smile.

They said their goodbyes and then it was just Mr Sidhu and Rose alone in the street.

'He seems like a nice boy,' said Mr Sidhu.

'Divorced, two kids, lives in Sheffield,' said Rose matter-of-factly. 'He works up there; it's nice he came down to see her.'

They both nodded and also knew that she needed him, but they didn't say anything more about that.

'Please let me walk you home, Rose,' said Mr Sidhu, still feeling the warmth of the alcohol in his body.

'Thank you, David, that's very gentlemanly of you.' She offered her arm for him to loop his arm through. They walked past the post office with its red pillar box outside. Mr Sidhu resisted the urge to check the shutters were properly locked.

'You know, I'll have more time with the new system coming in,' he said.

'Oh, that's nice,' said Rose. 'What will you do?'

'I want to see Richmond Park and the seaside,' he said firmly. He'd always enjoyed the little trips he and the family had made to the seaside when the children were young. He'd never seen the sea before he came to England, and the way the sea and the land came together was like nothing he'd ever known. In Punjab the rivers were fierce and powerful, especially after the monsoon rains. The sea in England with its beaches was gentle in comparison, even if the water was freezing.

They arrived at Rose's house. She took out her key and opened the door, walking into her house without addressing Mr Sidhu, who stood on the threshold, not sure what to do.

'Come in, David, and close the door. You're letting the cold in,' said Rose as she took off her coat and indicated for Mr Sidhu to do the same.

He sat on the settee while Rose prepared a cup of tea. He looked at her lounge anew. The whisky in his blood relaxed him and he looked at the paintings he'd noticed earlier. He wanted something like that in his own house. He'd never felt the urge before but now he did: to have a picture of the bridge he'd driven over so many times in his life yet never stopped to look at. It was made of a pale, whitish stone and was small and narrow, with black lamps at intervals. In the picture the sky held a reflection of the bridge, as if the water was above it.

'Where did you get that picture from?' he asked as Rose came in with a tray with the tea.

'Oh, do you like it? Min painted it for me.'

Mr Sidhu tried not to show his shock. Min had made this beautiful painting?

'She's good, isn't she?' Rose added. They both looked at it.

'Yes, I must ask her,' said Mr Sidhu, feeling out of his depth suddenly.

'It wasn't so bad, was it? Coming to mine for Christmas?' asked Rose.

'No, it was wonderful. Thank you, Rose. It was my first time,' said Mr Sidhu, perking up.

'What, you've never had a Christmas lunch before?'

'No, not like today.'

'Well, I feel honoured that I was able to show you how we do it.'

They laughed together and then a silence fell between them. Mr Sidhu thought about leaving; he didn't want to outstay his welcome.

'I've a confession to make, David,' said Rose, breaking the silence.

Mr Sidhu looked confused.

'I know this may come as a surprise, and I don't want to scare you, but I took something that didn't belong to me this evening and I wanted to ask your advice.'

Rose looked at Mr Sidhu. His mouth was ajar.

'Hahn?' he managed to say, unsure that he'd heard her correctly.

Everything had been going so well and now he was getting involved in some kind of conspiracy. 'What are you saying, Rose?'

'I couldn't help myself, David. I saw this in the pub and took it without asking.' Rose held out a stick of mistletoe. 'Do you know what it is?'

Mr Sidhu nodded slowly, unaware he was frowning. Rose reached her hands towards his face, and in the next second she had taken off his glasses. The world became a blur. A warm, wet sensation hit his lips and even though he immediately went to recoil, Rose's soft hands gently but firmly held the sides of his face through his beard and slowly he allowed himself to kiss her back.

Chapter 6

Mr Sidhu woke up to a glorious sunny day. It was Boxing Day, so he didn't have to go to the post office. As he did his morning exercises in the garden he noticed his fingernails were yellow. After he finished his exercises and examined his hands more closely in the bathroom, he could see that the grey patches in his beard were yellow and orange too. Slowly he remembered coming home the night before and devouring a cold lamb curry with his hands. He had needed to feel the warmth of chilli inside him.

Last night's event seemed far away, here in his house. He tried to stop himself thinking about what was going to happen when he saw Rose again.

Mr Sidhu soaked himself in the bath, ducking his head below the water and letting the warmth of the water soothe him in a way nothing else did. As he poured water over his body, he thought of his father doing the same thing every morning at 5 a.m. Sikhs traditionally bathed in the cold of the morning, when everything was still and silent – a time called Amrit Vela. As a boy he'd watched his father bathe and then recite prayers in the morning darkness. He'd missed him when he'd come to England. He'd only ever seen him twice after leaving India: his own wedding, and then once again to take money to India. He'd also been to his funeral, but he didn't count that as seeing him.

Mr Sidhu cleaned and thoroughly rinsed his long, grey hair, leaning his head to one side and combing it from root to tip. His hair fell down straight when wet, even though it was loosely curled when dry. Mr Sidhu stopped. He'd been thinking about the cottage he'd found. Today, the idea of living there made him feel giddy with excitement. He quickly got dressed and rushed downstairs to find the property details.

Mr Sidhu spread the property listings out onto his dining table. The house was a ten-minute walk to the post office. He studied the description more closely now. 'Two bedrooms and a small garden to the rear', it stated. Perfect, he thought. He'd need to increase the mortgage as the house was worth more than his five-bedroom house in Hounslow. But what about Meenu? She'd been behaving strangely recently, becoming more involved in his life. He didn't know why, but it made him wary. As Mr Sidhu considered which curry he would have for lunch, the doorbell rang.

His first instinct was that it might be Meenu, but she was in Shropshire with Craig and his parents. Then he started to sweat; he thought it might be Rose. Had he done something to offend her? He looked at himself in the mirror and pushed in hair that was escaping from the back of his turban. Through the spyhole he saw Darshan and his wife, Tharlochan. Mr Sidhu sighed and opened the door.

Darshan was from Mr Sidhu's ancestral village, Bughipura, in Punjab. He'd known Darshan his whole life and there was a bond between them that spoke of their origins and where they were today. At weddings and other functions they would seek

80

each other out to talk and share news about the village – who had married, died or gone to Canada. However, since Sarabjit's passing, their relationship had changed. Darshan now saw Mr Sidhu as someone who needed looking after. Their village looked upon Darshan to protect and offer help to Mr Sidhu in the absence of a wife and the rest of his family, which consisted of two brothers he never spoke to and a half-sister he hardly knew. The visit, and everything it meant, annoyed Mr Sidhu. Ordinarily he would have tried to get rid of them as quickly as possible, but today their visit was a welcome distraction from thinking about Rose and their kiss, and what he would say to her when he saw her again.

'Hello! Hello! Sat Sri Akal!' Darshan almost shouted as he walked into Mr Sidhu's house.

He was one of those Sikhs who had a nasal voice. It seemed as if his voice box were in his nose, rather than in his throat. He sounded silly. His wife was a small, energetic woman who muttered to herself constantly. Whether she was praying or talking to herself, or both, was only known by Tharlochan.

'Have we disturbed you?' asked Darshan.

'No, no,' said Mr Sidhu.

'Post office closed?'

'Yes, Boxing Day, you know,' he replied.

And then silence. They took off their shoes with practised ease, using one foot to take off the shoe from the other. Tharlochan wore sandals and the pale-coloured, knee-high stockings that Mr Sidhu sold to elderly women in his shop (Sarabjit used to wear the same ones), and Darshan wore leather loafers and black-ribbed socks. As they wandered inside, Mr Sidhu wondered why they had come to see him. Tharlochan had been close to his wife, but now, without his wife there, he felt her presence more than before. She looked around his house as if looking for something.

'Cha?' Mr Sidhu asked.

He knew Tharlochan would jump to the task of making tea, refusing Mr Sidhu's perfunctory offer to do it himself. On her own in the kitchen, Tharlochan started to sing a devotional song: loudly enough to be heard, so that there would be no doubt in the minds of the two men of the goodness of her character. And just in case, she tugged at her chunni to cover her face, tucking a corner of it into her mouth to keep it in place as she dealt with making the tea.

'Looking for property?' asked Darshan, looking at the listings on the table.

'Something to pass the time, hunnah?' lied Mr Sidhu, gathering up the papers and placing them out of sight.

Darshan and Tharlochan had two children who'd married at the time that their parents wanted them to, in their mid-twenties, to people their parents had found for them. The boy, Gagan, was a dentist and the daughter, Daljit, an accountant. Gagan lived with his wife, along with Darshan and Tharlochan, and Daljit lived with her husband's parents. Their lives were set, and now that Mr Sidhu's life needed managing they set about improving it.

'People are worried about you,' said Darshan. Mr Sidhu knew Darshan was only doing what was expected of him. Mr Sidhu's situation would have been discussed by the village and the elders would have decided that someone should help him. It fell to Darshan to alert him to their decision. Mr Sidhu's life was their responsibility, even if three thousand miles separated them. He was one of them, even after all these years. He didn't like it.

'I am fine,' said Mr Sidhu.

'Yes, fine, you are fine, that is good, but your children are unmarried,' Darshan waved his hand in the air. 'A man must take responsibility for his life and his children's lives. While you are here they have your guidance, but if suddenly you are not here, then what?'

Darshan glared at Mr Sidhu.

'Suki, I am only thinking of you. I know it has been more than five years now and it was such a sad thing. She was a good woman. She is looking at you now thinking the same thing. Hundred per cent,' he added for emphasis.

Although Darshan was an educated man, he had worked at the airport for the last thirty years, having been promoted from cleaner to baggage security checker. His real passion was his work and involvement in the Sikh community. He'd helped with the building of a Gurdwara, firstly in Bughipura in Punjab, and then with the reconstruction of the local Gurdwara in Hounslow. He was a man of the community and people trusted him and looked up to him. However, Mr Sidhu had his suspicions. Darshan hadn't always been a devout man. In the early days when he came to England, he'd had the reputation of a philanderer, which most Punjabi men, unused to talking to women, were envious of. However, something must have happened, because from one day to the next Darshan had gone to India, got married and come back with a beard and turban. Rumour was that he'd seduced the wife of a small-time gangster who'd found out and wanted to kill him in revenge. But no one really knew, and no one asked him. These days he was always asking for donations, and Mr Sidhu had given in to his wife's demands to be one of the larger donors so that their name was engraved on a plaque inside the Gurdwara with the amount they had bequeathed underneath. There was no accountability for those who ran the Gurdwara. Not like the weekly accounts he had to fill in for the post office, which was government business.

Tharlochan was still muttering when she hurried in with the tray of tea. The men stopped talking as she carefully placed the cups onto the table, poured the tea and served it with aloo bhujia. Mr Sidhu loved aloo bhujia. Tharlochan must have brought some with her. He would have to be on his guard; they were up to something. He spooned a pile of the small, dry, spicy yellow pieces onto the palm of his hand and ate it down in one go, quickly followed by a sip of hot tea. Darshan and Tharlochan did the same.

Mr Sidhu looked at Tharlochan, who looked pleased with herself. People who met Tharlochan might say that she was a nervous woman – a little shy and perhaps wanting to impress too much. But they would be wrong. Tharlochan was a strong woman, and among other Punjabi women she would swear and curse like a sailor. Mr Sidhu had overheard her with his wife over the years, talking rudely about women they didn't like and calling them saali kuttis. It always shocked him to hear Punjabi women speaking like that with each other; they would never talk like that in front of him.

Darshan cleared his throat.

'We have found a girl for Raju,' he announced.

Mr Sidhu's ears rang with the words.

'She is a good girl, good family, some education, but she

will take care of you and Raju, of course,' said Darshan matter-of-factly.

Tharlochan studied Mr Sidhu. Thoughts raced through his mind. He stood up slowly, and calmly walked to the windows facing the back garden. He placed his hands behind his back. The sun was low and bright and he felt its warmth. He and Sarabjit had told each other many times that they would not interfere with their children's lives. They would choose for themselves. They had been born in England, and as long as the person was respectable and earned enough, that was that. Race, religion had nothing to do with it. Of course, they secretly harboured the wish that their children would marry a Sikh or at least an Indian, and definitely not a Muslim or West Indian, but if that's what happened then that was what would happen. Mr Sidhu turned back to face them.

'You are very good people coming here to help me,' he said. Tharlochan's face tightened.

She interjected, 'Such a good man you are, Sukhdev. And hai, hai, life has been unkind, taking your wife; she was a good woman and mother to your children. Who can ever find a woman like her? She was special. She understood the way things are done and the sacrifices you have to make for your family.' She paused, looking directly at Mr Sidhu. He turned away.

'What happened is more than some people can take, but you are strong like your father before you.' She allowed the mention of his father to hit its mark. 'You have carried on being a good father, but life is telling you that you need the help of your people to take your children to the next stage in their lives. Give them opportunity. This is what your father did for you.

He understood that he had to do his duty. How many times did he try to marry you? How many times did Darshan have to bring messages from your father? You were so busy. Now it is your turn to do your duty.'

'She is a very good girl, only twenty-two.' Darshan raised his eyebrows at Mr Sidhu. His turban rose up too.

'We know everything about her and she will make Raju very happy,' said Tharlochan.

Mr Sidhu was unable to hold on to his thoughts. Their words penetrated his mind and he started to feel weak. He sat down. Tharlochan reached into her bag and picked out a framed photograph. Silently, as if she were handling stolen goods, she handed Mr Sidhu the picture.

The woman was beautiful. He had half expected to see an old black and white picture like the one he had been given of his wife all those years ago, but this photo was in colour and he could tell it had been taken in a photographic studio in India. She was made up to look like a princess, gold everywhere, the eyes big and dark. She looked a little like Sarabjit when she was young. He looked at Tharlochan and Darshan.

'Who is she?' said Mr Sidhu, staring harder and harder at the picture – there was something familiar about her features. It was the eyes, there was definitely something there.

Darshan cleared his throat, 'She is Tharlochan's niece. She lives in Moga district. He is willing to give thirty thousand pounds. He has a big farm. Fifty acres.'

'He' meant the girl's father; 'thirty thousand' was the price of the dowry, so the rest of her family could come to England once they were married. This was the way things were arranged, but Mr Sidhu didn't like it. It was ignorant and uneducated and it made him angry. When he'd got married he made a big show of insisting on no dowry. It had been a modern idea then and he'd even made sure the wedding was a simple affair, with none of the brashness that some people insisted upon. Moreover, that this bride was related to Tharlochan cemented his resolve.

'He will choose for himself,' Mr Sidhu said finally and then added, 'just like Meenu. She is engaged to Craig. Very good boy. Journalist. Professional. And we do not do all this dowry and this and that.'

Darshan and Tharlochan looked at each other. Tharlochan began to talk but Mr Sidhu stopped her. 'Please, I have made up my mind.'

'Are all our elders wrong?' asked Tharlochan, her voice softening. 'Are all the people who came before us from the time of the gurus to now, are they all wrong?'

Mr Sidhu stared at her, not really able to fault what she was saying. He thought about how Raju would react to this kind of arrangement and almost smiled to himself.

'No, they are not wrong, they did what was right for them. But they did not have children born in England like mine.' Mr Sidhu smiled, thinking he'd won the argument, but then realised both Tharlochan's children had been born here too. He didn't want to offend them.

'I know you are trying to help me, but please, we are OK.'

'We are not English, Sukhdev,' said Darshan, looking directly at him. 'They do not look at us and say, there goes an Englishman. They will always see us as different. Your children are Punjabi. If we do not give them a sense of who they are, they will be lost.'

'They will be lost if they try to live as we did. They are born here, go to school with English friends, not like us,' replied Mr Sidhu, and there came into his mind something Raju would say to him whenever he tried to make him speak Punjabi, *'I didn't ask to be born in England. You came here. Nobody forced you to come here and have kids here. Why are you making me speak a language I don't understand?'*

'We raised our children to be whoever they want to be. It is not better or worse than how you raised your children; it is just the way,' and here he emphasized for Tharlochan's benefit, 'Sarabjit and I chose to do it.'

They sat in silence for a while before Tharlochan and Darshan exchanged a glance and said 'Chulo fer,' and got up to go.

Mr Sidhu thanked Darshan and Tharlochan for coming and told them that he'd come over to see them at some point, even though he knew he wouldn't do any such thing.

As they left, Darshan turned to Mr Sidhu and placed a hand on his shoulder.

'Suki, we are your people. Sarabjit kept the connection with the community, but now you are alone we have to look out for you. Make sure you do come and visit sometimes, hunnah?'

Mr Sidhu nodded. 'I will try, Darshan, but I am busy at the moment with the new computer system at the post office and everything.'

'Acha,' said Darshan and thought for a moment before adding, 'I am organizing a visit to Maharajah Duleep Singh's grave in the summer. Many people are coming. Bring Raju and Meenu. It will be good for you. It's very nice.'

Mr Sidhu was surprised to hear that Maharajah Duleep Singh – the last Maharajah of Punjab, son of the great Maharajah Ranjit Singh – had a grave in England. Sikhs didn't have graves.

Was Maharajah Duleep Singh buried here in England? He had no idea. He was about to ask Darshan about it, but he stopped himself. If he showed interest, he might end up being persuaded to go. And he definitely didn't want to go with them. Sarabjit used to go on those trips with the Gurdwara community, but Mr Sidhu preferred to stay in the post office in Richmond. He doubted that Meenu and Raju would go either. However, he made noises to the effect that he might come, to keep Darshan happy. Once they'd left, he picked up the property listings and spread them out on the table again. He looked at the house he liked and got his car keys. He needed to see with his own eyes where he might live.

Chapter 7

'Dad!'

Mr Sidhu woke up. Meenu was staring at him. People seated around were also staring at him. Of course, he was at the theatre. Raju had invited him and Meenu to watch his latest play. He'd been dreaming about his village and could still feel the heat of the sun on his skin. He sighed loudly without thinking and the scowling faces of the theatre-goers turned to face him again. He looked straight ahead at the stage, ignoring the looks. He didn't like going to the theatre. There seemed to be too many rules and conventions that no one bothered to tell him about. He was there to see Raju's show. Raju was in the centre of the stage with a spotlight on him; he was curled up on the ground, talking about being entombed in the Taj Mahal. He couldn't remember, or wasn't following the storyline, and the next moment Raju was whirling around in a white sheet to loud Qawwali music, which Mr Sidhu appreciated – it stopped him from falling asleep again when the lights dimmed.

In the theatre bar after the show, he waited with Meenu for Raju to come out.

'You were so embarrassing, Dad, falling asleep like that. Did you realise that you were sort of wailing when you woke up?'

Meenu stared accusingly at him. He felt an anger rising up within him. Why was she siding with strangers against her own father?

'I was tired,' he replied with a note of annoyance.

'Is everything all right, Dad?'

He didn't like it when Meenu asked him that question. Her eyes penetrated his being, making him feel naked and his reply hollow.

'Everything is fine, beta.'

Everything wasn't fine, but he didn't want to worry Meenu about something that even he didn't understand. Since the new year, money had been going missing in the post office accounts, and so far, he had no idea where it was going. It was April, three months since the new system had been installed, and every week for the last three months his balance had been out by a thousand pounds. It was something that had never happened before. He was worried that he was somehow not using the new computer system properly and that in turn only made him even more worried that the Post Office might then tell him that he couldn't work there any longer as he was too old to work the new system. When he did hesitantly contact the helpline, the Post Office told him it was nothing to worry about and that it would sort itself out, but so far it hadn't. So, every week the new thousand pounds added to the previous week's thousand pounds. For Mr Sidhu, who had always prided himself on his meticulous accounts, it didn't sit right. He'd spent evenings going over every transaction in his post office, trying to find out why there was a deficit, but each time he came up with nothing. It was affecting his sleep and he had noticed himself getting more irritable. Mr Sidhu pictured the computer screen in his post office with the discrepancy amount in the weekly balance blinking at him repeatedly.

Raju arrived to join Meenu without acknowledging Mr Sidhu. He talked to Meenu as if Mr Sidhu wasn't there.

'What did you think?' he asked Meenu.

'Well done, Raju, very good,' interrupted Mr Sidhu, desperately trying to hide what he was really thinking about.

Raju turned slowly to him, only to stop to wave and blow kisses at someone. Mr Sidhu was disturbed to see it was a man.

'He's amazing,' said Raju to no one in particular. 'I'm so lucky,' he added. Mr Sidhu looked at Meenu, who raised her eyebrows at him.

'So, you came. Well done, Father,' said Raju, glancing at Meenu.

'He fell asleep and started wailing,' Meenu grinned.

'Was that you?' Raju finally looked directly at his father.

Mr Sidhu tried to look apologetic, but Raju's expression didn't break.

'At least when Mum came she actually watched my plays,' and with that he left Mr Sidhu and Meenu to order a drink and chat to someone at the bar.

Anger rose up in Mr Sidhu's body but he said nothing. They didn't know he'd been up until midnight, checking over his figures which weren't adding up. He didn't want to burden them. He dug his thumbnail into one of his fingers to change his thoughts.

'How is Craig?' he asked Meenu.

Meenu sighed heavily, 'Yeah, he's fine, Dad.'

'And any news of the wedding?'

Meenu stopped and looked at him as if she might hurt him in some way.

'Want to get rid of me, Dad?'

'No, of course not,' he said softly, but knew that it was what he actually wanted: that she become part of Craig's family and not solely his responsibility. It might make it easier then for Raju to do the same, to get married and have responsibilities that weren't just about his own career and nothing else.

'I promised your mother I would settle you and your brother, and time will not wait for you.'

Raju returned, dipping a straw into his glass and making the ice inside tinkle.

'Are you sure there isn't another reason you're trying to get rid of us?' he said, sliding onto a seat next to Meenu. Mr Sidhu noticed Meenu nudge Raju with her foot.

'What?' asked Mr Sidhu.

Raju smiled. 'Nothing, Dad, you seem a little bit preoccupied, that's all. Doesn't he, Meenu? He looks tired. What have you been up to, Dad? What or who's been keeping you up?'

Meenu smiled at Raju. 'Dad, we have to look after you, too. If there's anything you want to talk about, we're here for you.'

'Well said, sis.'

'Thank you. Oh, who was the guy you were blowing kisses to?' Meenu asked Raju.

'He's the director, Omar. He's amazing,' said Raju, his eyes bright with excitement.

Raju carried on talking about how amazing Omar was. Mr Sidhu wasn't really following what he was saying but pretended he was, looking at Raju and nodding occasionally. He glanced at Meenu, who raised an eyebrow at him and then returned to looking at Raju, with a hint of a smile on her face.

What was she trying to tell him?

'Isn't he gay?' Meenu asked Raju, her eyes darting to Mr Sidhu as she spoke.

'He's bi,' said Raju seriously.

'Bisexual means he goes out with men and women,' said Meenu to Mr Sidhu by way of explanation.

Raju and Meenu started giggling. Mr Sidhu stayed silent, not engaging with their childish behaviour. Meenu carried on smiling to herself as she left the table to use the toilet.

Alone with Raju, Mr Sidhu looked at his son, hoping for some spark of maturity that would allay his fear that Raju was wasting his life.

'Are you seeing Rose, Dad?' asked Raju out of the blue.

'What?'

'Meenu said you are.'

Mr Sidhu felt his face blush. It was the part of his life that he cherished the most at the moment. Since Christmas he and Rose had become a couple, he supposed. They worked together but also went for walks, to restaurants and the pub. It was a life he never imagined he might have. His heart grew as he thought about her.

'Dad?'

'We are friends, Raju. She is a good woman.'

'Right,' said Raju slowly.

'What did Meenu say?' asked Mr Sidhu, trying to sound casual.

Raju stirred his drink with a black plastic straw, not looking at Mr Sidhu.

'She said you went to Rose's for Christmas lunch,' he replied, finally looking at Mr Sidhu. 'And that you weren't really busy over Christmas, you just didn't want to be with us.'

Mr Sidhu hoped his blush wouldn't show through his beard.

'I told Meenu about the house you want to buy, too. I don't think it's fair the way you don't tell her these things and then complain when she gets annoyed.'

Mr Sidhu didn't know what to say.

'I'm happy for you, Dad, but I think you need to be more honest with Meenu. She's not happy.'

Mr Sidhu didn't like the way he was being talked to. He knew Raju was right, but he couldn't just become something he wasn't. He'd never had that kind of relationship with her and he didn't think he could start now.

'I promised your mother I would make sure you and Meenu were settled. You know your chacha, Darshan, came to me with a marriage proposal for you, Raju. And I tell him no. This is not what we do. Raju will decide for himself. I don't tell you because you don't need to know.'

'All right, Dad, calm down. She knows now, anyway,' said Raju, holding his hands up.

Meenu arrived back and stared at both of them.

'Everything all right?' she asked.

Mr Sidhu left them, muttering that he needed to go to the bathroom, even though he didn't need to go. He locked himself in a cubicle and tried to understand what was going on. He was arguing with his son, and Meenu thought he was a liar. It was madness. He wanted to tell Meenu that it was up to Craig to look after her now, not him. She would become part of his family and Raju would bear the family name. It was all he knew; it was what had been done in his family since forever. He knew Sarabjit had explained all this to them. But here in England everyone was told they could be anything,

96

break every rule and damn anyone who stood in your way. Apart from the Royal Family, he mused – they still did things in the old ways.

He returned to Raju and Meenu, who were talking intensely with each other. They didn't notice as he approached.

'You don't get it, Raju, he's lying to us. If he can lie about where he was at Christmas, what else is he lying about?'

Raju didn't say anything as Meenu continued, 'Dad's never lied to us before, has he? So why now? What's changed? She must have put him up to it. She doesn't want us to know about their relationship and she convinced him not to talk to us about it too.'

'She doesn't seem that bad,' said Raju, and Mr Sidhu was filled with a rare moment of pride for his son.

'Don't be so naive, Raju. She's got a son, too, you know. Who she gave up for adoption, by the way. And now suddenly he's come back. What do you think that will mean for you?' said Meenu, her lips tightened against her teeth.

'What are you talking about, Meenu?'

'What do we know about her or her son? Dad's alone and vulnerable. We have to protect him.'

The chair Mr Sidhu was leaning upon suddenly moved and scraped along the floor, making a noise which made the last few people in the bar look up, including Meenu and Raju. He made a show of moving some chairs and making a noise as he made his presence known.

'Right, I need to go,' said Mr Sidhu, trying to be upbeat. 'Well done on your acting, Raju, good work. See you soon, Meenu.'

They all looked at each other for a moment.

'Bye, Dad, see you soon,' said Meenu, breaking the silence.

'Take care of yourself, Dad. If you need to talk about any-thing, let me know,' Raju added.

Mr Sidhu nodded and left.

Driving home, Mr Sidhu thought about his children's behaviour and how it made sense now. They knew about him and Rose. And Jay. What was he to do? And what did it mean? He wanted to focus on it, but for some reason all he could think about was what Raju had said to him about Sarabjit coming to see his plays. He knew that Sarabjit couldn't stand going to see Raju's plays.

'I don't understand anything,' she'd told him. 'Hopefully it is just a fad which will pass.' Together Mr Sidhu and Sarabjit had gone to see Punjabi plays at the local community centre in Hounslow. They were comedies about newly arrived immigrants unable to be understood by English people, or Indians pretend-ing to be like white people, or a Punjabi man pretending to be a woman married to a man to get into the country. How they'd laughed along with all the other Punjabis, even though Raju and Meenu thought those kinds of plays were stupid and backward and never shied away from telling them so. Yet with Raju's plays, he and Sarabjit were always confused and no one laughed or said anything during the shows. They couldn't understand what and who they were for. Mainly English audiences would clap tremendously at the end as if they had witnessed something amazing, and Mr Sidhu and Sarabjit did so too, not wanting to be seen doing the wrong thing.

It turned out that acting wasn't a fad and so Raju carried on making next to nothing as an actor and squandering the opportunity to buy more property and become financially well off. As he drove, Mr Sidhu didn't feel Sarabjit's presence in the way that he did sometimes when he was doing something foolish. He glanced into the night sky, looking for something, but all he could see were the streetlights passing by rhythmically, one after the other.

Without Sarabjit, Mr Sidhu felt that his children wanted to make him do what they wanted, without thinking or caring about what *he* wanted. And like his schooling when he was a boy, he felt shame at his newfound happiness with Rose. His children were suspicious of it. Mr Sidhu stopped at a red light. It was drizzling and the red light illuminated the windscreen, momentarily creating hundreds of red spots which the windscreen wipers then swept away. Meenu had known for a while, he was sure. That was probably why Raju had been curter with him than usual. Mr Sidhu sighed and let the emotion he felt flow out of him. Part of him didn't care. He was happy. That was enough.

Since the new year he and Rose had taken walks around Richmond. He'd learned how to navigate Richmond by foot, something he'd never done before. He saw how the Green behind the main high street was connected to the river. You had to pass through what had been an old palace. Rose had shown him a blue plaque which told people Queen Elizabeth I had lived there. From there they walked along the river, passing Richmond Bridge until they reached Richmond Hill, which was connected to Richmond Park (TW10). You could walk everywhere without even crossing a road. He'd stood with Rose in Richmond Park, amazed that deer lived in the park and that you could get so close to them. It was so strange. And when Rose told him to look where she was pointing, he saw Central London. There was the London Eye, all the new skyscrapers and even the old Post Office Tower. It was almost too much to take in. Could he live here and see these sights every day? He hadn't told Rose anything about what he was thinking, but it made sense to him. Why be in Hounslow with aeroplanes roaring overhead with never a hello from anyone when he could walk along a river and see people who knew him and what he did? It made more and more sense every time he thought about it.

Mr Sidhu turned his van to go to the post office. He wanted to check one final time before he called the helpline again the next day. Perhaps he'd made a mistake with the stamps. He knew in his heart that it was impossible, but he might have missed something. So for the second evening in a row and the umpteenth time, Mr Sidhu sat in his post office late in the evening and counted every stamp, every note, every penny until there was nothing else to count. And yet there it was on the screen, a discrepancy of just over a thousand pounds. It was the tenth time since the computer system had been installed that he had registered a loss in his balance. It was the tenth time during his tenure as sub-postmaster that the balance had been more than a few pounds out. And again he couldn't find the discrepancy. Tired, he locked up, trudged to his van and drove home tired and alone. He remembered that Meenu had said he'd been wailing when he was asleep in the theatre. And he remembered why. He'd been dreaming about his village again. Something he'd been doing more and more. Remembering and dreaming of when his life was simple and everything made sense. He giggled to himself as he remembered the day Billoo, his older brother, had thrown him into the chuppar. That's what had made him wail – he'd been trying to get out and the soft mud was sucking him down into the earth.

Darshan stopped Sukhdev on the way to school. They were the only boys to go to school from the village (and no girls were sent).

'Look,' he said, pointing.

There was Billoo, Sukhdev's older brother, herding buffalo into the chuppar, a small pond in the middle of the village where boys took turns to cool down the buffalo and clean them, holding on to their backs and scrubbing them with wooden brushes. Darshan took his trusty slingshot, which he'd made himself from the wood of a mango tree. It was smooth through use and at each end of the 'Y' he'd tied a thick piece of black rubber which used to be the inner tube of a bicycle tyre. He picked up a stone the size of a baby's fist, aimed and fired. The stone sped through the air and hit the buffalo on its hind quarters, which made the dark buffalo bellow loudly and run out of the chuppar. Billoo, who was still on its back, went flying into the water and the commotion made all the other buffalo run away too. Sukhdev laughed nervously along with Darshan.

'Do you think he'll be all right?' asked Sukhdev, thinking that Billoo might be trampled under the water by all the buffalo running out of the chuppar.

'Billoo can handle himself,' said Darshan dismissively.

That was true, as Billoo was only 15 but could pass for 18. He was broad-shouldered and already had the beard of a man. Despite that, Darshan and Sukhdev walked tentatively towards the chuppar. And suddenly, like some kind of deity, Billoo rose up out of the water, his beard matted, his joora undone and his long hair all tangled up around his face like seaweed. He dipped his head in the water and flung his head back, his hair falling onto his back, clearing his face and vision.

Rather than running away, Darshan started laughing, 'Oh Billoo, your face!' Darshan imitated Billoo falling off the buffalo.

'I'm going to break your face, bhenchod,' Billoo replied, coming in close to Darshan to make good on his threat. Darshan stopped laughing.

'Come on, Billoo, I didn't know it was going to do that. I'm not that good a shot,' he lied. And then added, 'Anyway, Suki told me to do it,' and winked at Sukhdev as if they were in some kind of conspiracy.

Sukhdev struggled to say it wasn't true. Darshan had that power – he could make people do things they didn't want to. Billoo didn't need any more reason to turn his focus onto his brother, whom his father favoured over his two other sons who did all the work on the farm while Sukhdev went to school. Close to them now, Billoo grabbed Sukhdev violently, turned him around and took his satchel off his back, ripping the strap. Sukhdev looked at him, hoping he wouldn't do anything more. His hope was misplaced. He turned to look at Darshan to see if he might help, but Darshan was now walking on as if this incident had nothing to do with him.

'Do you think these books will help you now?' sneered Billoo as he emptied the satchel and looked at the contents. Books, apart from religious texts, were rare in Sukhdev's village and were looked upon with suspicion by his own family. These were algebra books which Mr Panesar had given to Sukhdev because he knew Sukhdev would read them. It was an honour that he had even been allowed to take them home. If anything happened to them, he would be punished severely.

'Let me go to school, you've already made me late,' he said, kneeling down and picking up the books.

Billoo kicked him, not aiming at any particular area of his body but just wanting him to stop what he was doing. His foot made contact with Sukhdev's jaw, and it hurt (later, Billoo would stare at him at dinner time, watching him painfully chew his roti). Sukhdev held on to his books, but a few more kicks into his body opened his hands and Billoo took what he wanted. 'Hey Billoo, come on, stop,' groaned Sukhdev, but Billoo ignored him as he walked to the chuppar where the egrets with their long legs had returned to the shallower areas after the earlier commotion with the buffalo. Billoo flung in the books and grinned.

'You think you are better than us with all this school non-sense,' Billoo declared, voicing the opinion he shared with his other brother and his mother, who had emotionally given up on Sukhdev, because of his slight stature, but were wary of him due to their father's interest in his schooling.

'That is because you are stupid,' declared Sukhdev. He was surprised by his reply but was glad he was able to find the words.

Billoo looked hurt and stopped. For a moment, Sukhdev

thought he might be able to get away and not be late for school, and thereby avoid a beating. However, Billoo had other ideas. Sukhdev could feel his brother's powerful arms grabbing him and picking him up effortlessly before throwing him into the chuppar. Billoo then picked up his satchel and other books and threw them in too.

'They can't save you from me,' said Billoo, smirking at him.

'No!' Sukhdev shouted. The opened books floated on the surface of the water, the covers spread out and the pages submerged. It would take an age for them to dry.

Sukhdev was chest-high in the muddy water. He walked to get the books, his bare feet sinking into the soft mud at the bottom of the chuppar, slowing him down. Billoo stood at the water's edge looking down at Sukhdev, smiling at him.

'You know Guru Gobind Singh could read and write, you imbecile,' quipped Sukhdev as he gathered up the books.

Billoo looked uncertain for a moment. 'The land and the rivers give us everything we need. Without them you would have died, you sister fucker,' he replied. 'You can't eat books,' he added, and kicked some sand into Sukhdev's eyes. Sukhdev tumbled backwards into the water, trying to hold on to the books, but somehow the weight of the books sank him to the bottom of the chuppar and the soft mud felt as if it was sucking him into the earth. He had a small moment of calm as if being under the water was where he was supposed to be. Then suddenly a force pulled him back into the sunlight. It was Billoo. He hauled him out of the chuppar and threw him onto the ground, then walked away to collect the absconded buffalo.

Sukhdev did not go into school that day. He spent the whole day drying his books and avoiding the laughter of the villagers to whom the spectacle of a boy drying his books was comical. The next day he was beaten by Mr Panesar, so as not to show favouritism. And Sukhdev knew that even as he was getting beaten with a cane, bent over in front of all the other school kids, it wasn't really because of what Darshan had done; it was because his father loved him more than his brothers. That's why Billoo had ruined the books.

Now Mr Sidhu felt sad that he'd not gone back more often to see his father, and that his brothers and mother might have treated his father without the love he deserved as he'd got older. However, one thing he did know was that his father never stopped him being what he wanted to be.

And for that he was grateful.

Chapter 8

Mr Sidhu took a deep breath. He knew the number off by heart now. He waited. The voice interrupted the music.

'Your call is important to us and we will be with you as soon as we can.'

The music came on again. He only had half an hour during his lunch break to get through to the helpline and explain the problem. As the music played on, with the voice repeating that the call was important to them every twenty seconds or so, Mr Sidhu's motivation for the call waned. He looked at Rose happily serving customers. She glanced at him and smiled. Alan was coming today to see what the problem was with his accounts. This was his last chance to sort out the problem before he arrived. He so desperately wanted things to go back to the way they were and to tell Alan that everything was fine.

'Hello, can I help you?' said the female voice on the phone.

'Hello, yes. Hello, hello,' exclaimed Mr Sidhu, making sure she could hear him and moreover that he was being listened to. He explained once again about the discrepancy in his weekly accounts and how it had not been automatically corrected as they'd said it would be.

'It will be corrected, sir. The system knows that there is a shortfall and I've noted it.'

'So I put the discrepancy into the holding account again?' asked Mr Sidhu, wanting confirmation that he was not doing anything wrong.

'If that's what you do normally, then yes.'

'But why is there the wrong amount every week? Why?' asked Mr Sidhu. He didn't understand why his accounts were not adding up. There was nothing in his post office to show why there was a loss every week.

'The system automatically calculates the balance for the week and if there's an accountable difference then it will correct it later. It's a computer system, so it can't be wrong.'

It was the same conversation he was having every week with the helpline. The losses in the holding account were nearing fifteen thousand pounds.

'You are sure it will be corrected?'

'Yes, of course, sir. Provided that all is as you say it is.'

Mr Sidhu was outraged by the idea that something was amiss in his post office.

'I have never had a wrong balance in over twenty years,' he stated.

'That may be the case, sir. However, as I'm not physically there I can't verify what you're saying to be true. I'm sure you—'

'You come here and you can see. No problem,' said Mr Sidhu, interrupting her.

'Sir, raising your voice will not help.'

'And what will help? I ring, you tell me everything will be corrected, nothing happens; I ring again and what? Nothing. You are telling me money is missing from my post office? Yes?'

'Sir, I'm afraid I will have to ask you not to raise your voice.'

A silence followed and Mr Sidhu bit his tongue, allowing his anger to be quelled for the moment. The female voice continued, 'I understand your frustrations, sir. However, no one else is having any problems with the new Horizon system, and from my notes I can see that the area supervisor will be visiting you today to find out more about what's happening in your branch.'

Mr Sidhu didn't like the idea that anything was happening in his branch, but he held his tongue. Horizon sounded like a word that was calm and neutral. However, for Mr Sidhu the word only meant stress.

'Is there anything else I can help you with?'

'No.'

Mr Sidhu felt like a child at school being blamed for something they'd not done.

He didn't think there was anything helpful about the helpline. He always rang off more confused and more anxious than before. He needed to get this problem sorted out; he was finding it hard to think about anything else. He looked at the computer terminal which looked so harmless. On its screen were little icons which he tapped for the sale of stamps, or a pension payment from a card which replaced the different coloured pension books. He missed them now. It sat there humming away with the wires coming out of the back, and next to it was the little printer, which duly printed out receipts and the incorrect balances every week. They felt like a personal rebuke against him.

'Still on for later, David?' asked Rose.

He was peering at the figures printed on a roll of paper,

holding the paper taut, scanning it up and down, his face in a grimace.

'What?' he replied without looking up.

'With Jay? The trees in your garden,' said Rose, lowering her head to try and meet his gaze.

Mr Sidhu looked at Rose, his mind unable to focus on what she was saying. He was replaying the conversation with the helpline, *'Provided that all is as you say it is.'* Had he done something wrong? Is that what they were saying? Was the computer telling them something he didn't know about? Was it able to see everything he was doing? He might need to ask Meenu about this. She knew about computers. He turned to look at the computer terminal with its touchscreen again. He felt it held some kind of unnatural power.

'You know where the fairies live,' continued Rose.

'Fairies,' repeated Mr Sidhu, trying to show he was following the conversation.

'With Snow White and the Seven Dwarfs. David!' Rose laughed. 'Are you OK?'

Mr Sidhu blinked repeatedly, 'Sorry, Rose. I don't under-stand,' he said vaguely.

'What's wrong?' asked Rose, looking concerned.

Mr Sidhu placed the printout down and it curled back into its roll as if it possessed life.

He took off his glasses and rubbed his eyes then cleaned the lenses as he spoke.

'There is something wrong with the accounts and I don't know what it is. They say "don't worry", but I am worried. I am very worried. This never happened before.'

He really wanted Rose to hold him and tell him everything

would be OK. But they were separated by the bulletproof glass and he didn't have a good reason to come out of the post office.

'David, you said this has never happened before?'

'No, never,' he said, a little too loudly.

'Well then, it must be a fault in that new computer system. A loose connection or something. Did you tell them?'

'Yes.'

'And?'

Mr Sidhu told Rose about his chats with the helpline.

'Well, there you go then, it'll sort itself out. It's not like there's anything missing, is there?'

'No. They said they are sending Alan.'

'He'll see that nothing's wrong. He knows you.'

Mr Sidhu didn't want Alan to be sent to check on him. It meant that something was wrong, and if something was wrong it would be his responsibility. It was what he'd been told by Alan many times.

'When's he coming?'

'This afternoon.'

'Oh, that's why you're getting yourself all worked up, is it?' she asked.

Mr Sidhu nodded.

'I'll make you a nice cup of tea. Take your mind off it.'

'Thanks, Rose.'

The tea did take his mind off the losses for a moment, and his mind even allowed him to think of the possibility that Alan might come and find out what the problem was.

'We are still on for later, then?' asked Rose, collecting his cup once they'd finished their tea.

'What?' asked Mr Sidhu, pretending to look confused, but then he smiled and Rose shook her head at his attempt at humour.

Mr Sidhu smiled at the thought of showing Rose his house. 'Maybe we can go to a restaurant after?' he said.

'Sounds lovely.'

Rose's eyes met his and all thoughts about anything else evaporated as he imagined Rose coming to his house, showing her how to make tea the Punjabi way he liked it, and then taking her to his favourite restaurant. He thought about what dishes he would order and what dishes Rose might eat. He didn't think she would like very spicy food; he would ask them to tone down the spices for her. And then Jay too, did he like spicy food? A cold shiver went through him as he thought about taking Jay and Rose to his local Indian restaurant. He hadn't dined there for years and when he had, it had been with Sarabjit. What would they think of him, going there with Rose and Jay? He stopped to take a few deep breaths. It was fine. He was fine. Or perhaps he wasn't, he didn't know. But what he did know was that Rose made him feel happy. And more than that, she knew when he needed cheering up.

The door to the shop opened and Mr Sidhu saw Alan coming in, exchanging pleasantries with Rose. Mr Sidhu pretended not to notice. He'd tidied up the post office and placed all the paperwork Alan would need to look at in neat piles. The post office was small, and with the two of them in there space was tight. One person could not go around the other easily.

'Dave,' announced Alan, 'What's all this about, eh? Why are they telling me to come and see you, eh?'

'Oh, hello Alan,' Mr Sidhu pretended to be surprised and opened the door.

Alan walked in with his usual aroma of stale cigarettes and cheap aftershave. He was wearing his grey suit with his tie fastened slightly loosely as if it didn't want to be there.

'I think it's because of the computer system,' said Mr Sidhu casually, as if it was a small matter that could be easily rectified.

'Well, I doubt that, Dave. In fact, that's the last thing it would be,' said Alan, setting his briefcase down and getting some papers out and a notebook. Mr Sidhu's heart sank. He kept his nerve and stayed silent, trying not to appear anxious. If it wasn't the computer system, then what could it be?

'Right, let's see what we've got here then, shall we?' Alan started to look at his notes as Mr Sidhu opened the safe (it was normally locked but he'd timed its opening for Alan's visit) and started to empty the safe of its contents, which were in neat piles of stamps, plastic bags of different denominated notes, bags of coins and traveller's cheques.

Mr Sidhu was used to the post office officials coming into his post office in this fashion. They often audited sub-post offices, which meant they came in unannounced and closed the post office for a couple of hours while they checked stock and cash to make sure it tallied with the figures the head office thought it should have. They'd done it every year when he'd first bought the post office but, after five years of impeccable accounts, the audits came every other year. Mr Sidhu never minded because, once they'd finished, his figures always added up. There was always talk among sub-postmasters in the cash-and-carry about sub-postmasters who had been suspended due to taking money and not returning it, which was easy to do. In fact, taking cash out of the post office was very easy. You just wrote down in the accounts that it was there. But if you never put it back and then got audited, you would be suspended immediately and risk losing your post office licence and being prosecuted. Mr Sidhu had only ever heard of one postmaster being found out, and everyone knew he was an alcoholic and a gambler. But the way postmasters talked about it, it sounded like there were lots of them.

Mr Sidhu had made it easy for Alan, placing everything neatly with totals noted on them so Alan could easily discover any total that didn't tally. Mr Sidhu found he was not really needed as Alan got on with the job without making small talk. However, Mr Sidhu didn't want to leave him there alone. If there was anything wrong, it would land on his head, and he wanted to be there when the totals were finalized.

Mr Sidhu tried not to get in Alan's way as he counted up totals, noting them down in a practised manner, then moving quickly on to the next total. He looked over to Rose, as he saw her serving Min, taking a note and some coins out of her purse and giving her back the change. Min's hands were trembling slightly as she carefully placed the coins into her purse. He so wanted Rose to turn and smile at him as she did now and again, but she didn't.

'Where are the traveller's cheques?' asked Alan, breaking the silence. He looked at Mr Sidhu without any glimmer of familiarity. Mr Sidhu felt panicked that the traveller's cheques weren't where they should have been. He knew he'd got them out of the safe earlier, but he couldn't see them anywhere. Alan stood staring at Mr Sidhu, his face serious, Mr Sidhu's eyes darting around the post office as he tried to think where they were. Alan sighed and Mr Sidhu could smell his breath. Mr Sidhu lifted up his ledger where day-to-day stamps were stored, and there they were underneath it. The traveller's cheques were held together by a rubber band with a Post-it noting the totals. He presented them to Alan proudly with a smile of relief on his face. Alan took the bundle and shook his head, sighing again. Mr Sidhu kept silent as Alan got on with the balance. After two and a half hours it was done.

'Right so,' said Alan, looking down at the totals he'd jotted down on a piece of plain white A4 paper with various headings: 'stamps', 'coins', 'bank notes' and so on. He logged on to the computer terminal and entered the amounts.

He was doing the account balance for the week, which was something Mr Sidhu normally did himself. They both waited for the printer to give them the balance amount that the centralized computer system, Horizon, said the amount should be. Alan tore the paper off the printer and checked the totals against his own written down ones. He took Mr Sidhu's totals and checked them too. He laid them all back down and looked at Mr Sidhu with a serious expression.

'What does it say?' asked Mr Sidhu, trying to have a look at the printout.

'Over a thousand out. Don't know why it's saying that,' said Alan.

'You see,' said Mr Sidhu, trying not to be too enthusiastic.

'What have you done with it, Dave?'

'Hahn?'

'That's what they'll be asking you,' said Alan, picking up the landline telephone in the post office as if it was his to use without having to ask. Mr Sidhu didn't know what to say.

Alan spoke into the phone.

'Hello, Alan Dankworth, yes, here now. That's right. All correct but still out.'

Alan stayed on the call, listening and nodding, and then held the handset between his ear and shoulder as he started to press buttons on the post office terminal. Mr Sidhu saw that he was re-entering the numbers. Then, to Mr Sidhu's amazement, the terminal seemed to be working on its own as if a djinn was operating it. The arrow on the screen moved on its own and pressed icons on its own. Alan and Mr Sidhu looked on silently. Mr Sidhu could hear Alan's heavy breathing, and then suddenly the printer started to whir and out came a new printout. Alan tore it off and looked at it. His brow furrowed and he spoke into the phone.

'It's just doubled the loss. Yeah, I've got it right in front of me. Yeah, yeah. OK. No, he's been putting it into a holding account.' Alan looked at Mr Sidhu and shook his head at him. 'Of course, I'll inform him,' Alan wasn't looking at Mr Sidhu any more. 'And what about the loss that just appeared?' The voice at the other end was talking again. 'OK. Fine. OK. Sure. Right you are. Bye.'

And with that Alan hung up. Mr Sidhu waited for Alan to talk to him. Instead, Alan ignored him and started to pack away his papers, even taking the curly printouts.

'Alan,' Mr Sidhu said as calmly as he could. 'What did they say?'

Alan finished packing up his briefcase and looked at Mr Sidhu.

'Couple of things, Dave. The Post Office has stopped you being able to put losses into the holding account.'

Mr Sidhu's mind started to process a hundred thoughts at once, his eyes blinking repeatedly. He needed all his powers of concentration to keep up with what Alan was saying.

'That means you have to make good on any losses which occur in the week as per your sub-postmaster contract,' Alan paused to allow the information to be absorbed.

It meant the missing money would have to be put right by Mr Sidhu, no matter what. He would be responsible. It was a stipulation of the Post Office contract that there could never ever be losses in the weekly accounts. So if there was a thousand-pound deficit, the sub-postmaster was responsible. And if the money was not paid back, then they could suspend him, even take the post office back off him and take him to court to recoup the missing funds. However, sometimes losses could not be accounted for and the Post Office created holding accounts for the those sums to be placed in until the losses could be investigated and accounted for. But if there was no holding account, the loss needed to be 'made good', which meant Mr Sidhu would have to put in his own money unless the Post Office corrected the loss.

'But what about the balance? You saw it. Everything is right, we checked it,' pleaded Mr Sidhu. 'And when they did it with you, it doubled the loss. I am not responsible for that,' said Mr Sidhu, his voice rising now. He pressed the print button on the terminal, so it would print the last thing it had printed. He showed it to Alan. The initial loss of just over a thousand pounds had doubled exactly, to the penny. It could only be a computer error and they both knew it. Alan and Mr Sidhu looked at each other for a moment. Something had changed; Alan was not being the usual way with him. Something had been said to him.

'No more holding account, Dave. Make it good or else the Post Office will take action.'

'Why? They say that every week and nothing happens. Loss, then another loss and another and everything is fine. You know that, Alan. You know me. Come on,' Mr Sidhu could hear the desperation in his own voice. It was alarming. Mr Sidhu looked at the terminal and at Alan. He had a sudden urge to rip the thing out and throw it at Alan.

'Look, I've got to go, Dave. I need to go to Head Office.'

'What will you tell them?'

'The truth, Dave. What else?'

Mr Sidhu wanted to know what the truth was, because as far as he could tell, everything about the losses was a lie.

They didn't say anything to each other as they exited the small space of the post office. At the shop counter Mr Sidhu saw Rose, Jay, Meenu and Richard chatting away. His heart started to thump in his chest in a way that made it hard for him to swallow.

'Hi Dad,' said Meenu, striding over to him, dressed in her work clothes, a tight dark skirt and a jacket with a pastel blouse. Just as he was about to say hello, she turned to Alan.

'Hi Alan. How are you? What are you doing here?'

'Hello darling, lovely to see you. Just been helping your dad with the new system,' said Alan, his silent demeanour having disappeared – he was all charm and smiles now.

Mr Sidhu could hardly believe his ears. What help was that exactly?

'My dad has his own ways of doing things, don't you, dad?' Meenu said, laughing and glancing at Rose and Jay, then back to Mr Sidhu.

Sukhdev sat in the big cart along with his father, mother, brother and others from the village, including Darshan. It was being pulled by two big horned buffalo, who that morning had been scrubbed clean and adorned with flower garlands. There were two other carts travelling with them with people from his village on the way to the wedding. Children were excited, unused to being bathed and cleaned so early and made to wear stiff, clean clothes; the boys wore kurta pyjamas and the men the same. The women and girls wore their best salwar kameez. The men looked bored, more interested in talking to each other about how long it would take to get to their destination and who had travelled this road before, and who the bride's father was and how many acres of land he had. The women bristled with expectation at the day's events; they were unused to being around their husbands all day long like this and they all held on to their chunnis with their mouths so as to not uncover their heads now that they were outside their village, the place they knew so well.

Billoo was sitting on a white horse, his face covered by a sehra, made from flowers which hung from the front of his bright red turban. A small boy from the village also sat with him.

Sukhdev and Darshan had come back from Chandigarh, where they were studying at the University, to attend his brother's wedding. Increasingly, Sukhdev disliked coming back to his village, where his mother openly treated him as if he didn't really belong to the family and was someone she only tolerated. Both his brothers treated him in the same way, and it was only his father who was now elderly and less interested in the farm who showed interest in what he was doing. It was apparent to him that when his father passed away, he would be excluded from his own family. It made him resolve to escape the village and work in the city, and earn his own money and make his own life. So it irritated him that Darshan was poking fun at him.

'Oh Suki, now Billoo is married, your turn is coming soon. Who do you think your mother will choose for you? Do you know what to do on the wedding night, hahn? Do you know your way into the gates of heaven?' said Darshan, sniggering. Sukhdev disliked that Darshan said these things to him. Darshan was much better at talking to women and could openly flirt with them in a way that Sukhdev couldn't. His fellow villagers eyed him with disdain. This was because he wore trousers, shirt and a tie. No one else wore such things and he knew it made them think that he thought that he was better than them. It wasn't the impression he intended. His learning simply made him think about more than his village. About all the people who had written the books he'd read, whether on algebra or the necessary but boring English novels he had to read. It was required reading to learn English at his university. But that was the least interesting thing. He liked to think about the engineers who built ships and buildings,

who planned entire cities, like Chandigarh, which had been designed by the French architect Le Corbusier. He imagined them wearing trousers and shirts and ties, perhaps smoking cigarettes and deep in thought as they imagined a new world. A world that he was desperate to be part of, and so wearing those clothes made him feel that bit closer to it. Darshan had already been making plans to go to England, and Sukhdev was jealous, but he didn't want Darshan to know that.

'Suki, going to England is the only chance I will get to improve my lot,' Darshan would often say while they sipped tea and ate samosas in the college canteen. Darshan was one of nine children and his three older brothers would have much more claim on the land that was passed down to them when their very fit and active father eventually died. Both Darshan and Sukhdev knew they could get jobs teaching in India, but the system was corrupt, with rich students openly paying their lecturers to pass exams, and even to get into the civil service required money and influence, which they did not have.

'How can you go to England?' Sukhdev asked him one day. He wanted to know what he needed to do to get there. He knew more and more Indians were leaving, and it felt as if he might lose out if he didn't go soon.

'Suki, they need us! They have no men left. They had two world wars in the last fifty years. Everyone is dead. Why do you think they want us? They need workers to rebuild. They will give people like us, the educated ones, a voucher to go and become teachers and professionals. Over there it is not like here. Even an illiterate can earn good money'

The very idea that he might go to England was overwhelming to Sukhdev. That he might walk along Pall Mall, see Piccadilly

Circus, talk with intellectuals in the cafés in London. Become part of a big organization and solve the world's problems. And then perhaps one day come back to his farm with plans and ideas to make it into a modern, efficient farm that would enrich the village and make it into a kind of model village that people would come from all over India to look at. And he would be there to talk to everyone about it, but at the same time be called to the United States to talk at the newly formed United Nations and speak about his work.

'Are you listening to me, Suki?'

Sukhdev smiled his thin, silent smile and nodded.

'What kind of girl do you want? Because your mother will choose a girl with the face of a buffalo's backside for you.' Darshan laughed at his own joke, which was not entirely a joke but sort of true, in that whoever Sukhdev married was low on his mother's list of priorities.

When they arrived at the village where the Anand Karaj, the wedding ceremony, was to take place, the villagers were out in the lanes to look at the Baraat arrive. At the front of the Baraat, someone from Sukhdev's village led them all with a dhol drum strapped to him, which he beat on both ends with angled sticks; it announced the arrival of the groom and his family to the village.

The Haldi ceremony, which had taken place at Sukhdev's family house the previous day, was when the wedding had really begun. Billoo was cleansed by the village. He sat half-naked while the villagers and his family lathered him in a mixture of turmeric, oil and milk. Each person took a turn to place their hands on him with the oily yellow mixture, which in a previous era perhaps had the purpose of cleansing but now was an opportunity for everyone to have fun at the groom's expense by plastering his whole body in the mixture. Everyone enjoyed it, especially as it was Billoo, who was generally thought to take himself a little too seriously. Once he'd been smeared and not one part of his body was not covered in the oily mixture, the women of the village started the Jago. They held staffs in their hands which they pounded into the earth while lighted diyas were balanced on their heads and all the while everyone sang. The men drank and once Billoo had washed off all the oil and turmeric, he too joined in with the men and women of his village to have one last night with them. It was during this time that a drunken Billoo got hold of a trouser-wearing Sukhdev.

'Who do you think you are?' said Billoo, looking him up and down. 'You've always thought you're better than us. But I am the eldest and I will carry the name of this family, not you.'

Billoo dared Sukhdev to say something back to him, but Sukhdev had no wish to have an argument with Billoo on his wedding day and so stayed silent. This tactic didn't seem to help.

'You think you are a big gora angrez, hahn? Wearing all these stupid clothes.' Billoo took hold of Sukhdev's tie and started to tighten it round his neck, choking him. Sukhdev tried desperately to stop him, but his own soft hands were no match for Billoo's large, powerful farmer's hands.

'Why do you hate your own people so much, Suki?' continued Billoo. 'The land gives us everything. Your silly books give us nothing. You are a waste. Why our father thinks so much of you and pays for this silly education I do not know. But when he is gone, you will get nothing, I promise. And when I am married I will have five sons who will work this land and their sons after that! No one will remember you.'

Billoo let go, and Sukhdev rubbed his neck and got his breath back. He looked at Billoo, who sneered at him and then turned and left, laughing.

Sukhdev looked at Billoo walking away and then said in a low whisper, 'I will go to England and I will become something you can never imagine.'

When the Baraat arrived outside the bride's house, the Dhol player drummed even louder, then, after a few final flourishes of the Dhol, everyone fell silent and the bride's family opened the doors to their house with the characteristic mud walls and courtyard, and the Milni ceremony began. The bride's family welcomed the groom's family by exchanging garlands with them to show that there was no one in either family who was opposed to the match. Billoo waited at the rear – no one was allowed to see him or the bride until the religious wedding ceremony took place later.

Once inside, the villagers were fed and watered by the bride's family until the time came for the wedding ceremony. It was at this point that Billoo met his bride for the first time.

Gurcharan was chosen for Billoo, not because anyone thought they were a good match but simply because she was of age and so was he. The two families had been introduced to each other at the bride's house and had spoken, and it was felt that the bride's family was of good enough character. At the initial meeting, Gurcharan had come in to serve tea, which allowed Billoo's father Mantinder and his wife to have a look at the girl, to make sure she was physically fit and did not show any signs of illness, mental or physical, and that she was respectful to her elders. It was understood that if anything was found out to be wrong with her after the wedding, that would bring great shame on the bride's family, which they would pay for in some way to correct. Because what was also understood was that it was the groom's family who would be bringing someone into their house, not the other way round.

Sukhdev sat next to Darshan in the morning sun on the men's side while the wedding ceremony took place. The men sat on the right and women on the left, a path between them leading to the front where the groom sat cross-legged in front of the Guru Granth Sahib from which a granthi would read. Billoo sat there initially until the bride's family led the adorned bride to sit next to him. This was the pinnacle of any Punjabi woman's life in terms of her outfit. It was always a bright-red lehenga, the same colour as the groom's turban. She wore as much gold as the family had for her, which was passed down from her mother and her father's mother too. Her chunni covered her head (as everyone was required to do in the presence of the Guru Granth Sahib) and if Billoo was lucky, he might have a first glance at her when she sat down next to him with the help of her sisters, but it was also not good form to actively take a look. The bride's father then placed one end of a scarf in Billoo's hands and the other in his daughter's. The ceremony involved Billoo leading his new bride four times around the holy book, each circle representing a different aspect of married and spiritual life. The ceremony could be long or it could be short, and it was during this time that Sukhdev pressed Darshan about how he would get to England, feeling more determined than ever.

129

'You will get a voucher from the government, no problem, Suki. The big obstacle is getting to England.'

'Why is it hard to get to England?'

'The plane fare is three hundred pounds,' said Darshan and paused, allowing the amount to register with Sukhdev. 'My cousin brother is already in England for two years and he is helping me buying my ticket.'

Sukhdev fell silent. The wedding ceremony carried on, but he wasn't paying any attention to it. Three hundred pounds was an astronomical amount. How would he get that much money? That was more than three years' salary for a teacher, and he didn't even have a job yet. He began to feel that he might have overstepped the mark in deciding to go to England, which was not certain at all now.

After the ceremony had finished, all the guests blessed the bride and groom by giving them gifts of money, placing notes in their laps. Sukhdev eyed the money as everyone placed it, thinking that perhaps if he got married he might be able to raise the money with the gifts he might receive. The thought subsided when he realised his mother would be arranging his marriage, as Darshan had rightly told him earlier.

Sukhdev sat in the cart on the way back to the village, still deep in thought. The bride had made an emotional farewell to her family as she'd left her family house for the last time and made her way to her new home in Sukhdev's village and in the house she would share with her mother-in law, father-in-law, brothers-in-law and husband. On her wrists she wore elaborately decorated red bangles, which she would wear for at least six months, a sign that she would not be required to do any kind of physical work for that time. However, Sukhdev did not know about the significance of the bangles; he had no sisters and no knowledge about these things.

Back at the village everyone welcomed the new bride and groom by lighting up the house and making merry. The bride's family were invited too, and this was the final celebration of the uniting of the two families.

'You know what the bangles are for, Suki?' grinned Darshan.

Sukhdev shook his head. To him they simply looked like one of the many elaborate adornments a Punjabi bride wore on her wedding day.

'You have to break them,' said Darshan in a low voice.

'What?'

'Before you enter the gates of heaven you have to make sure she knows you are her master and break the bangles,' he looked at Sukhdev seriously.

Sukhdev stared at the bangles on the bride's thin wrists, thinking how much force might be required to do such a thing.

'Won't she be hurt?' he asked seriously.

And with that Darshan laughed hysterically and started to tell everyone about what Sukhdev thought he had to do with the bangles on his wedding night. Everyone laughed at him. Darshan's humiliation of him was complete, once again.

Sukhdev removed himself from all the mocking laughter, and it was then that a woman the same age as his mother approached him. She had features which looked familiar to him, and with her were five serious-looking children. They looked uncomfortable, if not a little fearful.

'Sat Sri Akal, Suki,' she said, and then went to him and did the Punjabi sideways hug men did with women.

'You don't know me, but I am your sister, Bitu,' she said.

'Sorry I couldn't come to the ceremony, but I wanted to say hello.' She then introduced her children, three teenage girls with tightly plaited hair and a boy who was about ten. Sukhdev was lost for words. He had no idea he had a sister – he vaguely knew that his father had been married before, but not that he'd had a daughter.

'Sat Sri Akal,' said Sukhdev. Bitu told him the names of her children which he instantly forgot.

'My eldest daughter is married, she is twenty-four.'

Sukhdev realised he was younger than her eldest. It was strange to think of having a sister, and one that was almost the age of his mother.

'I used to live in this house with your father, it was just the two of us. But one day the elders told him he needed to marry again to have sons. My life changed that day because I had to leave this house and marry. I was sad but I did my duty and now I have my own family.' She gathered her children around her as if to emphasize where her loyalty lay now.

'Does my father ever talk about me? Or my mother?' Bitu looked at him, her eyes hopeful, and now he placed the feature that was so familiar about her – it was her eyes; she had the same childlike, innocent gaze as their father.

'No,' he said truthfully. 'I'm sorry, I didn't even know I had a sister,' he added.

'Oh, it's no matter,' Bitu replied, not allowing any disappointment to bubble up, 'that is the way. I am no longer part of your family any more.' She half smiled but her eyes expressed the sadness she felt at being forgotten in a place where she had been loved and would never be loved again in the same way. Sukhdev wondered if he ever had a daughter whether he would *do that to her: give her up to another family. It didn't seem to bother his father, but then his father didn't have that worry any more, only having sons in his new marriage. And perhaps it was a condition of getting married again – putting the past behind and looking forwards.*

'I am going to England,' *he said suddenly.*

'Oh, how exciting!' *said Bitu, smiling, reflecting his enthusiasm back to him.*

'I am going to do big things there. I am at university studying mathematics.'

'Is England a good place to go?'

'Yes, it is a fair country, anyone can succeed if you work hard.'

'Maybe I will send my son there,' *she said, rubbing her hand over her young son's back.*

'Yes, you should. You can send him to me. I will look after him, paanji,' *said Sukhdev. Hearing the word sister (paanji) caused Bitu to become emotional.*

'Thank you, Suki, you are kind. Just like our father.'

Sukhdev didn't know why he'd wanted to tell Bitu about his plans to go to England; perhaps he just wanted to say it out loud to someone to make it real. Maybe he wanted to say it to someone who would be impressed, rather than dismissive, and share the same optimism that he felt. Whatever had made him say it, it had worked. It felt more real.

Later he saw Bitu touching his father's feet, and him holding her for a long time. He also saw his mother looking on with a scowl. Later still he was introduced to her husband, a drunken man with a pot belly and a red face who was making a fool of himself. Bitu was trying to get him to leave but he wouldn't. So with Darshan's help Sukhdev bundled him onto a cart with Bitu and the serious-looking children.

'You Sidhus think you're so big, but you didn't give me enough to take her. Four girls, four girls! You need to give more,' the husband slurred.

It was a common refrain from the uneducated families who would try to get more money from a bride's family, especially when she'd given birth to girls, which meant paying for their weddings because that was the price you paid for the groom's family to take care of her for the rest of her life.

Sukhdev watched the cart disappear into the darkness and he resolved to get that money and get out of this place.

Chapter 9

Rose clutched her handbag close to her chest as Mr Sidhu indicated to turn onto the Great West Road to Hounslow. Mr Sidhu wished he'd kept Sarabjit's old car. They'd bought it after her remission. It was a green colour which matched how they'd thought about the new chance they'd been given, in the same way politicians talked of the green shoots of recovery. And more importantly the car was a Mercedes. Not one of the bigger Mercedes – a smaller one, which she found easier to navigate. But it being a Mercedes was important to Sarabjit. It was a sign that they'd made it, and it had always been her wish to have one. And so she'd had her wish. But then the news came that everything wasn't OK.

The car had stood on the driveway, and both Raju and Meenu had told him they didn't want it, so he'd got rid of it. He continued to drive his useful Ford Escort van, which he'd got cheap from the Post Office when it changed its fleet. Since then, he'd never worried about getting another car – until now. And it wasn't just because he wanted to impress Rose; it was because Jay was in Meenu's car. She was giving him a lift to Mr Sidhu's house because he hadn't thought through how Jay would get to his house. There were only two seats in the van and

Mr Sidhu had naively thought Jay would be prepared to go in the back with his dog. But then Meenu, quite enthusiastically, had offered to give him a lift.

When Meenu had said to Alan, *my dad has his own way of doing things*, she'd had a glint in her eye. He knew she was up to something. It was the same look she'd given him and Sarabjit when she was a child. It meant she wanted something and would not stop until she got it. The idea made him shift in his seat.

He stopped at a red light at Gillette Corner. To his right was the big clock tower with a clock on all four sides that could be seen for miles around. Further behind it was Sky Television's studios and offices, a big, ordinary-looking building with differently sized satellite dishes scattered on its roof. The road ahead led straight to Heathrow Airport, where he'd arrived all those years ago.

'Penny for your thoughts?' asked Rose, taking his hand and holding it between both of hers. The lights turned to green and Mr Sidhu, not really wanting to share his thoughts, took his hand back to change gear and released the clutch, allowing the van to lurch forwards.

'Alan seemed to be happy about how things went,' Rose commented.

Mr Sidhu looked out of his driver side window, not wanting to show Rose the scowl on his face.

'But when I asked him, he said he couldn't discuss Post Office business,' she continued. 'Did you get to the bottom of it?'

'No.'

'Oh, that's not good, is it?' She looked at Mr Sidhu, who looked straight ahead, tightening his grip on the steering wheel.

'Well, he checked all the stock, didn't he? Did he check the computer system?'

'No, he said it wasn't the computer. They said the computer cannot be wrong. And no one else is having this problem.'

Rose looked puzzled, 'What are they going to do about it?'

'They said the loss is my responsibility.'

Rose turned to Mr Sidhu. 'Are they having a laugh? They can't say that. I mean there's nothing missing.'

'The computer says money is missing,' countered Mr Sidhu.

They both fell silent. Mr Sidhu turned off Henlys roundabout, where the Great West Road merged with Bath Road near Hounslow West, onto his road – a fairly good road by the standards of the area, he thought.

With everything that was happening, Mr Sidhu hadn't prepared himself for welcoming Rose and Jay into his house, especially now that Meenu was coming too. In his mind, Jay was simply coming to help sort out the overgrown trees at the back of the garden. And Rose was coming because? Mr Sidhu could not invent an innocent answer to his own question. She was coming because he wanted her to come to his house so he could make her tea and take her to a restaurant. But instead of simply inviting her, he'd made up this silly excuse for Jay to come and look at his trees so he could see him work. As if that really mattered. Why all this nonsense? He, and especially Sarabjit, had encouraged their children to be open about their relationships, and yet here he was hiding from his own children. What a fool.

He pulled the handbrake up with unnecessary force and turned the ignition off so all they could hear were small ticking noises coming from the engine as it cooled down. Meenu's boldly coloured red car was already there and she was standing with Jay outside the house. They were smiling together, as if sharing a joke. That was good. They were getting on.

'Nice house, Sukhdev,' said Jay, smoking a roll-up cigarette and squinting in the spring evening sunshine. His dog, Tubby, sat by his side, his tail wagging, looking at Mr Sidhu eagerly. He pretended not to mind Jay calling him Sukhdev, or that he was smoking so openly outside his house where his neighbours might see him. He nodded and went to open the front door. He'd cleaned the house that morning, knowing Rose would be coming. Meenu entered, taking off her shoes in a practised fashion, and Rose and Jay followed suit.

'No, no, you can keep your shoes on,' said Mr Sidhu. Meenu had already put on the slippers that she kept at the house for when she came to visit. Rose and Jay put their shoes back on. 'We're only going into the back garden,' Mr Sidhu added. Meenu looked at him and smiled.

'I'll put the tea on,' she said and walked to the kitchen. Mr Sidhu wanted to tell her not to; he'd already gone over it many times in his mind – how *he* would show Rose how to make 'proper' tea, as he thought of it.

'Rose, you can help me make the tea,' said Meenu briskly, filling up the kettle and acting as if she lived there.

'I will show Jay the trees,' said Mr Sidhu in a low voice seeping with disappointment only Rose could hear. Rose looked at Mr Sidhu as if she might say something but then turned away and followed Meenu.

'Come, Jay,' motioned Mr Sidhu.

Mr Sidhu and Jay left the kitchen via the back door. It led straight out into the garden, which was a big rectangular lawn with three large conifers at the back which protected the garden from the public path that ran behind the gardens to all the houses on that side of the road.

He thought about how different the garden used to be when he moved into the house. He'd bought it from an old English couple in 1985. It had been a beautiful, crazy-paved garden, carefully planned with rose bushes and a sunken garden that had a birdbath at its centre. There was a big pond with lilies, newts, frogs, salamanders and goldfish and a small potted fir tree. All this he'd made into a grass lawn. It wasn't what he'd wanted, but at the time Raju was young and energetic and would regularly destroy the rose bushes with his football and throw stones at the fish until they all died. Mr Sidhu told Raju off many times, scolding him about the destruction he caused, but Sarabjit would always side with their son, as would Meenu, blaming the garden for being unsuitable. So, harangued by his son and backed up by the family, he dug up all the crazy paving and buried the sunken garden himself. There was never even a hint of a suggestion that he would hire anyone to do it for them. It had taken him two months of weekends to complete it. All that was left now was the rectangular green lawn.

Sometimes, Mr Sidhu thought about how much effort must have gone into making that garden. He would have liked to tend that garden now. So, recently he'd started gardening again. Rather than just mowing the lawn he'd started to ask his cus-tomers about which flowers he could plant. He enjoyed turning the soil, tending to the plants and growing herbs in small pots to use in his cooking. It made him feel close to the earth as he had been when he lived in Punjab.

Together Mr Sidhu and Jay walked into the back garden.

Raju's old leather football lay on the lawn and Mr Sidhu held down the impulse to kick it. Tubby went to sniff it and then cocked one leg and urinated on it, looking at Mr Sidhu while he did so.

'You can cut them,' said Mr Sidhu, indicating the trees which were at least three metres high.

'You want me to cut them down?'

'No, just cut them a bit.'

'Trim them, you mean?' said Jay, looking seriously at Mr Sidhu.

'Yes.'

'I'll need a stepladder to have a proper look,' said Jay. 'It's a cypress. You can't trim the branches on the sides too much otherwise they'll die. I can take the top off it, though, and get a bit off the sides, maybe.'

Mr Sidhu nodded his acceptance of Jay's proposition and went to the garden shed to fetch a stepladder. Jay examined the trees.

'Yeah, the trees look healthy enough. I can do it.'

They walked back to the house together.

'She's nice, Meenu, your daughter.'

Mr Sidhu made a sound to indicate that he liked what Jay said.

'She told me your name was Sukhdev. You don't mind me calling you that, do you?' asked Jay.

'No,' said Mr Sidhu, but wondered whether he did mind or not. It was strange, because no one at the post office had ever called him Sukhdev, apart from Sarabjit.

'It's the name you've been given – you should use it more,' Jay said. 'She asks a lot of questions, mind. I didn't say anything about you and my mum, in case you're wondering.' Mr Sidhu nodded as the two men absorbed the moment. 'That's your business,' added Jay. As they both went to enter the house, Jay stopped Mr Sidhu with his hand. Mr Sidhu was surprised by the action. Jay stared at him for a few moments, not smiling or showing any kind of emotion. Mr Sidhu readied himself for what might happen next.

'You make my mum happy and I can tell you're a good sort, Sukhdev.' Jay held Mr Sidhu's stare for a moment longer and then added, 'You both deserve happiness,' and smiled before walking into the kitchen. Mr Sidhu stood for a moment, wondering if his own son had ever said such a nice thing to him.

'Everything all right?' Rose asked as Mr Sidhu and Jay came back into the kitchen.

'Fine, everything fine. Isn't it, Jay?' said Mr Sidhu quickly.

'Yeah, yeah, fine,' said Jay in his drawn-out Yorkshire accent.

Rose smiled at both Jay and Mr Sidhu as Meenu got out some cups and biscuits to lay out on the dining table along with the teapot which was filled with tea made in the English style with only hot water and tea bags as well as a small jug of cold milk.

'Here you go. Sit down,' said Meenu.

They all sat at the table.

'It's so brilliant that you're coming to help with the garden, Jay,' enthused Meenu, pouring tea for everyone and offering biscuits before sitting down herself, still with a smile on her face.

'That's all right, it's what I know,' said Jay, taking a cup and sipping from it. Meenu laughed as if Jay had said a joke and then took a sip from her own cup.

A silence in the kitchen grew as the tea was drunk (only a little bit by Mr Sidhu and Rose) and the biscuits eaten. The whole while Tubby sat looking at them, ready to pounce on any crumbs that might come his way.

'Dad, what do you want to eat tonight? I think there's some daal in the freezer I can heat up,' said Meenu as she placed her unfinished cup of tea on the table and got up to open the freezer. She took out a plastic yogurt container filled with frozen daal and was about to start to empty it into a saucepan.

'It's fine, beta, we have things to talk about. The shop and everything,' he tried to smile at Meenu. 'Don't worry about food. You go. Craig will be waiting for you,' he added, hoping he was sounding casual.

'Oh, right. Of course,' said Meenu, her eyes unable to meet any of theirs. She placed the plastic container back in the freezer and started to gather up her things, hurriedly putting her phone into her handbag, and was about to make her way to the front door to leave, but then she stopped. Meenu checked her pockets and then started to rummage around in her bag, peering into it to locate something. Mr Sidhu, Rose and Jay looked at her as she tutted and sighed.

'Oh, my keys, I can't find them,' she said, sounding irritated. 'No one one's picked them up by accident, have they?'

Everyone made a show of looking in their pockets apart from Jay, who stroked Tubby and was seemingly ignoring Meenu.

She stopped and looked at Jay. '*You* didn't take them, did you?' she asked, indicating that he should check his pockets.

'No,' said Jay simply, without moving.

'Are you sure?' asked Meenu, looking surprised.

'Yes. I can help you look for them though.'

Meenu guffawed.

'Sorry, how are you so sure you haven't picked them up? Why don't you want to look in your pockets?'

'I wouldn't pick up keys. I don't really use keys, so I wouldn't take any.'

Meenu looked at Jay and then the others. 'You don't *"use keys"*?'

'No.'

Meenu let out a few stifled laughs as if she wasn't sure whether Jay was joking or not.

'It's true, dear,' said Rose.

'What?' Meenu looked perplexed. 'Everyone's got keys – how can you not have keys?'

'It's not a big deal,' said Jay. 'I just don't do keys so I wouldn't have yours, that's all. I know what you mean about how people sometimes pick up keys without thinking, but I don't.'

Even Mr Sidhu was surprised at this revelation.

'Jay lives differently,' said Rose. 'He likes to sleep outdoors. So I leave my key under the gnome in my front garden. Don't tell anyone!'

Meenu turned to Mr Sidhu, whose mouth was half open. He could not understand what was going on.

'Did you check by the front door?' he asked, as that was where he would have put his keys.

Meenu said nothing and went to check. They heard the clink of keys.

Mr Sidhu, Rose and Jay all exhaled.

'There you go,' said Rose, smiling, as Meenu came back in. She picked up her handbag and checked for her phone again, her keys dangling from her pinkie finger, with various key rings and mini-loyalty cards among them.

'So where do you sleep, then?' asked Meenu.

'Here and there. Mostly there,' Jay replied with a smirk. 'Don't worry, I do shower and stuff, I'm not . . .' He hesitated and then added, 'Being inside, it's not me, that's all. I sleep better outside.'

'I've never known anyone like that before. I mean, apart from—'

'Tramps?' said Jay with a raised eyebrow.

'Well, yeah.'

'My father, your grandfather, always slept outside,' blurted out Mr Sidhu. 'He slept on the roof of our house in the village.'

'What, even in the monsoon season?'

'No, not when there was rain, but otherwise yes.'

Mr Sidhu and Meenu looked at each other for a moment. Mr Sidhu tried to smile to her but she didn't reciprocate.

'You learn a new thing every day, don't you?' said Meenu. 'Lovely to meet you, Jay. I look forward to seeing you again.'

'Thank you for giving Jay and Tubby a lift, dear,' said Rose. Meenu smiled in acknowledgement but said nothing to Rose.

'Have you got everything you need, Dad?'

'Yes, thank you, beta. Oh, Meenu . . .'

'Yes, Dad?'

'Maybe you could come one day next week to have a look at the computer system in the post office?'

'Yes, of course, Dad,' said Meenu, looking a little confused. 'Why, what's happened?'

'Oh nothing, something silly. Maybe you can check it for me?'

'I'll call you, Dad.' Meenu gave Mr Sidhu a sideways hug and then walked out the front door, closing it firmly behind her.

The three of them sat for a moment; they could hear Meenu's car being started and then being driven away. Mr Sidhu got up, taking the teapot and cups to the sink and emptying them. He turned to Rose and said, 'Would you like to see how to make proper tea?'

'I would like to know how to make tea the way *you* like it,' Rose replied.

Mr Sidhu's chest expanded.

'I might go and give the dog a run around in the garden,' said Jay, sliding a roll-up cigarette behind his ear.

Once Jay had shut the back door and Mr Sidhu and Rose were alone, Rose watched as he brought out the ingredients to make the tea. He took out a saucepan, filled it to about halfway up with tap water and placed it on the gas ring.

'The first thing to do is to boil the water,' he said. 'And while you wait for it to boil, you take these green cardamon seeds – we call them lachis – and crush them.' Mr Sidhu demonstrated by rolling the glass jar used for storing them over them as they sat on the kitchen counter. The cardamon broke open to reveal small, dark seeds inside. He dropped them into the water along with some fennel seeds, a couple of cloves and two PG Tips teabags.

'Now you wait for it to boil.'

'Smells lovely,' said Rose, her glasses misting over as she smelled the aroma from the saucepan. 'Oh look, David, I can't see anything,' she said, laughing, and held out her hands, trying to hold on to something. Mr Sidhu took her in his arms and raised up her glasses.

'Is that better?'

'Definitely,' Rose replied, looking into his eyes. As Mr Sidhu went to lean in to kiss Rose, she stopped him.

'Sorry, David.'

Mr Sidhu relaxed his hold on her.

'You know, I don't think your daughter is very happy about all this.'

Mr Sidhu swallowed, looking at Rose.

'Did she say something to you?'

'Not directly, but I could sense it. Sorry, I don't mean to cast aspersions.'

Mr Sidhu looked confused.

'I don't mean to say anything bad against your daughter. She has a right to feel the way she does.' Rose paused. 'Does it worry you?'

Mr Sidhu had never considered whether anything his children thought had any bearing on what he did. He raised them and they were (well, Meenu was) successful. What he did now didn't matter; their lives were set.

'No,' he said honestly.

'Well, you should talk to her. I get the feeling she doesn't want another woman in your life; I don't think it's against me personally.'

The tea boiled angrily, demanding attention. Mr Sidhu didn't respond to what Rose was saying. Instead he went to get some milk out of the fridge. He knew Meenu had become protective of him since Sarabjit had gone. He couldn't blame her for that. He poured the milk into the tea. It was the moment he liked the most. Everything calmed down. The dark tea settled and the colour changed to that of his own skin: brown and milky. A new stillness was attained.

He lowered the gas and turned to Rose. 'She misses her mother,' he said.

'Of course. I understand.'

'I think she knows how I feel about you,' he took her hand in his as they both looked at the tea, which was now bubbling slightly. The brown, milky mix began to rise with a froth which threatened to spill out of the saucepan, but before it did Mr Sidhu took the saucepan off the stove and the whole thing lowered down to the final state. Proper tea.

'Well, that was quite something, David. I'm not sure I'll be able to do that with the kettle in the post office,' Rose said, smirking.

They both smiled and kissed, and in that moment he forgot everything that was trying to get in the way of their happiness.

Chapter 10

'David, have you got anything planned for the long weekend?' asked Rose, leaning on the post office counter.

The early May bank holiday was coming up. Mr Sidhu had vaguely thought they might go to Kew Gardens or for a walk in Richmond Park, but his mind was still distracted by the balance issues and the idea of planning anything was low on his list of priorities. Recently, he'd not seen Rose as much as he'd wanted to. She'd asked him to come with her for a drink at the Arms and even suggested dinner at hers, but he'd made an excuse about work. He'd also been busy making plans to buy his new house. He wanted to finalize everything so he could move in by the end of the summer.

'No,' he said vaguely as he sat in the post office, updating his unofficial accounts book, where he kept a running total of the mysterious losses. Current total: over twenty thousand pounds. He calculated he had another five to ten weeks to sort out the black hole in his accounts. After that the Post Office would come to collect the cash he pretended was waiting to be picked up. The Post Office allowed sub-post offices to hold a certain amount of cash, but when this amount went over twenty-five thousand pounds, the Post Office would flag it up as a security risk and come to collect it. The cash normally came from business accounts such as pubs depositing money after big weekends. Mr Sidhu was pretending his post office held cash which it actually didn't. It was the only way he could balance the books without putting in his own money, which he thought he might have to do at some point so that he was not in breach of his sub-post office contract. He was hoping that the problem would fix itself, that one week the computer would show the surplus that should be there instead of the constant losses. Then the problem would disappear and he could get on with his life again, as before. However, his hope that that would happen waned every week as the deficits mounted up.

Rose lingered at the counter. 'Is everything OK?' she asked. For some reason unbeknown to him he felt a rage at this question. Of course everything wasn't OK, he wanted to yell at her. He didn't need this right now. It wasn't only the losses which were stressing him out. It was Meenu too. Ever since making tea at the house, Meenu continued to come to the house every Wednesday, as before, but now there was a steeliness in her manner. She fed him, cleaned up, sat with him and went home, which was the same as before, but now there was no small talk. Everything she did was perfunctory, and Raju, who'd never been the best at checking in with him, was even more remote.

The effect of all that had been to make Mr Sidhu ruminate. Thoughts swirled around his head and it was only work that brought a distraction to them. He didn't want to bother Rose with all his problems. They were his and he needed to deal with them like he'd always done. There was a time when he thought that if his children left him alone, he would be happier. But the reality was that even as adults their happiness was something that mattered to him. Ever since they knew about Rose, he felt his position as their father had diminished. For Mr Sidhu, there was a new tension between him and his children, and it spoke of their belief that somehow, he was betraying his family with his relationship with Rose. It was never articulated, never brought up in conversation, but it was there in their behaviour towards him, and for Mr Sidhu it felt as if he was being asked to make a choice. And the thing that disappointed him more than anything was that he and Sarabjit had never interfered with their children's choices. Who they chose was up to them and so now being treated in this way filled him with a quiet rage that he couldn't share with Sarabjit and didn't want to tell Rose about.

'I was thinking we should go away to the seaside, David. The weather's going to be nice on the bank holiday,' Rose added.

Mr Sidhu looked up and smiled. All the anger ebbed out of him.

'We could leave on Saturday afternoon when the post office closes and then come back Monday evening. Unless you've got something on?'

Rose looked at him, waiting for an answer. 'I would love that,' he replied. She remembered, he thought. He'd told her about how he'd loved going to the seaside in England and she remembered. When he'd been suffocated with his own problems, she remembered what he loved.

A couple of weeks earlier Meenu had come to the post office to look at the computer system as he'd asked her to. He regretted having asked her afterwards, but at the time he was eager for anything that might help him with the losses. After examining the terminal a little, Meenu told him she couldn't do anything about it.

'Every week it says there is money missing,' he pleaded.

'Does Alan know?'

'Yes,' replied Mr Sidhu.

'So, if the Post Office knows, then what's the problem?'

'They say I have to pay it back.'

'But you haven't taken it, Dad, have you?' asked Meenu, genuinely wanting to know if he had or not. Mr Sidhu kept his outrage in check.

'No, beta, but they say I am responsible.'

They both stood in silence looking at the terminal as if it might reveal its secrets, but it was only the whirring of the small cooling fan inside it that they could hear.

'And you've checked everything?' asked Meenu.

Mr Sidhu told her how he'd checked the stock multiple times, sometimes staying until midnight, but nothing turned up.

'I can't believe it,' she said, suddenly walking out of the post office cubicle. 'I know you haven't done anything,' she called out. Her back was to him but he could see her shaking her head to herself. The shop was closed so it was only the two of them there. She turned and looked at the post office counter with its bulletproof glass.

'How much is missing?' she asked urgently.

Mr Sidhu did not want to worry her and told her it was only a few thousand pounds.

'The same amount every week, it must be the computer,' he added, hoping that her work in IT would help her intuit that what he was saying had to be true.

'Or someone wants to make you think it's the computer,'

Meenu replied, her arms folded, her head to one side and with both her eyebrows raised, looking directly at Mr Sidhu.

He had never thought about it in that way.

'Has anyone else got access to the post office?' she asked.

'No, no one can get in here,' he said.

'I thought Rose had a spare set of keys, Dad?'

'Yes, Rose has spare keys at hers in case I lose mine,' he replied. Meenu stared at him for a few moments and then smiled. 'Of course, Dad. Of course.'

There was a knock at the door to the shop. Meenu and Mr Sidhu turned to see Bill standing outside in the darkness, bits of him visible through the glass door, which also held the 'open' and 'closed' sign and the opening times.

Mr Sidhu went to open the door and Bill came in, his eyes glassy and his face unshaven.

'I'm not too late, Davey?' he asked.

'No problem, Bill, come. Everything is downstairs,' said Mr Sidhu.

Bill came into the shop. 'Hello, Meenu.' Meenu said nothing to him but gave him a slight nod. 'I remember when you were a wee bairn only this high,' he said, indicating a height around chest level, 'and two little pigtails too.' Meenu ignored him and Bill waited a moment before nodding to Mr Sidhu and going down to the basement.

'What's he doing down there?' asked Meenu once Bill was out of earshot

'Taking out the boxes and rubbish and everything,' Mr Sidhu replied.

'Are you OK, Dad?'

Meenu's question penetrated his mind. It was as if she could access a frequency which bored into his brain. What did she mean? 'Yes, I am fine, beta,' he replied, as calmly as he could.

'Why are you getting Bill to take the rubbish out?' Her question was filled with strained surprise.

'He needs money and I need the rubbish to be taken out,' Mr Sidhu said simply, trying to keep everything calm.

'Money for whisky.' Meenu said it as a statement rather than as a question.

It was an open secret in the community that Bill was a drunk. However, he rarely caused any trouble, he was retired and his pension barely got him through the week, so Mr Sidhu obliged him. Mr Sidhu liked Bill because he had always come to the shop. He'd always spent his money there (apart from for alcohol) and it was only right that he help him a little.

'Is he hurting you or me, hahn?' asked Mr Sidhu, losing his cool a little. He disliked Meenu's black and white way of dealing with people. He knew that Bill was someone she looked down upon. He and Sarabjit hadn't done their job properly, he thought. Bill was a good man who would help anyone who needed it.

Bill came up the stairs, huffing, carrying up the pile of flattened boxes, bound together with string.

'Just one more to go,' he said as Meenu opened the shop door for him and he deposited the boxes outside the shop, ready to be collected by the bin men in the morning.

'Of course he's not hurting me, Dad,' said Meenu a little petulantly, once Bill had gone back down into the basement to take another load out. 'But . . .'

'What is it?' asked Mr Sidhu.

'Nothing, Dad. I'll talk to Alan. I'll explain everything,' said

Meenu in her businesslike manner, gathering up her things in the busy way she did – laptop bag, handbag, keys and phone.

'That's good, beta,' he replied, but he didn't know how she would be able to talk to Alan, since she didn't work for the Post Office. Then he remembered that Alan had given her his business card.

Meenu was in the doorway and just about to walk to her car, some early summer rain gently falling bringing in a little chill in the air, when she suddenly turned back around. She looked at Mr Sidhu with her mouth open as if she was about to say something. She stopped but then started to speak.

'Such a strange way to live, don't you think, Dad?' He was a little taken aback – what was she talking about? She softened her voice so he had to lean in to hear her, 'I mean Rose's son, Jay,' she said.

Mr Sidhu could tell that Meenu was up to something, but feigned ignorance, 'Hahn?' he said.

'Do you remember he made such a fuss about the keys?'

Mr Sidhu remembered it was actually Meenu who had made such a fuss, but didn't say that.

'Everyone is different,' he said, trying to sound casual and break the conspiratorial tone that Meenu had adopted. 'He's a good boy,' he added.

'Not really a boy, is he, Dad? He's in his forties. He's lived a lot of life. Can't have been easy for him with everything.' Mr Sidhu could sense Meenu trying to push an idea into his mind. He nodded silently, while thinking about what he knew about Jay's early life. She knew he'd been adopted but he didn't want to talk to her about that. Jay had told Mr Sidhu he'd travelled the world and even been to India and visited Amritsar (143001).

Mr Sidhu admired his adventurous spirit, especially since Jay had told him he'd never had any money but earned as he went, working in markets and bars and anywhere where he could, eventually returning to England set on finding his real parents. And that was how he'd found Rose. Mr Sidhu didn't know if Jay had told Meenu about all that but didn't want to say anything in case he hadn't.

'Dad, you're too nice,' said Meenu, in a jokey way so it wasn't clear whether she was being serious or not. 'You need to be careful,' she said, like a mother to a child. He didn't like being talked to this way. 'People might take advantage of you,' she added.

'I am always careful,' he replied. Was she trying to imply that Jay had stolen the money? Surely not.

Meenu looked at him in that scrutinizing way she did and then broke the silence by telling him she loved him and only wanted the best for him. Mr Sidhu was happy to hear such words from Meenu. He felt relieved that the tension which had been there was somehow lifting.

'I know Raju hasn't been in touch recently, but you know what he's like, Dad. I'll talk to him.'

Good, thought Mr Sidhu. It would give him a chance to talk to him about the property he wanted to buy. Mr Sidhu wanted to show Raju how to go about buying and selling a house. Raju might need to know these things if he ever stopped acting. Mr Sidhu had finally put his house on sale quietly, without a board outside, and got a mortgage agreed in principle to fund the new house and renovations. The property market was still on the up even as interest rates were rising. Richard was of the opinion that the economy was overheating and that there would be a crash, but Mr Sidhu, who had studied the property market for years, knew that a property in Richmond was a sure bet. In fact, anywhere nice in London was the same.

'And don't worry about the losses. I'll talk to Alan,' said Meenu. 'I'll explain that it's got nothing to do with us.'

At the time, Mr Sidhu was grateful that Meenu was so involved in helping him. He'd hugged her and she reciprocated, and it felt that a corner had been turned. Of course it was natural for her to be protective of her father, he thought, but she knew that he was happy and that was what mattered. Life goes on, he thought.

Bill finished taking out the rubbish and hung around, waiting for his payment.

'That's nice she comes and sees you, eh?'

Mr Sidhu nodded and took out his bundle of cash from his back pocket. He gave Bill a ten-pound note then returned the bundle to his pocket.

'Nice one, Davey,' said Bill and paused as his nose twitched, something he did when he was nervous. He wiped his nose with his hand and then spoke, 'I couldn't get twenty Embassy Tip, could I? Or ten if it's no bother. Put it on the book.'

Mr Sidhu fetched a packet of twenty Embassy filtered cigarettes and gave them to Bill.

'You're a good man, Davey,' said Bill as he left the shop nodding to Mr Sidhu (as he did every week).

Mr Sidhu waited to hear from Alan after Meenu told him she would talk to him. He tried to stop hoping that Meenu would talk to him and that it would make everything all right. And he couldn't help thinking about and fantasizing that Alan would come in to apologise for the mix-up. But he heard nothing, which only added to his anxiety about what would happen to him and his business. He tried not to think about it. But it was the only thing he could think about.

Raju, however, did call, which always made him happy even if Raju didn't have much to say.

'Meenu said you need Bill to take the rubbish out now for you. Are you OK, Dad?'

'I'm fine, beta.'

Mr Sidhu was saying this more and more these days to his children. 'I'm going to put an offer on the house I showed you. You know, to be closer to the post office.' He allowed the comment to hang in the air. He found it easier to say things like this to Raju. With Meenu, she made him feel more like he was being parented rather the other way round. And even though he didn't need anyone's permission to move to Richmond, he knew he was seeking Raju's.

'Meenu bought her place to be near you and Mum. You know that, don't you?'

'Mmmm . . .' he replied. Raju had said that to him before. Raju had told Meenu about him buying the house in Richmond already, but Meenu hadn't mentioned anything to him. Which he liked. He didn't think he'd be able to handle Meenu talking about where he should or shouldn't live. Meenu had bought her flat (in her own way, not heeding his advice about not buying a leasehold property) when Sarabjit was ill. But now he didn't need her to be near him. He wanted her to be married and be busy with her children and her own life, not be so interested in his life. He didn't say anything more about the property and then listened to Raju telling him about his new project in Avignon in France.

So when Rose asked him to go with her to Southwold (IP18), it turned out to be just the thing he wanted to do – to be away from all the losses, the haranguing of his children, and to have a weekend by the sea with Rose all to himself.

Chapter 11

The sun shone overhead as London disappeared behind them and the green of the countryside enveloped the road. His van sped along the A12 making a steady noise, which wasn't too loud but loud enough that neither he nor Rose needed to talk. Mr Sidhu was often surprised at the quietness of newer cars like Meenu's, in which you could barely hear the engine when it was going along at low speed. So whenever he got back to his van, the noise of it all felt reassuring to him.

Mr Sidhu liked the calm of driving on the open road. It was not something he did often, but the stretch on the A4 from Hounslow West to Brentford, before he turned towards Kew Bridge, took a good twenty minutes and he would often find himself pondering during that journey – about property matters or financial decisions, and even figuring out how to get Raju to stop acting. Often on the way home from the post office, he would talk to Sarabjit, but since Christmas she had not spoken with him. It did not feel wrong as he supposed it might. He thought she would be angry with him, but it was more that she seemed to have just slipped away. He had tried a few times to initiate a conversation with her, but recently, and without really wanting to, it was Rose he found himself talking to and reaching for when he lay in bed at night.

Driving away from London and the post office had the effect of making Mr Sidhu less anxious about everything that was going on. His worries ebbed away and he wondered, if he kept on driving, whether they would just disappear altogether. He doubted it. Meenu would find him somehow, he was sure. She would ask him in the concerned way she did about why he was away, why he hadn't come home. Since Sarabjit's death, the thing he was least able to deal with was Meenu. He felt Meenu was trying to fill his wife's shoes. But it bothered him that she was so focussed on his life rather than her own. Her life was still to be lived with a family and all that that would bring. Mr Sidhu decided he would go and see Craig when he got back to London. He needed to see what was taking so long; they had been engaged for over five years.

'Where does Jay live?' asked Mr Sidhu as casually as he could.

'In the world,' said Rose, opening her hands out like a magician.

Mr Sidhu glanced over and saw Rose smiling at him.

'That's what he says when you ask him,' she added.

Mr Sidhu smiled too, but actually did want to know the answer.

'He stays by the river when he comes to see me. He says he likes Richmond.'

Mr Sidhu had more questions about where exactly he lived – and how, and why – but he didn't want to spoil the atmosphere by saying something wrong.

'Isn't it cold?' he asked.

'I'm sure it is, but he doesn't mind the cold. He often swims in the river in the mornings.'

'Oh,' said Mr Sidhu, as if it was normal, and nodded his head slowly as if absorbing the information.

Rose had told him that she used to go to Southwold as a child with her family and that she would like him to see it too.

'If you like the seaside, you'll love it,' she'd told him.

Mr Sidhu wondered if Rose expected him to swim in the sea. He didn't know how to swim and didn't want her to be disappointed if she found out he couldn't. Then he thought that if they were to go swimming, he would need to get some swimming shorts. He'd only ever owned one pair of swimming shorts which he'd never used for swimming, only to go into the sea when he'd gone with his family to the beach, during a golden period in their lives. It was the time before he'd bought the post office, when the weekends really were theirs entirely, and the children were curious about the world, and playful, and not sullen.

Sarabjit was the one who planned days at the seaside. Sometimes a whole troupe of Punjabi families would go to the seaside on the south coast; pebbly Brighton and sandy Littlehampton were places they'd gone to and enjoyed. Sarabjit had bought him a pair of blue checked tie-up shorts for going into the sea and bought herself a yellow swimming costume too. None of the other families had bathing costumes – Mr Sidhu had to be cajoled by Sarabjit to put his on, and at the same time be OK with Sarabjit in her new attire too. There were no pursuits like this in the India he and Sarabjit came from. Even by the rivers in Punjab, men could go in without their tops on, but women would nearly always be completely clothed when they went into the water, and they continued that tradition here.

Salwar kameezes were rolled up and the women paddled into the sea, tormented by their children to jump into the waves, which they didn't want to do for fear of getting their clothes wet and then remaining so for the rest of the day. The men rolled up their trousers and wore short-sleeved shirts, whereas he strode out on the beach with his swimming trunks on. He had no idea why they called them swimming trunks, until the image of an elephant's trunk came into his mind and he felt himself blush. And it was at that point that Mr Sidhu saw that there were lots of women on the beach wearing swimming costumes and bikinis and he found that he was becoming aroused at the sight of them. A slow panic seeped into his body as he tried to look to Sarabjit for help. He was lucky. At that moment Sarabjit along with his children grabbed his hands and they all ran into the sea together.

The further they got from London, the fewer cars there were on the road and the more it felt to Mr Sidhu that it was just the two of them in the world. Now and again he wound his window down and felt the wind rushing against his beard. He didn't know anything about the East of England. He knew about Dover (CT16) and he had heard of the towns in East Anglia: Norwich (NR1), Bury St Edmunds (IP32, IP33), Great Yarmouth (NR30), Ipswich (IP1) and the like, but his knowledge of what these places were like was nil.

'Did you ever get to the bottom of that computer problem?' asked Rose casually.

Mr Sidhu felt his stomach turn. He shifted in his seat.

'No,' he said, not really wanting to talk about it on their weekend away.

'Oh, so what happens now?'

'They said it will sort itself out,' he replied, which is what the helpline had said, not that he held out much hope for that, but at the same time he hoped the answer would satisfy Rose enough so that they wouldn't have to talk about it any more.

'Oh, that's good,' she said, and Mr Sidhu felt pleased at how he'd dealt with it.

The land around was mostly farmland and as they penetrated deeper into East Anglia, everything was getting flatter and flatter.

'Just like Punjab,' Mr Sidhu muttered.

'Sorry, David?'

'The land, it's flat, like Punjab.' He looked across to Rose and placed his hand in hers. Mr Sidhu felt he ought to say something, to find an expression of some kind, as he felt more and more conscious of Rose's hand in his.

'It's nice to be out of London,' he said at last.

'Yes, it is, David. I'm glad you wanted to come away with me,' replied Rose and squeezed his hand. 'I've got you all to myself,' she said.

They held hands in silence until they approached a roundabout, which meant Mr Sidhu had to change gear and use his hand. The movement woke them from their happy quietude.

'It's been about twenty years since I've been to Southwold,' said Rose. A road sign indicated there were fifteen miles to go. Mr Sidhu nodded.

'What is there?' he asked, a little curious now as to what he should expect.

'It's a little seaside town. I'm sure you'll like it,' Rose added.

It was coming up to seven o'clock when they finally arrived in Southwold. The lovely summery May day was now turning grey and slightly windy. Mr Sidhu parked the car outside the hotel that Rose had directed him to. It was a Georgian building, a big house with flat rectangular windows at evenly spaced intervals. It had a small, triangular green in front it, the grass perfectly mowed, and Victorian lamp-posts positioned to illuminate the area. It would stay light for another couple of hours, but the town looked empty and it felt odd to Mr Sidhu, being used to the busyness of suburban London. Rose got out of the car and put a hand to her mouth as if trying to remember something, her eyes squinting and far away. Mr Sidhu unloaded the two small suitcases from the van and placed them on the driveway to the hotel. He looked around, thinking he might see the sea, the air thick with its aroma. He waited for Rose, not wanting to disturb her first moments in Southwold.

Mr Sidhu could spy a man wearing a blue waistcoat and tie standing behind the reception desk inside the hotel lobby which was visible through the front door of the hotel. He was peering at Mr Sidhu, expressionless.

'It's changed, David. That hotel used to be a house and the roads were wider,' said Rose, looking a little confused.

'It looks nice. Shall we go in?' said Mr Sidhu.

They walked into the hotel together and Mr Sidhu placed the two small suitcases by the front desk. The man in the blue waistcoat welcomed Rose and gave a small nod to Mr Sidhu, but without looking at him. Mr Sidhu had never been in a hotel in England before. It was something he had an idea of but not an experience of. In India, he would know what to do. He would not have had to bring his bags in; a boy would have done it and he would have been fussed over by the hotel manager. However, Mr Sidhu didn't want to spoil anything so he kept his mouth in a thin smile.

The waistcoat had no hair on his head or face, the opposite to Mr Sidhu, who had never cut his hair in his life. His face was lean and Mr Sidhu could not help thinking there was something wrong with him. And then it dawned on him that this man had no eyebrows either. Mr Sidhu didn't realise he was staring at him so openly until Rose nudged him, bringing him back to the present. Mr Sidhu smiled and felt for the reassuring touch of his beard.

'We've a room booked, we've come down from London,' said Rose, looking at the waistcoat. Mr Sidhu smiled to himself. Rose was using the same tone as she would in the post office, telling people they had come too late. Rose spoke to the man while Mr Sidhu looked around the hotel. It had a small reception desk with a couple of cushioned chairs and a coffee table with a small pile of magazines.

'So . . . that's a double for two nights,' he glanced up for a second to Rose to confirm the details and she nodded.

Mr Sidhu looked at himself in a mirror on the wall next to the reception desk. His turban was a little lopsided and his beard windswept from the open window of his van, and he was frowning. He smoothed his beard down and adjusted his turban. As he looked in the mirror, he spied the receptionist stealing glances at him.

'Good evening, sir, madam,' the waistcoat was speaking.

Mr Sidhu turned to see an older couple walking out the

front door. The waistcoat bowed his head slightly and smiled to them. The couple smiled and nodded their heads but changed their expressions when they saw Mr Sidhu. He looked at them and said his soft 'hello'. They smiled again and left without saying anything.

'Room seven, on the first floor, breakfast is served from six-thirty till nine, full English. Do you need a hand with the bags?'

Mr Sidhu looked at the man, happy that he was helping them, but still feeling a certain awkwardness which was deepened by his inability to make eye contact with him. He could not stop looking at his lack of eyebrows or any hair at all. The fact that there was no hair trying to push through his cheeks, chin or upper lip made him look like an adult-size child to Mr Sidhu. Although now, with a ceiling light shining at the right angle, Mr Sidhu could see a few blonde hairs rising from the top of his head. The man scratched the back of his head as Mr Sidhu continued to stare.

'David. The bags?' prompted Rose.

'Oh, yes,' said Mr Sidhu, picking them up and forgetting about the offer of help.

'I can take them if you want?' offered the man again.

'Yes, please,' interrupted Rose 'We'll be here all day other-wise.'

They followed the hairless man up the stairs to their room. The man wasn't old and was fit and strong enough to carry the two small suitcases up the stairs without stopping or breaking his stride. He opened the door and stood aside to let Mr Sidhu and Rose in.

Until that moment it had been the idea of having to show himself to Rose in swimming trunks (which he'd not brought with him) that had caused Mr Sidhu some anxiety. Now it was the double bed. Since their first kiss at Christmas, they had kissed often – when saying goodbye or when walking and looking at a beautiful view in Richmond Park. But they had not stayed at each other's houses and slept together. They never spoke about it because, for Mr Sidhu at least, everything was perfect. They saw each other every day at the post office, and on Sundays when they went for their walks, and that seemed to be enough. However, secretly, he did fantasize about his new house and the idea that he and Rose might live there together one day. He dared not mention the house to Rose yet; he wanted to surprise her with it and invite her over for dinner. Perhaps then, in this new house with his newfound happiness, they might lie down together. But he could see now that Rose had beaten him to it. Rose had booked them a room with a double bed.

The room itself was nice enough. It had a wooden-framed bed with two bedside tables and matching table lamps with shades made of the same green cloth as the curtains. There were paintings on the wall of the coast: one above the bed and several smaller ones dotted about the room. The furniture was made of good, well-polished wood. Mr Sidhu had no idea what type of wood it was or even what style of furniture it was. It looked good, though, he thought.

The man coughed. Mr Sidhu looked at Rose, who fished a five-pound note out of her purse and gave it to the man. Mr Sidhu did not like it that she had done that. It should have been him, but his mind was still absorbing the bed.

'Have a nice weekend, madam, sir,' said the man. He hesitated and added, 'If you don't mind me saying, you have a magnificent beard, sir.'

'Thank you,' Mr Sidhu started to say but as he gazed at the man, he couldn't help looking at his head and eyebrows again – and then it struck him. He remembered when he'd gone to see Sarabjit in hospital and he'd seen the patients with headscarves and some without, all hiding their hairless heads. Mr Sidhu was about to say something—

'I suffer from alopecia,' said the man. Mr Sidhu looked confused. 'It's when your hair falls out,' he added helpfully.

'Alopecia,' repeated Mr Sidhu, never having heard the word before.

'Oh yes, I knew someone who had it but it wasn't so . . .' Rose trailed off.

'Pronounced? Yes, it's pretty much everywhere. So I do appreciate someone like yourself, a Sikh, who doesn't cut their hair, is that right?'

Mr Sidhu nodded proudly and added, 'I have never cut my hair.'

The man didn't say anything but his eyes were softer now and he was able to look at Mr Sidhu. As Rose went into the bathroom, the two men absorbed each other and then after a few moments spontaneously shook each other's hands.

The waistcoat left and Mr Sidhu sat on the bed imagining what it would be like without any hair. He couldn't fathom what he'd look like. The drive had made his body a little stiff, so they said they would go out for a walk and then have some food. Mr Sidhu placed his hands on the bed, feeling the firmness of the mattress. He got up quickly, not wanting to linger on the bed and give off the wrong signals to Rose. He looked out the window as if he would find what he was really craving for out there: an Indian restaurant. He so wanted to feel the heat of chilli inside him.

Rose came out of the bathroom, wearing a long pink-coloured dress. She had more make-up on than he had seen her with before, but it did not look overdone or cheap. Mr Sidhu was speechless.

'So? What do you think?' Rose asked.

All thoughts about the bed were forgotten.

'Beautiful. You look like a princess.'

Chapter 12

They walked along the streets of Southwold, trying to find a restaurant in the evening dusk. A huge white lighthouse towered over the town, the first one Mr Sidhu had ever seen. Rose explained its purpose, which Mr Sidhu found mysterious having grown up in landlocked Punjab without any kind of nautical knowledge. They found the big main road which the hairless receptionist had told them was where they would find restaurants. It was the main high street for Southwold. There were lots of tourist shops, as well as the odd pub and restaurant. The first restaurant they passed was French and busy, but was unable to accommodate them unless they were prepared to wait half an hour. They weren't. The next restaurant was Italian. It was empty. For Mr Sidhu that was a bad sign. 'A busy restaurant is a good restaurant,' he told Rose. As they neared what they thought was the end of the restaurant area of Southwold, Mr Sidhu saw what he was looking for – an Indian restaurant – the Eastern Promise. There were people inside and there were tables free. Rose looked at Mr Sidhu who was already salivating.

'This isn't what I was thinking when I thought about coming to Southwold,' said Rose, frowning a little, 'but I suppose you do deserve something for driving,' she added and took his arm and led him to the entrance. Mr Sidhu beamed.

Inside the restaurant Mr Sidhu noted the usual kind of Indian restaurant décor: a picture on the wall made of plastic with an electric light inside it that created the effect of a moving waterfall, a model Taj Mahal, Rajasthani ladies painted onto a wall, wearing long plaits, colourful clothes and lots of jewellery including pierced noses. Inside, there was music Mr Sidhu didn't recognize. It had a heavy beat and loud Hindi lyrics. It was probably modern Bollywood music, which he didn't listen to. It disturbed Mr Sidhu's mood, but the need for spicy food usurped any obstacles.

'Hellosirmadam, tablefortwo?'

The waiter, wearing a cheap polyester black waistcoat, white shirt and black bow tie, rattled the words off quickly and did not wait for a reply as he indicated the way they should go with his arm. Mr Sidhu didn't like the way the waiter was acting so stood his ground, holding on to Rose's handbag so she would not follow him.

'What are you doing, David?' asked Rose, a little annoyed.

A look of surprise flashed through the waiter's eyes as he heard Rose calling him David. Mr Sidhu understood the look of the waiter. It was the idea that Mr Sidhu, a turbaned Sikh, might be called David. It would make no sense to him. The waiter addressed Rose with a thick Indian accent.

'You are from London?' he asked enthusiastically.

Rose blushed as she was addressed. She placed her free hand on her chest and smiled with embarrassment.

'Yes, we're down for the weekend. I used to come here as a child, you know, it's a beautiful town.'

174

'Oh yes, very beautiful,' the waiter shook his head side to side with one hand raised in the air as if it were impossible to express how beautiful the town was. Rose tugged her handbag free of Mr Sidhu's grip as the waiter led them to a free table and left them with the menus. Rose studied the descriptions of the various dishes carefully, now and again asking Mr Sidhu what something was. Mr Sidhu, however, had never used a menu in an Indian restaurant; he knew what he wanted.

'Hellooo!' Mr Sidhu bellowed. For Mr Sidhu this was the way of getting the attention of an Indian waiter. It came naturally to him and most other Indian men he knew. It worked every time. All the waiters instantly perked their heads up. They looked around until they saw Mr Sidhu with his hand in the air beckoning them in the Indian way; the palm of the hand facing down, pawing the air. The waiters looked at each other to see who would be the one. Nervously, a young, slender East Asian-looking waiter came to their table. Mr Sidhu was happy that his methods had worked; Rose, by contrast, was embarrassed by the attention Mr Sidhu was creating.

She muttered at Mr Sidhu, 'David, there's no need for that, you're drawing attention to us.'

'Don't worry, Rose. I know how to deal with them.' Mr Sidhu smiled as the waiter approached.

'Punjabi bolday ha?' asked Mr Sidhu. The waiter smiled at Mr Sidhu, who waited for a reply. Most northern Indians could speak a little Punjabi in Mr Sidhu's experience, and even though the waiter looked more East Asian than Indian, Mr Sidhu knew he wouldn't be Chinese or Taiwanese or even Japanese, not in an Indian restaurant anyway. The waiter turned to Rose, smiled and let out a little sigh. He looked towards the other waiters who were ignoring him, letting him know he was on his own.

'Ney,' he replied finally, shaking his head side to side.

'No problem,' said Mr Sidhu. 'Now, I want keema muttar and bhindi.' He turned to Rose, 'Rose? Rice or chapatis? Or both?'

'I don't know,' said Rose vaguely as she looked down the list of food, muttering names under her breath. Mr Sidhu sat back in his chair and looked at the waiter who looked nervously back at him.

'I come back?' the waiter asked.

'Nay!' Mr Sidhu wanted his food quickly. 'What sort of food do you want, Rose?'

'Don't rush me, David.'

Mr Sidhu continued to study the waiter.

'Where you from?' Mr Sidhu asked in a manner that sounded curt to western ears, but normal to eastern ones. The waiter looked embarrassed. Like a shy child, he smiled, unable to make proper eye contact. Mr Sidhu encouraged him, speaking more kindly now.

'Bolo . . .'

The waiter looked around for the other waiters and, noticing they were busy doing other things, he whispered, 'Nepal.'

Mr Sidhu knew that Nepal was a poorer country than India; therefore, by this logic, he wondered, because he would not put it past them, if the Nepalese waiter was paid less than the Indian ones. He was about to ask him this question, but Rose had chosen.

'I'll have the chicken korma, not too spicy, mind.' The waiter smiled and nodded as he carefully wrote down the order in his notebook.

'I want mine spicy, desi style, you know . . .' Mr Sidhu looked sternly at the waiter, who looked away. Mr Sidhu got hold of the waiter's wrist and looked at him seriously.

'Good spices, you know, proper desi style.' The waiter smiled again but looked nervous. Desi was the word for homegrown – from the village, or more precisely, authentic. It was the adjective given to anything that came from India.

'Oh, and bring me a Kingfisher.' Mr Sidhu chuckled to himself; he was enjoying himself in a way he could never do in purely English company. He would never get away with treating waiters like this in Southall, but then again he surmised he wouldn't have to treat them like this either. These ones were only used to dealing with English people, he thought.

'David,' said Rose, looking at him sternly.

'Oh yes, what do you want to drink, Rose?'

'I'll have a glass of white wine, please,' said Rose, smiling at the waiter.

After he left Rose scolded him, 'David, leave the poor waiter alone.'

'Rose, these are not your silver service this and that. No. These are idiots. They come from India. They do not know anything.' Mr Sidhu looked around until he saw the Nepalese waiter.

'He's from Nepal. You know why he is from Nepal? Do you think they have run out of relatives or people in India that they need to bring the Nepalese over now?' Mr Sidhu did not wait for Rose to answer, he was on a roll.

'No! He is cheaper. I bet you he is earning less money than

the other waiters. I bet you he doesn't even mind. He understands his position, you see.'

Rose wasn't listening to Mr Sidhu. She took his hand in hers across the table and looked into his eyes.

'David, are you feeling OK?'

Mr Sidhu was lost for words. Her touching him like this calmed him down.

Rose spoke again, 'I know it was a long drive, but there's no need to be so harsh to the waiters. Can we just enjoy our first night?'

Mr Sidhu smiled but the image of the double bed came into his mind now too, and so he nodded to her to show her that he was listening, even if inside he was floundering. He gulped down his beer and stopped himself from burping out loud.

Finally, the food arrived and Mr Sidhu was ready to eat. The Nepalese waiter nervously went through the well-practised ritual of moving the food from the food trolley onto the table. Firstly, he lit the candles inside the latticed metallic platform which would keep the food warm. Next, he placed the dishes onto the platform, then the rice and chapatis on the side. The table was busy with lots of food. Mr Sidhu could not wait to get started but ordered a glass of whisky before starting. As he ate his food, his mouth was disturbed; the taste of his keema muttar was nothing like anything he was used to. There was no real flavour, hardly any spice; it was a disappointment. He looked at Rose who seemed to be enjoying her food, unaware of his disturbance.

'Do you like it?' asked Mr Sidhu.

'Sorry, David?'

'The food. Do you like it?' he asked, annoyed that he was being made to explain what was very obvious to him.

'Yes, it's fine, David.'

Mr Sidhu looked around to find the waiter.

'Please, I've already asked you to stop causing a fuss,' said Rose, looking at the other customers.

'This is not Indian food!' said Mr Sidhu loudly, unable to contain himself any more. A few of the nearby tables looked over at them.

'David, it's fine. Mine's very tasty.'

Mr Sidhu ignored her as he looked at the waiters, who were chatting quietly but urgently among each other before one went off.

An older man wearing glasses and long sideburns arrived at their table.

'Hellosirmadam, everythingisOK? I am the proprietor of this restaurant.'

Mr Sidhu looked at him with disdain but at the same time tried to place the darker skinned, short, round-faced man with fuller and darker lips. His hair was thick too. He instinctively knew that he was Bangladeshi.

'What is this?' Mr Sidhu pointed at his keema muttar. 'This is meant to be an Indian restaurant, this is not Indian food.' A few of the customers nearby looked across at the exchange. Rose looked around, smiling anxiously at them. She turned to look straight at Mr Sidhu, in silence.

'No, no sir, this is not Indian restaurant, this is Bengali restaurant,' said the manager.

'Bengali?' replied Mr Sidhu, feeling happy that he'd guessed correctly.

'Yes, sir.'

'But these are not Bengali dishes, these are Punjabi dishes.'

'Yes,' the manager replied weakly, smiling at them, 'I know. This is our,' he hesitated, trying to find the right word, 'interpretation. Like fusion dishes,' he said finally.

Mr Sidhu looked at him for a moment while the manager smiled at Rose, who reciprocated, her eyes telling him that she was uncomfortable. There was a moment when Mr Sidhu might have said more, had he been in different company, but he held back.

'OK. OK,' said Mr Sidhu and waved the manager away, having decided that he didn't want to make any more trouble.

As they ate Mr Sidhu explained how the Bangladeshis had come to England and touted this brand of nonsense food to the English. It was Punjabi food, the rich sauces, the chicken, the lamb, paneer, saag aloo, all Punjabi. Rose listened quietly, not saying anything. Mr Sidhu, feeling more and more relaxed by the whisky, shouted his 'Hellooos' to the Nepalese waiter whenever he needed anything, which was more often than not a raw chilli to spice up his food. At last, they finished their meal and Mr Sidhu let out a loud burp. Several pink faces turned to look at this turbaned, hairy man stroking his stomach and picking his teeth with a stick.

'David!' said Rose suddenly.

'In India it is very normal to burp. All you English always quietly doing this, doing that, I am not ashamed to burp, it's my body, it's natural,' said Mr Sidhu. He was unaware of how loud he was being and also of the slight slurring of his words.

'If this is the way you're going to be all weekend, you can drop me off at the station,' said Rose, looking visibly annoyed.

Mr Sidhu sat up straight. He didn't think he'd done anything wrong, but the way Rose spoke to him made his heart sink.

It was the way Sarabjit used to speak to him when he'd done something wrong. It took him back to another time and it unsettled him. He excused himself and went to the toilet. He looked in the mirror and took some deep breaths. He was being an idiot, he told himself. It was a lovely thing to be away with Rose like this and he was ruining it. He would go back in and be nice and listen to her.

As Mr Sidhu walked back to his table the manager was waiting in the small bar area near the toilets.

'Please, sir, come, it is not every day we have a Sardarji come to our establishment. Can I offer you a complimentary whisky?' and before Mr Sidhu could answer, he added, 'Johnny Walker Black Label, of course,' and placed two glasses on the bar with a bowl of ice and a jug of water next to them, while pouring out two large measures. Mr Sidhu looked at Rose, who was still finishing her main course.

'Thank you, but—'

'No, please,' the owner interrupted, 'it's the least I can do. My name is Faisal,' he added offering his hand.

Mr Sidhu relented, shaking his hand and introducing himself. He sat on a barstool next to Faisal and with practised ease, took a couple of cubes of ice and placed them into the glass, and then poured some water in too.

'You live in London? Which part?' asked Faisal.

'Hounslow,' said Mr Sidhu, sipping his whisky.

'Oh, near the airport.'

Mr Sidhu told him about his post office and being near Kew Gardens.

'Kew Gardens,' Faisal exclaimed. 'Very beautiful place. I have been.'

Mr Sidhu felt a glow of pride. And suddenly he and Faisal started to speak to each other with ease and enthusiasm.

'I came after the independence war between us and Pakistan,' said Faisal. 'The country was only twenty years old and they were doing what had been always been happening in Bengal. Violence, war and famine. Very bad time. I heard many Bangladeshis going to UK and luckily I managed to get out with my brother. I went to East London, learned restaurant business in Brick Lane. You have heard of it?'

Mr Sidhu hadn't. If he went to a restaurant, it would be in Southall.

'Then me and my brother we decide to make our own restaurant. London was already too many restaurants so we went further east to Sussex, Essex, Suffolk, looking to see where there was a place without a curry house. We went to every small village and town. It is good business. The English eat it all the time. Now they say it is favourite food in Yu-Kay.' They both nodded in agreement. Mr Sidhu didn't say anything more about the quality of the food he'd received earlier.

'My wife was ambitious for me, you know,' said Mr Sidhu. 'I was happy working for Post Office, in sorting office,' he paused for effect. A sorting office meant he was literate and could read and write; it was important that Faisal understood this. 'Post Office is government business, is important work; every year they give children Christmas party, good pay.' Faisal nodded, sipping his whisky. 'Then my wife say everyone is getting own business. Why we don't do same thing? She is a good woman and I listened to her. We went to look same as you, Shepherd Bush, Feltham, Windsor and then we find the post office in Richmond and we liked it.'

'Yes, when you know you know, right?' said Faisal. 'When I see this place I think I can be happy here,' they laughed and for a moment, Mr Sidhu felt as if he was back in Hounslow. Faisal topped up his glass with whisky. A waiter brought in a plate of chilli chicken which was not on the menu. Mr Sidhu devoured the pieces of red chicken using his hands, the mix of chilli, grilled meat and whisky creating a sensory experience hard to beat.

'So you married an English woman?' asked Faisal.

Mr Sidhu blushed, but hoped anyone would think it was the chilli chicken, 'No, no, she is a friend,' and for some reason he couldn't tell him that his wife was dead. It might spoil the feeling of bonhomie that he was relishing. Faisal raised his eyebrows and smiled, nodding his head as if they were sharing a secret. Mr Sidhu nodded too but knew he needed to go. Rose wouldn't be happy waiting for him while he drank whisky.

He paid for the meal in cash and did not leave a tip. Faisal and Mr Sidhu shook hands and then hugged each other, slapping each other on the back. And to his surprise Rose was nowhere to be seen. He asked the waiters, who told him she'd already left. The whisky dulled any urgency about the matter as Mr Sidhu's mouth glowed with heat and he simply meandered back to the hotel, smiling and nodding to people on the way.

Chapter 13

Rose stood over him. The curtains were open and so was the window. The cool air was soothing as Mr Sidhu slowly opened his eyes. His mouth was dry and he saw that he was still wearing his clothes from the night before. Rose seemed too far away from him as if she was floating above the bed. She was silent. As he used his arm to push himself into a sitting position, he realised that he was on the floor. He pushed the blanket that was covering him to the side and sat up, finding that he was a little stiff. He blinked a few times, remembering that he was in Southwold, and then felt a wave of nausea mixed with shame come over him. Rose remained silent but was still looking at him. Mr Sidhu could feel sweat seeping out of his underarms and forehead. He raised himself to his feet, feeling unsteady, but didn't want Rose to know that so he walked purposefully to the window and leaned over to pop his head outside even though the bright sun hurt his eyes.

The window looked out over the small green outside the hotel. He could see his trusty van still parked there and further away he could see the sea and some seagulls hovering overhead. He breathed in through his nose and out through his mouth a few times to try to feel a little more normal. He could smell the sea air, but it only made him feel more nauseous. He could quite easily have rested his head on the windowsill and stayed there, with the cool breeze soothing him. But he knew that was out of the question.

In the room Rose was sitting on the bed. She was dressed in a pair of jeans and a yellow top and was lacing up her boots.

'Got nothing to say for yourself?'

Mr Sidhu tried to think of something appropriate to say but at that moment felt an immediate urge to urinate.

'Excuse me,' he said hurriedly and went to use the bathroom. His body relaxed as he emptied his bladder, making him sigh over the noise of the torrent hitting the water in the toilet bowl. The noise hurt his head and at the same time made him conscious that Rose might be listening too. He immediately changed the angle, but overcompensated and urinated all over the floor. He regained his composure and found a position that hit the side of the bowl, making no noise.

After cleaning the floor with toilet tissue, he looked at himself in the mirror and was surprised to see that he felt worse than he looked. It was true that his eyes were a little bloodshot and his hair a little unruly, but other than that he looked fine. He was only wearing his under turban, the patka. He untied it, unplaited his hair and scratched his scalp, which was soothing but also hurt slightly. He poked his head out of the bathroom, aware suddenly that this was the first time he had his hair open like this in front of Rose.

'I'm going to have a shower,' he said.

Rose looked at him, her eyes betraying her surprise at seeing him like that, 'OK, I'm going to go down for some breakfast. Shall I see you there?'

The question felt loaded, so Mr Sidhu chose his words carefully. 'Yes, of course, Rose. I won't be long.'

He waited for a reply but Rose simply got her things and left the room.

In the shower Mr Sidhu remembered drinking whisky with Faisal, and then Rose not being there in the restaurant. He lowered his head. What a fool. How could he make it up to her? Maybe she might go out and leave him alone in the hotel. The idea disturbed him. He didn't know this place and he would be lost without her. He quickly washed himself and got ready. He hurried downstairs, the movement making him feel nauseous. It was all right, Rose was there sitting at a table waiting for him. He sat down, trying to be casual. Rose looked up from her book and said nothing.

They sat in silence as they waited for their breakfast to arrive. Mr Sidhu's eyes hurt. The paracetamol he'd taken had yet to take effect. He so wanted to just lean back in his chair and drift off to sleep. Rose started to speak casually without any anger or reproach.

'The way I feel right now, David, is that I shouldn't have bothered with this weekend. I don't care to be treated like that, to be honest. I'm fine to stay here on my own. If that's what you'd rather,' she said.

Mr Sidhu was surprised at Rose's casual manner as she talked about her being fine to stay at the hotel on her own, so he was glad when a young woman arrived with their breakfasts: two full Englishes with a pot of coffee for Rose and a pot of (weak) breakfast tea for Mr Sidhu.

'He's an interesting man. The restaurant owner, he is from Bengal,' said Mr Sidhu, trying to change the subject. He smiled as he knew he'd been right all along about the food not being authentic.

'I don't care where he's from, David,' Rose exhaled with impatience.

She had every right to be angry, he thought. She asked him to come away with her and he'd abandoned her. Suddenly a wave of nausea hit him; his mouth felt dry and he gulped for air.

'Are you OK?' asked Rose, half frowning, half showing concern.

Mr Sidhu nodded but said nothing. The food wasn't making him feel better. He burped silently, letting out the stale air as subtly as he could.

'Oh David!' Rose glared at him and a few other couples turned to look up from their breakfasts. He concentrated hard on stopping more gas rising up from his belly. 'I can smell the whisky,' she added, waving a hand in front of her face. They ate in silence. Mr Sidhu relaxed a little as his stomach returned to normal.

'I thought you wanted to come here with me, David, but I get the feeling that I'm not as interesting as whisky or a random restaurant owner whose food you didn't even like,' Rose said sadly.

He wanted to tell her that he'd had a nice plate of chilli chicken that wasn't on the menu but decided it wouldn't be appropriate.

'I do,' he said with a quiet, childlike voice. 'I do want to be here with you.'

'So why did you just abandon me like that, then?'

'I didn't think. I wasn't thinking,' he said. But it wasn't true. He'd just wanted to step out of his life for a moment. He wanted to forget everything that was waiting for him. He paused; he wanted to say something more about how he felt but knew he might say the wrong thing.

'No, you weren't thinking,' Rose replied. It felt as if they were far away from each other. 'Just ignoring me like that on our first evening out.'

She was right, he'd ignored her. She had let him go to an Indian restaurant and he'd behaved as if she wasn't there. It was bad mannered and disrespectful. And now Mr Sidhu was genuinely interested in talking about why he had done that.

'You are right, Rose. I think I wanted to forget.'

'What?' Rose asked. Mr Sidhu could feel her indignant veneer falling away.

'There is so much going on,' he said, his head bowed at his plate, unable to look at Rose. 'I don't understand. I don't want to think about it,' he said, and he felt good for saying how he felt.

'That's what this weekend is meant to be for, David. To get away from it all.'

Mr Sidhu didn't really understand what getting away from it all meant. But he nodded in agreement and dared to look up at Rose.

'Everything will still be there when we get back, but now it's just you and me, David. You work hard and I know there's lots going on, but I want you to myself and I thought that's what you wanted too, but now I'm not so sure.'

And finally Mr Sidhu understood what a fool he'd been. He was in danger of ruining the one thing that had given him happiness during this time of turbulence in his life. Was it gone? Had he succeeded in making Rose think he was a complete idiot? Would she just go, as she was threatening to do?

'I want that too, Rose, I want you to myself,' he said, feeling unsure about the words he was using. But Rose smiled and then took hold of his hand under the table and Mr Sidhu felt himself relaxing and smiled back. After a few moments Rose spoke again and all the distance between them had evaporated.

'We'll go for a walk after breakfast. I want to show you the beach, and one more thing, David . . .'

'Yes, Rose?'

'You're not wearing those silly shoes. I want to get you some proper walking boots.'

Mr Sidhu looked down at his white trainers. He'd bought them in Hounslow, the most comfortable shoes he'd ever worn. He'd always worn smart leather shoes to work, but in the late Eighties he started to notice fellow postmasters and shop owners wearing trainers on his visits to the cash-and-carry. At first he thought that it was unprofessional, or that they changed their shoes, but then he surmised that he spent most of the day behind one counter or another and so no one looked at what shoes he was wearing. And he loved it. Going to the cash-and-carry with his smart black leather shoes was painful, but with trainers he felt as if he was bouncing around the place. So one could say he was a little attached to those big white trainers – the bigger the better – more cushioning, he thought.

'Your feet will get wet in those and they look silly,' Rose added.

Mr Sidhu held his tongue and stopped himself explaining what those trainers meant to him. 'Of course,' he said.

It was a sunny day, but not warm enough to be without a jacket. As they left the hotel the receptionist handed Rose a key and winked at her. For a moment, Mr Sidhu felt a sudden panic; was Rose going to sleep in another room? He looked for signs from her but she gave nothing away and continued to walk at pace, which Mr Sidhu did his best to keep up with despite how he felt. Rose wore a fluffy jacket that could be zipped up all the way up her neck. Mr Sidhu was not used to wearing much apart from his work suit jacket and pullover for days like these, and wore his only other jacket – the down-filled hooded parka he wore for his morning exercises when it was cold. It could stand temperatures of up to minus ten, he'd read on the label. It was a big beige coat and Raju would tell him that he looked like a giant chicken when he wore it with his comfortable, straight-cut Farah trousers.

'You'll need to get a new jacket too,' said Rose. Mr Sidhu nodded again, wondering how much money these new boots and jacket would cost him.

Soon they were walking past small huts built one next to the other all along the beach front. They were all different. Some were pretty, painted in bright colours or made to look like a boat; others were open with people sitting inside or just outside them, drinking tea or eating a sandwich.

'What are they?' asked Mr Sidhu.

'Beach huts,' Rose had a hint of a smile on her face as she told him. It was the first indication to Mr Sidhu that things might go well today. But then Rose stopped. She looked at Mr Sidhu.

'Do you like them?'

Mr Sidhu wasn't sure what the answer should be. One that would get another smile was what he wanted.

'Yes, they're nice,' he said.

'We used to rent one when I was little. Every summer we'd

come here, and my mother and father would sit with sandwiches while Fred and I played in the sand. Fred's my brother.'

Mr Sidhu nodded gently. 'Where is Fred now?'

'He died. In a motorcycle accident. He was eighteen,' said Rose. There was the hint of a smile again, thought Mr Sidhu, but then he saw that it wasn't a smile at all; it was Rose stopping herself from crying. She turned and walked on. Mr Sidhu walked behind her, unable to match her pace.

Rose stopped and looked for something in her pocket, and then took out the key he'd seen the receptionist give to her earlier. She unlocked a padlock on one of the beach huts. The hut was made out of the same kind of wood that garden fences were made from. And that's what they reminded Mr Sidhu of, garden sheds.

'I haven't been in one since I was about sixteen,' she said matter-of-factly.

Mr Sidhu watched her carefully. The beach hut was small. It only had two chairs inside and a fold-up table. There were shelves with little trinkets, shells, model boats and even some ornate miniature fishing boats.

'What is it for?' asked Mr Sidhu.

'Well, you relax here, get changed, keep things here so you don't have to carry everything with you. And just look at the sea.'

'It's lovely,' half lied Mr Sidhu. It was nice but he could not see the point of it. They were only a ten-minute walk from the hotel and there was no electricity or way to make a cup of tea or cook parathas, which is what he was yearning for.

'I'm glad you like it. I wanted to give you an authentic Southwold experience. Now, leave your coat here, it's not that cold.'

Mr Sidhu took off his coat, feeling a little naked without

it. Rose was right, it was unnecessary, but its bulk had made him feel secure. He left it hanging on a hook but had to check each pocket twice as he didn't want to leave anything valuable in it. As they left, he patted his back pocket for his bundle of cash that he took with him everywhere. Sunglasses would be a good idea too, he thought, perhaps those ones that fitted over normal glasses. The day was clear and the sun was merciless on his eyes.

They walked back along the main street where the Eastern Promise was, but neither of them mentioned the restaurant or veered towards that end of the street. Instead, Rose navigated them to a clothes outfitter, which had an array of walking boots and jackets displayed in the window. They went in without having said much on their walk, which suited Mr Sidhu's mood.

'We'd like to see some boots for him,' said Rose, indicating Mr Sidhu.

'You've come to the right place. Please take a seat,' said the lady. Mr Sidhu didn't need asking twice and let himself fall into the seat. Rose smiled at him and walked off to look at some jackets.

He settled upon a pair of boots that Rose liked. They were brown, a mix of leather and strong canvas, with curved suede pieces around the toes and heel. The sole of the boot was raised and Mr Sidhu felt taller. He was also given the same kind of jacket that Rose had on. It was called a fleece, he learned. Warm and practical, it would be good to wear it in the big, cold warehouses in the cash-and-carry and in the mornings for his exercise.

'How much?' asked Mr Sidhu, readying himself for some haggling.

'It's been taken care of already,' said the woman serving them. She exchanged a look with Rose, who looked smug.

'No, please, Rose, you can't pay for this.'

'David, you are in no position to argue with me today.' She exchanged another look with the woman, who was younger than both of them, around forty, thought Mr Sidhu. He felt himself blush a little as if they both knew what had happened the previous night.

'Lucky you,' said the woman with a small nod of the head. 'You gonna keep them on?'

Mr Sidhu looked at Rose and nodded. The woman took his trainers and placed them into a bag.

Outside, Rose took Mr Sidhu's arm and they walked back to the path on the beach. They didn't head to the hut but walked along the path above it. They passed a pier which jutted out into the sea and went further on, where the beach huts ceased and there was just a beach and a car park. Rose kept walking and Mr Sidhu followed beside her. The air was chilly now, clouds having come in and blocked out the sun. Rose headed down a concrete staircase and they were on the beach with only a few other people dotted here and there, mainly dog walkers. Mr Sidhu felt as if she was taking him somewhere. The town centre and the pier were far away. There was only the sound of the wind and the gentle breaking of the waves on the shore. Rose stopped and looked out to sea. Mr Sidhu stood behind her, not sure what he should be doing. He felt much better now than earlier. The walk, the fresh air and breakfast had cleared his head.

Rose stood with her hands in her pockets, her hair blowing

a little in the wind as if an invisible hand was pushing it up. He slowly walked towards her and tentatively placed his hand on her shoulder and then in one movement she turned towards him and buried herself in his chest, sandwiching his hand between hers and laying her head on it.

It's the wind, he thought, that's what's making her eyes water. But he could not forget that she'd been crying earlier in the day when he'd thought she was smiling. He remained solid, not moving, hoping that it was comforting.

'I'm a silly old woman,' she said.

'No, you're not,' said Mr Sidhu without hesitation.

Rose remained where she was. Mr Sidhu looked out to sea, liking Rose's proximity to him. She could stay like that, he thought, he didn't mind that at all. But then he felt her juddering slowly, the rhythmic movement of her chest as she sobbed again. He held her. What else could he do?

'Shhh . . .' he said softly. 'It's OK.'

Rose lifted her head. She looked a little crazed, her eyes desperate for something. Mr Sidhu tried to remain calm as she looked at him, and then looked around her, as if she didn't know where she was. Mr Sidhu could feel a wave of uncertainty wash over him. He felt anxious. What would people think if they saw a man like him with a woman as upset as Rose was right now?

'What kind of woman am I?' she said suddenly. 'First Fred, then Jay,' she added and then stopped. 'What are you doing with me?'

Mr Sidhu was finding it hard to keep up with her.

'I thought I knew everything. I don't know anything,' she added.

At last they were on common ground, he thought.

Rose had lost her brother Fred when she was sixteen and he was eighteen. She loved him, and when he died her grief had nowhere to go, she explained to Mr Sidhu.

The conversation was stilted with silences and sudden flows of memory and the emotions attached to them. They were walking with no destination in mind, holding paper cups of tea, which were scalding when they'd bought them from a little kiosk, but were now too tepid to enjoy.

'He loved his motorbike and his music. I thought he was just amazing. Everyone loved him. And I didn't think I needed anything else. But it turns out that I did. After he died there was no music, no dancing, nothing at home. Dad had been in the war and Fred just dying like that affected him so much. He'd always been Dad's favourite, but seeing him unable to smile or even look me in the eye made me feel unwanted, like I was nothing. I couldn't stand it. So as soon I could, I left for London. I was eighteen. And London was amazing,' Rose looked out to sea, not looking sad any more but remembering something.

'What year did you come to London?' Mr Sidhu asked.

'Nineteen sixty-six, the year England won the World Cup. Bobby Moore was captain. It was a lovely moment. Everyone was so happy. There were street parties just like the coronation.' Again a pause as Rose remembered that moment. 'And what about you, David? When did you get to London?'

'October tenth, 1969,' he replied. He would never forget that date. His life changed in ways unimaginable to him. He'd never set foot outside Punjab before coming to London.

'I was twenty-three,' he continued. 'I told everyone I was going to London to see Piccadilly Circus and Trafalgar Square.

We all knew these places by name, but no one had ever been, and I had no idea what it would be like.'

Now it was Mr Sidhu's turn to look out to sea. Moments he hadn't thought about for so long entered his mind: not knowing how to use the escalators at Heathrow Airport, not being understood, being made fun of because of the way he talked and the way he dressed, being terrified of going on the tube, being amazed at seeing Big Ben and the Houses of Parliament, the nights when the air was so thick with smog it was impossible to see past your hand.

Work was all that mattered. Where you could find work and how much you could save made the world small. The routine of working and sleeping became everything. What the rest of England was like or what the English did, didn't matter.

'I was a maths teacher in India,' he said, smiling at a memory of being in a college in Chandigarh, with his shirt and tie even then.

'Were you?'

'Yes, I loved algebra.'

'Did you teach when you came here?'

'No, they said I needed to do a teaching course for three years. And I needed money, so I worked instead at a coffee factory in Southall, cleaning these huge metal vats. I will never forget that smell of coffee.'

'And did Sarabjit come with you?'

'No, only men came first. I lived in a house with twelve men, two to a room. My parents tried to marry me many times before I accepted. I wanted my own house for my wife and family. It took me a few years to get a deposit. Then I told my father I was ready.'

He explained to Rose about how Sarabjit had been selected for him and that she came from a good family. He'd been twenty-six then and she was twenty. Mr Sidhu remembered his first glance of Sarabjit on his wedding day. It was during the Anand Karaj, the wedding ceremony. She was dressed in a sea of red and gold, the colours of a Punjabi bride. She wore a red sari embroidered with gold thread, with a matching scarf that hung forwards over her head so that even he could not see her face while he was sitting next to her. Her hands were covered in mehndi and adorned with the solid yellow-gold jewellery loved by Indians. They sat next to each other while the granthi read from the Guru Granth Sahib, the Sikh holy book. Later, Sarabjit's father took a scarf which he tied to his daughter's hand, after which Mr Sidhu then led her around the holy book four times. Sarabjit's brothers and maternal uncles lined up to give their blessings to the marriage as well as looking Mr Sidhu in the eye and reassuring Sarabjit. As they sat back down, cross-legged on the floor, Sarabjit's sisters gathered behind her to make sure her sari fell gently to the floor surrounding the bride like a huge petalled flower. And there was a moment when Sarabjit moved her gold-covered hand to adjust her scarf and the movement had caught Mr Sidhu's attention for what seemed like a long time but could only really have been a second or two; their eyes had met and they held each other's gaze, smiling.

Rose told him about coming to London from Suffolk, working at Selfridges in London and having a wage and living independently, meeting Min and living together then meeting Reggie, Jay's father, and getting pregnant.

'We were just kids, really, when I think back. We were both

far away from our families, thinking we knew it all. I mean, we hadn't the experience – and he was sure he didn't want the baby – whereas I thought I did, but didn't know. I was so scared to tell my family. Being pregnant out of wedlock was the worst thing a girl could do. It was so confusing, and then it was too late; I had to have him. I'm so glad I did, but I didn't know anything. Min told me she'd spoken with some people, and they put me in this hostel with other girls and I had Jay there, and they took him away after he was born. I knew it was going to happen and I think I was in shock, because I would never have done that. Not a day went by when I didn't think about him. Not one day.'

Mr Sidhu held her and allowed her to cry. He would stand there and hold her for however long it took. Rose wiped away her tears.

'The funny thing is that since he's come back into my life, I don't think about him any more because I know he's all right. We're friends more than . . .' She trailed off. 'But that's OK because somehow, through some kind of magic, he's healed me. He did. He told me everything he went through and in the end he came to me. He's so lovely.'

Rose got a tissue out of her pocket and blew her nose. 'I'm sorry.'

'It's OK, Rose,' said Mr Sidhu. 'He's a good boy.'

'He is, isn't he?'

They both sat on the dry sand beneath them and stared out to sea.

'You see, I *am* a silly old woman, aren't I?'

'No,' said Mr Sidhu gently.

They sat silently. Mr Sidhu wondered why none of her story

199

bothered him. Had he seen too much of life and so now took everything in his stride? Is that what happened as you got older? He didn't think so. People did things all the time that annoyed him. Even recently as he was coming to the post office, and as usual not understanding the timetable of rugby matches played in Twickenham, found himself stuck in traffic. He was late and hooted at a taxi that had stopped to take a fare and was taking too much time. The men and two small boys who boarded the taxi turned to him and one of the men told him to 'Fuck off'. That had irritated Mr Sidhu for the rest of the day.

Rose got up and dusted herself down; Mr Sidhu was staring at her as she dusted her bottom.

'Want me to do yours?' she asked, looking at him.

'No, no, it's fine,' said Mr Sidhu, standing up quickly and brushing the sand off himself.

'Come here, silly,' said Rose, lightly brushing his bottom. 'That's better,' she added and then looped her arm through his. He felt his body expand.

I wonder why she's with me, he thought. And, as if the thought had a physicality of its own, he became increasingly aware of Rose's arm in his. So much so that he wanted to untangle himself from her. But what if I just asked her? Now he would have to; the question just kept repeating in his mind.

'Why do you like me?' he blurted out.

Rose kept walking and didn't say anything at first.

'You care,' she said finally. Nothing was said for a while and then she elaborated.

'You make everyone who comes into the post office feel like you're there for them. It's why everyone comes. You listen when they ask about this or that. You help people like Min, who would be lost without you. You let people have credit when you don't have to. I wonder why *you* like *me*.'

Because I can't stop thinking about you and every time you touch me my heart starts to sing, he wanted to say. But he didn't.

'You make me happy,' he said.

'Why?' she asked.

'You care too, Rose. You care like I care.'

Chapter 14

It was Monday bank holiday morning and tomorrow Mr Sidhu would be opening his post office. However, thoughts about the post office and the losses were not what Mr Sidhu was thinking about as he drove back to London. The receptionist had advised him to go back to London via Thetford on the A11 as there were roadworks on the A12 going down to Ipswich. Mr Sidhu had thanked him and resisted the urge he'd had to feel the man's hairless head with both his hands. Instead, they'd exchanged one last look at each other before they left.

As he drove with Rose by his side, neither of them said anything. They looked at each other every now and again, not smiling, not anything, just checking the other was still there.

After their walk along the beach the previous day, they had gone back to the beach hut and Rose said she'd like to just stay there a while. She had a small rucksack with her and she took out a book and started to read it, sitting on a chair inside the hut.

Mr Sidhu sat a while, looking at Rose as she read, and then looked out at the sea and beach where children were playing and parents and grandparents all sat together on blankets and fold-up chairs. Mr Sidhu was not used to just sitting still like this – unless he was at home in his armchair watching the news or looking at the property listings. He got up and muttered to Rose that he was going for a walk. She nodded but kept on reading.

Had it happened? Had Rose spoken to him in the way she did? Of course she had, but the way she was fully absorbed by her book had the effect of making it seem as if nothing had happened. That they hadn't just opened their hearts to each other. Mr Sidhu let her be rather than interrupt her. He walked onto the beach and up to the water's edge. A little boy ran to the sea to fill up his bucket with sea water and then ran back to his sandcastle where he poured the water into the moat. He continued to do this at a pace right next to where Mr Sidhu was standing in his new waterproof boots, the soles leaving intricate footprints in the wet sand.

'The water keeps going down so I have to fill it up,' said the boy.

Mr Sidhu realised the boy was talking to him, so he searched for something to say.

'That's good, keep doing it,' he said.

The boy, who Mr Sidhu thought was about six or seven, had freckles and ginger hair. He looked up at Mr Sidhu, holding up a hand to shade his eyes from the sun, nodded and carried on.

Mr Sidhu smiled and walked away. He thought about Jay and how he was so calm and resourceful. It was something Mr Sidhu recognized. Something Raju would never understand. It was how his own father had been. A man who said little but when he did say something you knew to listen. Even though it was his brothers who worked on the farm turning the soil and sowing the seeds and harvesting the crops, his father would now and again motion wordlessly to Sukhdev to come with him to the farm. He was older than many of the fathers and Sukhdev knew that he'd been married once before, but he never dared asked him about it. At the farm there was a clearing in the middle of the fields with a barn in which tools were kept, as well as a couple of charpoys that the workers used to rest in the afternoon heat. Sukhdev's father showed him how to unblock the irrigation canals using a kind of inverted shovel that scooped up all the silt from the bottom of the canals to allow the water to flow around the fields, water that came from the Beas River, one of the sacred five rivers of Punjab that began their journeys from the mighty Himalayas. His father showed him the workers who worked alongside his brothers. If there was one that was talking or making jokes, his father would look at Sukhdev and gesture at the worker as if to say 'don't turn out like him'. In his mind, Mr Sidhu couldn't remember his father ever talking a lot. It was as if language didn't do justice to what he wanted to communicate. And perhaps it was *that* that reminded him of Jay and *that* which annoyed him about Raju.

The beach was quieter now, and as he looked out to sea he could make out a big ship sitting in the water, so far out that it looked peaceful. But he knew that if you went near it there would be noise and smoke and danger. The sense of space he felt here reminded Mr Sidhu of when he used to stand on the roof of his father's house as a boy and look at the miles of green fields all around. He would pretend to be a maharajah viewing his kingdom. But that feeling had disappeared when he came to London with its endless roads and houses one against the other. But here now on the beach, and from the top of Richmond

Hill, that feeling of space had returned, and it felt soothing, healing almost. Mr Sidhu glanced at the big ship again out in the North Sea, looking so fixed and sure. He knew that at some point it would be gone. Perhaps if he came tomorrow it would be gone, just like he and Rose would be gone tomorrow. And what about the losses – would they be gone or would they stay? He had that sinking feeling again after such a lovely day with Rose. He turned and walked back to be with her.

Rose was still reading. She put her book down as he approached.

'All good?' she asked.

'Yes,' he replied, 'I like it here.' He was glad that Rose was paying attention to him again. She started to gather her things.

'Did you like the beach hut?' she asked.

'Yes, it's nice,' said Mr Sidhu.

'It's OK if you don't,' said Rose. 'I wanted to sit in one again, like my parents used to. Silly, isn't it?'

Rose pushed the chairs under the small table and then closed the door with them still inside, which felt odd. There was hardly any light in the hut and Mr Sidhu thought for a moment that Rose was going to make them sleep there, or that she had something terrible to tell him that she'd been holding back.

'I want to make a new memory,' she said and then turned to look at him, her eyes bright. Mr Sidhu hoped he wasn't frowning and moved his mouth into a smile position, but wasn't sure it was right. Rose didn't seem to notice. She took his hands and then lifted up her face to his and kissed him.

'There's no point living in the past,' she said. 'Now when I see a beach hut I'll think of this,' she added and Mr Sidhu felt his loins stir.

By the time they got to the hotel it was early evening and they were both hungry.

'I don't feel like going anywhere,' said Rose. 'What do you say to some fish and chips, David? We can get a takeaway and watch a film in our room or something?'

The double bed loomed in Mr Sidhu's mind again, as well as his behaviour the previous night, so he agreed, not really understanding what they were deciding.

As they stood in the fish and chip shop waiting for their fish to fry, Mr Sidhu remembered getting fish and chips for Sarabjit when she'd first arrived in England. It was the first time she'd ever eaten fish (or meat) and he'd not appreciated how anxious she'd been about pleasing him.

'What are these signs on the fish?' she'd asked, and Mr Sidhu had laughed at her, which she'd not been happy about. The newspaper which wrapped the fish and chips in those days would leave print marks on the food. They'd often laughed about it later in life, once the children had left home and they had space to think again.

'What's funny?' asked Rose.

Mr Sidhu told her and they both laughed. It was such a new thing for him to do, to remember Sarabjit like this and not feel sad, it was almost overwhelming. His eyes filled with tears and, as if Rose knew what he was feeling, she took his arm and leaned into him.

'Oh, I see you're a silly old man too,' she said.

Mr Sidhu focussed on Rose's face. Neither of them was wearing their glasses and the world was a little blurry for both of them. Mr Sidhu started to kiss her face and arms and hands. Rose giggled a little but soon stopped and quietened, allowing Mr Sidhu to explore her body without interruption. Mr Sidhu was conscious of his erection, but instead of feeling the need to be inside her straight away before it subsided, he carried on kissing Rose. When she was ready, Rose sat up and let Mr Sidhu know that it was his turn to lie down and for her to explore him. He wondered if his hairiness bothered her, as nearly his whole body was covered in hair, but she didn't say anything. Perhaps that is what she expects, he thought, just like he expected her to be almost hairless, which she was.

After they had made love they laughed and giggled and tickled each other, their bodies no longer their own, but part of each other. Mr Sidhu told Rose about how he used to lie down at night and think about Sarabjit, but that these days he thought about her. Rose looked a little uncertain, but Mr Sidhu reassured her.

'This is all new to me, Rose. I am used to being on my own and with my thoughts. I said the wrong thing. I—'

'It's OK, David,' Rose put her finger to his lips. 'Tell me about her. What she was like?'

And now it was Mr Sidhu who felt uncertain and suddenly very aware of his nakedness.

'It was like she always knew me,' he said after a pause.

'That must have been nice.'

'It was.'

He wanted to add that Sarabjit would always be with him even though he was so happy to be with *her* right now. But he didn't. Instead he reached over and kissed her.

Chapter 15

Mr Sidhu saw a sign that told him they were entering Elveden Forest. Tall pine trees grew on either side of the road, almost blocking out the afternoon sun. A column of red brake lights stretched ahead of Mr Sidhu's van. He slowed down and came to a stop. The cars ahead started to move again, slowly, stopping every now and then.

'There must be a tractor or something,' Mr Sidhu muttered. They were both now looking ahead, trying to see what was slowing the traffic. A lorry turned on its headlights behind him, flooding Mr Sidhu's van with light so that he was unable to see anything in his rear-view mirror. As Mr Sidhu played around with the rear-view mirror, to find an angle that didn't blind him, he didn't notice the traffic clearing in front of him. So he was surprised when the lorry behind him let forth its powerful horn at close range.

Rose and Mr Sidhu both jumped slightly in their seats. Mr Sidhu pressed down on the accelerator and his van lurched forward as it always did in first gear. As he pressed the clutch and pushed the gearstick into second, he looked up and saw a man standing in the road. Mr Sidhu slammed both feet down onto the brake and clutch pedals, while gripping the steering wheel and leaning back, bracing himself for an emergency stop. The suitcases in the back came crashing against the backs of their seats as the van stopped and then stalled. The man was untouched but glared fiercely at Mr Sidhu. Mr Sidhu glared back at the man, who was also wearing a turban. Then the thought came to him: *I know that man.*

'Darshan?' Mr Sidhu whispered and then undid his seatbelt and got out of his van.

'David? What are you doing?' asked Rose. Mr Sidhu ignored Rose and walked up to Darshan. Darshan's fierce expression melted away as soon as he saw Mr Sidhu.

'*Suki?*' exclaimed Darshan.

'Are you OK?' asked Mr Sidhu, suddenly forgetting where they were and worried that he might have injured him.

'Belcol teak ha, koshni hoiya,' Darshan replied, indicating that he had not been touched by his van.

The lorry behind them beeped its horn again, as did, it seemed, all the other cars and vehicles trying to get further down the A11 towards London. Darshan indicated a small car park where Mr Sidhu could pull in, just off the main road, overcrowded with cars and minibuses, with lots of Sikhs milling around talking, eating pakoras and samosas and drinking tea in white polystyrene cups.

Mr Sidhu got back in the van as Darshan shouted at a group of young Sikh men. One moved to stand fearlessly in the middle of the road, holding a hand up to the lorry, stopping it from moving.

'David? What's going on?' said Rose, her eyes darting around, hugging her handbag close to her chest.

He looked at Rose, wanting to reassure her in some way, but

with the presence of the other Sikhs he switched into automatic pilot and simply got on with the task in hand. Another Sikh man motioned for Mr Sidhu to drive into the car park, yet another found him a place and, before he knew it, a hand had slapped his van, letting him know that he was parked. Mr Sidhu's door was opened by Darshan, his expression changing when he saw Rose. His eyes darted between Mr Sidhu and Rose before he could say anything.

'Hello,' he said softly, which was the way he talked to English people.

'Hello,' said Rose, looking at Mr Sidhu for guidance.

Mr Sidhu froze for a moment, unable to grasp what was happening.

'Rose, this is Darshan, he is from the same village as me in India,' he said finally.

'Oh, nice to meet you,' said Rose, offering her hand which Darshan took and shook lightly.

'Yes, yes,' said Darshan, fractionally moving his head from side to side.

'Rose, I'll be back in one moment,' said Mr Sidhu. Darshan walked a little way away from them to give them some space.

'And don't worry, everything is all right. Are you OK, Rose?' asked Mr Sidhu.

'What's happening, David?'

'That's what I'm going to find out,' he replied and then left.

Mr Sidhu was surrounded by Sikhs. He could not believe his eyes. There were women in brightly coloured salwar kamcczcs and men in either kurta pyjamas or European-style suits. Children hung on to their mothers' hands, older teenagers grouped together, the females still wearing salwar kameezes, whereas the boys wore hoodies with turbans, or short hair and bandanas emblazoned with the Khanda. None of them wore a fleece and walking boots like him. The chatter was constant, broken every now and again by a cry of 'Waheguru Ji Ka Khalsa, Waheguru Ji Ki Fateh.'

'You are here, Suki! You made it!' said Darshan, trying to look enthusiastic, but Mr Sidhu could tell he wanted to know who was sitting in his van.

'Why didn't tell me you were coming to see the grave today?' said Darshan, looking at Mr Sidhu. *And why didn't you tell me you were coming this bank holiday?* thought Mr Sidhu. Even though it made perfect sense that the visit would be on a bank holiday: in his experience, Punjabis would never take a working day off to visit a place like this.

'So this is where Maharajah Duleep Singh is buried?' Mr Sidhu said, ignoring Darshan's question. He felt unprepared; he wasn't ready to show Rose his community yet. There would be questions and more questions, and his answers and his comportment – as well as Rose's – would be scrutinized for *signs* indicating whether it was good or not that they were being seen together.

'Yes, he owned a big estate here. Elveden Hall – all this used to be his,' said Darshan, indicating all the land around. Mr Sidhu was confused about why the Maharajah of Punjab was buried at all.

'Acha' was all he could manage.

Mr Sidhu understood what was causing all the traffic now. On one side of the road was a car park with coaches and cars, and on the other side of the road was a church and cemetery with Maharajah Duleep Singh, the last Maharajah of Punjab, buried there. In between those things was the A11.

'Sometimes the locals here complain, saying we are creating traffic, but I think it is good to do this. There should be something, a sign or a plaque, so when we come we like to make a tamasha,' Darshan grinned.

Before Mr Sidhu could go to have a look like all the other Sikhs, a small woman came rushing up to him. It was Tharlochan. She was wearing a bright yellow salwar kameez with a black embroidered shawl over her shoulders. He could smell the aroma of the coconut oil she'd used on her hair, which was pulled back into a small bun on her head.

'Sat Sri Akal, veerji,' said Tharlochan, looking more at ease here than she normally did when she came to visit him. 'Who is the woman sitting in your car?' she asked, as if reading his thoughts, looking directly at him. 'Where have you been? Where are you coming from?'

'Oh, bus kar, Tharlochan,' said Darshan, rescuing Mr Sidhu from Tharlochan's questioning.

They all turned as a group of Sikhs marched passed them chanting 'Waheguru Ji Ka Khalsa, Waheguru Ji Ki Fateh.'

'Come, Suki, I will show you the grave,' said Darshan. Mr Sidhu saw Tharlochan glancing at his van.

'Bring your friend,' she said, indicating the direction of his van with a movement of her head.

'Yes, I will,' replied Mr Sidhu, trying to sound confident, and then walked back over the road to his van and Rose. He took a deep breath and opened the passenger door.

'Rose, I have something to show you,' he said.

'What's going on?' she asked, her voice betraying her anxiety.

Mr Sidhu put out his hand and smiled, 'Don't worry, Rose, I know these people.'

Rose walked alongside Mr Sidhu. People stopped and stared as they walked past, some with their mouths slightly agape. Mr Sidhu pretended to ignore the looks but felt every single one of them.

He told Rose what was happening and why there were so many Sikhs around.

'My friend, Darshan, organizes it all. He is here with his wife. I will introduce you to her too.'

'Oh, so you're finally letting me meet your friends,' said Rose in a faux-aggrieved manner, her eyes letting him know that she was joking. This was a kind of humour that had disappeared from his life; to feel it re-emerging like this was almost overwhelming.

'Well, I think you've earned that right now,' he said, trying to keep his voice even, hoping she would understand the first joke he had made since he could remember.

'I hope you don't think I'm a soft touch either!' said Rose, still speaking in her faux-insulted manner with the same expression, but now looping her arms through his as they crossed the road.

'Oh, I know you're soft,' he said. 'Soft and sweet and beautiful,' he added. Rose leaned into him with a quiet smile on her face.

As they approached Darshan and Tharlochan, Mr Sidhu let go of Rose's arm and stood up straight with his hands behind his back. He felt the need to introduce Rose again in front of Tharlochan, whose powerful gaze was penetrating his skull.

'We are like brothers,' he said to Rose, hoping such a statement might make Darshan more open to Rose. 'And this is his wife, Tharlochan.'

'Hello,' said Tharlochan, but without offering a hand or any movement at all.

'Nice to meet you,' said Rose, offering her hand to Tharlochan.

'Yes, nice, thank you.' Tharlochan took her hand and held it then looked at Mr Sidhu and let out a giggle as if she were suddenly a little girl again and let Rose's hand go.

The four of them relaxed slightly.

'We were driving from Southwold to London. A little holiday, weekend away, you know,' Mr Sidhu said with a serious expression; this was the way things were said.

'Acha,' Darshan nodded.

'David's been working so hard recently, I thought he could do with a little trip away,' Rose added.

Tharlochan and Darshan nodded, as if they knew what Rose was talking about.

'David,' repeated Tharlochan and let out another little giggle. 'You are married, Rose?' Tharlochan added, looking directly at her. Mr Sidhu tried and failed to say something and then threw Tharlochan a glance, but she kept her gaze on Rose.

'No . . .' said Rose, looking bemused.

'I'm sorry, Rose, Tharlochan is very direct,' interjected Mr Sidhu, trying hard to hold down his impatience with Tharlochan. He knew she would keep on asking questions to find out as much as she could about Rose, so that she could tell the community about the English woman who was with one of theirs. He wanted to protect Rose from the questions, as Rose would be honest, and that honesty would be taken as a weakness.

215

'Bus kar hon, Tharlochan,' said Mr Sidhu, asking her to stop with her questions.

Tharlochan stopped and cast a look at Mr Sidhu. She started to speak in Punjabi, in the direct way most rural farming communities talked.

'*You come here with her and I am not allowed to find out who she is? You've not told us anything about her, how are we meant to know anything?*'

'*So tell me then, what do you want to know?*' growled Mr Sidhu.

'*It's OK, Suki, she didn't mean anything,*' interjected Darshan, wanting to calm things down.

'*It's fine, tell me what you want to know and then stop all this nonsense,*' said Mr Sidhu.

Tharlochan glared at Mr Sidhu.

'*Who is she? How do you know her? Is she married, does she have children, where is her family? Does she work?*'

'*She works in the shop with me; she has been very helpful since everything . . .*' Mr Sidhu paused as Tharlochan raised an eyebrow and smiled at the word 'helpful'.

'*There is no family, she never married,*' he added, to stop Tharlochan from prying any more. Mr Sidhu hated that he was being made to talk about Rose in this way. It felt like a betrayal of sorts, although he thought he did well to swerve the question about children by saying she had no family and had never married. He knew Tharlochan would assume she had no children and that this would keep the story about Jay from coming out, which Tharlochan would be bound to use as fodder for gossip.

Tharlochan seemed satisfied and then addressed Rose again.

'Suki is very good man. He has successful post office business he built with his wife.'

'Suki?' Rose asked, looking puzzled.

Mr Sidhu broke in 'Suki, short for Sukhdev.'

'Oh, I see. I call him David,' said Rose.

'David?' Tharlochan started to giggle again. Then she said it again, 'David,' this time imitating a posh English accent.

'You know his wife, Rose?' asked Tharlochan, ignoring Mr Sidhu's effort to leave.

'Yes, Sarabjit, I had the pleasure of knowing her,' said Rose, looking more keenly at Tharlochan.

'She was a very good woman,' said Tharlochan. 'The best. She did everything for her family. She sacrificed so much. You understand, hunnah?'

Rose looked at Mr Sidhu and Darshan for guidance. 'Yes. She was a wonderful woman,' she said, adjusting her cardigan.

'So sad,' continued Tharlochan. 'She give everything but then, ek dum, she gone and children without mother.'

They all stood in silence for a few moments while the chatter and movement of people swelled around them.

'Shall we see the grave?' said Mr Sidhu, clearing his throat and breaking the silence.

Darshan told them to follow him. Mr Sidhu and Rose joined a long line of Sikhs snaking into the small church graveyard. Mr Sidhu saw women's heels digging into the soft green turf, leaving blades of grass clinging to the soles of their shoes as they walked. There was an uneasy silence as they made their way to the grave. The line thinned into single file as they neared the gravestone. He looked at the people around him who were oblivious to anything except what lay beneath the ground ahead of them. Even Darshan had become silent. He looked at Rose, who was looking at the church and the groups of turbaned Sikhs milling around it. The mourners laid flowers and bent down to pay their respects to the Maharajah. Mr Sidhu looked at the people as they passed him, some of them smiling, some of them with teary eyes, women covering their faces with their chunnis. And suddenly he found himself at the front of the line and there it was, a headstone with the inscription:

IN

MEMORY OF

DULEEP SINGH, G.C.S.I.

MAHARAJAH OF LAHORE

BORN IN THE PUNJAB

4TH SEPTEMBER 1838

DIED IN PARIS 22ND OCTOBER 1893

AGED 55

Mr Sidhu found that later he could not remember what it said on the gravestone. He might have wondered why the Maharajah had died in Paris and why he had died at such a young age. He might also have wondered who had decided to call him Maharajah of Lahore and what the letters G.C.S.I. meant, and, probably most interestingly of all, why it was that a Sikh was buried and not cremated as they usually were. He didn't even notice the gravestone next to it:

IN

MEMORY OF

BAMBA DULEEP SINGH

MAHARANEE

BORN JULY 6TH 1848
DIED SEPTEMBER 18TH 1887
THE LORD GAVE AND THE LORD
HATH TAKEN AWAY. BLESSED BE
THE NAME OF THE LORD.

The name Bamba was not Punjabi. He might also have noticed the other grave of a young son of the Maharajah, Albert Edward Alexander Duleep Singh, who died at the age of thirteen. But he hadn't.

Mr Sidhu looked at the Maharajah's grave and was overcome with emotion, feeling something stirring deep inside him. A few tears fell from his eyes as he knelt down at the grave and did as the others before him had done – said a little prayer for the Maharajah. The grave was in a place where there were no Sikhs or Punjabis. Mr Sidhu was helped up by Rose. People patted his back as he walked past the line; men shook his hands even though he didn't know who they were. He looked back at the grave to see an elderly Sikh soldier wearing full military clothes, including a huge turban, saluting the gravestone.

Darshan came to him. A few comments on the Maharajah were exchanged as they both felt the weight of the occasion. Rose, who was being patient but hanging on to Mr Sidhu's arm, was conspicuous among the Sikhs, who were segregated by their sex and certainly not holding hands or linking arms. A silence fell upon them. Mr Sidhu was still thinking about the Maharajah.

'Sorry, did I miss something?' asked Rose. 'Why is he here again, if he was the Maharajah of Punjab?'

Darshan and Mr Sidhu looked at each other, and Mr Sidhu indicated that Darshan should tell Rose who he was.

'He was the last Maharajah of Punjab,' said Darshan. 'He was the youngest son of Ranjit Singh, the first Sikh Maharajah. He ruled from Delhi to Kabul. The British never fought him, they were too scared of him,' said Darshan proudly. 'The British waited until Ranjit Singh died and then Maharajah Duleep Singh was only a child when he became the last heir to the throne. Then the British captured him, took him away from his mother and his people and brainwashed him into wanting to be a Christian.'

Darshan paused for effect. Rose showed no sign of offence at the previous statement, so Darshan continued.

'Then he came to England and, thinking he was an Englishman, he cut his hair and lost his way. They never let him go back to his home. He lived over there,' Darshan pointed in the direction of the church. 'Behind the church is Elveden Hall – a big estate. That was his home. He used to shoot with Queen Victoria's son. But he didn't live here at the very end. He realised what the British had stolen from him and tried to get his kingdom back, but in the end he died with no money in Paris and with no heirs either,' said Darshan mysteriously. 'He is our history, even if he is buried here in Suffolk like a Christian.'

Darshan looked sad for a moment.

'That's extraordinary,' said Rose.

'Yes,' said Darshan, 'it is extraordinary', repeating the word slowly for emphasis.

'Waheguru, Waheguru,' Tharlochan approached them, one hand tucking her chunni behind her ears. With the other she held an oversized handbag. She eyed Rose, but before she could get to her Mr Sidhu went to Tharlochan, telling her how sad it was about the Maharajah. This allowed Rose and Darshan to walk ahead of them, which he liked because Darshan was always so polite to English people. He made noises to Tharlochan about how good the turnout was and how important it was to know one's history. However, he was also listening to Darshan speaking to Rose, which he imagined Tharlochan was also doing.

'The sad thing is that even though he had many children, none of them had children, so there were no heirs. Sorry, I hope I am not being rude,' said Darshan.

'No, you're not being rude. What do you mean?' asked Rose.

'I was saying that it was sad that he had no heirs and Suki mentioned you don't have children either. I'm sorry if I said the wrong thing.'

Rose stopped and Mr Sidhu's ears started to burn.

'No, Darshan, you weren't being rude, but you did say the wrong thing because I have a son, actually.'

Tharlochan stopped and looked at Mr Sidhu.

'You have a son,' exclaimed Tharlochan.

Rose and Darshan turned around.

'Yes, Jay,' said Rose proudly.

Mr Sidhu, Rose, Darshan and Tharlochan all stood together.

Tharlochan smiled and her eyes widened until her smile turned into a grin. Mr Sidhu stood stuck to his spot.

'We have to go now,' he said, his eyes betraying his nervousness. Darshan placed his hand on Mr Sidhu's back. 'Don't worry, you go, Suki,' he said encouragingly.

'We need to get back before traffic,' said Mr Sidhu, trying to explain the sudden departure.

'Why did you tell them I didn't have a son?' Rose asked Mr Sidhu in front of Darshan and Tharlochan.

Mr Sidhu hesitated; he couldn't find any words and didn't want to say anything more in front of Darshan and Tharlochan.

'So lovely to meet you both,' said Rose and turned to go.

Mr Sidhu shook hands with Darshan and nodded to Tharlochan, who still had the same smile on her face. He turned to Rose but she had already walked to the van, far away from him. He indicated that he needed to go and Darshan and Tharlochan both gave him his leave. He trudged back to the van thinking what a fool he was. He could have told the truth and let them know about Jay, but that would have also involved explaining that they didn't need to worry that Jay – or Rose – would make some kind of claim on his wealth. None of that was part of his life with Rose. And they'd had a such a nice time in Southwold and now he'd betrayed her trust. He got into the van and sat next to Rose. It was a while before they spoke again.

'You're embarrassed by him, aren't you?'

'No. No. It is not like that. You don't understand,' pleaded Mr Sidhu.

'Just drop me at the station. I can make my own way home,' said Rose, buckling her seatbelt.

'What?'

'You can drop me at Thetford Station and I'll get a train from there,' Rose looked straight ahead.

'Rose, please,' said Mr Sidhu.

Rose turned round and stared at him. Her face was quivering before she exploded at him.

'Explain it to me, David. Explain to me why you can't tell people who you've known your whole life that Jay is my son.'

Mr Sidhu knew that Darshan and Tharlochan would be

surprised and shocked if they met Jay, just like he'd been at first. And for the same reasons. Because where they'd grown up everyone looked the same. But of course the same wasn't true here, especially in London.

But that wasn't the whole reason. So he tried to articulate something he'd never had to explain to anyone before.

'Rose, they don't believe in boyfriend–girlfriend, things like this. If we are together, then they will think we will get married. This is how they think,' Mr Sidhu paused because it was also how he used to think, but not any more. Not now he was with Rose. Marriage didn't feel necessary. How he felt about her was something outside of everything he'd known. It was something completely new. Rose said nothing and looked straight ahead.

'They will think that if we are together then we will get married and Jay will be my son too. And that you and him are after my money.'

Rose's mouth opened and then closed. Whatever she was about to say, she kept to herself. Another lorry horned loudly on the A11 nearby, making them both turn to look as it passed.

'You know that's not true,' she said at last.

'Yes, but they don't,' Mr Sidhu replied.

Rose sighed and studied the tissue she held in her hands.

'David, who are you trying to please? Them or me?'

'I cannot stop being who I am or where I am from.'

'I'm not asking you to stop being you. I'm asking you to be kind.'

Rose clipped her seatbelt back in and looked straight ahead.

'I thought you cared, David. Let's just get back to London.'

Mr Sidhu looked at the church and graveyard and all the Sikhs. If that Maharajah hadn't been buried here, all the good feeling that they'd brought together over the weekend might still be here, he thought bitterly. He was about to start the van, when he heard a knocking on his window. It was Darshan. Mr Sidhu wound down his window.

'What is it?'

'Suki, there is someone here who wants to see you.'

Mr Sidhu looked at Rose who was staring straight ahead. 'Just a minute, Rose,' he said and got out of the van for the second time.

'Who is it, Darshan?' he asked impatiently. Darshan turned and behind him Mr Sidhu saw Tharlochan and a young turbaned Sikh man helping an elderly Sikh woman in a salwar kameez walking with the aid of a walking stick towards them.

'It's your sister, Suki, Bitu,' said Darshan.

Bitu struggled to walk alone but was still mobile. Mr Sidhu stood watching and then started to walk towards her.

'Bitu,' he said gently.

Bitu looked up. Her hair was all white and tied up into a bun on the back of her head, which was covered by her chunni. She wore the old type of dark-framed square NHS glasses which he'd not seen for many years; the corner of one of the frames was wrapped in a sticking plaster to hold it together.

'Suki,' she called out with a thin, raspy voice and smiled. 'Ki haal chaal?'

Mr Sidhu had the urge to bend down and touch her feet. But she was his half-sister, not an elder, and that wouldn't be appropriate. Instead, she reached out a hand to pat his shoulder by way of greeting.

Mr Sidhu stood rooted to the spot. The last time he'd seen Bitu was as a young man and she in middle age, perhaps only in her early forties then. He was over sixty now, which meant she was in her eighties at least.

'What are you doing here?' was all he could manage to say.

'I am here to see my great-grandson,' she chuckled. 'Can you believe it?'

Mr Sidhu stared into her eyes and he saw his father's eyes, and the familiarity caused him to stop and take her hand.

'Oh Suki, what are you staring at?' She laughed and her eyes smiled at him in a way that spoke of their shared history.

'Sat Sri Akal,' said the man who was with her, who wore a small, tight turban and a trimmed beard. He bent down to touch Mr Sidhu's feet.

'My name's Jesse. Glad we met you here, mate,' he said, standing back up and speaking with a Birmingham (B1) accent. 'My dadima was all 'ell bent on us coming down to London to find you.'

Bitu being Jesse's dadima meant that he was her grandson through his father. Her son had only been around ten years old when Mr Sidhu had met him at Billoo's wedding. He remembered telling her how she could send her son to him in England. But she hadn't, and he hadn't thought about that moment until now. He'd only seen her once after that – at his own wedding – and then she'd been alone.

'You didn't send your son to me. Why not?' said Mr Sidhu, half joking.

Bitu smiled, 'You remember, hahn? Well, my son was just like you. He wanted to do things his own way. I told him about you, but . . .' Mr Sidhu remembered how her husband had spoken about their family, so perhaps they saw him and his brothers as adversaries, a family who'd not given enough dowry for their daughter. Maybe her son still carried some of that attitude. It was a different time then. And this Jesse boy seemed nice.

'Nice to meet you, Jesse, and is it your son who she's come to see?' asked Mr Sidhu.

'Yes, it is, mate.'

'How are you, Suki? I heard about your wife,' said Bitu matter-of-factly.

'Yes, Sarabjit, she passed,' he said. Death had always been talked about without great emotion in his village. When you lived on a farm, it was part of the way of things.

'Children?' she asked.

'Yes, Meenu and Raju.'

'Marriage?'

'Not yet, Meenu is engaged,' said Mr Sidhu, trying to sound upbeat, but even he could hear the uncertainty in his voice.

'Here is different, hunnah, Suki?' said Bitu quizzically. 'Jesse is living with a gori and their son and they are not even married!' she added.

'We're gonna get married one day, Dadima, but I'd rather buy a house than spend all that money on a wedding with five hundred guests who I don't even know,' said Jesse, smirking. Mr Sidhu marvelled at the exchange between his sister and grandson. He and Sarabjit thought that they were modern by letting their children choose, but here was Bitu, who hadn't seen much of the world, having the same ideas as them.

At that moment Rose got out of the car and everyone fell silent. Rose looked at Mr Sidhu for guidance.

'Rose, this is my half-sister Bitu and her grandson Jesse,' said Mr Sidhu, indicating with his outstretched arm.

'Hello,' said Rose, standing next to Mr Sidhu. 'You never told me you had a sister, David.' Mr Sidhu blushed at being called David in front of Bitu. He heard Tharlochan sniggering again.

'My father married twice,' he said to Rose.

'My mother, she pass when I born,' said Bitu, surprising Mr Sidhu with her English and forward manner with Rose. 'I live with father for sixteen year. Only me and him. Before Suki and his brothers born. Very happy time. Then he want to get second wife. And they say I need to marry. But they marry me to idiot man,' she said, shaking her head, 'too much drinking. But he pass when he is young and then my life better. My son coming England and making good life. Sending money for me to look after my husband mother,' said Bitu proudly.

Rose smiled at Bitu who smiled back at her.

'Pleasure to meet you, Bitu,' said Rose. 'I'm sorry you lost your mother and your husband.'

'My life much better when husband dead,' she said, nodding her head.

'I lost my brother when I was sixteen. It broke my heart. We were close,' said Rose.

'When I leave my father I feel same. Like he death happen.'

Mr Sidhu looked on in amazement at Rose and Bitu getting to know each other. He was unsure what to do with himself as they spoke about Bitu's five children and multiple grandchildren and now her great-grandson. Jesse helped Bitu understand what Rose was saying with certain words.

'Your friend is very nice,' Bitu told Mr Sidhu as she finished talking with Rose.

'How long are you here for?' asked Mr Sidhu.

'One week more,' she said. 'You should come back and see the village. When was the last time you went?'

'When our father passed away,' he said. It had been a quick visit, not enough time to notice anything or even process anything. It was during the early Nineties when interest rates had gone up to 15 per cent and they'd hardly had any money left at the end of each month. He'd gone and come back in five days on a cheap standby flight. They both nodded, remembering him.

'He was a good man,' said Bitu.

Mr Sidhu nodded. 'I'm sorry we didn't see more of each other, Bitu.'

'It is like that, Suki. People leave the village for England or Canada and you might never see them again. But when I came to England I make sure I see you. Then when I see Darshan here and he tell me you are here, oh, it make me so happy. Your brothers are idiot like my husband, they tell everyone they don't have any sister, but you, you are same like your father. Good man.'

The compliment struck a chord with Mr Sidhu. There were only a few people in the whole world who could say that to him. He'd always felt the love of his father, but Bitu saying it out loud like that almost overwhelmed him.

'Thank you, Paanji,' he said to her. He suddenly thought how lonely it must have been for her to marry her 'idiotic' husband, as she called him, without a mother or father to come back to when things got tough. He knew Sarabjit struggled with that when she came to England. His mother never spoke about Bitu and their father knew not to talk about her with his new wife. And then Mr Sidhu realised that perhaps he was the only person in the world that she could share her love for their father with, and that this might be the last time he saw her.

'I don't think our father wanted to marry again, Bitu. I think

228

he was happy with being with just you. But the village elders told him he had to, so he did his duty. He loved you very much.'

Bitu smiled and they embraced.

'We should go now,' said Jesse, approaching them. Mr Sidhu nodded and shook Jesse's hand.

'Sat Sri Akal,' they all said to each other as they parted. Mr Sidhu thanked Darshan for bringing Bitu to him and he walked back to the van, hoping Rose wasn't still cross with him. He understood a little more now how lonely it must have been when Rose had Jay taken from her at such a young age and why she would be so protective of him now.

'She seemed nice,' said Rose, as Mr Sidhu settled himself in the van and tugged at the seatbelt. 'You never told me you had a sister.'

'I never really knew her, but she knew my father,' he said, remembering her eyes.

'I've still not forgiven you, David, in case you're wondering. You'll have to be patient. That was hurtful, even if you think otherwise,' Mr Sidhu nodded and accepted her words. And that was the last thing they said to each other as they drove back to London. The good feeling they'd built up over the weekend had lessened. The van's reassuring noise held the silence between them as they approached London and came back to all the problems he was running away from.

Chapter 16

Since coming back from their weekend away, Mr Sidhu's world was turning upside down. Rose came to work on Tuesday as usual, but she was distant. She didn't come and have the usual chats with him and he felt anxious when he saw her talking to the locals. Was she telling them about him? About how he'd embarrassed her? All this was new to Mr Sidhu. Rose was unknowable to him in many ways, especially when she was annoyed with him. Mr Sidhu felt unable to broach the subject with her. A simple sorry didn't seem appropriate. She'd shared so much with him about Jay and her brother, and all he'd done was worry about what (mostly) Tharlochan thought about him and Rose. Again he missed Sarabjit; she'd kept all these people at arm's length from him and now they were penetrating his mind and he was unable to deal with it, just as he was unable to deal with Meenu. So now, rather than bringing them closer, which it had done for a moment on the beach and in the hotel, the holiday had created a new atmosphere between them, which neither one of them could find a way of lifting themselves out of.

On Wednesday, as usual, he came home to find Meenu at his house. He wasn't really in the mood to be scrutinized by Meenu and didn't have the energy to put on a front about how everything was fine, but he was surprised to see Raju there too. He would have preferred to see Raju alone as he was simpler to deal with. Also, he wanted to talk about the house in Richmond. Everything was ready, the offer and the mortgage. He could show Raju how simple it was to acquire property. Just as his father had acquired land before him and showed him how to tend to it and manage it, Mr Sidhu wanted to pass on that knowledge to his son. However, he didn't want to talk about all that in front of Meenu.

Meenu was in the kitchen cooking while Raju stood silently nearby. Something was in the air.

'Hello, hello,' he said, hanging up his coat and taking off his shoes.

They didn't look up.

'Did you have a nice trip?' asked Raju.

Mr Sidhu entered the kitchen. 'Yes, beta, it was nice to have a break,' he replied. He was pretty sure he hadn't told them he was going away. They were definitely up to something.

'Weather good in Suffolk, was it?' Tharlochan must have told them about it, he thought.

'See the coast? Dip your feet in the sea, did you? Bet that felt good,' said Raju. His face was flat, with no hint of the warmth or silliness that he usually exuded.

Mr Sidhu stood looking at his two children, wondering what was going on.

'Auntie Tharlochan was asking about you, Dad. Everyone's wondering if you're OK. Are you OK, Dad?'

'She's your chachi, Raju, not your auntie,' he replied. Raju had never learned all the different names for relations in their culture. He and Sarabjit had tried, but Raju thought it too confusing. However, Meenu did know. And it was probably Meenu who had been told about the meeting at the Maharajah's grave. So it was Meenu who'd put Raju up to this. Raju wasn't one to involve himself in family matters unless there was some drama to it. Mr Sidhu sighed. He knew he needed to be on his guard as Meenu had been acting strangely ever since knowing about Rose. Now she was making Raju into her mouthpiece.

'Why didn't you tell us you were going away?' asked Raju, with a hint of betrayal in his voice. 'And why didn't you want to tell us you were going away with Rose, Dad?' he added a little more firmly.

Mr Sidhu clenched his fists. He would never have spoken to his own father like this. This was just like Raju, thinking he was in one of his plays, rather than being respectful to his father.

'That's enough, Raju,' he said, trying his best to remain level-headed.

'And when were you going to tell me about the losses?' Raju continued.

Mr Sidhu looked at Meenu. Her head was lowered, looking at the daal.

'I thought he should know, Dad. He's your son,' she said without looking at him.

What difference would it make if he knew? thought Mr Sidhu. He wouldn't be able to do anything about it.

'Dad, please. What's going on?' said Raju, persisting in his questioning. 'Where's the money gone?'

For a moment Mr Sidhu didn't know what Raju was referring to.

'We only want to help,' Raju added.

Those were Meenu's words. Raju never helped. Meenu

looked up and there was silence in the house, apart from the sound of gas heating the thuvva and the daal bubbling away.

'Who's Jay?' asked Raju softly, continuing his questioning.

Mr Sidhu could feel his chest tightening.

'Meenu told me about him. I can't believe Rose's son is a tramp,' said Raju.

Meenu didn't look up, but kept stirring the daal slowly.

'Meenu told me everything. He's homeless, isn't he?'

'Enough,' said Mr Sidhu firmly.

'I couldn't agree more, Dad,' said Raju, not letting up. 'That's enough of you being taken advantage of. I'm not going to let you take the rap for this. If there's money's missing, we need to know where it is and who's taken it.' Despite Mr Sidhu not liking what Raju was saying, he was pleased that Raju was being strong; he would have to remind himself that Raju was capable of that.

'No one has bloody taken it,' said Mr Sidhu, surprising himself with a rare swear word, anger rising in his voice.

'That's not what Alan says, Dad,' said Meenu, speaking calmly. 'I spoke to him. He says the computer can't be wrong. And if it was, it would have happened to other post offices, but it hasn't. They've checked everything and there really is money missing.' She looked at Mr Sidhu with concern.

For the first time the thought crossed his mind that perhaps his children were right. Could it be true? Was there money missing? No, of course not. He'd seen it with his own eyes when the loss doubled on the system. Everything was wrong. Upside down.

'Stop all this nonsense,' he said. Raju and Meenu looked at him, waiting to see what he would say next. He needed to regain control; his children were trying to tell him about his own business, his own life. This was not the way things were done.

'Meenu, this weekend you bring Craig here. I want to see him and talk to him,' he said, looking at her.

She stood silently, and Raju persisted, 'Why did he say he never uses keys, Dad? I mean, who even says they don't use keys?' He turned to Meenu. 'I mean, that's a giveaway if ever I've heard one.'

Mr Sidhu was lost for words. It did sound strange now that Raju had said it. Meenu turned away and started to bring plates out from the cupboard.

'Meenu,' said Mr Sidhu.

'Yes, Dad?'

He didn't want a confrontation. He needed to be careful.

Raju interrupted, 'Dad, who else has keys to the post office?'

Raju was beginning to irritate him.

'Does Rose have keys?' Raju continued.

'Raju, chup,' Mr Sidhu said. He hardly ever told his children to shut up, but they were really grating on him.

He hoped Raju had finished, but there was more.

'Dad, you can't be that naive. I mean,' Raju sniggered, 'the lady doth protest too much, don't you think? I'm talking about Jay, Dad. You know, about not using keys. Shakespeare? No?'

Mr Sidhu didn't know what Raju was talking about. He was smiling at Meenu.

'I can't believe he's actually fallen for her so much that he's been blinded,' Raju whispered loudly to Meenu. 'I never thought he had it in him.' Raju stared at him now as if he were a child. 'He probably took the keys from Rose's house, Dad. You know, Rose might not be aware of any of this.'

'Meenu, I want to see Craig this weekend. You understand?' said Mr Sidhu, trying to maintain his authority.

'Yes, Dad,' Meenu replied with a deference that was missing from Raju.

'Meenu, do what you want,' said Raju. 'He can't tell you what to do. We don't live in some village in Punjab, for god's sake.' His face showed his disdain.

Mr Sidhu looked at Raju. 'Yes, you are right, we don't live in a village any more, but your mother and I did. We grew up in Punjab. We came to this country with nothing. Everything we did was for you.' Without wanting to, Mr Sidhu was close to tears as he thought about Sarabjit and how much he missed her in this moment. He breathed in deeply to regain his composure.

'Raju,' said Meenu, 'that's enough.'

For the first time, Raju looked lost for words. Mr Sidhu noted that Meenu had not said anything against him or Rose. He looked at her as she made herself the woman of the house.

'Food's ready,' Meenu declared bracingly.

Raju and Mr Sidhu ignored each other as Meenu poured out the daal and placed a small silver bowl full of mixed pickle and a large bowl of yogurt onto the dining table. They all ate in silence before Mr Sidhu confronted Meenu.

'Meenu, what did you say to Alan?' Meenu looked at her food for a few seconds before she looked up at her father.

'I spoke to him about the missing money, Dad. I wanted to see if I could help. Alan is on your side. He doesn't want anything bad to happen to you.'

'Bad?' Mr Sidhu didn't understand what she meant.

'You have to pay the missing money back unless they find out what happened to it. Alan told me it's a lot of money.

I don't want anything to happen to you, Dad.' Meenu gave him a reassuring smile, as if all he needed to do was accept what she was saying and then everything would be all right.

'Beta, nothing bad is going to happen to me. It is a mistake. They will correct it. Nothing is missing. 'Over twenty years I have done this. Don't worry, OK?'

'Yes, Dad,' said Meenu unconvincingly.

'And Meenu, we don't talk about family business with strangers, OK?'

Raju smirked. 'Jesus, Dad, this isn't a dictatorship. You can't just tell us what we can and can't do.'

'It's OK, Raju,' said Meenu. 'Yes, Dad, I won't talk to Alan about our business any more, I promise.'

He could feel his family breaking apart. He had no idea how to keep his children from thinking the worst of things. Sarabjit would have dealt with this, smoothed things over, made him feel calm. Was life punishing him for being with Rose? Was it true, what Meenu was saying about her? Was he blind?

After dinner, Meenu cleared up. Raju made perfunctory efforts to help, but Meenu, well practised in the kitchen, did not need his help and quickly made the kitchen and dining room sparkle. It was as if the dinner had never happened. Everything was reset. Meenu gathered up her phone and handbag and told them she was going.

'Yeah, I might go too,' said Raju.

'Raju, you stay here,' said Mr Sidhu and Raju sat back down. 'And Meenu, Craig this weekend. OK?'

Meenu nodded.

'And remember, don't talk to Alan. You don't tell him our business,' he repeated.

Meenu nodded to her father and left.

Mr Sidhu and Raju sat on the sofas in the lounge listening to Meenu start her car, music blaring out loudly before being quickly turned down. The car revved up a few times before the gear was engaged, and then reversed out of the driveway. Then, both music and accelerator were turned up again and Meenu zoomed off, the noise trailing in her wake. Mr Sidhu got up and went to the kitchen. He got a couple of glass tumblers and was about to take the bottle of Famous Grouse from one of the high cupboards, which served as his liquor cabinet, before changing his mind and taking the unopened bottle of Johnny Walker Black Label. This was important business.

'This looks serious,' said Raju, his boyish silliness returning.

Mr Sidhu poured the amber liquid into the two tumblers, using the good sized measures that were normal to Punjabis.

'Ice?' he asked. Raju nodded.

Mr Sidhu dropped ice cubes from a bowl into both glasses and took a jug of water, pouring a little into his glass. Raju indicated he wanted the same. Mr Sidhu took a sip and placed his glass back down.

'You know your place in the family, Raju?'

'Yeah, Dad, I'm the boy, I carry the family name, blah blah.'

'No, not blah blah. This is important, Raju. You know why you are here today?'

'Just say what you want to say, Dad. You don't really care what I think.'

Mr Sidhu let the latest barb from Raju wash over him and spoke as calmly as he could.

'Your grandfather had three brothers. But he was the only one left when his father died.'

'Why, what happened to them?' asked Raju, suddenly interested.

'My father never said. But many people died in that time. There was an illness or something. And when he married he only had one daughter before his wife died.'

Mr Sidhu could see that Raju was about to say something but then stopped himself. Mr Sidhu stopped too, because for the first time he could see that he was connected with his own father in a way that he'd never thought about before. They'd both become widowers. He would so have liked to have spoken to him about that now.

And there it was: a memory from his wedding day when he'd stolen his first glance at Sarabjit. After the wedding, everyone came to bless the couple as they remained seated in front of the Guru Granth Sahib. It was February in Punjab and the ceremony had to be performed before midday, which meant it was starting to heat up. And all he'd wanted in that moment was that the people would hurry up and bless them so he could get a tumbler of water. And then his sister Bitu had come to bless him and Sarabjit; it was only the second time he'd met her. She was as old as his mother, with grey hair and a hairy upper lip. It had taken him by surprise, as he never thought about her, and his father never mentioned her. Since there had been so many people coming to congratulate him that day, he hadn't thought about it much, but he'd seen her later touching his father's feet as she'd done at Billoo's wedding. His mother, who never really had anything nice to say about anyone, told him, 'She killed her own mother at birth.'

His own father had been through what he himself had been through later in life. His wife had died. It wasn't the same, of course, but it was the first time since Sarabjit had gone that he'd thought about that. Was that what Raju had seen and wanted to say to him? Mr Sidhu carried on.

'Your grandfather was sad after his wife died and didn't want to marry or have any other children. So he lived with his daughter, sometimes sending her to his sister's house, until she was old enough to look after the house all by herself. And he carried on farming his land, waiting for death to take him away. Everyone in the village could see this and one day, when he came back from the fields, one of the village elders stopped him and asked, "Who will look after your land and your daughter when you are gone?"'

Mr Sidhu and Raju each took a sip of their whisky before he continued.

'So my father found a new wife and remarried. But before he did, he married his daughter Bitu so she could start her life with her husband. Your grandfather had three sons and his land was safe and his house was safe. He didn't want to do it, but he knew he should do it because it was his duty. And years later, when I wanted to come to England, he sold some of his land so that I could buy a plane ticket. No one had ever sold land before, but he did it. My brothers were so angry that they do not even speak to me any more. Even my mother was against it, but he knew it was his duty to help me. And he did it. And my duty is to my family, too. And so, Raju, I have accepted who you are and what you want to do with your life, but I know I must help you to have security, because that is my duty. One day everything I have will be yours. Not because you are a boy but because you are my responsibility.'

'And what about Meenu?' asked Raju, his eyebrows raised.

'She is my responsibility, but when she is married her husband will take care of her. That is his duty. And Meenu is not like you. She works hard and has a property; she can buy another one if she wants. But you, Raju, you are different.'

Raju smirked. 'Très controversial. Not sure Meenu sees it like that.'

'Raju, what you do in your life is up to you. Not me. And what I do, I do to honour my father and his father. I have to do my duty, and one day you will too.'

Raju leaned back in his chair as if absorbing all that had been said.

'So, Raju, I put my faith in you, but I am not you. You do with it what you want, but understand what those who came before you did for you. Don't forget.'

Raju nodded slowly as he absorbed all that his father had shared with him.

Mr Sidhu wanted to follow up his little chat with Raju by showing him what he meant. 'I will make an appointment to see the house I want to buy,' he said, 'and you come with me to see it. And then you will understand how to buy a house, OK?'

'OK, Dad, if you think that's important.'

'Yes, it is important,' said Mr Sidhu firmly.

After they had finished their drinks, Raju asked Mr Sidhu about the losses again. Mr Sidhu told him about what had been happening since the new computer system was installed.

'There's no money missing, Raju. All the actual money in the post office is accounted for. It's only the computer that says there is missing money. For over twenty years I have always balanced the books. Now a new computer system comes in and suddenly there is a loss. The Post Office have given us a good life and a community who respects us. They have nothing to gain by all this. Once they understand it is the computer, everything will be fine. This is government business, not like Robert Maxwell and the pensions he stole.'

'And what if that doesn't happen?'

'Raju, it happens all the time. How they say it? "Clerical error" or "mistakes happen". Why would I steal my own money? It makes no sense. And all this nonsense about Rose and Jay, this is just your sister. She doesn't like it that Rose is my friend. She thinks Rose will replace her mother, but nothing can do that, Raju. No one can do that.

Raju nodded but Mr Sidhu could tell he wasn't convinced, and Mr Sidhu in his heart wasn't convinced by his own words either.

After Raju had gone, Mr Sidhu drove to Rose's house. He rang her doorbell and waited.

'What is it, David? It's late,' said Rose, in her dressing gown.

'Sorry, I wanted to see you,' he said, looking a little pitiful.

'You'd better come in, then,' she said, turning back into the house.

He followed her in and placed his hand on her shoulder. 'I'm sorry,' he pleaded.

Rose turned to look at him. 'You really are a silly old fool, aren't you?' She let out a sigh. 'What is it? Meenu again?' He nodded. 'I told you she doesn't like me, didn't I?'

Mr Sidhu explained what had happened at his house, but left out the bit about Raju and Meenu thinking Jay had taken money from the post office.

'Why do they care who you go on holiday with?' asked Rose, looking confused.

'Tharlochan told them and she makes it worse.'

'Because I've got a son?' asked Rose.

'Please, it is different for us. They will think—'

'Whatever they want to think, David, what do you care?' said Rose, interrupting. 'The point is, do you think there is anything wrong? With us being together?'

'No, I don't.'

'Well then, stop worrying about what other people think. What do *you* want?'

'You, Rose.'

Rose smiled. 'You have me, David, just about. You just about have me.'

'Only just about?'

'Yes,' said Rose, smiling now.

'And what do I have to do to have more of you?'

'You have to show me how you're going to make it up to me.'

Mr Sidhu smiled. 'Thank you.' And for a moment everything felt wonderful again.

Chapter 17

A few weeks later, at 8.50 a.m. on a bright, sunny Thursday morning, there were two men waiting outside the post office, standing next to Rose and Richard. They wore dark grey suits and everything about them said they were not customers. Auditors, most likely, thought Mr Sidhu as he parked his van. He walked towards them as calmly as he could, breathing deeply. One was younger looking, fresher-faced than the other, who was older and portlier.

'Hello. Mr Sidhu?' said one of the suits, coming to him before he could get to Rose and his customers.

'Yes, can I help you?' asked Mr Sidhu, hoping his eyes were not betraying the panic he felt. Rose looked at the men, her body stiff and ready to deal with whatever might be coming her way.

'They were here before me, David, and haven't said who they are,' said Rose, walking towards him and glancing at them as she spoke. His thoughts slowed and calmed as Rose said his name.

'We're auditing this branch today, so unfortunately the post office won't be open for a couple of hours. Could you let us in?'

'Well, that's all very well, but what about all the people waiting here?' said Rose, indicating Richard and a few other pensioners who always came early on a Thursday, it being the start of the new week to get their pensions. 'They were here before you. We should at least serve them before you do your audit or whatever,' Rose added.

'That's not how it works,' said the younger suit. The other auditor was talking into his mobile phone a few paces away, making it hard for anyone to hear him.

'Well, I suppose it couldn't be any other way, could it?' replied Rose. Mr Sidhu felt proud of Rose, seeing her defend their customers.

Mr Sidhu opened the shutters and unlocked the door. He could hear Richard and the others grumbling with Rose about the audit. The auditors followed Mr Sidhu into the shop and went to the post office end without speaking to him. Mr Sidhu opened the post office and the three of them stepped inside.

'Open the safe,' said the older, portlier man.

Mr Sidhu obliged, opening the time-locked safe, which made its usual beeping noises and then clicked open. Mr Sidhu waited for a moment.

'You can go,' said the man, without looking at him.

Mr Sidhu left the post office with the auditors inside. They started talking to each other as soon as he left. He walked to where Rose was standing behind the shop counter, where a few of the locals were chatting to her.

'When's the post office going to open again, Sidhu saahab?' asked Richard.

'Maybe a couple of hours. But don't worry, Richard, I have some stamps for you,' said Mr Sidhu.

'Won't they be needing them for the audit, David?' asked Rose.

Mr Sidhu froze for a moment. 'Yes, thank you, Rose, that is true.'

He went behind the counter and retrieved the sheets of stamps he left there for out-of-hours customers or when the queue was too long at the post office. He approached the post office counter and knocked on the glass. The auditors both looked up.

'These were . . .' he trailed off as he pushed the sheets under the bulletproof glass. He didn't say any more because he remembered that he kept Min's pension book and card in the post office safe.

'Why aren't these in the post office?' asked the older one.

'Sometimes there's a queue, so I put some in the shop,' said Mr Sidhu.

'They shouldn't be out of the post office,' the auditor replied, taking the sheets and sighing and shaking his head. He spoke to the younger one, but again Mr Sidhu could not hear what they were saying.

Mr Sidhu apologised to Richard about the stamps and then tried unsuccessfully to make himself useful in the shop but was only getting in Rose's way. He went to sit in the cellar and get out of everyone's way, and waited for the auditors to finish. He still hoped that somehow the losses would be rectified and that they would know that there was nothing missing. It was a possibility, he thought.

Mr Sidhu sat alone and waited. He didn't know what would happen, but he knew what was right and what was wrong. He'd always tried to do the right thing, just like his father before him. But here in this country, in this city, the idea of what was right and what was wrong felt old-fashioned. His father would always take a long time to make a decision, just like when he had asked him for money for his flight to England. His father had nodded in acknowledgement of Sukhdev's request but told him to wait for an answer. Sukhdev wondered what his father was waiting for, exactly. He knew his brothers would kick up a fuss, because he'd already got money from his father for his education, and now he wanted more for something that would not benefit the farm or the family, only him. When his father finally agreed to sell some land to pay for the plane ticket, Sukhdev, after thanking him, asked what had taken so long for him to make the decision.

His father told him that he'd worked out all the different scenarios in his head, even the bad ones (the brothers wanting to beat Sukhdev up) and he knew he'd be able to deal with them all. 'But what if there was something that happened that you'd not thought about?' he'd asked his father.

'The only thing I can't know is whether you are sincere about going to England,' he'd said. 'Whether it is a small idea or a big idea, whether you will go and become successful or come back with your tail between your legs. That I cannot know. And neither can you until you do it.'

It was all Sukhdev needed to hear from his father to become determined to succeed – and he had, he felt, in some way or other, succeeded. So what now? What were the consequences of what was happening now, with the missing money from the post office? Mr Sidhu knew there were big consequences if things didn't go his way. The worst that could happen was that he could lose his licence to run the post office. But how would that benefit the Post Office? Surely that wouldn't happen. But if it did, it would mean his salary could go, which would then mean he could lose his house if he couldn't afford to pay the mortgage. He calculated that the shop takings would just about cover the outgoings for the business and the shop lockup, which he leased. Mr Sidhu sat and thought, as calmly as his own father used to, about what might happen, to prepare for the course he was taking. And of course the move to the new house in Richmond would be impossible, too. But nothing had happened yet.

It was tiring for Mr Sidhu to think of his life in this way and the consequences of what might happen, and before long he was walking on a dusty road near his village, following his father, who was ahead of him using a staff to walk with, placing it in time with his feet into the dust and making an 'O' shape in the ground which Mr Sidhu stepped onto.

'There was something wrong,' his father said in that matter-of-fact way farmers talked about such things. 'She lost a lot of blood,' he added.

He continued walking in front of Mr Sidhu, his shiny, sun-drenched, dark brown hand gripping the wooden staff, his back and head straight. Mr Sidhu wanted to tell his father about Sarabjit and her cancer, but his mouth felt closed shut. He couldn't say anything. However, his father turned his turbaned head along with his long white beard and nodded to him, as if he had told him.

All around were wheat fields, still green and not ripe yet. They carried on walking until they reached a village which was just as Mr Sidhu remembered in his childhood – full of small boys with topnots, girls with double or single plaits playing outside, having fun, the odd dog lying happily in the sunshine. Eventually they arrived at a simple single-storey house. His father stopped, placed his staff down and squatted effortlessly in the shade of a tree, his elbows resting on his knees, his arms outstretched, motioning with his head in the wordless way he used to that Mr Sidhu should go in.

Mr Sidhu pushed open the double wooden doors, small square panels in the fascia, decorated with painted flowers, slightly worn away by the constant combination of sunshine and monsoon rains that distressed everything man made over time. Inside the house – which was made half from bricks, half from straw and mud – it was dark. There was a shaft of sunlight which shone onto a door where he could hear what sounded like someone straining with something. He walked over to the door and pushed it open. And there was Sarabjit. She was younger than he last remembered her. She looked like she did when they were first married, big brown eyes, shiny black hair plaited into a long, single plait hanging elegantly down her back and her slight figure. She wore a beige, hand-embroidered salwar kameez and was kneeling on the ground, tightening thin ropes around the wooden frame of a charpoy, a traditional Punjabi bed. She threw one of the ropes to Mr Sidhu who, having done this many times as a child, took it and wound it round his end of the frame and passed it back to her. She began talking without looking at him.

'Where have you been, Sukhdev?' She smiled as she said it.

Mr Sidhu found that he could move his mouth now.

'I tried to look for you,' he said.

'I know,' she replied, still not looking at him. 'I had things to do.'

She tied her end of the rope and passed it back to him.

'Don't worry, Sukhdev, everything will be fine. You are a good man.'

Hearing those words made Mr Sidhu feel guilty. He wanted to tell her about Rose but couldn't find the words. Should he tell her? As he was about to speak, he felt her arms holding him close. He leaned into her and felt her warmth. When he looked up at her he saw that it was actually Rose holding him. Sarabjit was still there, looking at him and smiling. She turned to Rose and they exchanged a friendly look that reassured him in a way that he hadn't experienced in a long time. He heard heavy footsteps coming towards him, which made him look around. The footsteps became lounder and louder and then he heard an English voice,

'Mr Sidhu?'

Mr Sidhu opened his eyes to the glare of the lights in the cellar; it was the big auditor. His expression was serious. The younger one stood at the foot of the stairs behind him.

'We need to talk to you. There's a big shortfall in the post office accounts.'

Mr Sidhu listened as they explained to him what he already knew.

'You need to make it good.'

'It is a mistake,' he replied.

'Be as that may, Mr Sidhu, I refer you to section twelve, clause twelve in the sub-postmaster's contract,' he said, and then quoted the clause: 'The sub-postmaster is responsible for all losses caused through his own negligence, carelessness or error, and also for losses of all kinds caused by his assistants. Deficiencies due to such losses must be made good without delay.'

They stood looking at each other while Mr Sidhu remembered Sarabjit's smile and the feeling of seeing Sarabjit and Rose together.

'Are you in a position to make it good?' the big auditor asked again.

'No, I haven't taken any of this missing money,' said Mr Sidhu.

'It doesn't really concern us who's taken the money or even where it is. The point is that it's missing. The accounts don't lie. So, now, it might be you. It might not be you. That is for you to sort out. If you can make it good, we can all go home right now,' he paused, allowing the last remark to remain in the air. He leaned in closer to Mr Sidhu, his face a little sterner, 'But if not, then it's on you. You are responsible, whoever might have taken it. And we will go after you.'

Mr Sidhu looked at them, perplexed and worried. If he paid the money like they said, then things would go back to normal. His children would stop haranguing him and he'd go and serve his customers with Rose by his side. Everything would be good again. But then he had another thought.

Mr Sidhu looked at the men and spoke slowly to make sure they knew what he was saying, 'If I pay the money to the Post Office but then the money keeps going missing, then what? What will happen to me then?'

The younger one replied with a slight grin, 'I'd suggest you find out who's taking it and have a word with them.'

Mr Sidhu could not believe what he was hearing. He leaned back in his chair, bewildered. And then an image of Meenu came into his head, looking at him with her concerned expression. It couldn't be Jay, could it? he thought.

'I'm not going to ask again,' said the big auditor. 'Can you make it good?'

'No. I won't do that. I haven't done anything wrong,' said Mr Sidhu.

'Well, in that case we are suspending you immediately. The Post Office will send a temporary postmaster to take charge tomorrow. It will be closed for the rest of today.'

'In over twenty years I have never had a loss,' said Mr Sidhu. He didn't like the words they were using. 'Make it good' – what did that mean? There was nothing to 'make good'.

'You need to come with us immediately.' They gathered up their files and stood up, waiting for Mr Sidhu to do the same.

'Where?' asked Mr Sidhu.

'To the Twickenham sorting office. We need to ask you some questions.'

Mr Sidhu followed the auditors, telling Rose they had to sort out some issues with the post office. Rose came to him as he put on his jacket in the alcove.

'David, is everything OK? Is it the losses?'

Mr Sidhu managed to nod to Rose. She took his hand.

'What did they say?'

'I have to pay the money back,' he replied.

'What? Why?'

Mr Sidhu didn't want Rose to let go of his hand.

'How much is it?' she asked, her blue eyes searching his face.

'Thirty-five thousand,' he said, his voice trembling.

'*What?*'

The auditors called out for him to leave with them.

'Call me if there's anything you need,' said Rose, then pressed his hand and pecked his bearded cheek. He managed a smile.

Mr Sidhu sat in the back of the saloon car as the two auditors drove him the short distance to Twickenham Post Office Depot.

They got out and asked him to follow them. The depot was on the side of a train track next to Twickenham Station (TW1).

'Come with us.'

The two auditors walked together with Mr Sidhu following them. They walked into the sorting office where trolleys were filled with bundles of post tied up with rubber bands. Men stood around sorting out the letters into pigeonholes where other men took them and placed them into more piles, ready for them to be dispatched to wherever the address stated they should go. It was the life he'd had before buying his post office, when weekends were free and overtime was paid. They walked through more swinging double doors which no doubt allowed the movement of the trolleys around the depot. At last they opened a door with a handle and entered a simple room that smelled of cigarettes, with grey square carpet tiles and a table with four chairs around it.

'Sit down and wait. Someone's gonna come and see you. Ask you a few questions,' said the big one and then he and the younger one left.

Mr Sidhu sat and waited. The room was bare with no windows, and the only light was provided by fluorescent tubes hidden behind obscured plastic. There was a brown plastic cup on the floor in the corner of the room, like the ones that came out of vending machines that he saw in cash-and-carry. Mr Sidhu thought about what might happen. They had no proof that he had stolen anything. It was only the computer system that was saying it. The auditors were only repeating what the computer said. It was a waste of time them coming. He would tell them about when Alan came and that the loss doubled and then went away again. Alan could tell them and then they would have to look at the system again. It would be there in the records somewhere. He could tell them the date and then they could find it. And if they could change it then, well, they could change it now.

The door opened and two men came in. They could have been wearing identical suits to the auditors as they looked the same to Mr Sidhu. These two looked the same age, around fifty or so. One had a big, fat face like a child's and the other sterner, thinner, with thick-rimmed glasses and a thin, red nose matched with red cheeks, which made him look like he was continually blushing.

'Good morning, Mr Sidhu, we're from the Post Office investigations unit. We'll be interviewing you today, having a chat and getting to the bottom of things. Do you understand?'

It was the man with the child's face who was speaking. He said the last bit about understanding unusually slowly, while placing a tape recorder onto the table between them, and then pressed a button on it. They both sat down opposite Mr Sidhu.

Mr Sidhu nodded.

'Is that a yes, Mr Sidhu?' said the stern one.

'Yes,' he replied but was surprised at how dry his mouth had become.

'Mr Sidhu has indicated that he understands the nature of this interview,' the round-faced man said into the tape recorder. He continued, 'We're obliged to ask you if you require someone to represent you? You don't have to, of course. It can be a chat with us like this if you want.'

'No, that's fine,' said Mr Sidhu, finding his voice again and relaxing slightly, thinking that it wasn't a legal matter they were talking about yet.

The men looked through a folder on the table.

'So look, there's money missing and you're responsible for it. So where is it?'

Mr Sidhu was taken aback.

'I haven't taken it.'

'The accounts state that there's thirty-five thousand in cash at your branch. And the problem is that it's not at your branch. Would you make us believe that it's just vanished into thin air? Is that what you want us to tell Head Office?'

Mr Sidhu explained that he'd started putting the losses in as cash held at the branch in order for the accounts to balance each week.

'That's false accounting. That's not gonna look good, is it?' said the thin one.

'Thirty-five thousand pounds missing and an admission of false accounting. Well, is there anything else to add?'

'I never had any problem until the computer came. Look at my accounts for over twenty years, no problem. And it has only happened since the new computer. Maybe it is the training.'

'Oh, it's the training now, is it? Somehow when you were trained it wasn't up to scratch? Is that what you're saying?'

'Have you spent it? Did someone tell you to do it?' asked the baby-faced one.

'Where is it, Mr Sidhu?'

The two of them continued to alternate questions, making Mr Sidhu feel slightly nauseous with the constant barrage. He told them about the computer system and the losses.

'No one else has had these problems, Mr Sidhu. We've rolled out tens of thousands of these systems and no one has had a problem. Only you. Is that what you want us to believe? A hundred-million-pound computer system is wrong and you, a sub-postmaster, are right?'

They both laughed. Mr Sidhu told them about the losses on the system when Alan was there with him and how they had been rectified.

'You can rectify the losses,' Mr Sidhu told them.

The round, pink, child-faced man guffawed, 'Rectify your losses? Are you mad? This computer system is state of the art. The system can catch a mistake and correct it automatically, but it doesn't correct a balance with missing money. That is called theft, Mr Sidhu.'

The thin, thick-lensed man leaned into Mr Sidhu. 'Do you know a woman called Winifred Ogilvy, Mr Sidhu?'

He nodded; they were referring to Min.

'Could you explain why her payment card was in your post office? Also, they found written notes with payments and dates, some of which were future dated along with payments to the local pub. Can you explain that?'

'She is getting old so we help her,' said Mr Sidhu, thinking they would understand.

'It's fraud, Mr Sidhu. And theft. Also, there were stamps being stored outside the post office. That doesn't paint a pretty picture, I'm afraid.'

The two men looked at each other, shaking their heads.

'I have not stolen anything!' Mr Sidhu was starting to get angry. By now he would have had a nice cup of tea from Rose along with a digestive biscuit. Instead he was stuck inside this room with the brown plastic cup in the corner.

The men stopped and looked through their papers. The thin,

red-nosed, stern one started to speak, his eyes magnified by his thick-lensed glasses.

'Mr Sidhu. You are, whichever way you choose to look at it, responsible for the losses at your branch. That is just a fact. It might not have been you, but you are responsible. And false accounting too. Doesn't look good.'

Mr Sidhu clenched his fists. He was the only one who worked in the post office, so if it wasn't him it was obviously the computer. When would they address that!

'It could be,' the child face began, 'that someone else had access to the post office.' He looked at Mr Sidhu.

'It could be,' the pink, child-faced one continued, 'that someone else had access to the post office without your knowledge. Sometimes it's someone you know and trust, but their circumstances change and suddenly they need money, and they abuse their position.'

'You think everything's the same, but you don't know what's going on with someone else.'

'We've seen it happen before, haven't we, Keith?'

'We have, Colin.'

'A new pressure in their lives.'

'A sudden change of circumstances.'

'An old flame stirring things up.'

'A new flame stirring things up.'

'A drug-addicted son who needs money to feed the habit.'

'A mother who feels guilty about giving her son away for adoption and wants to help him. Or she just turns a blind eye to what he's up to. Uses her close relationship to the postmaster to hide what's really happening. We've seen it all, haven't we?'

'We have indeed.'

They both stopped talking. Mr Sidhu's mind whirled with all the information being thrown at him. Were they talking about Rose and Jay?

'Thing is, Mr Sidhu,' carried on Keith, the thinner one with thick glasses, 'Dave. I hope you don't mind me calling you Dave? Alan speaks highly of you. And we've looked at your file.' Keith stopped the recording and after a moment spoke.

'This is off the record, but we kind of know it's not you,' he said, his eyes softening.

The pink one, who Mr Sidhu knew was called Colin, now interjected, 'You're still responsible for the losses, mind.'

'Yes, the losses are on you as per the contract, but we know who it is,' said Keith, edging closer to Mr Sidhu.

'Who?' asked Mr Sidhu.

'We've been given information by a very reliable source that a man named Jay, who is the son of your employee Rose, had access to the post office and most likely took the money without your knowledge.'

'No. There is no money missing. Only the computer is saying it is missing. I have checked, double-checked and triple-checked.'

'Listen, Dave, if you confirm this information, then we can get the police to investigate him. We've got a good relationship with them. And it is highly likely they will get a conviction, given his circumstances and background,' the men exchanged a look. 'But that won't happen unless you make it clear that he had access through your employee, Rose. That you saw him with the keys or in the post office on his own. We can also make the false accounting go away. Then you can have what we all want. You keep the post office, carry on serving your customers. Or else we'll have no other choice than to prosecute you.'

Mr Sidhu sat open-mouthed. What was this nonsense? Was he being arrested? Why did everyone think Jay took the money? He rubbed his face with his hands, hoping this moment might be erased somehow.

'I want to see the balance,' he said finally. 'I want to see all the money going in and out. I will find it, I will find the money. I used to teach Mathematics.'

Keith and Colin exchanged a smile and then Colin turned to look at Mr Sidhu. 'You're clutching at straws here. I understand this is stressful. Of course it is. No one is saying it isn't. But remember, Dave, the computer cannot be wrong. It's a fact. You have to accept that. And if you accept that and that we also have evidence of someone having access to your post office . . . Well then, there's only one outcome, isn't there? Tell us about this man Jay.'

'Jay is a good boy.'

'Not really a boy, is he? Forty odd years old, according to our source.'

Mr Sidhu stopped. Was he going mad? Could everyone else see something he couldn't?

Was it Jay? Even Raju and Meenu suspected him. Mr Sidhu looked at the two men who were both staring at him with looks that said they had already made up their minds. He held his head in his hands, his palms covering his eyes so he couldn't see anything. 'Sarabjit,' he whispered silently to himself, 'help me. They are trying to ruin us.'

Chapter 18

'Dad, do you mind if I come with Craig next week? We're a bit busy this weekend.'

'No, beta, that's fine. Everything OK?'

'Yeah, fine. Everything OK with you, Dad?'

'Fine, fine.'

'OK, bye, Dad.'

'Bye, beta.'

Mr Sidhu hung up the phone. It was morning and unusual for Meenu to call at that time. However, he didn't know if he could face his children right now and he was grateful for the delay. Today he had to go to the post office and let in a stranger who would work in the place he'd worked and served for over twenty years. He also had to tell Rose she would no longer be required to work in the shop, as he wouldn't be able to pay her. He'd told the post office investigators to pursue him and not Jay. He'd done nothing wrong, and that would be proved in a court of law.

'But you've already admitted to false accounting, and the computer has got the evidence of theft. You're looking at prison,' Keith had told him coldly. 'We're going to send investigators to find the stolen money.'

It was outrageous, and Mr Sidhu told them, 'Fine, go ahead, the truth will come out in court.' He would not be cowed by these people who knew nothing about him.

So when he told Meenu he was fine, nothing could be further from the truth. Everything was far from OK. His children would find out eventually, but maybe, just maybe it would all work itself out before then. Even he knew a computer only did what it was told; surely the mistake would reveal itself at some point. He had to hang on to that idea. What was the alternative? That Jay had taken the money? No, that was wrong, he knew it in his heart. But he'd have to wait and see. He didn't like it that a nagging thought in his head kept repeating, 'Two different sets of people think Jay took the money. Could it be true?' He shook his head to get rid of it. At least there was some good news. He was going to see Meenu and Craig, and he didn't want anything to stop that happening.

Mr Sidhu went into his garden. He swung his arms and lifted his feet. He kicked the football and made himself breathless. It was summer, which meant the flowers were out and the grass needed mowing. He looked at the trees which Jay had cut back and made neater and less overgrown. Jay might be able to help him. He would try and find him. He needed to talk to him, explain things. Tell him about the stupid stories people were saying about him. Maybe he could talk to the investigators and tell them it was all nonsense. Maybe they would look at the computer system then. He finished his exercises and went into the kitchen to eat his porridge and then shower.

A noise filled with violence shook Mr Sidhu. He stopped drying himself and waited. There it was again. Someone was hitting the front door repeatedly. And now the doorbell was performing its long chime along with the very loud knocks. He went to have a look out the window. There was a police car and another car parked outside his house. He peered down at the four men standing outside his door. Two were policemen and two were the men who'd questioned him at the Twickenham depot: Colin and Keith. The thin one, Keith, looked up at him with his thick-lensed glasses and Mr Sidhu stared back and waved without thinking. Mr Sidhu's hair was exposed and he hesitated before going down. He wound his hair up into a joora on top of his head and then wrapped it in a patka. He put on his kurta pyjama and slippers, walked down the stairs, opened his front door and stood staring at the men, his legs in a wide stance.

'Hello, Mr Sidhu. We're from the Post Office special investigation unit – we spoke to you yesterday. We're here to conduct a search of your property in order to ascertain the location of some stolen money. Can we come in, please?' asked Colin, his pink, round face making him look earnest.

Mr Sidhu stood, not quite believing what he was hearing. He looked up and down the road, hoping no one was watching all this.

'If you don't let us do our job, it might make things worse for you,' said Keith. And then one of the policemen spoke.

'We're just here to keep the peace, so if you don't mind, I think you should let these men in so they can do their job.' His face showed no emotion. 'Is there anyone else in the house?' he asked.

'No,' Mr Sidhu replied, his voice breaking slightly. He turned away from them and walked back into his house.

263

'You know, you could make things easier for us and yourself too,' said Colin.

Mr Sidhu turned to look at the man.

He continued in the same matter-of-fact way. 'If you just give us the information we require, we can get the right person. Or else tell us what you've done with the money so we can all just save ourselves a lot of hassle.'

Mr Sidhu looked the man up and down. Whenever anyone was invited into his house they were treated as an equal, if not more. But now, this man who looked like a child and was a stranger wanted to come into his house and had already presumed him to be a thief. The world was upside down.

Mr Sidhu indicated for the men to come into his house.

'You want tea, coffee, water?' he asked.

The investigators entered, exchanging an amused glance with each other.

'No, that won't be necessary.'

They told one of the policemen to stand at the front of the house, the other to accompany Mr Sidhu wherever he was. And then the two men went upstairs and started to go through the rooms where his children used to sleep, and where he and Sarabjit had slept for so many years, and polluted his house with their presence.

The last time he'd felt like this was in the early Nineties when the British economy had crashed out of the European Exchange Rate Mechanism and interest rates had doubled and tripled in one day. The pressure had put a strain on his family. Even though Meenu and Raju were small, he'd noticed how quiet they'd become in that time. He and Sarabjit had had a terrible time, blaming each other for all the financial problems the business had created for them. If he could go back, he'd have protected his family from all that and allowed them to carry on not knowing. Because eventually the economic storm had passed, and even though so many of his friends had gone bankrupt, somehow he'd survived. And that, he always thought, was because his post office was in Richmond. A green and pleasant borough, as Richard called it. This time, he felt he could protect his children from all of this and keep his promise to Sarabjit.

The investigators finally finished looking through his house. They looked under all the beds, all the cupboards, even lifting up the carpet where it was loose and checking to see if any of the floorboards had recently been lifted. They'd scanned the garden as well, perhaps looking for recently dug patches.

'Well, it isn't here,' said Keith, cleaning the lenses of his glasses, his eyes looking small and his face narrow without them on.

'There's nothing because nothing has been taken,' said Mr Sidhu, even though for some reason he thought they might find something. He felt guilty but he didn't know why. It might have been because of the policemen; they added extra gravitas to the situation. He'd seen several neighbours looking with not curious, but fearful eyes. It was the look of anxious immigrants thinking, *What have you done? Why are you bringing shame to us? We are not with him!* He felt bad for that. But then he didn't really know anyone on the road. Each house had, over the years, been transformed from normal and semi-detached houses into small palaces with electronic steel gates, lion-topped pillars and expensive German cars filling the driveways, one for each occupant. But no one was ever seen. They came and went in

265

their cars and talked only to each other in their homes. It was nothing like his post office where people came in for a stamp or a pint of milk and lingered for a little gossip, knowing he would look after them. A tinge of regret came over him as he thought about the house he wanted to buy. He might never live in Richmond now. It would be careless to buy a new house with a bigger mortgage. He might lose his post office if all this craziness continued. Even his current house had a mortgage which he and Sarabjit had taken out to fund the deposits for their children's properties. Meanwhile the policemen and the investigators left, leaving Mr Sidhu to clean up after them. He'd be late at the post office.

'What's going on, David?' Rose peered at him through her glasses. She looked worried. It was 11 a.m. and he'd just arrived at the post office.

'I had to open up myself. And why's he in the post office?' she asked. He paused at her reference to opening up. Could Jay have borrowed her keys to let himself in to take the money? No. Impossible.

Mr Sidhu looked at the small, balding Indian man standing in his post office.

'Are you OK, David?'

He wanted to feel like he had in his dream when she was holding him, but he couldn't. And he needed to tell her about working in the shop, but again he couldn't find the words.

'I haven't seen Jay for a while,' was all he could muster.

'What?'

'The trees in the garden. They look wonderful. I wanted to tell him.'

'David. What are you talking about? Min was asking about her card. Is it in there?' Rose asked, indicating the post office.

Mr Sidhu could barely look at the post office. The temporary postmaster was finishing up with a customer and when he glanced up they exchanged a look. Once he'd finished with the customer, he came out of the post office and walked to Mr Sidhu, his hand outstretched.

'Hi, Ken Kukadia, nice to meet you. I'm the temporary postmaster.'

Mr Sidhu shook his hand limply and introduced himself. The name was Gujarati. East African, most likely, thought Mr Sidhu. There had been an influx of Gujaratis into the UK from East Africa in the Seventies when Ted Heath had welcomed them after they had been expelled by Idi Amin, for reasons Mr Sidhu knew nothing about. To Mr Sidhu, being East African made him once removed from India, unlike he himself who was Indian born. He didn't want to like this man. He knew the losses and the circumstances were nothing to do with Ken, but he resented him for standing in *his* post office.

'I hope I am not being insensitive, but it would great to get a set of keys. This morning you were not here and it was inconvenient to the customers,' said Ken, looking at him with a friendly smile.

Mr Sidhu wanted to drag Ken out of the post office, *his* post office, but instead he said nothing, just staring at him. The mention of keys again made him feel uneasy.

'And how long are you going to be here? It's not your post office, it's David's,' said Rose, coming to Mr Sidhu's side, instantly calming him down. Mr Sidhu breathed out, not realizing he'd been holding his breath.

Ken held his hands up, perhaps sensing Mr Sidhu's anger. 'Don't shoot the messenger, I'm just following instructions from Post Office head office.'

'Just following orders, I suppose,' said Rose. Ken and Mr Sidhu could sense an undertow, but only Rose knew what she meant.

'How long?' asked Mr Sidhu.

'They didn't say,' said Ken, looking a little unsure.

Mr Sidhu and Rose walked away together as if they were going to discuss something, but that wasn't actually what they were doing. Mr Sidhu simply couldn't bear looking at Ken inside his post office.

Mr Sidhu sat silently behind the shop counter with Rose as she served customers. The regulars noticed Mr Sidhu wasn't in the post office. 'Everything all right?' he was asked a few times, to which he just smiled and Rose responded with 'Something wrong with the computer. They have to check it.'

When the shop was quiet, Rose made Mr Sidhu a cup of tea and didn't offer to make one for Ken. 'What can we do?' she asked, cradling her tea, blowing steam off the top of it, her eyes searching for instruction. It was the nicest thing anyone had said to him for what seemed a long time.

'I don't know. I need to speak to Jay.'

'Why do you keep on about seeing Jay? Has he done something?' asked Rose. Mr Sidhu paused. *Had he done something?* 'Anyway, he's not around,' added Rose.

'What?'

'He's gone. Don't ask me where.'

'Why did he go?'

'You'll have to ask him, David. He does as he pleases. Why did you want to see him?'

'The trees in the garden look nice,' said Mr Sidhu, lying, 'I wanted to thank him.'

But that wasn't the real reason. He needed to ask Jay about the money and hear it from his mouth. But why had he gone now? Mr Sidhu couldn't shake the thought away.

'David, don't you think we need to talk to someone? Perhaps we could get Richard to have a look into this, see if there's anything he can do?'

Mr Sidhu didn't want help from his customers; that was his job – to help them. The other way round made him feel like a failure.

'No, please, Rose, I can manage this. I will do it.'

He didn't know what he meant by that, but he didn't need other people's gaze on him. He liked the customers being just that – customers. But for how much longer would they be his customers?

'David, come to my house this evening. I'll cook dinner,' said Rose.

Mr Sidhu didn't know what to say, even if the urge to go was overwhelming. 'Yes, OK,' he uttered finally.

*

That evening, they sat opposite each other and ate sausages and mash covered in beef and onion gravy. 'What can I do to help?' asked Rose.

Mr Sidhu was lost for words; nothing made sense. He didn't want Rose involved in all this. What if she found out what

269

Meenu and Alan were saying about Jay? She'd be furious. He'd already let her down.

'I'm going to speak with Richard next time I see him. Make sure you know what's going on. I mean legally. The Post Office can't just do this to you, David.'

'No, I don't want—'

'David, stop being proud,' said Rose, interrupting him. 'It's OK to ask for help, it doesn't mean you're weak.'

Mr Sidhu nodded. He needed to be honest with Rose. 'I can't afford to keep you working in the shop,' he said.

'I know that,' Rose replied, as if they'd already spoken about the matter, 'you don't have to pay me, David. It's fine.'

'No, Rose. That is not fair.'

'David. I said it's fine,' Rose stared at him, daring him to counter her. He knew he had to say more. He had to be in the shop to see what Ken was up to and to help his customers, because Ken wouldn't understand their particular needs. And he wanted a role. He wanted to be useful. If Rose was there with him, she would do everything, that's just the way she was. And more than all of those things, he didn't want Ken to be looking at Rose from the post office window. That was his view and he wanted to honour it. Since Sarabjit's passing, that view of Rose tidying up, putting away the stock and serving customers was something he cherished. He secretly hoped those moments would return. That he would be back in the post office and Rose would be back at the shop counter and everything would be back to what it should be.

'Please, Rose, just for the moment. It won't be for long, but I need to work in the shop, until all this blows over.'

Rose nodded. He could tell it wasn't what she wanted. But

she didn't say anything. She cleared the table and took the dishes into the kitchen. As Rose washed up and Mr Sidhu dried them in silence, Rose said casually, 'Stay here tonight, won't you?' He ignored her question and carried on drying the dishes, until Rose took the dishcloth off him. He could feel her looking at him as he stood, unable to say anything. By denying her place back in the shop, he felt he was in no position to accept her generosity. Rose gently laid her hands in his and tried to meet his gaze, which he reluctantly yielded to her. Looking into her bright blue eyes helped to break the spell and slowly he smiled.

Chapter 19

The following week, Meenu kept her promise to bring Craig over to Mr Sidhu's house. It was the first time in a long time, at least a couple of years, that he'd seen Craig. He liked Craig, and he and Sarabjit had been satisfied that his family were good and that they had no objections to their relationship. Their engagement had happened when Sarabjit was still alive. He thought it was a reaction to her illness, perhaps a ploy to keep her alive, but he never said anything about it. However, since the engagement, nothing had happened and now he wanted Meenu and Craig to be married. So, when Meenu confirmed that she was coming, he'd gone to the bank.

Almost every Punjabi he knew had a safety deposit box in a bank. His was at the local bank in Richmond. It was only opened in preparation for weddings or other functions, when Sarabjit would go and get some jewellery sets to wear. The 'gold', as he thought of it, was what the Punjabi women dealt with. The gold was actually a series of sets: a necklace with earrings, or bangles and bracelets or rings. As a man he had no interest in wearing it, only how much it weighed. The gold Indians wore was pure twenty-four-carat gold, soft and yellowish, unlike most of the jewellery he came across in

England, which was pale, hard and impure. And so whenever gold prices went up (usually during a recession or economic crisis), Mr Sidhu felt good. When it went down, he wondered if he should buy more, because there was never a thought or suggestion that it should be sold, even in the most desperate times, because it was not really theirs; it was something passed on by the women to the women. Sarabjit's mother had passed on the gold to her, which Mr Sidhu's mother had added to herself from the gold her mother had given her, and so on. That was the way it worked in Punjabi families. Mr Sidhu felt that the time was right for him to pass it on. And even though Meenu and Craig were not married, they were in his eyes pretty much married. It was sad for him that Sarabjit was not there to do her duty, but he would do it in her place. But he needed to see Craig first and do his duty as a father.

They arrived in the evening. He heard Meenu's car pull into the driveway. She'd offered to cook food, but Mr Sidhu told them it was unnecessary as he'd ordered lots of food from his favourite restaurant, Priya's. He didn't want Meenu to be fussing over food; he wanted them to be relaxed. He'd also bought a lovely selection of burfi to sweeten their mouths when the moment of handing over the gold was meant to happen.

'Hello, Kerayg,' said Mr Sidhu loudly, standing on the threshold as he motioned for them to come in. Craig looked the same as he always did except his brown hair was shaved short, making him look a little severe. He wore a tight-fitting blue shirt, which emphasized his slight paunch, with a pair of jeans and shoes. He was tall and Meenu looked impishly small next to him. Mr Sidhu shook his hand and then lightly embraced him with both hands as he walked into the house after Meenu.

'Hello, Mr Sidhu,' said Craig. He wasn't a big talker. He would speak to Raju if he was around, but without him there he didn't say a lot.

'Please, you can call me Dad. Come, come,' said Mr Sidhu, ushering them into the living room.

They arranged themselves in the front part of the lounge, next to the bay window which looked out onto the street. Meenu and Craig sat together on the two-seater while Mr Sidhu sat in his favourite armchair.

'It's been a long time, what happened?' asked Mr Sidhu, enjoying his role as the father-in-law. Meenu and Craig exchanged a look before Craig started speaking.

'Oh, you know what it's like, work's been busy,' said Craig.

'I understand, Kerayg. I missed to see your parents at Christmas,' said Mr Sidhu. He glanced at Meenu to let her know he hadn't forgotten the invitation, but her face looked stern.

'Of course, we missed you at Christmas too,' said Craig and turned to Meenu and added quietly, 'different priorities, I suppose.'

'Christmas is a busy time at the post office, you know,' said Mr Sidhu, feeling as if he had to explain himself, 'and there was a new IT system being installed, and it was taking a lot of my time up.' The enthusiasm in his voice was no longer present as thoughts about the IT system and the losses came into his head. He pinched his hand to change his thoughts. Christmas lunch with Rose flashed through his mind. It felt so long ago now. Meenu got up and mentioned tea.

'I made some already,' said Mr Sidhu.

'I'll get some cups,' said Meenu.

'There are some samosas too,' said Mr Sidhu.

Meenu went to the kitchen and the two men sat silently.

'Mum, Dad OK?' asked Mr Sidhu.

'Yes, they're OK, thanks,' Craig said without elaborating.

After he'd asked after Craig's brother and whether he was married or had children (he did not), Mr Sidhu decided there was nothing untoward and that he would pass on the gold, perhaps privately to Meenu, and do his duty.

Meenu served the tea, and they all ate the samosas, which Mr Sidhu loved along with the taste of hot tea. Once they'd finished, Mr Sidhu invited them to sit down for dinner.

'Dad, I know what's going on,' said Meenu as they tucked into the ginger chicken and muttar paneer dishes.

'What, beta?' asked Mr Sidhu, his body suddenly becoming heavy and leaden.

'The post office. I went to see you, and I saw a man standing in the post office. And it wasn't you, Dad. I didn't know what was happening and I'm sorry, but I called Alan to find out and he told me what had happened.'

'Don't worry, beta, everything will be OK,' said Mr Sidhu, waving his hand in the air, dismissing her comment.

'Dad, it's not you. I know that,' continued Meenu. 'I know you haven't taken anything, but one of the neighbours told me the police had come to search the house. What's going on, Dad? Why does everyone else know apart from us? Raju's very upset too,' said Meenu, deflecting away from her own feelings on the matter.

It was ruined. This was not how the evening was meant to be going, especially in front of Craig. Mr Sidhu explained that the losses had led to an audit and while they worked out what had happened, the Post Office had, for a short while, suspended him. It was a story he'd made up in case anyone asked him, and it sounded plausible every time he told it, even if the truth was that he feared the worst.

'Mr Sidhu,' said Craig, interrupting a short silence, 'it's been known to happen before.' His voice rang with a believable authority, which even Mr Sidhu listened to as if it were a BBC news reporter speaking – it was the same kind of serious plummy English accent he'd heard in Richmond. 'So don't feel ashamed or feel as if it's just you,' Craig continued. He was a journalist, thought Mr Sidhu; maybe he'd heard about other cases like his. Mr Sidhu listened attentively, 'People like him are used to deceiving well-meaning people like yourself. They don't have any remorse; they only want the money. I mean, thirty-five thousand pounds is a significant sum. He's probably done it before. The whole "*I'm a hippy*" thing, I mean, really, it's all a facade. I bet he's not even around any more. I hope I'm not being disrespectful; I do understand that you are in a relationship with his mother, but you should know he might have encouraged the relationship. There you are.'

Mr Sidhu could not believe his ears.

'Who told you this?' he asked. 'Who told you it was thirty-five thousand?'

Craig and Meenu looked at each other.

'Dad,' said Meenu, 'there's still a chance. I spoke to Alan. If you tell him about Jay and pay the money back, then you'll have your post office back. We can help you if you need, Dad.' She looked at Mr Sidhu with a supportive smile as if he were pathetic and needed help.

Mr Sidhu closed his eyes, feeling a tightening in his chest.

'I'm sorry I spoke to Alan, Dad,' said Meenu, every word cutting into Mr Sidhu like a dagger. 'I know you said not to, but I'm not going to stand by while you throw away everything that you and Mum worked so hard for.'

Mr Sidhu inhaled deeply, letting his belly expand, and then exhaled slowly. The feeling was not going away. He nodded and arranged his face into expressions that he thought would convey that he was pondering what they were saying. And they had a lot to say. They talked about something called catfishing and romance fraud committed by men in Nigeria. He wasn't really listening and hoped it would stop soon.

'Alan told me that if there were any discrepancies in the accounts, they would automatically be corrected,' Meenu continued. 'So you see, Dad, the losses are real, money has gone missing. The theft is real. And no one else is having these issues. Why can't you see what's happening?'

'I hope you're not planning to run away with . . .' Craig paused, unable to say Rose's name, 'back to India or something. You'll make yourself very vulnerable alone without the support of your family,' he added in the same serious manner as Meenu.

Mr Sidhu looked at them, so earnest in their belief. They belong together, he thought. Yes, they definitely belong together, they think as one. The idea of running away was ridiculous. If he was going to run away, it would be to Richmond. Although not in the way he'd thought he would. Now Raju would be angry with him, too. Meenu would have told him, and he would be thinking in the same way. Mr Sidhu cleared his throat and spoke:

'For over twenty years my accounts balanced perfectly, and since the new computer system has come in every week there is a loss.' It was all he wanted to say. He knew he could not change their minds, but they should know that at least.

'Wasn't it at the same time that you went to Rose's for Christmas lunch? Was Jay there? Did he ask you any questions about how the safe worked or anything?' asked Meenu, her face condescending and pitying at the same time. Mr Sidhu was dumbstruck. Meenu had never spoken to him like this. He needed to get them out of the house; their presence was starting to cloud his judgement. He needed to do his duty and not be engulfed by the torrent of accusation. He knew he couldn't stand up for Jay or Rose in front of them, as that would only make them firmer in their belief that he had been manipulated. He took a deep breath and put his feelings to one side.

'I have something for you,' he announced, getting up and leaving the room. He went to the kitchen cupboard where he had the grey metal box. It was locked and had a key. Inside were all the contents of the safety deposit box he'd kept in the bank and which he no longer needed. A while ago he'd swapped many of the necklaces that were no longer worn for thick, simple bangles to make it easier to store the gold.

Mr Sidhu walked into the living room and sat down with a box of burfi and a box of gold.

'Kerayg, in Punjabi culture when a woman is married, she is given the gold from her mother. When Meenu's mother married me, she was given the gold from her mother and also my mother gave her some too. That gold will be passed on to your daughter and daughter-in-law.'

Mr Sidhu opened the box of burfi and chose the patissa, his favourite burfi made from wheat and sugar with a hint of cardamon.

'So, is this a dowry?' asked Craig. 'Do I get to keep it?'

Mr Sidhu glared at him; he had the urge to slap him across the face. Instead he placed the patissa back into the box.

'Is this what you tell him, Meenu?' asked Mr Sidhu, hoping his voice was even.

'Dad, what are you doing? We're not getting married,' said Meenu, smiling for the first time. But he knew her smile masked an anxiety.

'You live together and share your life. This is same as marriage,' he said, raising his upturned hands. They both shifted in their seats.

'Marriage is a bit old-fashioned, Dad,' said Meenu, breaking the silence.

'A bit like the male heir getting the family wealth, or a bride belonging to her husband's family like chattel,' Craig added, grinning at Meenu as if they were sharing a joke. Mr Sidhu clasped his hands together so that he wouldn't slap him.

'He's just being funny, Dad.'

Mr Sidhu glowered at Craig. This was the second time he had been insulting and Meenu had not corrected him, even if he didn't know what chattel meant.

'Do you like living in Meenu's flat?' he asked Craig, who blushed. However, he was not here to be angry; he was here to do what Sarabjit couldn't do and what he might not be able to do if he wasted any more time. He took a moment and spoke directly to Meenu. It wasn't going at all as he'd anticipated.

'This is from your mother,' he handed the metal box to Meenu and at the same time took a piece of patissa and placed it in her mouth. 'You too,' said Mr Sidhu, indicating to Craig to open his mouth. Mr Sidhu chose a particularly large piece of burfi and slightly pushed it into Craig's panic-stricken mouth.

'Can I have a look?' asked Meenu, while Craig chewed and tried to swallow the burfi, his eyes watering.

'It's yours now, Meenu. But remember, it is only for you to hold on to until it is time to pass it on again. There is fifty thousand pounds' worth of gold there.'

Craig was finally able to swallow the last piece down as Meenu opened the box to reveal the bangles and rings and necklaces, which shimmered in the light. Meenu's eyes were watering now too.

'Dad?'

'Yes, beta.'

'Won't you change your mind? I mean, all you have to do is pay it back and let them investigate the real culprit. You can use this gold, Dad.'

Won't you change your mind and believe your own father? thought Mr Sidhu. Meenu had always had this streak in her. Even as a child she'd get an idea in her head and would make the world bend to her. When she'd lost one of her toys as a child, she accused everyone of stealing it, including Raju, who had been devastated that Meenu thought he'd stolen it. And when she'd found it (stuck behind a chest of drawers) she never spoke about all the drama she'd created. She acted as if she was entitled to have been angry and accusatory.

'I will talk to Alan,' said Mr Sidhu, being diplomatic and not wanting to spoil a moment which should have been a happy one.

'That's good, Dad. I think that's for the best,' said Meenu, nodding her head vigorously as if he'd already spoken to Alan.

They left soon after and Mr Sidhu sat alone in his house, wondering how long it would be until he would have to move out. He'd already put the house up for sale.

Chapter 20

Two months later and things were getting serious. Without his wages from the post office, Mr Sidhu found that everything was falling apart. He was behind on the rent for his lease and his mortgage. Most embarrassing of all was his inability to keep the shop stocked, leaving bare shelves and gaps in product lines. Sometimes he would go to the big supermarkets to buy single items (he could not afford to buy in bulk any more), just to keep the shelves looking stocked. The worst of it was that he had to see Ken Kukadia every day, knowing that he was getting his wages. The wages had been virtually nothing when Mr Sidhu first bought the post office, but with hard work, Mr Sidhu and Sarabjit had boosted them by encouraging local businesses to bank with them, and having stamps and travel cards available at the shop so customers didn't have to wait in the post office queue, making more and more people use it and turning it into what it was today. Now, seeing him take his wages so easily was heartbreaking on top of everything else. Ken was prone to coming to talk to Mr Sidhu during the quiet moments, as if they were friends.

'It's a good place here, David,' said Ken, taking on the name that his customers had given him. Mr Sidhu knew what Ken was up to. 'Good people, good place,' he continued. 'I had a place in Hampstead, same as this, but it was a main post office. Then the landlord put up the rent, he measured every square inch and charged me so much I had to leave it. Who is the landlord here?'

Mr Sidhu pretended not to listen to him, and Ken didn't seem to mind. He knew with every day that passed, it was getting harder for Mr Sidhu. There were bills to pay, business rates, electricity for all the fridges, and suppliers. Mr Sidhu knew he had a couple of months, but after that he'd lose everything.

The usual morning routine no longer gave Mr Sidhu any pleasure. The customers were there, but with Ken being in the post office, the noise was different. People knew what was going on and asked when he'd be back in the post office; he would simply say it was out of his hands, which was the truth. But there were comments he overheard too.

'No smoke without fire,' he'd heard someone say.

Customers didn't linger to gossip any more like they used to. And then there was Ken. Always jovial, walking into the post office as if he'd been there forever and would be there forever.

'David, did you ever have any problems with the balance?' asked Ken one afternoon.

Finally, thought Mr Sidhu, now they will know. This was a conversation he actually wanted to have with Ken.

'What's wrong?' he asked, trying not to sound excited.

'Each week the balance is coming up as *in arrears*. I've checked everything and I can't find anything wrong, but the damn thing says there is money missing.'

'Did you ring the helpline?' asked Mr Sidhu, suppressing a smile.

'Yes, they said it would correct itself, but it hasn't.'

'That's strange,' said Mr Sidhu. 'Perhaps you should call Alan Dankworth, tell him all about it.'

Mr Sidhu watched Ken behind the bulletproof glass talking into the telephone. He couldn't hear anything, but his heart was racing. Should he tell Darshan to stop the sale of the house? Mr Sidhu had approached Darshan about selling his house and the post office. Darshan had been surprised but also knew Mr Sidhu well enough to know he didn't make rash decisions. So he did what he was told. Mr Sidhu told him he wanted it done quietly without it being listed on the property pages or having a sign outside. Darshan had contacts, cash buyers, mostly Sikhs from Afghanistan who'd left after all the troubles and come to England to set up businesses with cash. They would buy – for a discount, of course – and quickly.

'Any joy?' asked Mr Sidhu, one of the few times he'd tried to start a conversation with Ken.

'Alan said he will come tomorrow, to check it. Thank you for helping, David.'

'No problem, no problem,' said Mr Sidhu. 'So, he's gonna do an audit?

'I don't think so,' said Ken, looking slightly confused. 'It must be the terminal, I think, someone is coming to look at it.'

Mr Sidhu's heart leapt. They're going to find the problem, he thought and then everyone will eat their words. He liked that expression. It summed up perfectly how he felt. That evening he went home with a spring in his step and called Darshan.

'Darshan, I think it is OK. Tell them the house is not for sale any more.'

*

The next day Alan arrived at the post office. It was a warm August day, and he was wearing a short-sleeved shirt and tie. He ignored Mr Sidhu and walked straight to the post office counter to talk to Ken. They spoke for a little while and then Mr Sidhu saw Ken and Alan looking at the terminal and then he saw the little printer roll whirring and delivering its verdict. At that moment, Alan looked up and met Mr Sidhu's stare. Alan looked away first. In Mr Sidhu's mind, even though it was childish, he felt that the moment was his; Alan had looked away first because he had something to hide, whereas Mr Sidhu had nothing to hide. Alan spoke into his telephone and then came out and walked to Mr Sidhu.

'The post office will be closed for the rest of the day. Could you tell the customers to go to the main branch in the town centre, please.' Alan didn't wait for a reply and simply left. Mr Sidhu wandered up to the post office counter to find out from Ken what was going on.

'Sorry, David, this is Post Office business,' said Ken. 'I'm not allowed to talk to you about it because, you know, you are suspended.'

'You asked my advice before, Ken,' Mr Sidhu reminded him. 'Is everything OK?'

'Sorry, David, Alan told me not to talk to you about it. You understand.'

Mr Sidhu nodded and returned to the shop, passing the half-empty dairy cabinet and empty shelves. He didn't feel as excited as he did earlier.

Later that day, Alan returned with two men carrying bulky laptop bags over their shoulders. They too wore short-sleeved shirts, and both wore glasses and had pens sticking out of their shirt pockets. Again Mr Sidhu was ignored as they went to the post office and stayed in there for the rest of the day. Mr Sidhu spied the men opening their bags and getting out laptops which they connected to the terminal. Mr Sidhu had no idea what they were up to. The two men stayed in the post office while Ken and Alan left for some unknown purpose, perhaps just to not be around.

Mr Sidhu served in the shop, unable to focus because of what was happening in the post office. It was a slow day, and he felt the disappointment more than any customer did every time he had to tell them he didn't have a particular product, like cigarettes. Cigarettes were an expensive stock to hold and buy but were essential for passing trade. When a person bought a packet of cigarettes, he might make five or ten pence on the packet but might make more on a lighter, chewing gum and maybe a drink or chocolate. But if you didn't have the cigarettes, they left without buying anything.

'Oh, hello, Mr Sidhu. How are you?' said Rita, pulling her pram into the shop. He noticed her hair was a different colour, a dark red rather than the black it used to be. She looked much better than he remembered.

'Good, good. Sorry, Rita, post office is closed.'

Rita looked at the post office where the two men were still working.

'Oh, I thought it was open. Shit,' Rita clenched her fists as her mouth tightened. 'I can't do anything right.'

'No, Rita, is normally open. They are fixing a problem.'

'Oh,' she said, her face brightening, 'I didn't get the wrong day then?'

'No. It's not your fault, Rita,' said Mr Sidhu, attempting to smile.

Rita looked at him.

'Everything all right, Mr Sidhu?' She looked around the shop. Mr Sidhu felt the shame of all the empty shelves.

'Yes, yes, fine,' he replied. 'I think post office will be open tomorrow.'

'And how come you're in the shop now? Why's that other bloke in there instead?'

'Oh, it's nothing. They are just trying to sort out a problem. Where are your other children? Please take some sweets for them,' he said, placing some Cola bottles and Cherry Lips into a paper bag for her to take.

'You don't have to do that, Mr Sidhu,' said Rita, taking the bag, and as she did so, she took his hand. 'Thank you for all your help. You're such a kind man.' Mr Sidhu did everything he could not to start to cry. Any acts of kindness towards him recently made him want to cry. He didn't know why.

'Hey, what's going on? Are you OK, Mr Sidhu?' asked Rita.

'Nothing, nothing. I am just a silly old man,' he said, taking his handkerchief out of his pocket to wipe away his tears. They stood together for a few moments.

'The kids are at school,' Rita said, changing the subject. 'It's my favourite time of day.' She smiled, 'Means I can have more time for her,' she said, indicating the now growing baby in the pram. 'I know what people are saying, you know, about the post office. But I want you to know that I know you're a good man, Mr Sidhu. You've a got a good heart, and if there's anything I can do, please just ask.'

Mr Sidhu nodded and, perhaps sensing that Mr Sidhu wasn't up for talking about it, Rita left. Maybe everything would turn out OK, he thought. Over the past year Rita had slowly become calmer and less in a rush all the time, and come back to herself. If that could happen for her, maybe it would for him too. Because he didn't feel like himself at all. However, things were not in his hands.

Finally the men finished and came out to buy some cold drinks.

'Everything OK?' asked Mr Sidhu.

'Yep, it is now,' replied one of the men, who sported a moustache and looked a little like the racing driver Nigel Mansell, in Mr Sidhu's opinion.

'What was wrong with it?' he asked, his pulse starting to quicken again.

At that point Alan and Ken pushed open the door, making the door chime go off, and they stopped talking as Alan saw Mr Sidhu and the two men standing together.

'What are you doing?' Alan said to the two men. 'You can't talk to him.'

Mr Sidhu felt a surge of anger. His chest rose and fell as he stood there witnessing the strangers who were telling him and everyone else he was a thief, that Rose and Jay were thieves too. He could have happily pulled out the rounders bat, hidden behind the shop counter, and knocked both Alan and Ken out. But he did nothing. The men went back into the post office and started the terminal. After a short while the printer whirred, rolling out its piece of paper. They examined the paper and passed it to each other, nodding and smiling. Alan and the two laptop men left, leaving Ken alone with Mr Sidhu. It was five-thirty so there was no point opening the post office now. Ken gathered his things, which consisted of a satchel with a thermos flask and steel tiffin boxes.

'It works OK now. They fixed it,' said Ken, coming over to talk to Mr Sidhu.

Mr Sidhu was lost for words.

'Listen, why don't we have a chat, David? You can't carry on like this.'

Mr Sidhu indicated for Ken to carry on talking.

'I'm a businessman, David, same like you. What would you do in my position? This is an opportunity for me, and you too. Your customers deserve better than this. I understand this is hard, but there is no point waiting until it is too late. My wife can work in the shop. She can take over tomorrow. Give yourself some peace, David.'

'What will you give me?' asked Mr Sidhu, his voice shaking a little. This was the first time he'd entertained the idea of actually selling the business to Ken.

'I will give you twelve thousand. I know it's not what you want, but even that is generous.'

So that was what he was worth now after twenty-seven years of building up a business. Only a year ago he could have sold the business for two hundred thousand pounds, but that was all lost now. Mr Sidhu looked at the post office and spied a little statue of the goddess Durga inside. It was Ken's, of course; she had multiple arms and sat on a tiger. In one of her arms was a stick of incense, smoking away. What if the incense stick fell onto the floor and started a fire? What if the whole place went up in flames? He would get an insurance pay-out. After all, Ken was the one who was burning incense sticks. He could tell them that.

'I will think about it,' he said. They looked at each other and Ken nodded. There had been a moment when Mr Sidhu might have considered his offer, but his voice had returned, it was no longer weak and shaky. They both knew there was no deal. Ken would wait and so would Mr Sidhu.

'See you tomorrow, David. Oh, and did you find the number for the landlord?' asked Ken.

Mr Sidhu ignored him. Ken lingered, weighing up something only he knew about. Was he going to offer him more money?

'Take the offer,' said Ken, looking around the shop. Mr Sidhu felt the presence of the empty shelves even more now. 'I know you need money. Think of your customers, David,' Ken pleaded. It was all Mr Sidhu could do to remain silent, to not grab the rounders bat, to not tell Ken that he would rather burn the premises down first before he let a stranger take what he and Sarabjit had built together.

'There will be a time when I will get this for nothing,' said Ken. 'I want you to have something. Have something for your children at least. Your pride will not help you.'

Ken left and Mr Sidhu was alone with his thoughts. He was opening his shop until 10 p.m. these days. There was no point in just going home and giving up. He could sell a few more items, get a little bit more money. But he knew whatever he did it would not be enough for all his outgoings.

Around eight in the evening, Richard came in for some milk, which Mr Sidhu had, making him feel good. Mr Sidhu was surprised at himself. What had his life become that he was thankful to have a pint of milk to sell to Richard?

'Sidhu Sahib, have they sorted out the issue? I saw the men come in today.'

'Not yet,' replied Mr Sidhu.

'Well, you can't go on like this, can you?'

Mr Sidhu put on his thin smile.

'Did you hear about Min?'

'No, what happened?' Mr Sidhu had completely forgotten about Min. He'd not seen her for a while and had not spoken to Ken about her pension card and book, which had been in the post office. He felt a pang of guilt and anxiety.

'Her son put her in a home, she was having a terrible time. I think between you and Rose, she knew she had some support, but they found her confused – not your fault, of course – she'd forgotten to turn off her oven and her house nearly burned down. She was in such a state.'

Mr Sidhu felt awful. He and Rose had always made sure they checked in on Min. There was a routine with her money and getting her shopping, but it was true he hadn't seen her come in for a long time.

'She is OK now?'

'Rose went to see her, but said she seemed very medicated and wasn't really like her old self.'

They both fell silent as if a death had been announced. Mr Sidhu wondered why Rose hadn't told him. Probably didn't want to worry him, he thought.

'Time waits for no man, Sidhu. We might be in her shoes one day. Hope your problem gets sorted. Can't have some random person running the post office. We need you back in there.'

That night, Mr Sidhu called Darshan again to tell him to carry on looking for a buyer. As he lay in bed, his mind was agitated. He thought about the way Alan hadn't spoken to him and what he would do if he saw him again. He thought about pretending he couldn't find the keys to the shop in the morning so Ken wouldn't be able to go into his shop and post office. So many thoughts. Silly old man, thought Mr Sidhu, and tried to repeat the mantra his father had taught him to relax his mind. It must have worked, because the next moment it was morning. And the feeling of dread returned. He wished he could have savoured his sleep; instead, he felt tired and groggy. He got up and started his routine: put on the porridge and went outside to do his exercises. Each movement felt laboured. Each mouthful of porridge felt like it might stick in his throat and suffocate him, no matter how much honey he put in it. Soon it would be autumn and then it would be cold and the winter would make it harder for his plan to work. He would need to talk to Jay about the plan.

Chapter 21

The next day listening to Ken talk to his customers made Mr Sidhu feel jealous. It was something he'd never felt before. He wanted to interrupt the conversations and tell the customers not to talk like that to Ken. The people in the area were *his* people. He had thought they came in for him, but now he saw things as they really were. They talked to everyone like that. The more time went on, the more customers got used to Ken being in the post office and Mr Sidhu being behind the shop counter. It was hell. Was Mr Sidhu the only one who could remember how things used to be?

Mr Sidhu called Alan.

'Ah Dave, how are you?' Mr Sidhu was surprised by the question and how genuine it felt compared to Alan's visit to the post office the previous day.

'Yes, fine, thank you, Alan. So you fixed the terminal?'

'What's that, Dave?'

'Yesterday you came, and you fixed the terminal. There are no more losses. Ken told me.'

'Oh, that. No, it was just a software update, Dave. You've still got to make good your losses. Is that what you want to do?'

'No, it is not,' said Mr Sidhu. There was a pause while Alan shuffled some papers. Mr Sidhu imagined that someone might be putting information in front of him. A piece of paper that told him that the losses had nothing to do with him.

'Dave, no one wants this to happen. The Post Office has always liked you. Just make it good, Dave,' he paused again. Mr Sidhu said nothing and waited for him to say something and then he spoke again, 'Or tell us who really took it. It's not too late. And then it can go back to what it was.'

Mr Sidhu could feel the energy seeping out of his body. Even the telephone felt heavy.

'No, Alan, I have done nothing wrong. Why are you doing this to me?'

'Dave, this is your last chance. Even your lovely daughter has offered to pay the money. Why are you being so stubborn?'

'Don't you dare ever speak to my family again!' shouted Mr Sidhu into the phone.

After a short silence Alan spoke again. 'Well, in that case, Dave, you are no longer suspended, you are sacked from the Post Office, and you will be charged for false accounting and theft. See you in court, Dave, and say hi to Meenu from me,' and the line went dead. It took Mr Sidhu a few moments to put the receiver back down. Court? What was happening?

The rest of the day was a blur. He served his customers; the smell of the incense from the post office was overpowering and the whirring of the fans of the dairy cabinets seemed louder than normal. He remembered telling Ken that he shouldn't light the incense; it was a fire hazard, and what would happen if the whole place burned down? Ken had looked at him and it felt like he might say something important, but then he just agreed that it was not a good idea to have incense.

'Good, that's good,' said Mr Sidhu. And it became his mantra for the rest of the day. Inside his head, he just repeated 'Good, that's good' – somehow it was comforting to know he'd done something good. Ken left at the usual time, around six.

'David, why don't you close up early today and get some rest? You look tired.'

'You make sure the incense is not burning, hahn, Ken?'

'Yes, I made sure, David. Get some rest, please.'

'You know, in the early Nineties they doubled, tripled the interest rates in one day. Seventeen per cent interest I was paying for this place. Can you imagine? Seventeen per cent. I survived. So many went under, but me and my wife, we worked hard, and we survived.'

Mr Sidhu could not remember Ken leaving. The shop seemed unusually empty. He checked that the open sign was showing and that he'd not changed it to closed by accident. He did that a few times, not remembering if he'd already checked it or just thought about checking it. Then he heard the door chime go off. It was Raju.

'Raju!'

'Hello, Dad,' his voice was flat. 'Why are you still open?'

'Oh, you know, keeping busy,' he replied, trying to stay calm, but suspecting Raju would notice how anxious he was. He suddenly remembered that Raju had been away in France.

'How was your play in France?' he almost shouted.

'Yeah, fine. Fine. Calm down, Dad.'

Mr Sidhu wondered why Raju was telling him to calm down. A moment passed.

'What's going on, Dad?' asked Raju.

'What is it, beta?'

'Stop it, Dad! Just. Please. I know what's happened. Meenu's told me everything.'

Mr Sidhu stayed silent.

'Where is he?' asked Raju aggressively.

'Who?'

'Jay! I'm not going to let some wanker ruin what you and Mum worked so hard for. Why are you protecting them, Dad?'

Mr Sidhu smiled for first time in a long time. Raju wanted to help him. He went to Raju and hugged him, even though his body was stiff and unyielding.

'I'm glad your play went well, Raju. We will talk soon. But not now. I have things to do.'

'What are you talking about, Dad? This is serious.'

Mr Sidhu's face fell. Raju was right. It was serious. He was going to court.

'Please, Raju, not now, please.'

Raju looked at him and shook his head. 'Meenu told me, but I couldn't believe it. He took the money, Dad. It's so obvious. Why don't you tell them Rose had keys too? Dad, please. Why are you protecting them? This is madness. You're going to lose everything.'

'I will talk with you, Raju, but please, not now.'

'Dad, why are you doing this?' pleaded Raju.

Mr Sidhu couldn't find words to say to his son. It was not up to him to try to defend Rose and Jay; Raju's mind was made up, he only wanted Mr Sidhu to do his bidding. Mr Sidhu thought about Ken and how he himself had made his mind up to not sell the post office to him. Here they were, father and son, stuck in their stubbornness. Raju said some more things to him but he could not remember what they were; he just waited for Raju to finish shouting at him. He was young and perhaps one day he would understand and come to him with the respect he'd shown for his own father.

Raju left as abruptly as he came. Mr Sidhu sighed with relief. It was too much for him right now. He needed quiet. The whirring noises of the cold fridges and dairy cabinets was loud again. The fluorescent lights seemed unnaturally bright. He was drawn to the post office. Had Ken left the incense burning? He looked. He hadn't. Mr Sidhu jangled his keys in his pocket. He still had a set of keys to the post office. He hadn't been in since the suspension. He wasn't allowed. 'Click', the door opened easily. He walked into the space he'd served in for so long. He sat on his chair. It was higher; Ken had adjusted it for his own height. He moved the leaver on the side of the chair, and it dropped down several inches. There, that was the correct height. He looked out through the bulletproof glass to the shop end. It was empty. The view he'd loved so much, which had given him a new lease of life, was gone. He looked down and spied the hockey stick he kept on the floor out of sight, next to the emergency foot alarm. He'd never used it. It was only for security reasons he kept it, just like the rounders bat. He'd brought the hockey stick with him to England from India. It was one of the few possessions he'd held on to. It felt firm in his hands. It took him back to his university days when he used to play. Neither Raju nor Meenu had ever been interested in the sport. He lightly tapped the

Horizon terminal with the stick. Then he did it again, a little harder. Then again and again and again. That felt good. He raised the stick above his head and smashed the plastic box with wires coming out. Oh, that felt really good. The hockey stick was well made, and it did not crack or break like the terminal had done. Bits of plastic splintered off this way and that. Some beeping noises came out of the machine but a few more whacks sorted that out. And finally it was done. It was dead. There were no more lights or noise from the whirring fan. Before leaving, Mr Sidhu smashed the little printer too. All that was intact was a spool of paper which spilled out of it like white blood.

To get to the river Mr Sidhu had to walk through the park. There was a footpath running through it, and even in the darkness there was light bleeding into it from the lights on the main road which hugged the park on one side. The other side of the park was bordered by a golf course, where Richard played, and joined up with Kew Garden further up the river. Mr Sidhu walked along the footpath which veered away from the main road and went deeper into the park and deeper into the darkness. As he walked he could feel the air getting cooler, and around him he could make out strange silhouettes on the regularly mowed grass. He approached the shapes and slowed down; they appeared to be about two feet tall – animal-like with thin, spindly legs. He couldn't make out what they were. He almost stopped walking as he neared the first one. Suddenly, it moved. It unfurled a pair of what seemed to Mr Sidhu huge wings. He crouched down, readying himself for an attack, but the thing just lofted up silently. It was a heron. There were about thirty or forty of them stood on the grass, all still like statues. Mr Sidhu relaxed and continued to walk, and they all one by one did the same as the first one – unfurled their wings, flapped them a few times and then settled a few metres away. Were they always here at night? he wondered. What were they doing? Were they wondering the same about him?

The path carried on ascending a small mound in the middle of the park where tall trees grew. One tree had what looked like a huge branch that had snapped off the trunk. It lay next to the tree with the tree innards exposed – all pale and in contrast to the dark bark. The fallen branch had old leaves which were brown and would never grow again, but the main tree was green and seemed unaffected. Mr Sidhu descended the mound until the park ended and the footpath joined the main path next to the Thames. In the summer months the banks were covered in green vegetation which was cut down now and again by the council. Now it was short, and he could see the river clearly. He walked towards Richmond, looking at the lights on the river path and on the bridges which were reflected in the water. He passed under the arch of the road bridge, which the main road heading towards the M3 passed over. His footsteps echoed under it, and he hoped it would not wake the person he presumed was a tramp. There was a construction made of cardboard and inside it was a sleeping bag, which was occupied. The zip was done all the way up and whoever it was looked asleep. Was it Jay? Mr Sidhu had never seen where he slept at night.

'Jay,' he said loudly. There was no response. He said it a few more times. The word 'Jay' echoed under the bridge, but apart from a grunt, he heard nothing. Mr Sidhu kept walking. There was another bridge fifty or so metres further along. It was an old metal bridge, coloured a pale green, with the date of its manufacture: 1908. A red and yellow South Western train suddenly passed over it, making a huge rumbling noise. The violence of the noise of the train on the metal tracks stopped Mr Sidhu, who admired the way the train passed seamlessly over the river. The lights were on in the train, and he saw a few anonymous heads inside it. He wondered if they were aware of how fragile the train seemed to be as it travelled over the hundred-year-old railway bridge. If anything happened to the bridge, the train would just fall into the river.

Mr Sidhu could see another bridge in the distance: Richmond Bridge. It was the one he drove over every now and again in the town centre. The one Min had painted. He suddenly felt sad thinking about her. The bridge was made out of a pale whitish stone and was lower than the rail and road bridge. He knew that near that end were pubs and benches where people would be, and he didn't want to see anyone or for anyone to see him right now. It was quiet where he was and it felt right to be here. He walked to the water's edge, looking at the rippling river and the reflections of the lights. Another train danced loudly across the bridge. Mr Sidhu let out a huge shout. There were no words, only noise. He let the noise of the train drown out his voice. And there, for a second, a memory bubbled up to the surface of his mind. When his children were small and Concorde was still flying, whenever it passed over the house it would make windows, doors, glasses and plates rattle – but above all it made every other noise redundant. He'd seen his children scream at the top of their lungs in the garden while Concorde roared overhead and he couldn't hear them, even though he was only yards away from them. Afterwards, both Raju and Meenu had told him that they hadn't even been able to hear their own screams. One step more and he'd be in the river. He wondered if he'd hear the train going over the bridge.

'Sukhdev?' a voice said.

Mr Sidhu was momentarily startled and took a step back from the river. He looked behind him and saw Jay smiling at him.

'Lovely evening, isn't it?'

'Jay?'

'Yes. You OK, Sukhdev?' asked Jay, looking at him intently, but still smiling.

'Yes, yes, I'm fine,' replied Mr Sidhu.

'You look a bit cold.'

'No, I am OK,' said Mr Sidhu.

'You're shaking, Sukhdev,' said Jay, taking Mr Sidhu's arm and guiding him back towards the path and away from the river. Mr Sidhu was unaware of himself shaking, but as he looked down at his legs, he could see them trembling. Now even his mouth was surrendering to it, and his whole body was in some kind of spell. What was happening to him?

Jay took his hand and led him back to the path until they found a bench. They both sat down; Mr Sidhu couldn't stop shaking.

'It must be the cold,' said Mr Sidhu, unable to talk properly.

'Let's warm you up, then,' said Jay, placing Mr Sidhu's hands in his and rubbing them. Mr Sidhu felt a sharp pain.

'What are you doing?' Mr Sidhu said accusingly.

'It's OK, I think you've done something to your hand,' Jay said gently.

They both looked at Mr Sidhu's hands in the light of a lamp-post. There were cuts and blood and what looked like a shard of plastic in one of them. Jay pulled it out.

'Doesn't look too bad. What did you do, get into a fight with a cash register?'

Mr Sidhu remembered what had happened.

'Oh, just something in the shop,' he said by way of explanation.

'We should get it bandaged up.'

'Where did you go, Jay? I wanted to see you.'

'Went to see some friends in Devon. What did you need to see me about?'

'Jay, did you do it?' asked Mr Sidhu, turning to look at Jay.

'Do what, mate?'

'The money. Did you take it from the post office?'

'Why do you think I'd do that?' replied Jay in his usual untroubled, unreactive way.

'They said you did it. Rose has keys. Did you?'

Jay looked at Mr Sidhu and held his hands, 'No. Sorry, Sukhdev, I didn't.'

Mr Sidhu wiped his eyes.

'I'm sorry, Jay. I didn't want to ask you, but I am not feeling well today.'

'Hey, it's OK, mate. No harm, no foul. Stand up, Sukhdev.'

'Hahn?'

'Please, just stand up,' insisted Jay.

Mr Sidhu stood up and Jay gave him a hug. It was a long hug; he'd not been embraced like that for a long time.

'I'm sorry, Jay,' said Mr Sidhu.

'It's OK, Sukhdev. It's totally OK.'

Jay led Mr Sidhu along the path and back to the park. As they passed the tramp under the bridge, Mr Sidhu told Jay he'd thought it was him.

'That's Johnno,' Jay said simply and then added, 'he used to be a soldier.'

'Where do you sleep?' asked Mr Sidhu.

'Under some of the railway arches.'

'Is it cold?'

'It is in the winter.'

'What about if you are in a van. Is it better?' asked Mr Sidhu. He had the idea that if he lost his house he could still perhaps sleep in his trusty van. It would save money and he could park it near the post office, which would save time in the morning. He might ask Rose if he could shower at her house.

'Well, yeah, you can heat up a van with the engine, but the metal will make it cold at night.'

Mr Sidhu nodded.

'How do you keep warm in winter?'

'Tubby keeps me warm and a bloody good sleeping bag and tent,' said Jay, pausing before adding, 'Thinking of joining me?'

'Maybe,' said Mr Sidhu. 'It's not a good time for me, I might lose my house.' He paused and then added, 'My father used to sleep outside.'

'I remember you said,' replied Jay. 'Why don't you stay with your kids? I'm sure they'd be happy to have you.'

'No, no. It is not good. They are busy. They work hard. I don't want to be a burden to them.'

Jay nodded and they carried on walking in silence.

'Where are we going?' asked Mr Sidhu suddenly, thinking Jay might be taking him back to the post office which he didn't want to go to after the damage he'd done there.

'Rose's house. I left Tubby there.'

Chapter 22

Mr Sidhu sat at the kitchen table looking out the window. The garden was small but he'd got used to its array of flowers in pots on the ground and in beds against the wall, some even hanging off the back wall, giving colour to the space. An overhanging apple tree from next door delivered big green apples onto the concrete ground which were now in various states of decay. Tubby knew the apples weren't tennis balls but would play with them for a little while, more to show Mr Sidhu he was up for fetching rather than for his own benefit, as he didn't really like apples, Mr Sidhu believed.

Jay was away again, this time at a music festival, something Mr Sidhu knew nothing about, and had left Tubby with him and Rose. Mr Sidhu was ready and so was Tubby. They walked out of the house together and made their way to the park by the river. The park was nearly always empty and Mr Sidhu enjoyed walking Tubby there, which Jay had sensed and let Mr Sidhu walk him regularly. At first Mr Sidhu and Jay would walk Tubby together, but over the last couple of months Mr Sidhu found that the dog was quite intelligent in his own way and responded well to him, almost coaxing him to walk him. Mr Sidhu hadn't been close to an animal since his days as a boy in his village, when he'd lead the buffalo to the chuppar, or milk them in the courtyard in his father's house. And being with Tubby, seeing how he turned to look at him when he'd wandered too far to check if Mr Sidhu was there, made Mr Sidhu wonder if it wasn't that Tubby was actually checking that he was all right.

The morning walk consisted of following the path that went through the park. Then strolling through the trees at the top of the mound in the park, where the grass was longer and felled tree trunks lay horizontal and Tubby leapt about and sniffed. After the park he walked along the river, under the two bridges and then left down Old Palace Lane, where Rose had shown him the Old Palace, and on to Richmond Green, where at the weekend there were games of cricket. He was only 63 but he felt as if he was retired. He had no work; his children were, if not settled, at least secure. From the Green he'd walk back home and avoid going towards the post office where Rose was working in the shop now and also try not to think about the immediate future. Would he survive all this? He couldn't believe things had gone so wrong. He expected at any moment that someone would call him or visit him and tell him that they were really sorry about all this confusion and that they had found the problem and it was all fixed. But no one did. Instead the Post Office, the company he had worked for almost half his life, was doing everything it could to ruin his life.

When Rose had cornered Richard one evening in the Arms about Mr Sidhu's plight, she insisted he do something about it.

'Rose, my dear, I haven't practised for years,' explained Richard.

'But you know how it works, Richard, you know David. Are you really going to tell me you can't help? After everything he's been through. I expected more from someone like you,' said Rose in the manner few people found easy to disagree with.

The pub was all interested now. Gerry stopped drying glasses and people looked up from their newspapers and drinks. Richard could feel the expectation in the air. He looked at his pint of ordinary and as he made up his mind, he finished the last of the beer inside it and placed it down on the bar.

'Fine. Rose, I can't promise anything, but I'll see what I can do.'

'Richard, you are a gentleman.'

Gerry poured out a pint and placed it in front of Richard. 'On the house, Dicky boy,' said Gerry, never having called Richard by his full name. Mr Sidhu didn't go to the Arms in the evenings any more; he found himself shrinking away from his locals. The burden of explanation and the anxiety about everything that was happening was too much for him to keep telling people about. Tubby asked no questions and gave him comfort. When Rose told him Richard would help, he felt bad that he was troubling people. 'David,' Rose admonished, 'you have helped everyone who comes to you for help, this is the least he can do. Will you please stop this idiotic idea that asking for help means you are weak. We all need help sometimes.' Even Tubby was cowed by Rose as she spoke. Mr Sidhu understood what she was saying but it wasn't something he was used to. He'd made it in this country with no help from anyone, and that was part of who he was. To change that idea of himself would be hard. But he tried as best he could, because he knew he had to.

It was a Saturday morning and Mr Sidhu was on his morning walk with Tubby, but today he was meeting Richard to talk about what could be done to help him. On the green, members of a cricket team were arranging white plastic flags to mark out the boundary, along with two sets of stumps perched on the neatly prepared wicket at the centre of the green. Tubby ran over to Richard as soon as he sensed him. Mr Sidhu joined Richard on one of the wooden benches set at intervals along the boundary of the green, sheltered by big plane trees.

'I'm afraid they're proceeding with a criminal trial,' said Richard, cutting to the chase. 'They want to get a conviction. It's ludicrous, they don't have any evidence of theft. But unfortunately they do have your admission of false accounting. That's the rub.'

Mr Sidhu said nothing. He didn't know what to say. Did it even matter if he said anything? No one seemed to be listening to what he said.

'Look, Sidhu, don't worry. I think I can get them to drop the theft charges if you pay the money back. But they insist you have to plead guilty to false accounting.'

'No, I haven't done anything wrong.'

'I know that. We all know that. Unfortunately, the Post Office have deeper pockets than us. They can afford to prosecute you on theft charges and get all sorts of specialists in, and if they lose they've still got you on false accounting. But if you only plead guilty on false accounting, it will be a slap on the wrist and you can move on.'

Move on? thought Mr Sidhu. How can I move on when they've taken everything? But what could he do? It was in the hands of the law now.

'I will get a good barrister to represent us, Sidhu. I still have some influence in those matters.'

*

That night he told Rose he would be going to court.

'*What?*' she exclaimed. And now Mr Sidhu felt that he needed to defend Richard from Rose's outrage. 'This is appalling, David.'

'Richard said I have to plead guilty to false accounting and then I will avoid jail.'

'Is he sure about that?' asked Rose. 'I wouldn't trust anything the Post Office say.'

Mr Sidhu couldn't believe what had happened to his life. No house, no business. The possibility of going to jail. And his children weren't speaking to him either. They held on to the belief that he was choosing Rose and Jay over them. He would never do that. He loved them, but he didn't agree with them. It was mainly Meenu's assertion that he'd been hoodwinked by Rose and Jay, and now Raju believed that too. The only people who believed him were Richard, Rose and Jay. Even some of his locals were frosty towards him, and he'd hear the odd comment about 'thieving' and 'cooking the books'. He tried to remain aloof, but the comments hurt. Even when people were trying to be kind to him, he could tell that they felt sorry for him, and he didn't need pity. He wanted the truth: that he'd never done anything illegal. He wanted someone to get to the heart of the matter – the bloody stupid computer system.

'Unfortunately, the law deems a machine to be just that: a machine which works as well as it should unless there is evidence to the contrary. In this case, we don't have that evidence,' Richard had said to him many times over the last couple of months.

Darshan had at least been understanding when Mr Sidhu had approached him again to sell the house. Darshan was practical when it came to sorting out such matters and he'd used his connections to get Mr Sidhu a buyer – an Afghani Sikh with plenty of cash. He'd paid him quickly, and for that Mr Sidhu gave him a 20 per cent discount. After the purchase, Darshan asked Mr Sidhu if he wanted anyone to visit Ken. Mr Sidhu didn't at first understand what Darshan was alluding to, but Darshan explained that he 'had some connections with the Afghans' and that if he wanted he could 'call someone who would let Ken know that he shouldn't make such a low offer to his friend'. When Darshan told him this, Mr Sidhu could detect the demeanour of the younger Darshan he'd known from the early days. It made him smile, but he told him, 'It's fine, there's no need.' Darshan had regarded him for a moment, then said, 'You know, Suki, everyone thinks it is this Jay boy who has taken the money. That is what Meenu is telling everybody.'

Mr Sidhu looked at Darshan, probably the only true friend he had in the world, someone who knew where he came from and what it took to make it in this country. But at that moment Mr Sidhu couldn't think any more about anything. His mind was full to the brim. He just needed to get through the next few weeks. Darshan squeezed Mr Sidhu's shoulder and smiled. He told him that the money for the house would be with him once the solicitors had sorted out the conveyancing. Darshan took a cool 1 per cent of the transaction, just like an estate agent.

Mr Sidhu had felt the discount he'd given on the price of the house was necessary, owing to his situation and needing money immediately. But then, by the end of the summer, a global banking credit crisis had hit and Mr Sidhu was happy to see property prices tumble.

The credit crunch, as it became known, was due to a mistrust between banks over who was holding bad debts. Over the previous ten years the banks had given out all sorts of mortgages without proper checks on the reliability of people to pay the mortgages back (which Mr Sidhu, Raju and Meenu had all taken advantage of). And as the banks bought and sold debts and financial products between themselves constantly, which was in essence the global financial system, when they stopped trusting each other, they stopped the flow of money. The property market was hit first, prices plummeted, and he realised he'd actually made a good deal. It was during that moment that Raju had called him in an anxious state.

'Dad, what have you done to me?' he'd implored like a kicked dog, seemingly having forgotten that his own father was possibly going to jail.

'There is no problem, Raju, just weather the storm,' he'd told him, happy that his son was talking to him again. Raju was worried because everyone was talking about a property crash and because he didn't follow the property market, he felt he was in danger or needed to sell his property. Mr Sidhu knew that in reality Raju was in a privileged position, especially for someone whose career path was as uncertain as his. Most people never had that kind of opportunity, but Raju didn't have the experience that he had. Mr Sidhu, however, had no idea that the credit crunch would deepen over the next nine months, making interest rates go to nearly zero and causing house prices (and asset prices) to soar, making Raju and Meenu even more secure. Not him, though. He only had a small pot of money left over from the sale, which he kept hold of for legal expenses and paying the rent on his post office premises. The only reason he kept paying the rent was for the idea that somehow the truth would come out and that he would return to his post office, and work and serve in the place that he loved. But Richard had told him repeatedly that this was impossible.

'They've got the evidence of the losses and false accounting, Sidhu. There's no way a jury will find you not guilty. Take the plea of guilty to false accounting and live the rest of your life without going to prison. This is serious.'

Richard urged him to make the plea and he said he'd think about it. The case was only a few weeks away and a decision needed to be made.

The night he'd arrived at Rose's with Jay, his hand bleeding and his body shaking, he was unable to understand what had happened. He looked like a lost child holding a bleeding hand, incapable of looking after himself.

'What happened, David?' asked Rose as she examined his hand, turning it over and checking it. Mr Sidhu cried and wiped away the tears from his face.

Rose smiled gently. 'You really are a silly old bugger, aren't you?' She cleaned his hand with a wet towel, red marks smearing onto it from the cuts.

'What happened to your hand, David?'

'I killed the computer,' he said finally.

'About bloody time, David,' she replied.

And they smiled at each other.

Jay and Rose went into the kitchen while he looked around Rose's house and remembered the first kiss they'd shared.

Christmas seemed like a lifetime ago now. A very different life. Min's paintings still hung on the wall and he remembered how Richard had described her.

'Why didn't you tell me about Min?' he asked Rose.

'I didn't want you to have any more worry, David.'

He wondered if that was what awaited him. To be in an old people's home (something unthinkable when he'd lived in his village in Punjab) and to be left there, medicated and no good to anybody. He'd rather be dead. He was so thankful to have this moment in Rose's house. The world was too big for him, it was swallowing him up, and the only thing that was protecting him was Rose's front door.

He gave his keys to Rose, who went to the post office to clean up. He was fearful. The damage he'd done to the terminal and the fact that he'd been sacked from the post office meant he'd become nothing. Yet, he had to keep reminding himself that he'd done nothing to deserve that. Luckily, Rose and Jay were on his side and wanted to look after him, something he was unused to but needed at the moment. That night, Rose told him he'd be sleeping in her bed. He tried to refuse but she told him it was OK. And he knew she meant it. He didn't want to impose anything on her, bringing all his troubles to her door, but the thing was that when he was with her, his troubles didn't seem so bad, so he went with that.

The next morning, Rose told him to rest and that she would deal with the shop and Ken. Mr Sidhu tried to resist, but she told him firmly there was no way she was letting him go to the post office. He gave in and spent the day at the house, mostly with Tubby as company. Whenever he entered the same room as Tubby, the dog started to wag his tail and look at Mr Sidhu with wide eyes and ears pinned back. It took all his willpower not to stroke him every time he did this. Rose came home at 6 p.m. that evening. 'What did he say about the terminal?' asked an eager Mr Sidhu.

'I said we were cleaning in the post office and the terminal fell over and broke.'

'What did he say?'

'Nothing. He said the Post Office would replace it with another one.' Mr Sidhu nodded silently and was relieved he'd not made things worse.

It was the first time in a long while that Mr Sidhu had stayed in the house for a whole day without leaving. He stayed in Rose's house without venturing further than the back garden and opening the front door. And it was only by Tubby's constant prompting that Mr Sidhu started to venture out with Jay and Tubby. But never near too many people, just into what Mr Sidhu learned was called Old Deer Park. A place where, during the day, you could count the number of people in it on one hand. It was during these walks that Mr Sidhu started to grow attached to Tubby. He'd worry about him when he went running after another dog, or ran out of sight. And in turn Tubby would nudge Mr Sidhu's hand with his nose whenever he felt the need, asking for a stroke, or to be fed.

Chapter 23

It was a brisk November day when Mr Sidhu went to court and pleaded guilty. He wore what he always wore: trousers, shirt, V-necked pullover, tie, shoes, jacket and of course his matted beard and turban. Richard and Rose took him to Kingston Crown Court in Richard's blue Jaguar. Mr Sidhu knew the date was coming up but when it actually arrived he wanted someone to tell him that there was a delay, or that it was on another day and not on this day, in this moment. In his mind he'd had all sorts of things to say, speeches that everyone listened to. Some were calm, some were full of anger, but now the day had arrived, all he wanted to do was run away. He could hardly speak for fear of the consequences of the day. He looked to Rose and Richard to tell him what to do; what time he had to be there and what was going to happen.

'It's all in hand, Sidhu, we won't let you down. A slap on the wrist is all you'll get,' Richard repeatedly informed him.

Mr Sidhu had agreed to plead guilty to false accounting. He would not be charged with theft as long as he paid the Post Office the missing money. Nearly fifty thousand pounds, it turned out to be in the end. He just wanted it all to be over. But it still hurt a lot to give them his money. He was glad he had the money to pay it, but he wasn't happy to pay it. The money left from the house sale was dwindling and he refused Rose's offer to stay rent-free at her house.

He'd had to attend several hearings at the local magistrate's court in Richmond, which was a modern white building where there was a blue plaque stating that someone called George Eliot had lived there. Mr Sidhu had never heard of George Eliot and he'd never been to a court before either. He'd watched television shows like *Rumpole of the Bailey* and *Crown Court*, in the Seventies, when he'd been working shifts. The tone had always been serious, and now the wigs the barristers wore didn't seem ridiculous. He knew some men who'd been to court and even to jail for theft and violence, but never him. Mr Sidhu had always obeyed the law.

Mr Sidhu pleaded not guilty to theft, which the Post Office had initially charged him with, and the Post Office had asked for time to investigate it. The fact that the Post Office wasn't in a hurry made him think that perhaps they had discovered where the losses were coming from. He'd kept in that way of thinking for a few weeks, feeling hopeful that things would work out after all. But in the end the Post Office said that they would agree to a lesser charge of false accounting and he would need to make good the arrears.

'You won't go to jail if you take this plea,' said Richard.

'But they are wrong. I haven't done anything,' replied Mr Sidhu as they sat on Richmond Green watching a game of cricket.

'It's your call, Sidhu, but if they get a conviction you will go to jail. Good shot!'

That evening he said nothing to Rose as they ate. She was

tactful enough to know not to press him. Even Tubby laying his head on his lap and looking at him could not get him out of his funk. So he'd agreed to the false accounting. It was true that he had pretended to have cash in the post office that he didn't, but that was only because of the losses.

So here he was, waiting to be sentenced for false accounting.

'Why didn't they want to charge me with theft?' asked Mr Sidhu, 'You said they had evidence. Why didn't they want to do that?'

'Sidhu, be thankful they didn't. They could have put you behind bars.'

It didn't square in his head. Just like the old balance sheets he used to fill out. It was like an empty column that needed to be filled. Had they found something? Had they found the error?

'If they know there is a problem with the system, then I shouldn't accept the false accounting charge,' he told Richard.

'Sidhu. The Post Office is doing you a favour. Rather than have a trial which will cost a lot of money and which could also land you in jail, they are saving time and money by getting the money back, giving you a slap on the wrist. The judge will also see it like that, which will be good for you. Now, please. Can we do this as we've discussed?'

Mr Sidhu agreed. But something smelled off. It was as if the law was also a business. He'd never thought of it like that. Not the law courts. He understood the business of law when buying a property or creating a lease, but he could see now that everything in a court of law cost money. The court, the barristers, ushers, solicitors, security guards, everything. And the longer it took, the more it cost. So he was just a problem that needed solving in the most efficient manner possible.

'A fine, and maybe a suspended sentence. We'll have character witnesses,' Richard told Mr Sidhu.

He waited with Rose while Richard disappeared to talk to his barrister, a nicely spoken woman, Louise, who came to inform him that she would do everything she could for him, but also that the judge on the case wasn't particularly lenient. Rose got a thermos flask out of her knitted bag that she normally used for shopping.

'Here you go,' she said, handing Mr Sidhu a small plastic cup full of tea. She got out a Tupperware box and opened one corner of the lid before opening it fully. Inside were two samosas.

'Something to get you through the day.'

'Thank you,' he said while he munched on the samosa and sipped the hot tea. And there, for a moment, everything else evaporated.

'If I was in your position, what would you get me?' Rose's eyes looked at him with a hint of mockery. 'Just in case it ever happens,' she continued, 'I'd have tea with a freshly baked scone with strawberry jam and fresh cream.'

An image of the jar of strawberries and cream sweets came into his head for some reason. It was always popular, the small candies coloured red and white with a sprinkling of sugar. He felt sad that he wouldn't be pulling down one of those jars off the shelves behind the till and weighing out a quarter of an ounce for a customer and letting the sweets fall into the white paper bags. Another bite of the samosa and sip of hot tea alleviated his melancholy.

At 10 a.m., Richard told Mr Sidhu to come into the court.

Rather than being a place which, in his mind, would be traditional and aged, the courtroom was bright and the furniture was made from new-looking wood – probably laminated, he thought. The idea that he would examine it when he got close to it evaporated once he realised that he was the focus of the proceedings in the court. There was a raised area where the judge sat, and in front of him were several rows of desks with chairs behind them. All the furniture looked new. Mr Sidhu sat where he was told by the court clerk. Richard had told him the judge would ask him his plea and that he should answer as they had discussed. He'd paid off the fifty thousand pounds that the Post Office had accused him of stealing in order to avoid going to prison. By giving it to them, he knew in his heart that he would no longer be running the post office. What else would he do? He had no idea. His landlord had also informed him that he would not waive the ten years' worth of rent that he owed on the lease. Added to all the credit for milk, bread, cards and other stock that he owed for the shop, he knew he'd be bankrupt.

'All rise,' said a court official in a loud voice. Mr Sidhu rose along with everyone else. A door opened and a judge wearing a wig and a gown entered the courtroom and swiftly took his place and sat down. Everyone sat down. One of the ushers told Mr Sidhu to remain standing.

'In the case of the Post Office versus Mr Sukhdev Singh Sidhu, how does the defendant plead to the count of false accounting?'

Mr Sidhu cleared his throat and said, 'Guilty.'

After the judge left the courtroom, Mr Sidhu watched as the barristers and solicitors talked with each other, smiling and relaxed.

Did no one care that he'd just admitted guilt for something he hadn't done? He wanted to shout at them to have some respect. But he didn't, of course. Richard told him he would have to return to the court for sentencing. So he went back to Rose's house as a criminal. And also bankrupt with no business and no property. They could fine him, but he wouldn't have any money to pay it with.

Chapter 24

It wasn't the way Mr Sidhu thought he would be living in Richmond. Not living in his own house and not working in his post office. Instead, he was walking through the park with Tubby, rotating his arms and walking with his knees high up. He wore his fleece jacket and the boots that he'd bought with Rose, which were perfect for the fresh November mornings. Jay was with him today. He hadn't said anything when Richard told him it might be better if he didn't come to court. It must have hurt him. But he took it in his stride and never mentioned it. Mr Sidhu could see now why Rose had been so angry with him; there must have been many times that she'd have felt other people's gaze on Jay.

'Why did you call him Tubby? He's not fat,' said Mr Sidhu, looking at Tubby, who was sniffing about in the long grass. Jay smiled.

'King Tubby was a music producer. From Jamaica. I love his music and wanted to say his name often. So Tubby became Tubby.'

Mr Sidhu nodded, not really understanding much of what Jay had just told him.

'How are you bearing up, Sukhdev?'

Mr Sidhu took a moment to absorb the question. He knew he was simply trying to get through all that was happening and not think about it at all. And if his mind started to dwell on a particular thing which might spiral his thoughts and make his heart quicken in a way that made him want to stop everything, then he did what his father had told him to do. He said '*Satnam Sri Waheguru Ji*,' and repeated it and repeated it until the thoughts subsided and he could feel his breathing coming back to normal.

'It is not in my hands, Jay,' he said. 'You know the situation. I have lost a lot already, but I can take it. My children are OK. That is the main thing.'

'I'd love you as my dad,' said Jay in his unforced way.

'My children don't think like that,' said Mr Sidhu, almost smiling. There was something about Jay that made him relaxed in the way that an old friend might do.

'They will, though. I'm sure, Sukhdev.'

And with that they carried on walking in a comfortable silence.

Mr Sidhu thought about his children, who hadn't been in touch since his suspension and sacking from the Post Office. They kept their silence and Mr Sidhu kept his. Jay's words comforted him a little, but he was still disappointed that they chose to believe the Post Office over him. Darshan had been in touch a few times, and even offered Mr Sidhu money if he needed, but he refused.

'You are always so relaxed, Jay,' said Mr Sidhu. They were walking along the river, not far from where Jay had found him that evening when he'd smashed the terminal. The riverside was quiet with only a few fellow dog walkers, joggers and cyclists venturing out in the calm of mid-morning.

'Yeah, a lot of people say that,' replied Jay. 'I used to be angry all the time when I was young. Perhaps I just got bored of it.' He smiled to himself as if remembering something.

Mr Sidhu remained silent, giving Jay space to express himself.

'I mean, I get annoyed in the moment and lose my cool. But I remember being angry when I was young and looking for things to feed it. Does that make sense?'

Mr Sidhu nodded. He remembered a foreman at the coffee factory he worked at in Southall. The Englishman didn't like the Indians or West Indians and kept finding things to be angry about, not doing this right or that right, or not saying words properly. And because he did it all the time, it became a joke where Mr Sidhu and his fellow workers would wind him up on purpose.

'I used to be angry at everyone. My adoptive parents, teachers, kids at school, the police and anyone in authority really.'

They passed Richmond Riverside, with its grassy banks which rose up to an office building that wouldn't look out of place in any European capital city. It was a busy place in the summer months – the pubs and restaurants there creating a kind of giant beer garden. But now in late autumn it was empty and peaceful. They continued along the path, passing under Richmond Bridge with buses and cars above them.

'But luckily I managed to get rid of all that,' continued Jay.

'How?' asked Mr Sidhu, genuinely interested.

'I travelled. I saw the world. Europe, Africa, Asia and the Caribbean and Australia, the States and South America. It was wonderful. And what you realise is that people are actually nice. Most people in the world are nice and want to be happy. And for some reason I didn't know that.'

They were walking towards Petersham now. The river meandered away as the path they were on forked; one branch followed the river and the other crossed through a meadow with Richmond Hill rising up beside it, with its big houses and grand hotels. They crossed through the meadow which had cows grazing in it, which Mr Sidhu had never seen before.

'They bring those cows in over the summer and soon they'll take them to their winter retreat to have their calves.'

'Really?'

'Yes, I spoke to the guy who looks after them. The grass here can't sustain a herd in winter.'

They reached the end of the meadow where there was a metal turnstile. Mr Sidhu paused as if to ask whether they should carry on or go back.

'You OK to keep going?' asked Jay. 'We can go to the park and then up the hill?'

Mr Sidhu nodded.

They passed through a turnstile and then along a track until they reached a small church. There was a sign which read 'Commonwealth War Graves' outside the graveyard. Mr Sidhu saw some well-tended gravestones not dissimilar to the ones he'd seen in Suffolk when he'd visited Maharajah Duleep Singh's grave. Were there Sikhs buried in this graveyard too? The thought troubled him. What if he was buried after he died? Did he need to tell Raju and make sure he was cremated?

The path ran behind the church and came out onto a main road, on the other side of which was Richmond Park. They entered the park through a black metal gate and immediately there was a big playground and a nice sandy path to walk on. Jay indicated for them to go up the hill which was on the left.

Mr Sidhu agreed. They walked silently up the hill, which was much steeper than he anticipated. He had to stop several times. Jay, however, kept up a steady pace which Tubby more than matched, turning to look at Mr Sidhu every now and again.

At the top they had a view over all the trees and a golf course next to the park. As they got their breath back, Jay spoke again.

'What was it like when you first came to England?'

Mr Sidhu had never been asked the question before. He'd only been a boy really when he'd left Punjab. With all the others, they'd left their land, their language, culture and their elders to live in a place where only money seemed to matter. They'd had no experience of this country and no elders to discuss it with. Mr Sidhu had only had the actions of his father as an indicator of how to live, and he'd tried to stay true to that, even if ironically now he had no money or wealth, whereas only a few months ago he was what most people would have called well-off.

Mr Sidhu didn't know how to reply to Jay's question. But he tried to answer truthfully.

'We kept to ourselves. I'd never met an Englishman before I came to England. I thought they would all be like in the films, wearing nice clothes. It was a shock to me when I saw poor English people. And the houses, row after row in the roads. It was like a labour colony – not what I was expecting at all. I don't really remember a lot. It was confusing. And cold.'

'I bet.'

'I was very angry when Sarabjit my wife died. She had cancer.'

'Sorry to hear that. Rose told me.'

'My children tried to comfort me, but I pushed them away. I was angry that I was alone. That Meenu wasn't married and that Raju was not serious. I felt sad that Sarabjit did not see a grandchild or her children married. I thought maybe we had been too relaxed with them. And I would get angry and tell them to be serious and get married. But in the end, I only pushed them away, and now when I need them they are not here. I think anger only hurts you in the end. Maybe all this is my punishment.'

Mr Sidhu looked at his hand. There was the scar from the piece of plastic that Jay had pulled out of his hand when he'd killed the Horizon terminal with his hockey stick.

'Look,' said Mr Sidhu. 'I only ended up hurting myself.'

Jay smiled and started to laugh. Mr Sidhu found himself unexpectedly joining in. Tubby sat waiting, his tongue lolling out of his mouth, his breath quick while he watched.

That evening Mr Sidhu, Jay and Rose ate out together as a kind of celebration. It was bittersweet, because the next day he would be sentenced and it would be the end of the saga. It was not only the end of dealing with the legal matters. He'd agreed a deal with Ken, too. Ken had upped his offer a little and paid cash for the stock, which meant Mr Sidhu wouldn't have to be liable for the lease any more. The money left over from selling the house was dwindling away since Mr Sidhu had no income from the post office and hardly anything from the shop. The rent and rates and bills ate away at his money, but with no post office and shop, his liabilities went away – but so did the possibility that everything would go back to what it was. So Ken took over the lease and Mr Sidhu didn't have his post office any more. It would be Ken who greeted his customers and made small talk with them. Mr Sidhu had never imagined it would be like this. He was glad Sarabjit wasn't there to see it happen. It was a sad moment for him, to see everything he had worked hard for be taken from him at a rock-bottom price. Ken had even given the moment some solemnity by bowing slightly to him when he'd signed the papers.

'You are doing the right thing,' Ken said. Mr Sidhu didn't say anything. Nothing was right about the situation. He was being forced into it. He was being made to leave, made to lose all his wealth and humiliated in front of the very people he'd served for so many years. It was done then, finally. It was always going to happen if the Post Office didn't reinstate him. And they hadn't. They'd done everything they could to disprove his version of events, and so there it was.

He gave Ken the keys and that was it. The landlord had agreed to reassign the lease and the Post Office had agreed that Ken could take it over. He walked out of the post office for the last time. He looked back at the post office end, where he used to look at Rose, the jars of sweets, the cards carousels, the cigarettes behind the counter. Mr Sidhu stopped; he'd forgotten something. His hockey stick. Ken went to retrieve it and handed it to Mr Sidhu. It felt good in his hands, like something that was part of him. He noticed a few dents in it and smiled. At least he'd put up a fight, he thought. He looked at Ken, who looked a little anxious with Mr Sidhu holding the stick. Mr Sidhu tapped the stick in his hands a few times, resisting the urge to smash the jars of sweets and cash register and even the big shop windows. He sighed and left without saying anything more to Ken.

*

In bed together, Mr Sidhu and Rose nestled up against each other, neither one able to say anything that might lighten the moment or allow them to forget what was happening.

'I'm sorry you've had to go through all this, David,' said Rose gently.

Mr Sidhu squeezed Rose. 'No, thank you, Rose. Thank you for everything. You are like the people in my village. They help when someone is in trouble. I am lucky to find you.' He thought about telling her about the dream he'd had about Sarabjit and her, but thought better of it. Instead he said, 'I never thought I would be living in Richmond.' He wanted to say something about Tubby too and how much he liked him, but he didn't think it was appropriate.

'We're all lucky to have had you, David; everyone around here loved the post office when you worked there. It will never be the same.'

'At least I have some money now for the fine,' he said, trying to sound upbeat, but both of them were silent as the idea of sentencing entered their minds. Mr Sidhu went to sleep, hoping that from tomorrow it would all be over and that he could start to build his life up again.

Chapter 25

The next morning Richard drove Mr Sidhu and Rose to court. No one felt like saying anything. They arrived and went into the court building. Richard told them to wait outside the court until they were called in by the court clerk for sentencing. As they waited, Rose handed Mr Sidhu a holdall, which she'd been carrying with her.

'What's that?' he asked.

'The barrister told Richard that the judge they were expecting isn't here today and that the one the court appointed isn't very lenient,' said Rose.

Mr Sidhu thought for a moment that Rose had given him a bag of money to pay for the potential fine the new judge might give him. Rose saw the confusion on Mr Sidhu's face.

'Richard told me yesterday that there is a very small chance of getting a custodial sentence.'

'What? Custodial. What is that?' asked Mr Sidhu.

'It's just a possibility, David, it's not a sure thing, but the barrister said the judge is a bit old-fashioned and can be severe. And it might mean that you go to prison. But I'm sure it won't happen. Richard called me last night to talk to you, and I told him I'd tell you.'

Mr Sidhu went pale. He had not considered that possibility. In fact, Richard had made him take the guilty plea for false accounting so he wouldn't go to prison.

'No, I don't want this,' he said, dropping the bag to the floor so it lay between them like a small dog.

'David, once you get sentenced you can give it back to me. But please just take it in case. For me. Humour me.'

Mr Sidhu didn't understand what 'humour me' meant, but he understood that Rose was doing this for him.

'What's in the bag?' he asked.

'Clothes, toiletries. Digestives and some samosas.'

'I can't do this, Rose.'

'David, it will be OK. It's only in case. It's just better to be prepared, that's all.'

Mr Sidhu stood in the dock, feeling self-conscious. He was shocked to see about thirty of his local customers all waiting in the public gallery.

'Before sentencing I believe the defendant has character witnesses?' said the judge, whose mood shifted between boredom and impatience. He noted things down in a book and told Louise, his barrister, to bring in the character witnesses. One by one they came to tell the court about Mr Sidhu.

The first was a middle-aged man wearing a suit. Mr Sidhu didn't recognize him straight away.

'My mother was a local customer and used the post office for her pension and shopping. Mr Sidhu always helped my mother, especially when she was getting elderly. He stopped a thief from using her pension book once and checked up on her if needed. He would even take her shopping to her house if she found it too heavy to carry. He arranged her bill at the local pub to be paid so she wouldn't have to worry. Without him she would have lost those last few years of independence which she cherished. She's in a home now, but thank you, Mr Sidhu, for all the help you gave to my mother. And I want to say on the record that I do not believe he is a thief.'

It was Michael, Min's son. He'd forgotten about him. Next up was Rita. Mr Sidhu felt embarrassed by his customers talking about him like this in public.

'Mr Sidhu has always been kind to me and my three children. After my husband died suddenly, leaving me with my three young children, I found it terribly hard to think straight and organize my life, and Mr Sidhu was always there to cash my giro, give me credit if I needed it and just be kind. He couldn't have stolen anything. He's too honest.' Rita turned to him and smiled as she finished. Mr Sidhu half smiled back out of habit.

Bill shuffled up to the witness stand and Mr Sidhu took a moment to recognize him. His Brillo pad grey hair was smoothed down over his head and he'd shaved and put on a shirt and tie. He looked smarter than he'd ever seen him.

'I've known Davey, I mean Mr Sidhu, for over twenty years. No one's got a bad word to say about him. He gives me work when I need extra cash, always happy to help any of his locals. Used to a be a tiny little shop and him and his wife along with their two wee bairns made it into a thriving business. Aye, he did more for our little community than anyone else. You ask 'em. They'll let you know.'

Bill performed a small salute to Mr Sidhu as he got off the witness stand. The judge looked annoyed and sighed audibly, but Mr Sidhu wasn't sure why.

Then there was the Harley Street doctor who'd told him to exercise to keep his heart strong, and the architect who'd advised him when he extended the shop at the back and made the basement deeper, the lady pensioner who was always made up and impeccable, Gerry from the Arms who described the tens of thousands of pounds he deposited into the post office after rugby matches and never had to worry because it was always correct and then finally it was Rose.

'He's been here for over twenty years and there's not one person who hasn't been served by his kindness: opening late, or unlocking the shop so you can get something, paying later, asking for something and the next day it's there. Even when his dear wife passed away he only closed for a few days, and you would never know anything was amiss. He served us well, and we miss seeing him behind the counter.'

The judge took a moment before saying anything after Rose spoke. He looked irritated, and toyed with his pen before looking up at the courtroom.

'Mr Sidhu, it is evident that your local customers hold you in high esteem. However, the crime you have admitted to is false accounting, and that pertains to Crown money which serves pensioners and others who are served by the state, and it is therefore important to show that the courts do not take this lightly. I am not sure why you committed such an offence; however, given the number of witnesses who attest to your good character and that you have paid the money back, I am reducing the sentence from twelve months to six months in prison. Court dismissed.'

And with that the judge hit his gavel and stood up.

'All rise,' said the clerk.

There were shouts and lots of talking. Mr Sidhu could barely stand, but two guards helped him to stand and started to lead him away. 'You need to come with us,' one of them said as Mr Sidhu grabbed the holdall that was next to him.

He looked around the court. He saw so many faces looking at him, but he kept scanning the room until he saw Rose. Her eyes looked powerless behind her spectacles and he could see her mouthing his name: 'David.' The guards led him away, but before he exited the courtroom, he turned one last time and saw them: Meenu and Raju. Their eyes had the same look as Rose's. He smiled reassuringly at them. He did not want them to feel bad about their beliefs. He was still their father.

He was ushered into a van and taken away. The whole time he thought he would be able to speak to Richard and tell him, 'You said I would come home', but there was no one. He sat in the prison van, looking out of the reinforced bulletproof glass window. The world looked far away and without sound. He had no idea where he was going or what would happen to him. He could hear someone else shouting in another part of the van. He didn't know it then, but he would get used to that over the next few months. After what seemed like hours, he was taken out of the van and into a prison courtyard. It was cold as he stood with other prisoners, their breath visible. They were ushered into the prison which would now be Mr Sidhu's home. He was taken into a room where he was told to empty his pockets and take off his clothes, including his turban. The prison guard looked unsure as Mr Sidhu untied his turban, revealing his patka underneath.

'You need to take that off too,' he said. So Mr Sidhu did as he was told. Another guard wearing rubber gloves rummaged around his head and beard and looked in his mouth. Mr Sidhu did not know why he was being searched in this manner. The strangest part was when he was asked to sit on a chair naked with a hole at its centre like some kind of toilet. The guard then examined his rectum. It was all Mr Sidhu could do to not shout and scream. He was given his clothes and patka and told to get dressed. The guards looked on impatiently at him as he tied his patka to cover his plaited uncut hair. He left his turban in his holdall.

He was taken to make a phone call. He waited a moment while the guard explained to him that he could make one call for two minutes. All his instincts told him to not make any call. This was not the real world. This was somewhere else, some kind of purgatory. He had no desire to talk to anyone, not even Rose. She would bring her presence to a place that was not for her. His children would become emotional and he didn't want that either. He called the only person who would understand.

'Darshan?'

'Suki?'

'Ha. I'm in prison!'

'Hahn?' exclaimed Darshan.

Darshan knew what was going on with the Post Office and the accounting issues but had no idea Mr Sidhu was going to prison. Mr Sidhu hadn't told him about the sentencing, not wanting his community to know about his problems. Mr Sidhu explained everything that had happened to him. Darshan quickly asked Mr Sidhu what he could do.

'My bank account details are at Rose's house. Tell everyone not to come. I will not call. I will come out in six months.

I do not want anyone to see me here. Tell Meenu and Raju not to worry.'

'Suki, you will be out in three months. I will come to see you. I know how it works.'

'OK. But I don't want anyone else to see me here.'

Mr Sidhu was taken to his cell. The guard unlocked the thick metal door which had a hole to see inside the cell from the outside. Mr Sidhu stood looking at his new home. The floor was a kind of grey plastic, there was a metal toilet in the far corner with no seat and a wash basin next to it.

There was a metal bunk bed and a thin man lay on the bottom bunk.

'Take care of the new boy, won't you, Harry?'

The thin man with lank brown hair sat up.

'Of course, boss.'

And with that the guard went away. Mr Sidhu was left with the stranger and his holdall. He was also given a bag containing a few biscuits, an apple and bottle of water, as well as soap and a cheap plastic toothbrush and tiny tube of toothpaste. He also had a sheet and blanket for the bed.

'First time?' asked the man, in a friendly manner.

Mr Sidhu nodded.

'Don't worry, you get used to all of this. It will become normal in next to no time. How long you in for?'

'Six months,' mumbled Mr Sidhu, unable to move.

'Oh, you'll be fine, you'll be out in three months. Just in time for spring. What's your name, pal?'

Mr Sidhu thought about what to tell him.

'Sidhu,' he said finally.

'Sidoo. I'm Harry. I'll show you what's what. You have the top bunk. You can put your things there.' He indicated the shelves attached to the wall. The walls were covered in layers of beige paint that just about showed the outlines of the bricks underneath. Mr Sidhu placed his sheet and blanket on the bed.

'It's time to eat; I can show you where to go.'

'No, thank you, Harry,' said Mr Sidhu. 'I am tired. I want to rest.'

'You won't get any food, Sidoo.'

'It's OK, thank you.'

Mr Sidhu heard all the prisoners making their way to the canteen to eat their dinner. He hadn't eaten since breakfast but wasn't hungry. He sipped water from the plastic bottle he'd been given. The idea of not being able to get anything he wanted felt like a kind of paralysis. He removed the clothes from the holdall Rose had got for him: seven pairs of pants and vests and socks as well as three pairs of trousers and four shirts and two V-necked jumpers. He also removed the toiletries bag and the Tupperware that had the samosas in. It was empty. The smell of the samosas lingered but that was all. He brushed his teeth in a room that smelled of urine and bleach. He lay on the top bunk with the lights on.

Over the next months he would mount and descend that top bunk many times a day. The worst thing was the light. There was no control switch. It was turned on in the morning and turned off at night by the prison guards. On the top bunk the light woke him up every day. Harry below him was able to keep sleeping. There was a window high up in the cell made with reinforced glass covered with metal bars; the only light it let in was from the floodlights outside, especially in this winter season. That first night he didn't sleep much. He awoke several times, hearing shouting and screaming. Harry seemed not to notice the noise and slept through. Even though it was dark, it wasn't cold, but more than anything it was terrifying not knowing the source of the noises and screams.

There were nights when he thought people were dying. The howls echoed around the prison. He found he couldn't eat a lot. He lost weight. His clothes became baggy. He came across people who were obviously in mental confusion. People hurt themselves, cutting themselves and sometimes banging their heads against walls. There were no other Sikhs in the prison, but there was a scattering of Muslims. He didn't want to befriend anyone in this place. It was not real. It was as if he were away from his own life. He didn't look too much at all those things that he found disturbing and instead got into a routine. Harry woke up late, around 7.30 a.m., so Mr Sidhu woke up as silently as he could around 5 a.m. before the lights came on. It was relatively quiet in prison at that time. He performed his exercises, raising up his knees and rotating his arms. In prison he did push-ups too, due to the space, and he did it all with his eyes closed, thinking sometimes about his village, sometimes about his old garden, but mostly about walking in Richmond with Rose and Tubby. After his exercises he sat cross-legged on the cold floor, a few feet away from the foul-smelling toilet which he had to share with Harry. He waited to use it when Harry went out of the cell, but other times he had to go with Harry there and it was humiliating. He had to clean himself and let the smell envelop the room. Invariably Harry would light up a cigarette, to get rid of the smell, something else Mr Sidhu had to put up with. But strangely, as Harry had predicted, he got used to it all in a short time.

The moment he relished the most was when he closed his eyes after his exercises. He sat cross-legged, hands open on his knees as the priest in his village had told him to do when he was a boy and had always done since, and then silently repeated, '*Satnam Sri Waheguru Ji*' over and over and over again. He could still hear all the noise of the prison, but he could equally be back in his garden or go to his village, sit with his father or Sarabjit, and even hold Rose or walk with Tubby. It was a skill that had begun when he was a child and found the mundanity of the Gurdwara too much. Along with his brothers and other kids, he would be taken to the village Gurdwara to listen to the priest reciting from the Guru Granth Sahib. It would last for hours and he discovered that he could disappear into his mind and go on adventures, or just work things out that troubled him. One day the priest scolded him for not listening, but he also took his hands which he'd been clenching and told him unclenching them would help him. And it was true. He sat cross-legged and placed his hands on his knees with the palms facing up, as if pulling the power of the world into his body. He didn't have to even try to disappear consciously; all he had to do was to repeat the words that every Sikh knew: 'Satnam Sri Waheguru Ji' – '*Great is the Divine, the teacher who leads me from darkness to light.*' And soon enough he was off, away somewhere in his imagination.

But it was hard to forget where he was now. It wasn't like when he'd arrived in England in the Sixties when everything was new to him and he had to pretend he understood the ways of this new land in order not to look stupid or backward. Here

340

in prison the constant noise of men talking or the odd scream, the frequent shouts and that clinking of keys and the slamming of metal doors brought you back to where you were; away from everything you cared about. And what was true here was that no one cared about you. Not even the guards. They laughed at prisoners in distress, and prisoners had to be subservient to them, like unloved children. Here he was in prison, with no house, no business and no relationship with his children. And without Rose too. He'd let them all down; that was how he felt about it all. Perhaps he should have paid off the losses himself when they'd first started, then he could have carried on working. But for how long? All paths led here to prison. Because the Post Office never believed him and had all the information they needed to convict him. He wondered where all the transactions he used to write out by hand in ledger books were. All those years of writing out the figures: the amounts of stamps bought, the money coming in and out, never a mistake, and now that was all forgotten. All it took was a computer to say he was wrong and the Post Office took everything away from him. These thoughts went round and round his head. He barely engaged with the world around him. He only hoped one day the truth would come out, but instead he had become the one thing he never wanted to be in his life: useless. He was no use to anybody any more. His days went mind-numbingly from one to the next. His covered head did not get the attention he'd thought it might and perhaps he had something written large on his face as everyone left him alone. Perhaps they could all see what he could see: that he was nobody. And if he was here or if he wasn't, it didn't matter.

Most days he stayed in his cell, apart from when he had to

shower and was allowed a little time to exercise. Mr Sidhu felt that the prison guards wanted the prisoners to stay in their cells. They didn't want them mingling with other prisoners. Mr Sidhu didn't mind that. He liked to touch the handles on his holdall now and again. It was where Rose had held them when she gave it to him.

'Suki, don't worry about your brothers, they are not like you,' his father told him. 'They will do what we have always done here. We are lucky the land gives us everything here. Now you must go and do something new. Find your life, puttar.'

He was remembering the day he'd left his village to go to Delhi to get his flight to London. Ahead of him had been a fifteen-hour bus journey, first to the district capital Moga, then on to Ludhiana and finally Delhi. It was October, a time when the rains had passed and everything was washed clean from the monsoon. The sun was less harsh, even in the middle of the day, and as he leaned his short-sleeved arm out the bus window he could feel the cool of the air against his skin. He passed miles and miles of fields, which grew sparser and the land more developed until Ludhiana, where the industrial world took hold. Hawkers crowded his bus as it stopped at the bus station, letting people off and others on. Ludhiana people were more brusque; passengers getting on pushed past others trying to get off, someone placed chickens stored in wooden crates on the floor, and there was even a goat, which passengers now had to navigate around. All the while a chorus of hawkers called out, trying to get their wares to customers – 'Chai! Chai!' and 'Coffeeee! Coffeeee!' and also 'Santra, Santra!' – the men using various vocal techniques to get the passengers' attention.

Sukhdev indicated to a plump man with freshly fried samosas to give him five to get him to Delhi. It was then and now Mr Sidhu's vice. They had got him through his exams at college; he was able to buy them and eat and work without stopping. They were the ideal meal in a snack. As the bus waited, a boy carrying a big blackened steel kettle and a stack of terracotta clay cups trod carefully through the aisle to serve tea to whoever wanted it. And Mr Sidhu relaxed. Hot, sweet, milky tea and samosa, it was all he needed.

He was only allowed to take three pounds with him to England under the currency laws in India. Being only twenty years into its creation, an independent and democratic India tried to stop large amounts of money leaving the country, so three pounds was all that men like Mr Sidhu had to create their new lives. The money was hidden in a specially stitched pocket under his shirt.

Before he'd left his father's house, his brothers were angry when they found out his father had sold land for his aeroplane ticket. They'd made a scene, making it hard for his father to say goodbye properly.

'When he comes back with his tail between his legs, then you will see Sukhdev is useless,' shouted Billoo, his wife looking on with their children looking frightened. His own mother was trying to calm Billoo down, but not with any authority or conviction.

'Go, beta, go and do your best,' his father told him. And he had. He'd travelled to England and worked as hard as he could with Sarabjit by his side to honour his father's faith in him. Mr Sidhu was happy his father wasn't alive to see what had happened to him. He must have been dreaming, he thought, because in this memory his father was beside him on the bus, enjoying a samosa and a cup of sweet, hot tea from one of the terracotta cups, which passengers would throw out of the window when they'd finished with them. It pleased him to feel close to his father again. And this time in this memory he could take his hand and thank him for all that he had done for him. His father smiled and as he got off the bus he looked in the mirror at himself and it wasn't him at all. It was Meenu. He looked around at his father and he wasn't there; instead, it was him and Sarabjit waving at him. He woke up with a start, nearly banging his head on the ceiling. He hadn't thought about Meenu since he'd seen her in court. He lay back down, thinking about what he'd just seen. It troubled him.

Chapter 26

The routine of prison life became normal, even if being in prison was far from normal for Mr Sidhu. However, it was the boredom that got to him the most, so he asked the prison guards if he could do some kind of work as he'd seen some prisoners doing various jobs. A week later he was told he could help clean the kitchen if he wanted. Mr Sidhu eagerly told the guards that he'd been a cleaner when he'd first come to England, but they didn't really seem interested in that.

'Anything goes wrong, you break anything, you'll be confined to your cell,' was all he got in reply.

Mr Sidhu accepted the terms; he was happy to have something to do rather than think about the current state of his life. He worked hard, getting great satisfaction in using the least amount of cleaning product and cleaning layers of grease and dirt in the kitchen. He scrubbed the ovens and stoves and mopped the floor until everything was clean. It was the most satisfied he'd felt since arriving in prison.

One morning as Mr Sidhu walked to the kitchen to do his cleaning, a scruffy-looking prisoner stared at him and then the man grinned, baring his yellow and missing teeth. It was not a friendly smile. Mr Sidhu felt something was wrong. Why was he staring at him? What did that grinning mean? Had he done something? He worked in silence with a frown which Joe, whom he cleaned the kitchen with, noticed. Joe stopped and asked him what was wrong. Joe was a Jamaican man in his sixties who wore his grey dreadlocks under a knitted hat.

'Somethin' happen?' he asked.

Mr Sidhu, who'd been scrubbing the same part of the stove for half an hour, stopped to look at Joe. Joe was in for manslaughter. He'd told Mr Sidhu it had been self-defence and Mr Sidhu believed him.

'I wasn't a good man then anyway, but this man he came to take my car from me and I told him no and then he come with a knife and I come with a hammer. I didn't want hurt him, but he come for we and me react quick. Him get hurt more than I realise' was how he told his story. He was a jolly man, who sang while he worked. He had an accent that Mr Sidhu would never have understood when he first came to England, but now his ears could decipher the words within the accent, although when Joe sang he didn't really understand most of what he was singing about. One day Mr Sidhu was thinking about Tubby and remembered his name came from a Jamaican music producer, so he asked Joe if he knew him.

'How you know about him?' Joe had said, looking at him side on, with his head leaning back as if Mr Sidhu was someone to be wary of. He explained about Jay and Tubby, and then Joe asked him if he'd ever heard his music, which he hadn't. The next day Joe brought in a small cassette player and played some King Tubby songs, which to Mr Sidhu's ears sounded slow and strange with big thudding drums which echoed around the empty kitchen. All the while Joe nodded his head, his eyes closed and smiling.

Mr Sidhu looked at Joe, whose playful eyes invited him to explain how he was feeling. It was rare anyone cared about how anyone was feeling in prison. So Mr Sidhu told him about the prisoner who was staring at him.

'You know him?'

'No, I don't think so.'

'You feel it, right?' said Joe, placing his hand on his heart.

Mr Sidhu looked at Joe and nodded. He was right, he could feel in his gut that something wasn't right.

'When you go back to your cell, you look at the floor, don't make no eyes at anyone. You understand?'

Mr Sidhu nodded again.

'Anything happen you tell them you want to see me, all right?'

On his way back to his cell, passing all the prisoners hanging around the corridors, and waiting each time the guard had to unlock a door and then lock it again once he'd passed through it, he did as Joe said and kept his head down. It was evening and having eaten, he brushed his teeth and scraped his tongue and got ready for bed. He heard footsteps coming into the cell, thinking it was Harry, but it wasn't. It was the scruffy prisoner with yellow teeth and he had two other men with him. Before he could do anything, one of them pulled him down off his bunk and stuffed a cloth, which looked like a pillow case, into his mouth and then held his arms behind his back on the floor. The third man kept a lookout at the doorway. Mr Sidhu felt as if he was going to throw up as he struggled to free his arms and breathe, but it was no use.

'You don't remember me, do you?' hissed the scruffy man,

pinning Mr Sidhu's body to the floor. He looked at the prisoner, who had tattoos on his arm, and there was something familiar about him.

'You couldn't cash me dear old aunt's pension, could ya?' he said, leaning in close to his face. 'How's the old dear doing, eh? Lost her marbles completely, I bet,' he added, laughing.

It was him, the one who'd tried to cash Min's pension. Mr Sidhu couldn't make any noise and couldn't move. What would he do? Mr Sidhu breathed through his nose, trying not to panic.

He addressed the two other men, 'This fucking smelly Paki wanker couldn't do me a solid one and cash in some old bint's pension. No sweat off his nose, but he gets all vigilante, doesn't he?' He slapped Mr Sidhu hard across the face. His glasses flew across the floor and under the bunk. The slap stung his face but he dared not move for fear of further violence. Like a scared animal, Mr Sidhu stayed still, hoping he could simply disappear.

'And guess what he's in for?' the man spat, grinning at the other prisoners. 'Stealing from his own post office. Can you believe it? What a fucking two-faced cunt.'

The man placed his mouth next to Mr Sidhu's ear. 'I guess I take payment now, if that's all right with you?' Mr Sidhu didn't move.

'I said, I'll take my payment now, yeah?' Mr Sidhu had no idea what was being asked of him. 'Yes, tell me "yes", you fucking piece of shit.' Mr Sidhu nodded his head.

'Don't mind if I do,' said the man in a normal voice, which for a moment made Mr Sidhu think he might leave. But he didn't, he punched Mr Sidhu in his stomach.

The two other prisoners laughed as Mr Sidhu curled up on the floor in pain. He felt his patka being taken off his head, his plaited hair being pulled ferociously, all the skin on his head being pulled with it. The pain was intense enough to stop his stomach from hurting from the punch. He kept his eyes focussed on his glasses under the bed as they carried on.

'Cut it off,' he heard one of them say.

'How?'

Mr Sidhu felt a mouth on his head. Were they trying to bite his hair off? He managed to spit out the cloth from his mouth and tried to shout, but his throat was dry and he only made a weak, hoarse sound. Immediately they were back on him, stuffing the cloth back into his mouth and holding his arms. He could feel a knee in his back while his arms were being pulled behind him. He had no fight left in him.

'Don't fuck around, you fucking thieving cunt. You and me,' the man said, now forcing Mr Sidhu to look at his face close up – his eyes were a pale blue, his skin pale with patches of beard trying to grow through – 'we're the same.'

Mr Sidhu looked at his glasses as he took several more blows to his body. He curled up into a ball, shielding his head and taking all that they could do to him. Their blows stopped and he could sense they were done with him. They told him that they'd be back for more payment. 'We'll bring something to get rid of that hair, give you a proper army cut, short back and sides.' They laughed and spat on him before leaving. Mr Sidhu lay on the ground crying into his arm, not wanting anyone to hear his pitiful noises. He stayed like that until he slowly lifted himself up and somehow climbed up onto the top bunk where he lay down with a jumper over his eyes and rested.

*

'Letter, Sid,' shouted a prison guard the next morning. That's what the prison guards called him. Sid, short for Sidhu; he didn't object. He didn't move; his body ached and he could feel his mouth and left eye were swollen. Mr Sidhu hadn't got up for breakfast because he could hardly move without causing himself pain.

'Come on, wakey wakey, Sid,' the guard shook him, causing him to groan. Mr Sidhu turned and saw the surprise in the guard's face, which disappeared quickly. 'Fell out of bed, did you? This might make you feel better. Hand-written – must be an admirer,' he added, throwing the letters at Mr Sidhu. The guard waited while Mr Sidhu slowly propped himself up and took a moment before looking at the two letters. He could tell who the top one was from. He carefully opened up the first one, but it was already opened. The guard looked at him, still smiling.

'Did you think we wouldn't open your mail? It's prison, Sid, not a holiday home. Didn't you tell him, Harry?'

Harry laughed along with the guard, who went off to deliver the rest of the letters. 'They don't read them. They check in case someone sends summink,' said Harry. Mr Sidhu hadn't heard him come into the cell after his assault. And it struck him that Harry might have known it was going to happen and that's why he'd been alone. This was prison, he reminded himself, not the real world. Like the guard, Harry made no acknowledgement of the fact that Mr Sidhu had been beaten up. It was completely ignored.

Mr Sidhu peered into the envelope and slid out the folded the letter inside. He opened it out. It was Rose, of course, writing to him. He took a few moments to calm himself before starting to read it.

David, how are you? I'm so sorry this has happened. It's been two weeks and I haven't heard from you. I tried to call the prison but I couldn't get through to you. I've been talking to Richard to see if there is any chance of an appeal. So far he doesn't think so. But we will keep trying, I promise. I want to see you, David, but they said you need to send a visiting order. Please send one. My address is on the letter if you need it. But I know you'll remember it like you remember all the postcodes. Nothing is the same now, David. There's a big hole where you used to be. Everyone can't believe what's happened. The truth will out, David. It's something my mum used to say to me. And soon you'll be out too. And don't worry, Darshan came to see me and I gave him your bank accounts and everything, he said he'll top up your account so you can buy anything you need there.

David, I know you're a proud man who doesn't want to ask for help, but please don't think you're asking anything of anyone. Just let me see you. Please. I can bring Raju and Meenu too. You are not alone, David. We all love you and Jay says that Tubby misses you too. I won't prattle on any longer. And of course if there's anything you want, let me know. But please let me see you.

Lovingly yours
Rose x

Mr Sidhu felt the paper. It was Basildon Bond paper from his shop. Richard had insisted he keep it in stock, and he had duly obliged. His tears fell from his swollen eyes upon the page, rolling down the letter and taking the ink with them, making long blue streaks. He held the letter away from him and placed it down to dry. He would read it many times, cherishing it like treasure. It was hard hearing Rose asking to see him. He didn't want to be seen here. He didn't want to create any memories here that could be shared with anyone. If Rose came, he wouldn't be able to be strong. He would crumble, and he didn't want to do that. It would make her worry to see him like this and that would make him feel bad. He looked at the envelope and saw her address and the idea of writing to her crossed his mind. He'd never written a letter, not a personal one, not since the days of the blue airmail letters he'd sent back to India to tell the village of his news. Then he'd written in Punjabi. He hadn't written anything in Punjabi since his brothers had installed a phone and he was able to call them. Which he never did. And for the first time he wondered what his brothers were doing. Still working the land? Was the chuppar still there? Were the buffalo still there? And suddenly he had the idea to take Rose there. To his village. Show her where he came from, just like she had shown him where she used to go on holiday when she was a child. The idea filled him with hope until he thought about how he'd pay for the flights and the travel expenses. The sinking feeling returned and his body ached and he thought about his real situation and not the silly dreams he was having.

'*You and me, we're the same,*' the scruffy man had said. Well, weren't they? In prison together and he was a convict just like him. His head hurt and his body ached. And then he remembered that the man had said they would come back for more payment and cut his hair off. He lay on the top bunk unable to move, knowing that if he did it would be painful.

Even getting down from the bunk would hurt. He placed Rose's letter under his pillow and then remembered he had another letter. He looked at the second opened letter and couldn't tell whose writing it was. He opened it.

Dad, I love you so much. I'm so sorry this is wrong, all wrong. What can I do? Just now I realise that I've never written to you ever. You or Mum. I wish I had. I wish I had a letter from you that I could look at now. How are you? I tried to call you but they said it has to be at a certain time and that you have to tell me to call you. Why haven't you called me? We need to know you're OK. I am fine. You must have seen that interest rates have been going down. It's good for me, the mortgage payments have gone down a lot! I really do appreciate everything you and Mum have done for me. I know that you love me and even though I don't show it very well, I love you. I'm so lucky to have you as my dad. I appreciate it every day. Meenu sends her love too. I'm so sorry I was angry at you and that we never talked properly. Everything that happened is wrong. I have been talking to Richard and we're going to do everything we can to help you. But first you have to send us a visiting order otherwise we can't come. Or just call me, please. My number is on the letter. Call me anytime and we can arrange a visit or even a call. Whatever works for you. I love you and I'm proud to be your son. Waheguru Ji Ka Khalsa. Waheguru Ji Ki Fateh.

Your son Raju

Mr Sidhu held the letter for a while. Time had no meaning in prison, there was nothing urgent to do. Raju wanted to see him, Rose wanted to see him. But he didn't want to see them. He folded the letter away and allowed a little smile to himself. Interest rates had gone down; he'd seen that and Raju had too. He was happy for that. Raju being interested in things other than acting, which he hadn't mentioned once. The letter gave him a boost. He would get up. He needed to pee anyway. And he would need to eat too. And he would go to the kitchen and get out of the cell and show everyone what kind of man he was. A man who would keep going and do his duty.

In the kitchen Mr Sidhu tried to keep his face away from Joe. Joe didn't say anything to him but as usual he came to Mr Sidhu with a cup of tea at breaktime.

'It him, the one you say yesterday?' asked Joe.

Mr Sidhu nodded and sipped his tea. The kitchen was empty; only trusted prisoners were allowed into areas like the library and kitchen. The job of cleaning required that prison guards felt you were not going to take advantage of being left alone in these areas. Joe passed him a packet of frozen peas.

'It help with the swellin,' he said, indicating his left eye.

The cold plastic numbed his skin and after a few moments Mr Sidhu did feel the pain ebbing away.

'I got letters from my son and my friend,' he said, trying to move the conversation away from the incident.

'Ah, that is nice.'

Mr Sidhu told him about Raju and how he was an actor.

'Is a good thing, him actin',' said Joe. 'Him showin' that they not only white people in this country. When I grow up, there no people like me on the teevee. We need that. Him brave. It's no easy to do that.'

Mr Sidhu nodded. He'd never heard acting being talked about in that way. He didn't tell Joe that Raju mostly did theatre and was only seen by handfuls of people a lot of the time. Perhaps he could tell Raju to go into television.

'And who this friend? Is man or girl?'

Mr Sidhu blushed and felt the blood move into various parts of his damaged face. Joe looked at him and laughed. 'Is always the quiet one. Wass she name?'

Mr Sidhu couldn't help but smile, which hurt his face a little. He explained Rose was the mother of Jay, who had the dog named Tubby.

'When they come see you?'

'No, no. I don't want anyone to see me in here,' said Mr Sidhu.

Joe stood up suddenly. 'What nonsense you talkin?' he exclaimed. 'You have people who love you, man. You must see them, because in this place' he waved his arms in the air, 'is no love, man. Is good for your heart to see the people you love. You understand?'

'You have people who come to see you?'

'I try, Sid. I have two boys. I write them. Soon one day they come,' he said looking away.

'Is problem with them?'

'No problem with them, Sid. Is problem with I. Me and the mother no talkin' and she say I no good. But is OK. I make them see with Jah love.'

Mr Sidhu nodded. He understood there was more to it than Joe let on and didn't feel he could ask what Jah love meant.

After they'd finished cleaning, Joe walked with him to his cell. 'You tell me who make trouble for you. We make it OK. You a good man, Sid.'

The scruffy man was there again with his two goons looking at Mr Sidhu. But this time they didn't grin. Joe, who was so nice to Mr Sidhu, had a sharp look in his eye and stared at the three men until they looked away. Joe grinned.

'They no make no more trouble for you, Sid.'

'How do you know?'

'Because Rasta man protect Rasta,' he stopped and looked at Mr Sidhu, placing a hand on his shoulder, 'you and me same, Sid, we no cut our hair like the devil man,' Joe looked around at the prisoners and guards, 'we keep our hair long as the Lord wanted us to and we find peace with that. But if Babylon come make trouble for we, we go fight them down.'

Joe was right and those men didn't come again. Mr Sidhu waited, unable to sleep that night, but no one came. The next day he woke up with a start as if something was about to happen. And then he remembered what Joe had said. He saw the men but they never looked at him again. It was as if it had never happened. But his body told another story. He wondered if it had anything to do with the black men Joe hung around with. A lot of them had long hair, shaped into locks like the sadhus in India. Not like his own hair, which he carefully combed every day and plaited and tied on top of his head before covering it with his patka. He looked forward to the day he would tie his turban upon his head again and wear it proudly.

*

The days passed slowly. It was December now and he would be spending Christmas in prison. It was only a year ago that Rose had invited him for a Christmas lunch. And even now the thought crossed his mind that perhaps if he'd not given in to his feelings for Rose and instead listened to Meenu, things might have turned out differently. Maybe he'd have focussed more on the losses and the consequences and less on his heart. He sighed as he lay on his bed. He spent so much time inside his cell and inside the prison building. There was nothing to do apart from the cleaning he did in the kitchen, but that didn't fill in his time enough. He didn't read books and he had no feeling for anything. The atmosphere was oppressive. Harry listened to a small radio with headphones lying on his bed. Occasionally Mr Sidhu would hear him laugh or giggle at something, but generally Harry left him alone. The incident that happened in the cell was never talked about.

Why was he being so proud? He would send the visiting order. He would see his loved ones. Joe was right, there was no love in this place and he needed to feel the love of his family and Rose. He needed to know who he was, and there was no one here who could do that. He waited a few weeks until the swelling on his face had gone down, and then he sent the visiting order to Rose, Raju and Meenu.

Chapter 27

Sidhu waited in line with the other prisoners to be let through into the visiting area. He had butterflies in his stomach. It made him think of what Joe had said – 'You feel it, right?' – when he'd asked if he knew the scruffy man was trouble. He'd felt something then, but what he felt now was completely different. He was nervous because he still had a few fading scars and bruises on his face, and he didn't want to make Rose or Raju feel bad about it or worry about him. He watched as prisoners entered the visiting area, a room with tables and chairs scattered around. And that's when he saw them: Rose and Raju sitting at one of the tables. Rose had her handbag on her lap, she was wearing her red coat. He could feel an ache in his heart as he approached them. Putting one foot in front of the other took a lot of effort and then finally he was with them. Raju came to him and hugged him a little too tightly so that it hurt his bruised ribs.

'I'm so sorry, Dad. I'm so sorry this has happened. I know you didn't do anything.'

'Shhh, it's OK, beta,' said Mr Sidhu, not remembering the last time he'd had to comfort Raju like this (perhaps never, he thought – his mother would have done it).

'How you doing, Dad?' Raju asked, looking a little too intently into his eyes.

'I am OK, beta. I am happy to see you,' he replied.

Joe had been right. He needed to feel the love of his loved ones. All his thoughts about prison disappeared. He felt happy in a way he'd forgotten about. And then there was Rose. She stood with her blue eyes looking at him. Her hand tentatively felt its way up his arm as if she was making sure he was real; the rest of her body didn't move.

'David,' she said.

'Rose.'

Neither moved before Raju interrupted. 'I'm just gonna get some water,' he said. Alone, Mr Sidhu stepped closer to Rose, who was examining his face.

'How are you, David?'

He nodded, fearing that words might let out emotions he might not be able to control. Slowly Rose came closer to him and they hugged. And for Mr Sidhu, everything was there in that moment. Everything that had been missing. He could feel something between them that was almost overwhelming in its intensity. He let go to look at her face and kissed her without thinking. Rose smiled and they stepped back a little from each other, embarrassed, glancing around at all the other visitors who were engaged in their own moments. Mr Sidhu remembered being on the beach and thinking about what other people might think of him being with Rose then. It was almost the same. They sat down, having unburdened themselves of their wanting to touch each other, and held hands.

'Richard's looking into everything. He says he won't stop

until he can find a way to help. He feels ever so bad. He's written to our MP, and so have I, and so has everyone else.'

'And Tubby misses you. He keeps one of your slippers in his basket.'

Mr Sidhu smiled. 'And how are you, Rose?'

'I keep busy. I'm working in the shop again.' She stopped to scrutinize his face. He nodded and indicated for her to carry on. 'He tried to get a young chap Indian working there, but he was useless. He tried, bless him, but he took too long and people complained, and so he asked me to come back and work. Which means people can get credit again. But it's not the same and everyone says so.'

Mr Sidhu sighed. He was glad Rose was there to make sure the customers were looked after.

'And how about you, David? Did you get my letter?'

'Yes. It was so nice to receive it. Maybe I will write one to you.'

'If you want to, David, I would love that. Have you made any friends?'

'Yes, Joe. He is Jamaican. We work in the kitchen together. He is a good man. He helped me,' he paused and felt his face. Rose knew not to probe.

'I'm glad you made a friend.'

Raju returned with some plastic cups of water. The water was cold, which felt nice as Mr Sidhu drank it down.

'Where is Meenu?' he asked Raju.

Raju hesitated. 'I asked her to come, but she couldn't.'

'How is she?'

'She's OK, Dad.'

'And Craig?'

'Yeah, he's OK, I think. I haven't seen him.'

Mr Sidhu thought about his dream when Meenu was in the bus. He wanted to see her. He couldn't concentrate on what Raju and Rose were talking about but nodded and smiled appropriately. He'd made his promise to Sarabjit and he didn't even care what Meenu thought about Rose and Jay and him. He just wanted her to be getting on with her life and for him to be able to support her. If she did that, then everything would be fine. But being unmarried and alone, being adrift and without her own family that would nourish her and make her become like her mother, a good woman, what would she be? Alone and without purpose. Just as he was now.

The time passed too quickly, and even though Rose never let go of his hand, he already missed them before they had left. Raju and Rose both offered help, but beyond coming to see him and writing letters there was nothing they could do. He was in prison. The courts had decreed it and so it was. He had lost his business and his house, but he didn't want to lose Meenu. That seemed more important than anything. It was the only thing he would give anything not to lose. He spoke to Raju and Rose before they left.

'Tell Meenu I am not angry with her. Tell her to see me.'

Raju and Rose nodded and told him they would try, but even he could tell they were doubtful. 'David, you're going be all right, aren't you?'

'Yes, don't worry.'

'You can't tell me not to worry, but I promise I shall try not to worry too much. I want you to call me and let us visit. OK?'

'Yes, OK. No problem. Raju, flat OK? No problems?'

'No, Dad,' said Raju and for a moment Mr Sidhu saw the little boy again who hated working in the shop. It made him smile inside.

That night in his cell he slept better than he had for a long time. When he woke the next morning there was a moment when he thought that Rose was lying next to him.

Chapter 28

Finally the day came when he was due to be released after ninety-four days in prison. It was a cold morning in February 2009.

'You gonna be all right, Sid,' Joe told him on their last shift working together. 'You a good man.'

'You have been kind to me, Joe. Is there anything I can do for you?'

'There's nothing you can do, Sid. I will miss being with you. We had a good thing. You got a good heart. Jah be with you. I'll be OK.'

The two men shook hands, which was more contact than he'd had with anyone in prison apart from being beaten up by the scruffy man.

Darshan came to pick him up in his Mercedes estate. The prison guards gave him back his turban, which was in a plastic bag along with keys and his wallet. In the car was Raju, Rose, Darshan, Jay and Tubby. Tubby was the first to greet him, ears flattened and almost knocking him over with his excitement, running round in circles, his tail wagging in a frenzy. They all took turns to give Mr Sidhu a generous hug each.

'How are you, Dad?' asked Raju, more earnest than he ever remembered him being.

'Beta, I am fine, I am fine. Where's Meenu?'

'She couldn't come today, Dad,' said Raju, his expression neutral now. Mr Sidhu nodded. He knew she was still upset with him. She hadn't visited him in prison or responded to any of the visiting orders.

'Let's get out of here,' he said, trying to sound hopeful but feeling sad.

They all climbed into the car.

'Where do you want to go?' asked Darshan, turning up the fans to warm the car up.

'Home to Rose's house,' said Mr Sidhu, looking at Rose. She smiled at him.

Darshan put the car into gear and off they went.

Rose handed Mr Sidhu a brown paper bag. It was full of samosas. Mr Sidhu munched into the first one and let the flavour fill his mouth. That was good. He ate another.

'There's tea in the flask, too,' said Rose, indicating a thermos flask in the door. Mr Sidhu didn't need asking twice. The prison grew more and more distant behind him. He was not there any more, but what had happened to him would always be part of who he was. He had a criminal record. He had been to jail. He could not deny it if anyone asked him. That was who he was now.

After coming home and having everyone fussing over him, he excused himself to have a bath. It was unnerving to have everyone around him, even though that was what he'd thought he wanted. Actually he wanted to be alone, or just with Tubby in the park outside with the trees and birds. He poured water over his head and sank down into the water. And he cried. Almost as a release. He was crying despite himself. The tears flowed out of him but he didn't feel sad; it was almost like something his body needed to do. And once he stopped, he felt better. What would he do? He had no business, no job to go to. Not enough money to do anything meaningful. He tried to sweep those thoughts aside. Rose was downstairs and so was Raju, they had missed him, the least he could do was show them he was happy to be home. And then the thought crossed his mind. *I am still useless. I serve no purpose. I might as well be back in prison. I am a criminal.*

He got up out of the bath and dried himself vigorously with the towel. He dried his hair. And he put on his patka and carefully stretched his turban cloth, tying one end to the doorknob as he stretched, folded and creased his turban and tied it onto his head until he looked into the mirror and saw himself again.

'Satnam Sri Waheguru Ji,' he whispered. He tied a cloth over his beard to matt it and went downstairs to be with Rose and Raju.

'Welcome home, David!' came the shouts of the locals. They filled the small living room and then they were silent.

'It's to keep his beard matted,' said Raju to the crowd of people.

Mr Sidhu realised his locals had never seen him like this. He came forward to be with his people once again.

Gerry hugged him, Bill shook his hand violently as he always did, Richard greeted him with a 'Sat Sri Akal' and a glass of whisky. And just when he thought he was being overwhelmed and might need to escape, Rose took his hand and everything felt better.

The next day Mr Sidhu called Raju and asked where Meenu was.

'She's away for work, Dad. I'll let you know when she's back.'

Mr Sidhu could sense that Raju wanted to end the conversation there.

'You said she was busy. Now she is gone away? What happened?'

Raju hesitated before answering, 'She didn't tell me, Dad, she just said she had to go away for work.'

'Why isn't she coming to see me, Raju?'

Raju was silent,

Mr Sidhu continued, 'I tried to call but she didn't answer. Where has she gone? Raju? Are you there?'

'Yes, Dad,' said Raju finally, a little wearily.

'So where is she gone?'

'Dad, just give her some space.'

'Hahn?'

'She'll come round, Dad, but right now she . . .'

Mr Sidhu waited for Raju to finish what he was saying but there was only silence.

'But what, Raju?'

'She doesn't want to see you, Dad,' said Raju, exhaling.

Mr Sidhu blinked repeatedly as he held the phone receiver and tried to absorb what he'd just heard. He knew he could go weeks without Raju calling him. But Meenu had always stayed close and kept the contact up. Before he went to prison he knew she was not happy with his relationship with Rose and the silly ideas she had about Jay, but it was over now. He'd gone to prison and he'd taken the punishment that was meted out to him for something he was innocent of. So why was she still ignoring him?

'Dad?' Raju said softly.

Mr Sidhu looked at the receiver, he'd forgotten it was there.

'OK, Raju. Thank you,' he said simply and hung up. He sat down and wondered what had happened.

Over the next few days Mr Sidhu tried to call Meenu, but his calls went to voicemail and the messages he left her went unanswered. He even went to her flat, but because it was inside a gated development he couldn't gain entry and the concierge wouldn't let him in without being invited. All this made Mr Sidhu sad. He tried to talk to Sarabjit, but she didn't seem to be there. Was she cross with him too? He'd thought the worst was behind him but a new feeling was with him, in his gut. It spoke of something that he couldn't grasp. At times the sensation turned into an acute pain that made him double over. *Perhaps my body has borne too much. Maybe it is my time to go*, he'd think. He knew he had to do something. He'd lost enough, he couldn't bear to lose anything more. He wanted to see his daughter and he would do whatever it took.

Chapter 29

Mr Sidhu wasn't one to sit around thinking about all that he'd lost. He did what he always did whenever he wanted to disappear. He worked. He was living in Richmond, as he'd wanted to, but it wasn't in the cottage he'd imagined; it was in Rose's house. He told Rose he'd pay her rent, which she flat out refused, but he paid her nonetheless from the income of his new job.

It turned out that finding a new job was not as easy as he'd thought it might be since he was now a convicted criminal. He was equally surprised by the job he did get in the end. He'd not applied for a job since the Eighties when he'd bought the post office. And now he couldn't work in a job that had anything to do with money, and it went without saying that he couldn't work at the one place he knew so much about: the Post Office. So he was happy and a little surprised when he got his job. His new place of work wasn't far. Just on the high street. He liked being among the hustle and bustle of shoppers. He was with his people, seeing them coming into the shop, picking items off the shelves and then queueing and paying – sometimes even leaving without paying. As a security guard he didn't say anything or stop those who didn't pay, because it was Tesco, and if anyone could afford to let a few goods go it was Tesco.

Mr Sidhu disliked the big supermarkets for the simple reason that they took away something that he and his fellow convenience store owners had created: local shops for local people. In the Eighties when the big supermarkets had been trying to copy the big American out-of-town supermarkets, he and his fellow immigrants had been creating small local shops which served communities. They knew their customers by name and opened when everyone else was shut. And the locals loved it and happily gave them custom. But by the Nineties, when the supermarkets had forced most small local greengrocers and butchers out of business, they took aim at the convenience store. The supermarkets realised there was even more money for them to be made in these local shops, so they swept aside the very people who had created the local market for groceries and put their own shops in those places and undercut them on price, because they could. And that was the end of the so-called Indian corner shop. Mr Sidhu had survived simply because people came to the post office for money and he gave them credit, which they needed.

Mr Sidhu thought about all that now because he had the time as a security guard, being paid minimum wage: £5.80 an hour. The new job meant he had to stand all day near the entrance to the supermarket and his legs ached, but he didn't complain. He wanted to work, even if it was for a supermarket. And sometimes he'd see his old locals and they'd say hello and talk about the day when they'd all gone to court and said good things about him. He spied a mother sneaking some baby formula into her pram. Mr Sidhu gave it no mind and when she (as the nervous ones always did) looked in his direction, he smiled and winked at her.

He ate his lunch, which was a two-pound meal deal from the supermarket, sitting on a bench on the green behind the high street. He ate his sandwich, looking at mothers playing with their children, the odd cyclist on one of the various paths that criss-crossed the green, and the lone dog walkers with whom Mr Sidhu now felt an affinity. It was calm. His life was calm, but still Meenu ignored him. He thought that she'd come round eventually and come to see him. Whenever he asked Raju about her, his face would betray the knowledge that he'd spoken to her and that she didn't want to see him. Three months had passed since he'd come out of prison; he'd kept going to try and see Meenu at her home, but he never got past the security gate of the development she lived in. At times she had replied to a message with a *'Sorry I missed your call'* or *'I'm away. Hope you're well.'* The messages gave him hope and he would then call her straight back, but he never got through to her.

A man in a pale linen suit was waving a newspaper at him. He was heading straight for him. As he approached, Mr Sidhu recognized Richard.

'Sidhu Saahab, good news!' called Richard. He threw the newspaper onto the bench next to Mr Sidhu.

'Read it,' he enthused, a little out of breath.

Mr Sidhu put down his chicken salad sandwich and chilli crisps and wiped his hands before picking up the paper. Richard's eyes were wide open, imploring Mr Sidhu to read the paper.

The newspaper wasn't one of the normal daily papers; it was a big magazine kind of newspaper called *Computer Weekly*. It was dated 11 May 2009. Richard had marked an asterisk in red biro to indicate which article to read.

'*Bankruptcy, prosecution and disrupted livelihoods –*
Postmasters tell their story', read the headline.

Once Mr Sidhu started he could not stop reading. One after
the other he read about postmasters who had found losses with
their balances after a new computer system had been installed.
And one by one the Post Office took them to court, telling
them no one else had these issues and the postmasters ended
up bankrupted or jailed, like him. Some paid the money back,
some didn't, but they'd all been criminalized – sacked and left
without anything. Mr Sidhu couldn't believe it. He stared at
the newspaper, unable to form a single thought.

'What does this mean?' he asked Richard.

'Nothing yet,' he replied, 'the Post Office hasn't responded.
We'll see what happens. But Sidhu, one thing we do know is that
they're lying. They told us no one else was having this issue.'

Mr Sidhu's mind whirled with thoughts as he remembered
being interrogated and told there weren't any others. They had
lied to him.

'Why did they do this?'

'Only the Post Office knows that. But it looks like they're
hiding something. They told everyone that it was only them
having problems. Exactly what they told you. Something's off,
Sidhu.'

'Maybe there are more,' said Mr Sidhu.

'I'm sure of it,' said Richard, his voice steady and controlled.

'It makes no sense,' said Mr Sidhu, still trying to fathom it.
'They took us to court for stealing from ourselves. Why would
we do that?'

'Looks like it has something to do with the computer system.
It has to be. They want to protect it for some reason.'

'By sending innocent people to jail!' Mr Sidhu stood up. He was angry now. 'They sent me to jail. They made me lose my post office, my house, everything I worked for. There are still some people who think I am a thief, a liar, a criminal. They did that to me. Why? Why did they do that?' Mr Sidhu looked at the sandwich in his hand and threw it as far as he could, yelling incomprehensibly as he did so. A few heads turned to look at him. He stared back at them as if daring them to ask him what he was doing. Some pigeons immediately came to feast upon the discarded sandwich and he watched as they started flapping their wings at each other, each trying to get the biggest piece to fly away with.

He walked away from Richard with his hands behind his back, unable to absorb what he'd just heard. Was it deliberate? Why would they do that? The Post Office wasn't a small organization, it was more than able to afford these losses. Why hadn't they believed them? Because even if the Post Office still denied it, he knew the postmasters were all telling the truth, because it was not in their interest to steal money they were responsible for. And what about the money he'd paid them? If there was no missing money, where had the money he'd had to pay them back gone?

Mr Sidhu looked at the clothes he was wearing. A pair of cheap, itchy black trousers, shoes which were heavy and ugly, a black polyester jumper. Had he come all this way for this? He knew there were people worse off than him. He knew he was lucky in most respects, but this! To wilfully incriminate innocent people who were serving their communities, this was too much, and just like that he doubled over and vomited on the green. He looked at the mess in front of him, steam rising from it like it did on Tubby's poo sometimes. He wiped his mouth and stood up straight, his eyes watering and an acidic taste coming up from his throat as well as a few bits of sandwich, which he spat out. He turned to look at Richard, who was staring at him. He walked back to the bench and took the bottle of water, and after rinsing out his mouth, he snatched the newspaper up and read it again.

'I'm keeping this,' he announced, looking at Richard and daring him to tell him otherwise. He went back to work, impatient for the working day to end.

At the end of his shift, Mr Sidhu strode back to Rose's cottage, paper in hand. He'd make a plan with Rose and Richard. Now the MP would have to listen. They had proof. He paused before inserting his key into the lock. He was outside Rose's house. He'd not been able to tell Rose about all the horrible things he'd seen in prison, the fights and screams and being beaten. He didn't want to pollute their home with that place. There were some moments in the night when Rose had woken him when he'd been asleep. She was gentle with him, and he'd not known that he'd been making howling noises in his sleep.

'You were just having a bad dream,' she'd say.

He knew that prison had done something to him. But slowly it had faded. Time took it away, but it was never forgotten and there were still nights when visions of prison came to him, and a feeling of helplessness invaded him. There were times when he felt as if he was awake and in prison and men were holding him down and he couldn't breathe. It took all his might to shout and get air into his lungs. And when Rose woke him up, for a split second he was back there. But when his body felt Rose and her soft skin, the feeling of relief was overwhelming enough to make his eyes wet with tears. The days when he woke up like that, the trauma stayed with him for the rest of the day.

He had to pause like this sometimes on the threshold before going in to see Rose to make sure he wasn't bringing in anything from the bad times. But with the paper in his hand he felt stronger. His resolve grew and he knew what he needed to do.

'I want to see Meenu,' he announced to Rose, who was darning his work socks. She looked up.

'That's good, David. Is that the paper?'

Mr Sidhu gave her the paper and pointed at the article. Rose sat reading it, her mouth opening wider the more she read.

'This is scandalous,' said Rose, standing up. Unable to sit back down, she paced the small living room.

'What are you going to do?' she asked, turning to him and looking as if she were ready for a fight.

'I need to talk to Meenu.'

'Yes, you said. But David, this is important. It's a miscarriage of justice,' Rose exclaimed. 'Someone has to pay for all this.'

Mr Sidhu had never seen Rose so angry about something that wasn't to do with tidiness or bad manners. It made him smile.

'What did Richard say?' she asked.

'Rose, my love, please,' he said. He only used the words 'my love' when he wanted Rose to calm down or actually listen to him. 'I will talk to Richard, we both will. But right now I need to see my daughter.'

'Do you want me to come with you?' asked Rose.

Mr Sidhu looked at her. The thought that she might come had not entered his head.

'It's OK, you go, David, I don't want to be seen to be interfering,' said Rose.

'You are not interfering,' said Mr Sidhu.

'Seen to be, David, seen to be.'

And they left it at that as Mr Sidhu called Raju and told him to come to Rose's house immediately.

Chapter 30

Mr Sidhu and Raju drove to Meenu's flat in the van. Mr Sidhu had made Raju call Meenu to tell her that he needed to come over to see her urgently.

'Is everything OK?' she'd asked.

'I'll explain when I see you,' he'd told her and she'd agreed.

They drove along the Great West Road to Isleworth (TW7), where she lived. She'd never invited him to her flat and he'd only actually been there a few times. He didn't like to go, as he knew she lived with Craig and he didn't like it that he lived in *her* flat. In his mind they would live in a house Craig would buy once they were married. He supposed not going to her flat was another way of him showing her that he wanted her to be married and settled. Sarabjit, on the other hand, was always interested in their children's lives and would go to see them at any opportunity. He and Sarabjit had actually offered to help Meenu buy a house. She'd agreed, but in the way that she did things, she'd then separately found her own property, a flat within a development, which Mr Sidhu had advised against due to there being a leasehold and service charges. But in the end Meenu got her own way and bought the flat (still with his and Sarabjit's help), which had been an old government building where Mr Sidhu had sent his income tax returns, but was now a development of flats.

Raju looked uncomfortable sitting next to him in the van.

'Dad, there's something you should know,' he said after a long silence.

'What?'

'Meenu isn't with Craig any more.'

'Hahn? What happened?' Mr Sidhu instinctively turned to look at Raju.

'Dad, the road!' said Raju, making Mr Sidhu look at the road. After Mr Sidhu had calmed down a little, Raju continued, 'They just got to the end of their journey, Dad. No big deal.'

Mr Sidhu thought it *was* a big deal. Meenu was getting old and he wanted her to get married, otherwise what would she be? And what would Sarabjit think? He stared out at the road ahead, trying to think of what he would say to Meenu.

'Why didn't you tell me before?' he asked Raju as they stopped at a red light. 'Did he do something?'

'No, no, nothing like that, Dad. It just wasn't meant to be, I guess. Meenu's fine with it.'

Mr Sidhu nodded to himself. Deep down he didn't really mind that she wasn't with Craig as he didn't like him that much anyway. But he didn't like the idea of her being alone. Maybe she might want to marry a nice Sikh boy. It was possible. There was still time, he thought hopefully. Maybe today would go better than he expected.

The lights turned green and he pushed the gear stick into first gear and felt the van lurch forwards. It was the only part of his old life that was still there. His van. He'd offered to sell it, but Rose insisted he keep it, and so he kept it. Jay borrowed it now and again to do his gardening jobs, and these days it had the smell of soil and vegetation rather than fresh tobacco, which it used to smell of when he bought cigarettes in bulk.

'I can't believe they did this,' said Raju, sitting next to Mr Sidhu in the van and reading the newspaper, the ancient windscreen wipers making a squeaking noise as they swished from side to side after the sky had darkened and a light rain began to fall.

You believed them before, thought Mr Sidhu, but he said nothing and carried on driving his van.

Raju went on to talk about his play and how it had been well received, and he told Mr Sidhu about his relationship with a French girl, Aurelie.

'She'd never met an Indian person before, Dad. Can you believe that?'

Mr Sidhu remembered his old university professor showing him pictures of Sikh soldiers in the First World War getting kissed by French women when they disembarked in Marseille. They had huge turbans and beards; it was the first time foreign soldiers had been used in a European war. His professor had told him how his father had been recruited to fight in the war by an Englishman who went from village to village recruiting Punjabis, because the British thought they were a martial race, whatever that meant.

'That's good, Raju. What is her job?'

'She's a costume designer.'

Mr Sidhu nodded silently and smiled his thin smile. 'How's work?' he asked and straight away he could see the discomfort in Raju's expression.

'A little slow, Dad, but—'

'Interest rates are low and rent is coming. So is OK?' interrupted Mr Sidhu, not wanting Raju to be disheartened.

'Yeah, I suppose,' said Raju, downcast.

Mr Sidhu wanted to say something about perhaps changing careers but stopped himself. He didn't want to get into that kind of discussion with Raju now. There was something more important to do.

Mr Sidhu arrived outside Meenu's building and looked at the black security gate which had barred his entry so many times recently. He wound down his window and stretched his hand out to press the round button on the grey intercom panel, which stood at the correct height for a car window. The rain landed on his outstretched hand. Would Meenu answer if he pressed the button? He had a thought.

'Raju, you speak when I press the button.'

Raju looked at him with a pained expression, as if he was asking him to do something arduous. However, magically the gate started to open before he pressed the button, furling out from the centre like a pair of wings. Mr Sidhu let out a grunt of relief and drove in, prompted by Raju, but felt as if he was trespassing somehow. A car sped past him, coming out of the development, and Mr Sidhu supposed it must be the reason the gates had opened.

Raju told him where to park in the underground car park. The spaces were all allocated to specific flats apart from a few which were there for visitors, Raju informed him. They walked up a damp, cold stairwell with wet, grimy footprints on each step and emerged on the ground floor. The development was large; the old building had been transformed into flats, each with a set of white UPVC windows that had been placed at a uniform distance from one another. There were people around, but something about the acoustics made it all sound quiet, and he could not hear any conversation or steps floating over his way. The only sound was the screaming of car tyres as they turned on the underground parking floor which had a glossy finish that allowed that to happen. He remembered when he'd first gone to see the flat, he was surprised by how big the place was. The development looked like a big, rectangular monolith from the outside, but inside there were courtyards with fountains, benches, trees and grassed areas almost like oases.

Raju rang the intercom on the outside of one of a series of doors allowing access into the monolith. There was a camera and a screen, but no image appeared, and after a short while the door buzzed and Raju pushed it open. They walked in as a woman wearing a hijab smiled as she exited. Mr Sidhu nodded and smiled back. They waited for the elevator and Mr Sidhu turned and was about to tell Sarabjit something. It was confusing, because for that moment, as happened every now and again, it was as if Sarabjit had never passed away, and her presence had never gone away. He looked at Raju instead and breathed.

The door to Meenu's flat had been left ajar and from inside he could hear voices and smell cigarette smoke.

'Raju!' he heard Meenu exclaim as Raju entered just before him.

Mr Sidhu took a breath and walked into Meenu's flat. He stopped as he saw Alan Dankworth sprawled out on the low, modern sofa, a cigarette poking out of his mouth. Meenu stood still by an open window, looking at him. He wanted to smile and go to her, but like everyone else he stood still as a statue, unable to say a word.

'Meenu,' he uttered.

'Dad?' said Meenu. His heart filled with emotion. He thought he might cry, but he kept himself together. He didn't want to show himself like that in front of Alan, even though every sinew of his body yearned to hold his daughter once again.

Her flat was sparsely decorated. Apart from the sofa, chairs and television, there were only a few plants. The open-plan kitchen's surfaces shone from the dim downlights above them and there was nothing out of place apart from a corkscrew and a piece of foil from the top of a wine bottle. The bottle stood on the glass coffee table with two glasses filled with wine. Even in this light, Mr Sidhu could see one of the glasses had lipstick on the rim. And there was also a grey metal ashtray with bent extinguished cigarette butts, some with lipstick on the filters. Meenu looked uncomfortable in her skirt and blouse, opened to reveal her cleavage and black bra. She tugged at her skirt to straighten it.

'I didn't know you were coming, Dad, I would have made some food,' said Meenu, glancing at Raju. Her voice sounded the same as always, not affected by everything that had happened. Alan grinned, revealing his yellow teeth, his tie loosened, his shirt spilling out of his waist on one side. He got up and came over to Mr Sidhu.

'Hello, Dave, always a pleasure to see you.' Mr Sidhu ignored his outstretched hand and kept his gaze on Meenu. Alan took it back and raised his eyebrows to Meenu, then sat back down.

'It's OK, beta, I am not hungry,' Mr Sidhu replied, still ignoring Alan.

Alan stubbed out his cigarette, his face serious, smoke coming out of both his nostrils as if the act required concentration.

'Always a pleasure to see you, darling,' said Alan and went to kiss Meenu; she moved away from him as he did so. Alan turned to Raju as if to share his surprise with him. Raju looked blankly at him.

'Well. I'll be off then,' said Alan to no one and gathered his computer bag and jacket. He stood up and looked at everyone in the room, nodding his head.

'No, Alan, you should stay,' said Meenu, now moving closer to him and making him sit next to her. Alan looked at Raju and Mr Sidhu as if measuring them up in case he needed to defend himself.

'Of course, darling,' he said, sitting back down and taking her hand in his.

'What do you want, Dad?' asked Meenu curtly.

'Meenu, do you know—' started Raju before Mr Sidhu interrupted him.

'Raju, it's OK. I can speak.' He turned to Meenu, 'Meenu, what has happened? Why aren't you answering your phone? Why you are not talking with me?'

Meenu turned to Alan and smiled. Mr Sidhu recognized the smile; he could tell that she was nervous. As she spoke she flitted between looking at him and the coffee table in front of her.

'Dad. I'm really sorry that you went to prison. I really am. I didn't want that to happen,' the words stung and even worse was the matter-of-fact way she spoke to him. 'But I've been through a lot recently and I needed space to work things out. Please don't take it the wrong way. I was going to see you. I wanted to, but it's been hard.'

Mr Sidhu tried to breathe but his breath caught in his chest. He felt as if the air could not fill his lungs. He tried again but the same thing happened. He tried not to panic and closed his eyes. Silently he repeated his mantra in his head,

Satnam Sri Waheguru Ji

Satnam Sri Waheguru Ji

And there it was, the air filled his lungs. What was that? What had just happened? As he opened his eyes he saw the concern in Raju and Meenu's faces. He cleared his throat.

'Are you all right, Dad?' asked Raju.

'Yes, I am fine,' he said, although the panic was still there in his chest. He gathered his thoughts. 'What has been hard, beta?' he asked Meenu, unable to conceal the disdain in his voice.

'Raju probably told you about me and Craig. We broke up. And that was hard because I think I stayed with him longer than I should have. I didn't love him any more and I felt trapped. That took its toll, because we got engaged when Mum was ill just before she . . . and then you kept on at me to get married and I didn't feel like I could tell you how I felt. So I wasn't being honest with you or myself. Which was making me unhappy. I felt hollow. In fact, I didn't feel anything any more.'

Mr Sidhu was confused, 'You both came to see me. You wanted me to see his parents.'

'I know.'

'I gave you your mother's gold.'

'You can have it back if you want, Dad. We weren't even together then. I had to make him pretend we were still together and come and see you,' she looked down at her hands and added quietly before looking up, 'I didn't want to disappoint you, Dad.'

'What? But you—' said Mr Sidhu.

'Dad, let me finish, please.' Meenu wiped her eyes and her face tensed and a steeliness seeped into her voice, 'You were fine, Dad. You were seeing Rose,' her voice was louder now, 'I wanted to know if I mattered to you. So I invited you to come to Craig's parents for Christmas to see if what *I* needed meant anything to you. Mum would have understood. But not you or Raju. Both of you talking about buying this place and buying that. What about me, Dad? Did you think about what I needed beyond getting fucking married and not being your responsibility any more? Going to see Rose at Christmas was more important than me, wasn't it? That's what's hard.'

The swearing smarted, but Mr Sidhu focussed on what she was saying. He'd never thought about what she was going through. It caught him off guard. He wanted to understand.

'What if I'd said yes and come to see Craig's parents?' he asked.

'Then I would have told you everything, Dad. I wanted you to come for me. But you didn't. She was more important. And I really needed you then.'

She was right. He hadn't thought about her. He felt silenced.

Mr Sidhu went and sat down on a chair. He felt tired. Raju came to him with a glass of water. What he'd wanted to tell her didn't matter any more. Not really. What Richard had told him earlier that day had seemed so important, but now it didn't, even though it was what he'd hoped for so much.

Silence filled the room. Mr Sidhu didn't know what to say.

'Well. I'll be off then,' said Alan for the second time to no one in particular, and gathered his computer bag and jacket. He stood up and looked at everyone in the room, nodding his head.

'You OK, Meenu, if I go? I think you and your dad have a few things to talk about.'

Raju stepped up to him and pushed the *Computer Weekly* article into his chest.

'What's this?' asked Alan.

'Read it,' said Mr Sidhu.

'OK,' said Alan, placing his bag down and glancing at Mr Sidhu and Raju.

A few moments passed.

'What is it?' asked Meenu.

'Well I'll be. That's something, isn't it?' said Alan, looking up, his eyebrows raised. Mr Sidhu couldn't tell whether he was genuinely surprised or just acting. Alan passed the newspaper to Meenu, who held it and read it carefully.

'Dad was right,' said Raju after a time.

'It's not true, is it, Alan?' said Mr Sidhu.

'What?' asked Alan, looking confused.

'It wasn't only me, was it? I wasn't the only one having problems with Horizon?'

'As far I knew, Dave. Yes, you were.'

'And now you know there are others,' pressed Mr Sidhu.

'Yes, I can see that's what the article says, but I don't know any more about it than you do.'

'You didn't believe me, Alan, all those years, the whisky, the cigarettes, you think I am a thief and a criminal?'

'No, Dave, no, it's not like that,' he looked around the room as if for the first time understanding that he was in potential danger. 'I just did what they said. They said the system was fine. I mean, it's not even our system, it's Fujitsu. They run it. That's what they told us,' he pleaded, looking at Mr Sidhu and Raju.

'But it was up to you to tell them to prosecute him or not, wasn't it? That's what you told me. Weeding out the bad ones. You told me that was part of your job,' said Meenu, joining in.

Mr Sidhu felt a rush of pride for Meenu.

'I just do my job. Head Office tell me to do this. I do it. They told me they had proof.'

'Did you even query it?' Meenu demanded, her eyes narrowed in disbelief.

'Listen, love,' said Alan gently.

'Did you know there were others?' Meenu pressed, rising to her feet, her gaze fixed on Alan with a mix of anger and revulsion.

'Look, I'm gonna go now. You're upset, and I think it's better we talk when we've all calmed down,' said Alan, his face cowed.

'You sent my dad to jail,' said Raju.

'I can't do that,' he replied, a little too quickly. He added with more measure, 'Only the courts can do that, and anyway, he pleaded guilty, so . . .' Alan trailed off, his throat gulping uncomfortably.

Meenu looked at Alan, shaking her head.

'You don't care, do you?' said Raju, blocking Alan from leaving the flat. Alan stood waiting for Raju to clear his path.

'As I said, probably best to talk about this when we've all calmed down.' His face was pink and sweat appeared on his forehead, which he tried to wipe away with the back of his hand.

'Calmed down? Don't you see,' Raju continued, gesturing towards Mr Sidhu, his manner aggressive, 'my dad did nothing wrong.'

'Listen, Raju. It's an article. It's not proof.'

'You knew there were others. You lied to me. You lied to all of us,' spat Meenu.

Alan was silent. His face was now red as his eyes flitted between Meenu and Mr Sidhu.

'For what it's worth, I never thought you did it, Dave, but I was told there was money missing and that you were responsible. Then Meenu told me about that Jay bloke having access to your post office. I was trying to get you off. We both were – tell him, Meenu.'

Mr Sidhu looked at Meenu and Alan and then spoke, 'Alan, go. Get out. Leave me with my family.'

'Are you going to be all right, Meenu?' asked Alan.

'Fuck off, Alan,' said Meenu.

Alan walked out of Meenu's flat. And then there was only Mr Sidhu and his two children.

After a silence Mr Sidhu spoke, 'Beta, what has happened to you? This is not you. Why you are thinking the worst in people? We are your family. We are not like this.'

'Sis, Dad did nothing wrong,'

'I know. I always knew he hadn't done anything.' Meenu stared at the floor, her hair hanging either side of her hands which were massaging her temples. Mr Sidhu looked at his daughter, wanting to go to her but still not knowing if she would accept him.

'Do you still think Jay stole the money?' asked Raju.

'I thought he could have, and so did you, Raju.' Meenu shook her head quietly, 'I didn't know about these other post offices who had the same problems. Alan told me the money had been stolen. I believed him. And I knew you hadn't stolen any money,

Dad. I knew that and so I thought it had to be Jay. I'm sorry. I never thought it would happen like this. God, what an idiot I am.' Meenu sat down and buried her head in her hands. And then looked up at Mr Sidhu, tears streaming from her eyes.

'I'm so sorry you went to prison, Dad. I'm so sorry. Raju was calling me, telling me to come and visit you and I was . . .' She stopped, searching for the right words, 'I was angry with you.' She got up and walked to her father and held his hands and squeezed his arms and shoulders. It reminded him of how Rose had touched him when she'd seen him in prison. He couldn't bear to see his daughter like this, so he tentatively placed his hand on her back and patted her. She buried her head into his chest and cried. He remembered how when she was little she'd come running to him, crying, demanding to be soothed. Yet now, with age and emotional distance between them, it was disturbing to see her cry; as if it spoke of a failure, which it did, he supposed. Perhaps it was the idea he held of her that she'd failed to hold on to, that the cry spoke of.

'Shhh. It's OK, Meenu. It's OK,' he said softly. He couldn't believe that when he was in prison he didn't want to see anyone he cared about. When you're on your own, you can think all sorts of things about other people, but when you are with the person you are thinking about, in the same space as them, all the thinking disappears. It only matters how they make you feel. Then, like now, all the distance between them disappeared once he had Meenu in his arms.

Mr Sidhu and Meenu stood together for a while before Raju announced that he needed a glass of wine and that if Meenu wasn't going to offer him one then 'I'll just have to serve myself', which he did, as well as subtly clearing up the ashtrays.

Mr Sidhu and Meenu sat together holding hands,

'I'm so sorry about you losing the post office. I can't believe what they've done,' said Meenu.

'House, too,' said Raju.

'*What?*' exclaimed Meenu.

'I had to sell it. I couldn't pay the mortgage and the rent and the bills when they suspended me from the Post Office,' said Mr Sidhu.

'I'm such an idiot for not helping, Dad. I'll help any way that I can, won't we, Raju? Where are you living, Dad?'

'I am fine, beta, I'm living with Rose, you don't have to do anything,' said Mr Sidhu, still not quite able to believe that half an hour ago she was still clinging on to her old beliefs and yet now here she was.

'He works at Tesco as a security guard,' said Raju.

'What? No, Dad, no,' implored Meenu as she continued to absorb the magnitude of what had happened to her father.

'What happens now? You have to take them to court. You have to get back what they took!' Meenu said, wiping her nose. She was angry now.

'I only read this today,' said Mr Sidhu, not caring much about the article now but pleased Meenu was talking to him again. 'But Richard thinks there might be a way to do it, get some compensation maybe. He is going to speak with the journalist and the other postmasters. Richard said there is a group of sub-postmasters who are talking about how best to do this.'

'That's a good start, Dad, but what about now?' said Meenu, looking concerned. 'Raju, he should live in your place,' she said. 'You've got the space for him. Dad, what do you think?'

'I've told him that already,' said Raju, sounding like a little brother again.

'Raju, Meenu, please. I am OK. I don't mind the work I do. And I live with Rose and everything is OK. There is nothing wrong with me, OK?'

Raju and Meenu fell silent.

'Me too, Dad,' said Meenu faintly.

'Hahn?'

'I'm OK too, Dad. I don't want you worrying about me. Getting married and everything, OK?'

Mr Sidhu's face dropped. It was his promise to Sarabjit.

'But beta, I want you to be happy.'

'I am happy, Dad. Not about what's happened. And just so you know, Alan is just, was just a friend,' said Meenu correct- ing herself and glancing at Raju. 'Nothing more, OK? I know I haven't exactly been in a good frame of mind, but please just listen, Dad.'

Mr Sidhu nodded and listened to Meenu.

'When I was with Craig I felt as if I was putting on a show with him, and so when I used to come to see you it was so nice to be in Mum's kitchen making rotis and eating with you and Raju. That made me really happy. And Craig was always saying how small-minded you were and that you were backward peasants, and part of me liked that because of how Raju was treated compared to me,' she paused and looked at Mr Sidhu and Raju. 'He never wanted to understand who we actually were. Even his mum would go on about immigrants, "not you, dear, it's the other ones", she'd say.'

Mr Sidhu nodded and smiled at Meenu. He took her hand. 'Beta, you are getting old. If you want to have a family—'

'Dad, I'm fine,' said Meenu, interrupting him.

'Beta, I made a promise to your mother that I would make sure you were both settled.'

'We are settled, aren't we, Raju?' said Meenu, taking her hand back and looking imploringly at Raju.

'Yeah, Dad, we're fine,' echoed Raju.

'Beta, me and your mum never said you have to be with this person or that person, but we both wanted you to be married and have a family. You're getting old, Meenu, beta, you need to settle otherwise it will be too late.'

Meenu exhaled and Mr Sidhu could see she was getting angry. This would not be easy.

'Dad, just leave me alone!' she said suddenly, breaking the good feeling that they'd just managed to recreate.

Mr Sidhu stood up. He couldn't stop tears coming to his eyes. He would never abandon his daughter, specially when she needed him.

'You are my daughter. I will never leave you,' he said, adamant in his conviction.

Meenu was silent and looked at him blankly. She turned to Raju, who wore the slightest smirk that only she would recognise.

'Dad,' said Meenu softly, which for a moment made Mr Sidhu believe that she'd come round to his way of thinking, 'I don't mean I want to leave you. I just want you to let me be me, that's all. Stop all your fussing. I'm proud to be your daughter, Dad. I'm not leaving you or going anywhere. What you and Mum achieved and gave us is incredible. But please, let me find my own way. I'm fine. There's nothing wrong.' Meenu looked at Mr Sidhu with kindness in her eyes. The severity had gone.

Mr Sidhu thought about Rose and how she had made her life on her own without a husband and how he was asking something of Meenu that he was not asking of anyone else. Meenu was right. She was successful. She had a good job. And she respected her family – what more could he ask?

'OK, beta. I will stop.'

'Thanks, Dad.' This time Meenu came and gave Mr Sidhu the kind of great big hug that he'd not had from her since she was a little girl.

'We're buying you a house, Dad,' said Meenu suddenly, looking at Raju, who immediately looked like a rabbit caught in the headlights. 'It's the least we can do,'

'Beta, please, I don't want that,' said Mr Sidhu, raising his hand to stop Meenu interrupting him. 'Don't put pressure on me. Just let me be me, hunnah?' He smiled, and Meenu looked at him for a moment, then her face relaxed and she smiled back at him.

Epilogue

Mr Sidhu looked at his grandson running into the waves, then sitting down and laughing as the waves washed over him.

'Would you like another cup of tea, Rose?' he asked.

'Yes please, David,' Rose replied and held his hand loosely before he got up and walked into the kitchen area of the beach hut. He didn't have his own house but he now had a beach hut. He'd not have allowed it, but it was given to him without his knowledge by his children. Rose had been delighted, and that really was the only reason he accepted the gift.

He'd made a thermos flask of proper tea, which Rose told everyone she couldn't live without now, and poured Rose and himself a cup each. He brought it back outside into the lovely summer day. He found that a kurta pyjama was the best thing to wear at the beach when it was hot, and sometimes he would undo his hair and let it all hang out. Raju told him he looked like one of those Indian spiritual gurus.

Raju and Aurelie were having one of their fraught discussions. Mr Sidhu had invited them with Meenu and Jay to come to Southwold to celebrate the news they'd had that year: that his criminal convictions had been quashed by the Court of Appeal. Mr Sidhu could not believe the lengths the Post Office went to to stop the sub-postmasters from discovering the truth of the matter, which was that the Post Office knew about the faulty computer system but carried on prosecuting innocent sub-postmasters because they didn't want to lose a lucrative contract with the government. The Post Office's legal team had been underwritten by the government, so they delayed and obfuscated everything. It took over ten years from the initial article in *Computer Weekly* until finally a judge ruled in favour of the sub-postmasters. Mr Sidhu had been pictured with his turban and beard, with a placard proclaiming victory. The picture was splashed across all the newspapers. The Post Office had spent hundreds of millions of pounds on their legal team, which Richard had informed him was 'being paid by you and me'. That was all over, but the Post Office was still making it very hard to get any compensation, even though the judge had declared that this must happen. Mr Sidhu let go of any expectation. If he got anything, it would be a bonus. Because he knew he was luckier than many. Several people had never recovered from the shock of being wrongly convicted and sent to jail. Mr Sidhu had listened to the stories and now there was to be a public inquiry into what had happened. Mr Sidhu would rather it didn't happen (and he suspected the people at the Post Office felt the same way), but only because he didn't want to think about that time any more. It was bad enough to pull yourself out of that moment, but then to relive it and tell strangers about it was not something he wanted to do. But he would do it for the others who needed it. He could do that.

Munni, his grandson, came running to him as he always did, his arms spread out, grinning ear-to-ear, and then launched himself onto Mr Sidhu, soaking his white kurta pyjama and covering it in sand.

'You naughty naughty ha!' shouted Mr Sidhu in a faux-cross Punjabi voice that always made Munni laugh even harder than he was already. Mr Sidhu hoisted him up into his lap and enjoyed the moment of connection with his grandson. He closed his eyes and was happy to see Sarabjit smiling too. Munni wriggled out of his lap and took Rose's hand and led her to the sea. They both stood with their feet in the sea looking out into the Channel, or was it the North Sea? Mr Sidhu didn't know. Jay and Meenu were talking together, smoking cigarettes; it was another thing that Meenu had told him that she didn't want to hide from him. He admired her strength in that sense, but he didn't like it, and neither did Sarabjit. She also didn't like (as he didn't) that Meenu was in no hurry to get married, have children or any of the things (apart from having a good job) that he and Sarabjit thought were normal. But what was normal? Being with Rose and still talking to Sarabjit?

Raju had finally got a well-paying job in *EastEnders*, a television programme which Mr Sidhu had heard of but never watched. Mr Sidhu was shocked when strangers would stop him to ask for a photo. He was happy for him, even if Meenu made fun of him because he played the role of a turban-wearing Sikh character, who was nothing like him. He could tell his wife Aurelie was good for him because she could see him for who he was: a boy full of himself. She complained that he was always on his phone and not concentrating on being with his family, and she was right. Yes, Mr Sidhu was finally happy again.

Meenu walked to Mr Sidhu and sat down next to him.

'You all right, Dad?'

'Yes, fine, beta.'

It was something his children asked more and more as he

got older, over seventy now, even though he felt no older than forty in his mind. Meenu leaned back in her chair, placing her sunglasses over her eyes and a cigarette into her mouth, lighting and exhaling and smiling. She looked content, Mr Sidhu thought. He wanted to say something but didn't know what. And the more Meenu sat there looking like a picture of happiness, the more Mr Sidhu wanted to get out of his chair and get away from her. But somewhere inside him, he told himself that would be a defeat of some kind. So he stayed sitting, fidgeting with his beard.

'Who's got your goat?'

'Hahn?' uttered Mr Sidhu, blinking, as Rose peered at him, the sun shining behind her as she stood over him.

'I can tell when you're bothered by something,' Rose insisted.

'Nothing, nothing,' he said quickly, not wanting to be exposed in front of Meenu. He exhaled loudly as Rose peered at him through her glasses. Mr Sidhu turned away from her, looked at Raju, Aurelie, Munni and Jay who were throwing a tennis ball into the waves which Jay's new dog Fela was happily jumping in to retrieve. He was surrounded by all the people he loved, but why was Meenu irritating him so much? He glanced at her and he could have sworn that her smile was growing as she exhaled smoke out of her mouth.

'Dad.'

'Yes, beta.'

'I've got a new job in San Francisco.'

'Hahn?'

'I'm moving to San Francisco, Dad. It's in America. In California, to be precise.'

Mr Sidhu's immediate reaction was one of disappointment and fear. Why was his unmarried daughter going to work halfway across the world? And even as he had the thought, the penny dropped. He looked at her.

'Good job?' he asked.

'Yeah, really good, Dad, working for a company called Google.'

'Oh, the searchy thing?' asked Rose.

'Yes,' said Meenu.

'They run the world, don't they?' asked Rose, grinning.

Even if he felt a little disappointed that Meenu was leaving, he still had to do his duty.

'Beta, I will buy your ticket.'

'What?'

'I will pay for your plane ticket to San Francisco,' said Mr Sidhu proudly.

'No, it's fine, Dad, they do that. They ship all my things over and pay for my travel.'

'No, beta, I will pay for your ticket.'

'But Dad—'

'Beta, please. Let me do this one thing, OK? When I come to this country, my father pay for my ticket. Now is my turn to do the same. No more discussion.'

Meenu placed her hand in her father's and squeezed it. Mr Sidhu felt her warmth flood into his body. He watched the waves crashing rhythmically onto the beach, the sun high in the sky; his skin glowed and his body relaxed.

'Rose,' he said finally. Mr Sidhu cleared his throat. He smiled and glanced at Meenu and then at Rose, whose blue eyes he would never tire of looking at.

'Will you marry me?'

Author's Note

I have always wanted to write about the sub-post office my father ran during the Eighties and Nineties in Richmond, and *Mr Sidhu's Post Office* is partly an attempt to capture the journey my father made from humble beginnings in India to serving an adopted community on the other side of the world.

We were a Punjabi family from Hounslow and were used to being around other Punjabis and immigrant communities. Richmond was almost completely English. Despite this, we were welcomed in and with my father's natural urge to serve a community we thrived. As soon as I was able (about 10 years old) I was 'encouraged' to work in the shop after school and at weekends. I saw how respected my father was and how the locals loved having a post office as a hub for the community where everyone came to get their pensions, travel cards, stamps, etc., and everyone knew about everyone.

It is a sad fact that post offices are no longer the community hubs they used to be. It was one of the reasons I wanted to write this novel. However, as I began to write and do my research I came across the Post Office IT Horizon scandal. Most of us learned about the Post Office Scandal from the brilliant, award winning ITV drama *Mr Bates vs The Post Office* in January

2024. The scandal had been reported upon repeatedly in the press since 2009, but mostly unnoticed.

I was amazed at the scale of the damage done to sub-postmasters by the Post Office – it was breathtaking. I read and watched everything I could about it and was often left in tears watching the human impact testimonies from the Post Office IT Horizon Inquiry. I was hearing about how families had been torn apart, suspicions sown, and lives completely ruined by a computer system that was known to be faulty. I knew then that I could not write this story without writing about the scandal. This is a work of fiction, however, I have tried as much as I can to stay true to the experiences of the sub-postmasters who suffered under the terrible Post Office Scandal.

But (as with all stories), it is also about people trying to live their lives as best they can, in the circumstances they exist in. Coming from a Punjabi Sikh background, I wanted to bring that texture into the story. I had also never come across a love story between a turbaned Sikh man and an English woman. Rose is a character wrought from the many working-class English women who lived in Richmond at the time and were at the centre of the community – there aren't many of them left. As the impact of the scandal grew within the novel, the romance between Mr Sidhu and Rose became a crucial foil to show how, at the end of the day and in the most difficult of circumstances, love conquers all.

Amman Brar

Acknowledgements

To my agent, Niki Chang, thank you for your patience and belief in Mr Sidhu's story. A huge thank you to all the staff at David Higham Associates who have supported me throughout the process, including Sophia Rahim for reading early drafts.

Manpreet Grewal, you created space for my debut novel, and for that I will be eternally grateful. Your guidance and expertise made Mr Sidhu better than I could have imagined. And without the cha and barfi, none of this would have happened. Thank you also to all the Juniper and HQ staff at Harper Collins.

Gillian Slovo, your expertise and love for the craft of writing a novel seeped into me and allowed me to write well, along with my cohort of generous Faber writers.

Tamasha Theatre Company was my first professional artistic home. They have and continue to bring up artists from the global majority. Even if I have written a novel (which started on a Tamasha / Hachette collaboration), it is to Tamasha Theatre Company that I owe my thanks for making me see myself as an artist.

Fiona Cairns, Tom Noble and Melanie Pennant, thanks for reading my work and being supportive when I needed it.

Luke Griffin for the legal insights and for introducing me to the judges at Isleworth Crown Court.

To those journalists who dedicated their time to uncovering the Post Office scandal – one of the biggest miscarriages of justice in UK history. In particular, Nick Wallis and Rebecca Thomson are the journalists who (in my view) have championed those sub-postmasters and families whose lives were turned upside down by the Post Office. '*The Great Post Office Scandal*' by Nick Wallis is the definitive work on how innocent sub-postmasters were pursued by the Post Office for crimes they did not commit.

The biggest acknowledgement is to all the mistreated sub-postmasters, past and present, whose fight this really is. You deserve justice, compassion and proper compensation.

To Mum, Anu and Kam – thank you.

Sukhjinder, Amandine and Fela, all my love – this is for you.

Juniper

Fiction to think about.

Juniper strives to reimagine what literary fiction can achieve. Our novels will resonate across generations, transcend genres, and break convention. Like the juniper tree and its berries, every story we publish embodies a spirit of wisdom, strength, resilience, and hope, and will stand the test of time.

Every Juniper author brings an undefinable spark of fearless creativity to their writing, which will surprise and inspire readers around the world.

Follow us
@ @readingjuniper